Lifelong romance a~~~ break from her caree~~~ a family and found h~~~~~~~~~~ as a Mills & Boon author instead. She now lives in New Zealand and finds that writing feeds her very real obsession with happy endings and the endorphin rush they create. You can follow her at jcharroway.com, and on Facebook, Twitter and Instagram.

### Also by JC Harroway

*Forbidden Fling with Dr Right*
*How to Resist the Single Dad*

### Mills & Boon DARE

*Bound to You*
*Tempting the Enemy*

Discover more at millsandboon.co.uk.

# TEMPTED BY THE REBEL SURGEON

JC HARROWAY

# BREAKING THE SINGLE MUM'S RULES

JC HARROWAY

MILLS & BOON

First published in Great Britain 2023
by Mills & Boon, an imprint of HarperCollins*Publishers* Ltd,
1 London Bridge Street, London, SE1 9GF

www.harpercollins.co.uk

HarperCollins*Publishers* Macken House, 39/40 Mayor Street Upper,
Dublin 1, D01 C9W8, Ireland

Tempted by the Rebel Surgeon © 2023 JC Harroway

Breaking the Single Mum's Rules © 2023 JC Harroway

ISBN: 978-0-263-30600-2

03/23

This book is produced from independently certified FSC™ paper to ensure responsible forest management.
For more information visit: www.harpercollins.co.uk/green.

Printed and Bound in the UK using 100% Renewable Electricity at CPI Group (UK) Ltd, Croydon, CR0 4YY

# TEMPTED BY THE REBEL SURGEON

JC HARROWAY

MILLS & BOON

This book is dedicated to
all the healthcare professionals of New Zealand.

You do an amazing job, thank you.

# CHAPTER ONE

Lauren Harvey expected the same promptness in others that she herself practised. As a consultant in the busy Emergency Department of Auckland's Gulf Harbour Hospital, she was rarely disappointed. Typical that today of all days, when she'd struggled to set aside her personal troubles, the minute she arrived at work brought one of those rare occasions.

'Have the surgeon paged again, please, Grady,' she said to her good friend and the ER's most senior nurse, then inserted an intravenous cannula into the sixty-six-year-old man's arm and attached an infusion of intravenous antibiotics.

The monitor displaying the man's vital signs—heart rate, blood pressure, oxygen saturations and respiratory rate—emitted an eardrum-popping alarm, telling Lauren what she'd already deduced. This man was seriously ill and needed to be admitted for an urgent laparotomy.

She needed the on-call surgeon. Now.

Grady silenced the monitor alarm and adjusted the rate of oxygen flow to the patient's mask and then ducked out of the curtained-off bay.

Lauren pulled up the erect abdominal X-ray on the computer screen in order to confirm her diagnosis: an intestinal perforation. Breathing through her frustration with the lack of response from the paged surgical registrar, she completed the required paperwork. She understood the clinical pressures of this job and shouldn't take out her volatile mood on her junior colleagues. As one of life's planners, she simply liked to run an efficient and reactive department.

Her mind wandered again to the reason for her distraction. Ben, her younger brother, had left home for university in Wellington, not flown a solo mission to the moon. He'd be back for visits. They would speak on the phone. She was overreacting. It was just that she'd been his only maternal figure since he was eight and she was eighteen; it was hard to switch off the caring gene.

Glancing again at the time, Lauren typed up the patient's clinical history and her observations at the man's bedside. She ordered a second raft of blood work, pre-empting investigations the surgical team would likely require. She would give the on-call registrar two more minutes to show up. Then she would place a personal call to them through the hospital switchboard. That should reset their priorities in line with how she ran the department. All junior staff quickly learned that Lauren Harvey ran a tight ship. She was fully aware of her reputation as something of a severe taskmaster, but she was fair and dedicated to patient care. Second to her little family, which comprised her father and Ben, her job was her life.

With her back to the entrance of the treatment bay, she registered a swish of the curtains and breathed a sigh of relief. The flash of green surgical scrubs in her peripheral vision, the vague impression of a tall manly shape confirmed that the on-call registrar had finally graced them with his presence. For now, she'd bite her tongue in front of their patient, but later, in private, she'd have a word with the surgeon about his laid-back timekeeping.

'Glad you could join us,' she said without turning away from the monitor. 'This is Mr Ellis.' She smiled at the patient and began reeling off the pertinent facts required to hand over the patient to the care of the surgical team. 'He's a sixty-six-year-old man with a history of peptic ulcer disease, well-controlled diabetes and ischaemic heart disease.'

She'd fully worked up Mr Ellis for admission. All the registrar would need to do would be to consent the man for Theatre and wield the scalpel. Clicking through the images on the screen, she located the relevant X-ray and continued. 'He presents with symptoms of peritonitis and has signs of perforation—free air under the diaphragm.' She pointed to the X-ray displayed overhead. 'He's tachycardic and hypertensive.'

She sensed movement behind her and, still without glancing his way, stepped aside so the newcomer could access the computer monitor, which displayed the relevant blood test results.

'Mr Ellis,' she addressed the patient, her hand on his shoulder, 'the surgical team are going to take over your care from here. Are you feeling more comfortable?'

At the patient's nod and muffled, 'Thanks, Doctor,' she adjusted the blanket over his shoulders.

'Our Clinical Nurse Specialist, Grady, is going to insert an NG tube for you,' she continued to address the unusually silent surgeon. The specialty was renowned for attracting doctors well versed in taking control of any situation. 'And we'll keep the patient nil by mouth, although he denies eating today.'

She finally turned to face the surgeon, expecting thanks.

'Mason!' The name flew from her lips before she could stop it, before she had a chance to dampen her shocked reaction at seeing her ex standing there in all his jaw-dropping glory. He was dressed like any other surgeon: green surgical scrubs, a theatre hat covering his dark unruly hair, a stethoscope slung around his neck, but as well as the last man she thought she'd see standing in her department, he was surely the sexiest doctor to have ever existed.

'Dr Harvey,' Mason replied with a twitch of his lips and a smile in his piercing grey-blue eyes. The look, which could have lasted a split second or a hundred years, somehow conveyed everything that they'd once been to each other, every intimate moment and whispered promise. But Lauren must surely have imagined those things, because on second glance she only saw polite recognition, as if they were total strangers, which of course they were now. It had been six years, after all.

Lauren swallowed, relieved to find that her mouth wasn't hanging open. What was he doing standing in her ER without explanation, resembling a surf bum not a doctor, all tanned and relaxed as if he'd just strolled in from the beach?

'What are you doing here?' she asked automatically, her feelings bruised and her mind abuzz with questions. But now wasn't the time or the place for an in-depth reunion. Despite what they'd once been to each other, he was just the registrar she would need to put in his place for keeping her and Mr Ellis waiting.

Relaxed, in control and in no way surprised to see her, Mason moved to the patient's bedside. 'You called me,' he said in an obvious and reasonable answer while mirth danced in his eyes. 'I'm the locum on-call surgical registrar.'

Fresh annoyance bubbled in her veins. He must have

known that she still worked at Gulf Harbour. He would have been prepared for their paths to cross when he took the locum position. Why hadn't he called, warned her that he was back? Had she meant so little to him that he hadn't given her a single thought?

Lauren cleared her throat, trying to gather her composure while her face burned with embarrassment. Thinking only of the patient and not her confusion and Mason's obvious indifference to her, she made introductions. 'Mr Ellis, this is…um… Dr Ward.'

Even saying his name made her throat scratchy with long-repressed emotion for that part of her past. Fortunately she'd had her family and her job to focus on after their break-up. And, over the years, she'd forced herself to shut down any painful and pointless moments of weakness and curiosity for Mason's well-being and whereabouts.

After medical school, despite planning to travel to Europe together, they'd gone their separate ways. Lauren had stayed in Auckland, lived in her family home and helped her widower father to care for her younger brother while she'd worked her way up the career ladder here at Gulf Harbour, the very hospital where she herself had been born.

And Mason? After his first job in outback Australia, she'd heard a rumour that he'd joined Medicine Unlimited, an international non-profit organisation that provided medical care in countries affected by conflict or natural disaster. She'd forced herself to deliberately lose track of which war-torn country he'd travelled to, which international medical emergency he had followed and finally grown accustomed to the fact that she would never see him again.

Now, for some reason, he was back at the hospital where they'd both trained, his diverse and comprehensive experience and confidence written all over his outrageously handsome and mature face.

In contrast to her shocked and fumbling introductions, Mason calmly and professionally took charge, the way she would have expected from a surgeon.

'I understand you've had some abdominal pain,' he said to Mr Ellis, taking the man's pulse.

Mr Ellis nodded, seemingly unaware of the tense currents swirling between the reunited ex-lovers. Lauren could barely breathe for the pressure those currents exerted on her lungs.

She took a shaky breath, blaming her temporary fragility over Ben's leaving home. It had nothing to do with her ex rocking up looking better than ever, a feat she would previously have deemed impossible. The younger Mason had made her insides quiver, but she was no longer that awed young woman who had struggled to see what outgoing, popular golden boy Mason Ward could have possibly seen in quiet, studious and responsible Lauren Harvey.

In fact, the only thing they'd had in common back then was the mutual absence of their mothers—Lauren's deceased from colon cancer and Mason's had abandoned him the year they'd met, moving to Australia after divorcing his father.

She snapped herself out of it, using her usual rational brain to deal with Mason's sudden reappearance. Yes, she felt ambushed, irrelevant, annoyed that he could resume that professional façade so quickly and act as if they barely knew each other, as if they hadn't known each other intimately, when for the last three years of med school they'd been an item. But this was *her* department, her hospital.

She even had seniority, a fact she would reiterate as soon as she could get Mason alone.

Her body heated from head to toe at that idea.

Disgusted with her own weakness, and cursing that, at thirty, she wasn't happily married or living with the man of her dreams, she tore her eyes away from the broadness of Mason's back and shoulders, which were more manly, more defined than she recalled. She had once known everything about him, physically and emotionally, as close as they'd allowed themselves to become, anyway. Two troubled students with nothing in common beyond the pressures of their demanding course and their rampant physical attraction.

'Any vomiting?' Mason asked the patient, the epitome of composed professionalism.

Another nod from Mr Ellis. 'Just once, Doctor.'

With that, a subdued-looking Grady re-entered the bay carrying a treatment tray for inserting a nasogastric tube. Mason flicked him an easy smile and then laid a large, capable-looking hand on Mr Ellis's rigid abdomen. Lauren shivered, discomposed by the sight of his tanned hands—elegant fingers, square nails, a smattering of dark hair across his knuckles—a part of him she'd always found insanely attractive. Especially when the touch of those hands had been directed at her.

She looked away. The last thing she needed to add to today's emotional milieu were hormones. How dare Mason be so unaffected, so blasé and arrogant as to swan into the department after being twice summonsed and act as if they'd never met before, as if he hadn't cared one jot for her, as if he hadn't moved on and never looked back. Not that Lauren herself had confessed any of her own feelings at the time. Then, like now, she'd had no desire to admit to anything so fragile as emotional vulnerability. She was a doctor, had responsibilities. She needed to be strong.

Reasserting her presence back into the consultation, Lauren interjected, 'There's been no history of haematemesis, but Mr Ellis reports two days of melaena suggestive of an upper GI bleed.'

She consciously slowed her breathing, battling the absurd irritation she felt that Mason Ward had disrupted her morning and her ER by simply showing up. She was a mature professional woman, despite the silly misplaced excitement or curiosity or whatever it was fluttering in her chest. Far too busy to have time for any sort of game-playing with this man from her past.

Staying in the hospital where they had been medical students might not have been the most daring or adventurous thing to do, but she'd had other responsibilities, to her family, to the memory of her mother.

Not everyone could run away from their problems the way he'd done.

Mason turned his perceptive eyes on her—a jarring shock that catapulted her back in time—as if he'd heard her uncharitable and unfair thought. She'd understood why he'd had to leave Auckland, just like he'd said he understood why she needed to stay.

'Cardiac markers?' he asked, tugging his stethoscope from his ears, as if he was used to barking out requests from juniors, as if *she* were subservient and he were the consultant.

Lauren tore her stare from his sculpted mouth, pressed her own lips together, lips that recalled his kisses all too well.

Forget kissing, where was his deference, his respect,

his decency? Had he lost those traits on his world travels? The younger man she'd known had a reckless streak, was driven but always polite.

Now he seemed far too laid-back, self-assured and indifferent to Lauren for her liking.

She reached for her own stethoscope where she'd left it on the foot of the bed and looped it around her neck. She wouldn't show him how much his appearance had dismantled her, nor would she berate him in front of the patient.

But he could rest assured that there would soon be a reckoning.

'Cardiac markers were negative,' she said, her own tone curt. 'Blood sugars, electrolytes and renal function also normal.'

Regaining control of herself and her emotions, she prepared to exit. 'I'll leave you in Dr Ward's capable hands, Mr Ellis.' She smiled reassuringly at the man who would soon be under Mason's knife. She could only hope that he was a good surgeon, that he'd worn away the chip on his shoulder that came from him being a part of a famous and infamous surgical family. In Lauren's opinion, he certainly had some work to do as a junior doctor in *this* hospital.

She might no longer know more about him than how his kisses, his touch, his whispered nothings had once, when she'd allowed her guard down long enough for feelings to escape, made her feel as if he was the centre of her universe, but she knew that with his confidence and hint of arrogance he'd more than likely made a name for himself overseas.

Too bad she'd have to take him down a peg or two, set him straight on how things worked in *her* department. Despite their past, he was just like all the other registrars in this hospital. Nothing special.

She swished aside the curtain, paused before leaving, settled her eyes on Mason, her heart beating like a rabbit's because, no matter what she told herself, her body seemed intent on reacting to the delicious sight of him. 'Please find me once you've admitted Mr Ellis. I'd like to welcome you to Gulf Harbour properly, elucidate you on the ER's protocols and procedures, now that you're back.'

With her missive delivered in what she hoped reflected cool, in-command professionalism, she turned on her heel and went in search of her next patient.

Every step away from his unsettling presence grew more sure-footed, the memories of them together fading. This was her turf. Mason Ward and the intense connection of their past were irrelevant, despite the fact that, physically at least, he appeared to still possess the skills to be utterly distracting.

# CHAPTER TWO

AFTER EXAMINING MR ELLIS and consenting him for Theatre, an impatient Mason left the surgical house officer to arrange the patient's transfer to the ward and went in search of Lauren.

His strides faltered, too many feelings running free now that the inevitable reunion had occurred. He'd expected to see her at Gulf Harbour Hospital of course, but that one interaction had blindsided him, sending him into a spiral of frustration, remorse and utter fascination. An impressive and unexpected outcome considering that he'd spent the majority of the past six years, after finally accepting that they were over and trying to block Lauren from his mind, on an emotional even keel while he'd focused on building his brand as a surgeon.

But the sight of her after so long was powerful, a violent jolt to his system, as if he'd been living in a daze and she'd just shaken him awake. She was beautiful. Whip-smart. A compassionate advocate. And still so sexy that his poor, jet-lagged body was now on high alert, his blood pumping determination through his veins as he paused to collect himself in the middle of the department.

He scanned the staff area for the only woman he'd ever allowed close, and despite his best attempts had always been unable to completely forget, still processing their reunion. Parts of today's Lauren had changed so much as to be unrecognisable. Other parts were exactly how he remembered. It made her both achingly familiar and delightfully new, each revelation unsettling.

He hadn't cyber-stalked her career path or her personal life after their first year apart for reasons of self-preservation but, whatever her marital status now, this unforeseen flare-up of interest in her needed to be nipped in the bud.

It didn't help his cause that she was still stunning, her dark and emotive eyes a place a man could lose himself if he wasn't careful, her glossy brown hair tamed into a practical ponytail for work and her figure a little more voluptuous than he recalled. And where Lauren was concerned, as soon as he allowed himself to imagine, the details came to him surprisingly undiminished.

All that was missing was her beaming smile, the one he'd coaxed out of her a million times, the one that'd had the power to quicken his pulse and pull him out of any funk. Now she seemed all hard edges, checklists and rules.

He sighed; he should have warned her of his return. Now he had some grovelling to do.

He quickened his pace, ducked his head into various parts of the ER and found Lauren at the work station in the minor injuries room.

His breath caught. With her back to him, his gaze lingered on the slope of her neck. If he chose to indulge that particular memory, he'd be able to recall the delicate softness of the skin there, the way his kisses and the scrape of his stubble in that exact spot had made her sigh or gasp or sometimes giggle. The scent of her skin and taste of her on his lips, however, eluded him, and a knot of frustration formed under his ribs because he shouldn't crave a return of those intimate details.

'You shouldn't creep up on people,' Lauren said without turning, her focus on the monitor as if it displayed the erratic and excited trace of Mason's racing heart.

'I was waiting for you to finish typing before interrupting,' he admitted, unable to hold in his smile, because she had always been one step ahead of him, always challenged his opinions, laughed with him when he'd taken himself too seriously. Their playful bickering had been one of the most stimulating aspects of their relationship.

A flood of nostalgia surged through his veins, warm and welcoming. Lauren had been the closest thing he'd ever had to a serious girlfriend. Since her, he'd moved around so much that his encounters with the opposite sex had been purely casual. Until this very second, he hadn't realised he'd missed having someone in his life who knew him so well.

'It's good to see you, Lauren.' Her name on his lips after all this time sent his temperature soaring, as if it were an intimate secret only they shared. Their chemistry had been off the charts when they had dated as medical students, their relationship driven by great sex, mutual support and too many good times to count.

But their intimacies had ended the day she'd called off their plans for travelling to Europe and declared it would be better for them both to make a *clean break*.

That was Lauren: neat, tidy, no loose ends. He'd learned to hate those two words.

Shutting down the memories of how, confused and rejected, he'd taken his mother's lead and fled to outback Australia, where he'd patched up his heart while training under surgery's answer to a crocodile wrangler, Mason cleared his throat.

'How have you been?' he asked. Time to clear the air, dispense with the distracting attraction he apparently still felt for her, so that they could go about their respective business.

Lauren concluded her typing with a flourish, spun her chair to face him and stood, no trace of warmth in her expression. His stomach sank. He should focus on his more immediate, work-related goals rather than flirting in order to coax out the dazzling smile he remembered. Only he didn't want there to be an atmosphere every time he came to the ER, and her welcome so far had been nothing short of frosty.

'I've been great,' she said, looking up at him with those easy-to-read eyes she'd always had, so he clearly saw her confusion and irritation. He had the height advantage, something that had often irked her competitive spirit, but he couldn't help remembering that when they'd embraced the top of her head had fit perfectly under his chin.

'But the bigger question is what are you doing back here?' She placed her hands in the pockets of her lab coat. 'Weren't you in Algeria?'

'Angola,' he replied, stomach sinking with disappointment. He should have stolen a handshake, a legitimate excuse to touch her, maybe defused some of this tension with a mundane professional gesture. Instead, she was looking at him as if he'd crawled unwanted from under a rock. 'Actually, that was several countries ago.'

So she'd said goodbye, moved on and forgotten all about him and everything they'd shared. But then what had he expected? That she'd embrace him like an old friend? They'd had little in common, but there had always been something about Lauren that he found enticing. That hadn't changed.

'So, tell me,' she asked in a cool voice, 'how long will Gulf Harbour have the privilege of your surgical skills?' She straightened her name badge, avoiding his stare, as if his answer mattered little, as if she'd only asked the question to be polite.

Mason clenched his jaw in frustration. He'd obviously inadvertently upset her, presumably by rocking up unannounced. He'd wanted to sit across from her, maybe with a drink, and explain everything properly. He'd just returned home in such a rush and then been occupied with hastily planning a funeral that he wished he didn't have to attend.

The idea of standing beside his father's coffin later this week made him shudder. He swallowed down the absurd urge to invite Lauren along, as if her presence would somehow soothe the part of him that was twisted into knots over his complex relationship with his father.

I don't know exactly,' he replied, reeling from how little he knew of this mature version of Lauren.

Before he could explain his plans further, she muttered, 'Of course you don't.' Something like hurt swept over her features.

He certainly hadn't returned to Gulf Harbour to rekindle what they'd had, but he'd at least hoped they could be civil, put this misunderstanding behind them.

In the same rather clinical way with which Lauren had declared their break-up, she said, 'Well, as you're here now, could you do me the courtesy of a quick chat.'

Mason sighed. It wasn't framed as a question. Without waiting for his assent, Lauren marched from the communal clerical area, away from the bustle of other staff.

So much for the cold reality of his fantasy homecoming, so unlike his dreams of reuniting with Lauren. Mason had always planned to return to New Zealand. Murray Ward's death had merely tightened the time frame.

He frowned as he followed behind her, growing more and more disgruntled. She'd been the one to call things off. Why was she acting as if he'd broken her heart? It was his heart that had been battered and bruised, his heart that had pined for over a year, while she'd moved on.

Lauren directed him into a small office labelled *Dr Susan Wallace, Head of Department*. When she saw his curiosity, she explained, 'Dr Wallace is on maternity leave. I'm acting head in her absence.'

'Congratulations.' Genuine warmth coloured his voice.

Her ambition and intelligence were things he'd found so compelling when they had first met as lab partners. Mason had instantly fancied the smart, serious girl and then quickly come to relish her dry sense of humour and readiness to prove that she was both always right and up to any dare he had set. And no one had worked harder than Lauren at med school, an impressive distinction considering that, when they'd met, she'd still been grieving the death of her mother.

Mason, by comparison, had always felt that he couldn't shine too brightly at med school. He was part of the Ward family, surgical royalty at Gulf Harbour Hospital. If he achieved too highly, there were whisperings of nepotism at play, and if his grades were low, tutors scoffed and compared him to his illustrious retired surgical professor grandfather and his dynamic Head of Surgery father.

He hadn't been able to win. But Lauren had been different. She hadn't cared either way. In fact, the first time he'd talked about the perils of following in some pretty large footsteps, she'd simply laughed at him, told him to pull his head in and shoved a microbiology textbook his way. No matter how messed-up the rest of his life had been, spending time with Lauren had always lifted his spirits, made him feel like himself, free from the expectations that had clouded the rest of his life.

'Take a seat,' she said warily, placing a literal barrier between them as she settled behind her desk.

He declined the chair, cutting straight to the chase. 'Actually, I was hoping I could buy you a coffee.' He smiled, raising his eyebrows in invitation. She'd practically mainlined caffeine as a student. He'd never arrived at her house without a takeaway. 'We could catch up on each other's news.'

He could explain why he'd returned so suddenly, why he hadn't had time to warn her that he was back. Why he hoped they could move past this distance between them and be...friends. If only he could persuade his libido to calm down and see her just as a colleague.

A *senior* colleague.

Lauren pursed her full lips, unimpressed, the move not helping his attempts to forget what they'd shared in the past one little bit. Lauren had done this thing that drove him crazy: talked while he'd been trying to kiss her so that they'd often kissed their way through entire conversations and even arguments.

'That's not possible, I'm afraid,' she said, aloof, as if she had no recollection of ever kissing him.

Mason faltered, wondering, not for the first time, about her private life. She could be married with children for all he knew. He'd have to pump Grady for information later.

His stomach lurched with envy—unless she and Grady

had taken their long-term friendship to another level in Mason's absence…?

'I'm busy,' she continued. 'You're about to operate on Mr Ellis, I would imagine. Anyway, this isn't a social chat. You missed that opportunity when you took a job at my hospital without a quick courtesy email to tell me you were back in New Zealand, leaving me to find out at a patient's bedside.'

She clasped her hands under her chin, her elbows resting on the table.

'I see,' he said. Every scrap of hope he'd had for an amicable reunion evaporated, leaving him hollow-chested. She had felt ambushed and it was his fault.

'I've upset you,' he stated. Although maybe she'd have forgiven his oversight but for their romantic past. He didn't want to discuss his father, something he avoided if he could, especially here at Gulf Harbour, where Murray Ward's once prestigious name had finally been tarnished by the scandal he'd caused by sleeping with a patient. A patient the same age as his medical student son.

'Actually, I'm more surprised…and disappointed.' Even sitting, she managed to look down at him with disapproval.

'Oh, no, that's even worse.' He tried an apologetic grin, hoping to soften her with humour. 'Not a great restart to our relationship.'

'We have no relationship.' Lauren flushed, as if remembering exactly the kind of passionate, flammable connection they'd shared.

Interesting…

'I meant professionally,' he deadpanned, hiding his smile. 'Come on, Laurie,' he teased, hoping to retrieve the playful banter that had been their second most commonly used form of communication after sex. 'I'm sorry that I sprang myself on you this morning, but I do have a good excuse, I promise.

'This is the part where you forgive me for messing up,' he said, trying to draw out her laughter, watch it light her pretty eyes, 'and then we make up.' At least that had always been the pattern to their fights, most of the making-up happening between the sheets.

She narrowed her eyes. 'Nothing about this, you just turning up out of the blue with a tan and cheeky grin, is usual, and please don't call me that.'

Mason winced; he seemed to be digging himself a bigger hole. 'Sorry, Dr Harvey.'

Of course he owed her the professional consideration he'd offer any other senior colleague. He'd once respected the hell out of this woman and still did, despite his bungled return, but nor could he deny that he wanted to smash through the barriers she seemed to be insisting upon erecting.

'That's right.' She raised her chin and met his stare. 'In case you missed it while you've been living in a jungle somewhere with no outside contact, I'm a consultant now. I run this department, and I expect junior members of staff, exes or not,' she clarified, her eyes hardening, 'to present themselves as soon as possible once they are called, to act with courtesy, not make blunt demands for results they are more than capable of looking up for themselves.'

He nodded, penitent, although he knew very well this wasn't about blood tests. 'My apologies. I'm simply used to taking charge of a situation. There's not too much call for strict protocol in a tent in the desert or a hospital basement that's being bombed.'

With impeccable timing, Mason noticed the absence of

a ring on her left hand. Not that it meant anything, or that her marital status mattered one bit. They were barely on speaking terms, let alone friends. And now that he'd been forced home prematurely, his plans didn't involve the complication of a relationship, even a physical one he knew would make the sum of all his other sexual encounters pale into insignificance.

'I did come to the ER as soon as I could,' he said, holding her affronted stare. 'Next time you call, I'll run.'

She looked mildly appeased, so Mason ploughed on. 'The truth is, despite knowing I was likely to bump into you at some stage, I was a bit thrown when it actually happened.'

He hadn't expected the visceral reaction to be so strong. At least eighty percent of his neurones had shut down.

Lauren flushed, the colour staining her neck and the vee of skin that the top of her scrubs exposed, luring his fatigued brain to recall every detail of what lay underneath the clothes. How had he imagined that he could ignore this woman who, for him, had always been the epitome of strong, sexy femininity, the gold standard when it came to undeniable chemistry?

*That* most definitely hadn't changed.

Lauren cleared her throat, seemingly flustered by his honesty. 'Well…um…apology accepted.'

With her reprimand delivered, she stood, came from behind her desk and walked towards the door as if about to usher him out. 'While we are on the topic, I'll also remind you that registrars don't invite consultants for coffee. That's not how things are done around here.'

Mason's feet stubbornly stuck to the spot as indignation slid beneath his skin. Oh, no, no, no. She'd dismissed him that way once before, all cold and clinical. Well, he wasn't young and obsessed with her any more.

'I'm sorry for forgetting myself. In future, I'll moderate my tone. You're clearly still a stickler for the rules.'

'And you are still pushing boundaries, I see.' Her pupils widened as she glared his way.

Mason shrugged. He'd rather push her buttons, these days. And if she didn't like his invitation for a harmless cup of coffee, she definitely wouldn't like the hot and steamy contents of his memories. Unluckily for her, she couldn't forbid how attractive he still found her.

She could kick him out of her office—she was, after all, his senior—but not before he'd delivered a few home truths.

Because he was done apologising, and because she kept checking out his physique, her stare sweeping over his chest and lower, he inched into her personal space. 'I can't believe how much you've changed.' The air in her small office was thicker than a desert sandstorm with sexual undercurrents.

Not one to miss out on the last word, she paced closer and quipped, 'And I can't believe how little you've changed.' She tilted her chin, eyes blazing, and he caught a hint of her scent, some sophisticated perfume that a younger Lauren would have eschewed but seemed to suit this older, professional version.

Her stare dipped to his mouth. A small sigh escaped her lips as if she simply could no longer hold it in. It made him forget all about his remorse, the respect she deserved, his explanations. It made him remember thousands of their kisses. Endless touches. The intense connection he'd never achieved with anyone but her.

Before she'd made a choice that hadn't been him.

'Oh, I've changed.' His voice grew husky of its own accord now that they were closer than they'd been since before that fateful break-up on *their* beach. 'The old me would have probably waited for you to invite *me* for coffee. But I'm more honest these days. I call things how I see them.'

An excited flush coloured her skin, the pulse in her neck leaping. 'What does that mean?'

'You and I have history.' Provocation bubbled in his blood. 'I figured we could dispense with the formality.'

He hadn't meant for his invitation to sound so suggestive. He wasn't here to reconnect with an old flame. He had a funeral to get through, a promotion to work towards, his own good name to establish here in Auckland. But older Lauren was still so intriguing, stimulating and unexpected, forcing all his good intentions to the back of his mind.

Her eyes danced between his as if searching, reacquainting, assessing. She was clearly not as immune to him, as uptight and coolly professional as she'd have him believe. Then her stare turned defiant. 'I'm afraid that I'm going to have to insist on the formality, Dr Ward.'

'That's fine by me, Dr Harvey. My invitation to coffee was purely a gesture of professional politeness.'

*Liar.*

'As is my refusal.' She loitered near her desk, arms crossed defensively over her chest.

'Okay then.' Mason raised his hands in surrender. 'I understand. I didn't realise that you still had unresolved feelings for me.'

Her outraged gaze clashed with his. 'Unresolved feelings? Don't be ridiculous. I've hardly given you a thought since you left.'

Oh, that had the potential to sting, if only her protestations were a little less vehement. If only she wasn't look-

ing at him as if she wanted to know more than where he'd
been working and why he was back. He remembered that
look in her eyes: need.

He nodded. 'Why else would you be so…hostile, so uptight towards me?'

Although behaving wildly inappropriately, Mason was
starting to enjoy himself. And so was Lauren. The door was
still closed and her eyes shone with the challenge.

'Uptight?' Her jaw dropped.

He nodded, adamant. 'Don't forget, Laurie, it was you
who dumped me.'

She huffed in disbelief. 'And you scarpered overseas
as quickly as you could, if I recall, never to return.' She
straightened her spine, trying to seem composed when her
pupils were deep black pools of excitement and her breaths
gusted past her parted lips.

'Beyond ensuring that my ER is run to the highest standards,' she added, clearing her throat, 'I have no more interest in you than I do any other doctor here.'

He clasped his chest, staggering back a pace as if mor-
tally wounded by her cutting admission. Then he straightened, his eyes boring into hers. 'That's a real shame
because, despite you reneging on our plans, despite you
practically shoving me onto the plane with a casual *Have
a nice life,* I've thought about you. A. Lot.'

He let the innuendo settle. She might want nothing to do
with him, she might be in charge here, might want to control everything that happened in the ER, but she couldn't
dictate the nature of his thoughts or the red-blooded reac-
tions of his body.

She stared, open mouthed, for a handful of seconds, as
if she couldn't believe his audacity, but her eyes gleamed

with fire, showing glimpses of the passionate woman who'd once craved him as much as he'd craved her.

'Just because we were pretty good together in the sex department, don't think for one second that your return means we'll be picking up where we left off,' she blustered behind a calm façade. 'I have other priorities now.'

Why, oh, why did she have to go and say that their sex life had been amazing? As it was, he was struggling to remember why he was here, the sight of her, the sexually charged standoff, the banter back and forth so unexpectedly distracting, so blood-stirring.

He held up his hands, palms out. 'Whoa, who said anything about us jumping back into bed? Wait, are you saying that you're too busy for sex these days?' He made a tutting sound. He shouldn't enjoy their verbal sparring, but he couldn't help himself. It reminded him of their endless debates over everything from global warming to beer versus wine.

'You're deluded.' She ignored him, this time swinging the door wide open, her intention clear.

He'd finally outstayed his welcome. He'd got under her skin just like she'd wormed under his, reminding him why they'd always worked so well together as a couple. Why they still could if either of them were so inclined. But it was clear that his absence had not made her heart grow fonder, and that suited him just fine because, unlike the younger version of the man she had dumped, Mason no longer sought the approval of others.

He stepped into the doorway, faced her, stared.

'Goodbye, Dr Ward.' She'd clearly meant to sound haughty and dismissive, but Mason couldn't resist one last provocation.

He smiled wide. 'I've missed this. The banter. The way an hour spent in your company seemed to shut out the noise of the world. We had so many good times.'

To his delight, Lauren cracked, her lips twitching, before her eyes rolled in mock disgust. 'I dare say we did in the way a young couple of twenty-somethings can.' She composed herself, growing serious once more. 'But we've grown up. I'm concentrating on building my career now.'

'As am I.' That had always been his motivation for every decision he made, including leaving New Zealand. Leaving her. Overseas, he was just Mason Ward, a name that, to his relief, meant only what *he'd* made it.

'Well, I doubt you'll be around long. I hear that they're desperate for hospital staff in Toruva,' she said, naming the Pacific Island recently ravaged by Cyclone Delilah.

Six months ago she'd have been spot-on with her observation. He hadn't been quite ready to return to New Zealand until circumstances had forced his hand. But now, with the right job on the horizon, he had a real opportunity to make his own name here in Auckland, to prove that, despite the expectations of the past and the impossible standards once set by his father, he was a good surgeon.

He passed over the threshold, throwing out what he needed to say in order to avoid future professional clashes, the last thing he wanted with Lauren. 'I'm thinking of sticking around for a while, actually.'

Shock sharpened her glare as she clutched the open door in a white-knuckled grip. 'Why? Whatever could GHH have to offer an adventurer like you?'

'Don't look so appalled. Is it so terrible a concept that we're to be colleagues?'

She huffed. 'For now.'

With their reunion over, he unexpectedly had no desire to be anywhere else. 'Or for many years to come.'

She frowned, confused.

Mason filled her in. 'If I'm successful in my application for the newest surgical consultant post here at Gulf Harbour, we'll be seeing a whole lot more of each other, Dr Harvey. As equals.'

And now they'd reconnected, now that he knew the sparks were there, hotter than ever, he was looking forward to each and every one of their interactions.

His statement left her speechless, a rare sight indeed.

'Admit it, Lauren,' he said in a low voice. 'You've missed me.'

He left her with a final smile and a cheeky wink, her flabbergasted stare burning into his back.

# CHAPTER THREE

GRADY, WHO OFTEN gave Lauren a lift to work when they happened to share a night shift, parked his car in the staff car park five spaces from Mason's distinctive motorbike and switched off the engine. Relief and trepidation that Mason hadn't yet left work for the day churned in Lauren's stomach. She couldn't avoid him even if she wanted to, so it was better to end this...thing between them once and for all.

She undid her seatbelt and fought the temptation to check her reflection in the rear-view mirror, taking full responsibility for her part in the flirtatious showdown that had transpired in her office yesterday. Clearly her libido didn't care how heartbroken she'd been after her last encounter with Mason Ward.

'You go inside,' she said to Grady, reaching for the door handle, preparing to exit the car. 'I won't be far behind you.' She'd confront Mason, say what she had to say and start her shift as if he'd never returned.

Grady's stare was laced with concern. 'Lauren—'

'Don't, Grady,' she warned with a shake of her head. She didn't want to hear her friend's opinion on Mason's reappearance. She wasn't interested if every female staff member of the hospital was swooning over him already— apparently he'd already earned himself the nickname Blade of Glory. She definitely didn't want to hear Grady talk her into or out of her course of action.

'I just need to talk to our newest surgical colleague. It won't take long.' She shot him a grateful smile, his calm, unflappable presence as soothing as always.

'Okay,' he said, and pressed his lips together. Then he sighed. 'I won't ask you how you're feeling about him working here. But I'm giving you fair warning—I'll struggle to stay quiet if he hurts you again.'

Lauren swallowed, her throat tight as she tried to keep her expression stoic, while memories flayed her: her mum, Mason, Ben. Before she'd ended things with Mason, she'd been torn in so many directions she hadn't known what to do for the best.

'I appreciate your concern, as always…' She'd known Nash Grady since her medical student days, when he'd literally taken pity on her one night. She hadn't been able to obtain venous access on a patient and had been on the verge of tears at the man's pincushion arms, when Grady had come to her rescue.

'But I simply need to have a professional conversation with Dr Ward, nothing else. You know me—I don't let anyone close enough to hurt me.' And she and Mason had already proved beyond all doubt that they were too different. He'd gadded around the globe and she'd stayed here, licked her wounds, tried to do the right thing for all concerned.

Sympathy clouded Grady's eyes and Lauren looked away. He'd been there to witness the fallout of that fateful decision she'd made six years ago. He'd picked up the pieces, literally holding her while she'd sobbed all over his uniform, her overwhelming hurt that their relationship was over matched only by the confusion and doubt she'd felt in being the one to end it. Without probing for details, Grady had turned up on her doorstep every evening for a month after Mason had left, never arriving empty-handed. He'd brought ice cream and tissues and listened while Lauren endlessly second-guessed her choice to say goodbye to Mason and stay to support her little family.

Talk about being caught between a rock and a hard place... Of course Mason must have been disappointed, but it hadn't really been any choice at all. Not for Lauren, whose grief over her mother's death had still influenced all of her decisions.

She glanced at the staff entrance at the back of the hospital, her heart climbing into her throat as Mason emerged and headed towards his motorbike. She stiffened. She'd been dreading this meeting since she'd opened her eyes that morning, the shock of seeing him at the hospital yesterday a fresh and startling reminder of his power to leave her both rattled and utterly turned on, for all her tough talk.

Not to mention infuriated. He'd waltzed into her hospital without warning. He'd deliberately riled her up and then he'd completely derailed her day with his revelation that he planned to stay at Gulf Harbour long-term.

Restless, she climbed from the car, vaguely aware of Grady discreetly locking up and heading for the entrance as she kept her focus on Mason and his long strides. She shuddered, her body ravaged by a jarring mix of déjà vu and desire as she watched his approach.

Why was he back? The Mason who'd left six years ago had been desperate to get away from the role he was forced to adopt in Auckland, desperate to be anywhere where he wasn't known, where he could make his own mark without speculation that he was any relation to Isaac Ward or, worse, Murray Ward.

Why had he applied for this particular consultant job? The timing couldn't be more inconvenient for Lauren when she needed all of her spare energy now that Ben had left home to focus on her own career goals—goals she'd already sidelined for years in order to spend more time at home with her brother.

She closed her eyes for a second's reprieve from the sight of Mason, but that simply conjured a memory of last night's dream. It had started out true to real events, her breaking things off with him on their beach, but then it had morphed into a chase scenario, where she'd literally run along the tarmac of the runway behind Mason's departing plane to tell him that she'd changed her mind. Of course she hadn't been able to catch up with the jet, waking with a sickening start instead. Not even recalling the sexy gleam in his eyes yesterday, the familiar Mason scent of his skin or the sexual tension that had clawed at her until she'd been lured into a dangerous game of verbal sparring in her office had been able to dispel the anguished hangover from her nightmare.

Now, just like six years ago, and too many other times to count, she wished that her mother was alive to offer sympathy and sage advice and, if all else failed, comforting hugs.

As Mason reached his renovated vintage Enfield, a backpack slung over one shoulder and his motorbike helmet under the other arm, Lauren stepped closer. She hadn't been able to believe that he still rode it, but his means of transportation was easily identifiable for anyone who knew him well, and more times than she cared to remember she'd loved riding pillion with him, her heart in her throat and a death grip on his waist.

Oh, how she'd trusted him then, believed that she was safe with him, at least physically. Emotionally she hadn't been that vulnerable with anyone. Her mother's death had taught her the benefits of emotional withdrawal in keeping her feelings protected.

Mason caught sight of her, faltered, then the confident smile that spread over his handsome face snatched at her breath the way it had when she'd first laid eyes on him at med school. Even tired from a night on call, he still made her pulse skitter. Blood whooshed through her head with foolish and misplaced excitement. He still had the power to discombobulate her with one look. Nor was it fair that his attractiveness, divine body and sharp intelligence made the rest of the human race look like a bunch of sad underachievers.

He was even a nice guy, for goodness' sake.

Abandoning her membership of the Mason Fan Club, she tilted her head towards the sleek black and chrome machine. 'Still riding around on a deathtrap, I see.'

Clearly her frayed nerves were in control of her speech, the delivered trite observation not what she'd planned to say at all. But, unlike yesterday, when his unannounced arrival had caught her off-guard, when he'd had the last word, she was there to set him straight. Them being anything other than polite work colleagues was not an option. It turned out Dr Wallace was enjoying motherhood too much and had decided to resign, and Lauren had strived too hard for too long for the permanent promotion in her sights: that of Head of the ER. She'd convey her message to Mason, ensure that he understood her boundaries and then try to forget that he was back.

There could be no more bickering. No flirtatious goading. No more talk of sex, past or future.

He shrugged, his fatigued but riveting grey-blue eyes reserved. She couldn't blame him after her tepid…no, outright rude welcome yesterday. It was a poor excuse, but she'd been completely overwhelmed.

'She's a classic.' He glanced lovingly at his bike, even stroked the leather seat. 'She's been in storage for six years and she still runs like a dream.'

Lauren stiffened, absorbing the twinge of jealousy. How could she be envious of a motorbike? He'd once looked at her with similar adoration, caressed her body as lovingly.

'I wanted to catch you before you headed home,' she said, pulling herself together. No more dwelling on the past or focusing on their attraction. With Ben at university, this was her time to concentrate one hundred percent on her career. She deserved it. That left no room in her life for… distractions. And unlike the sensible, busy professional men she occasionally dated, Mason was a definite distraction. More like an imminent heart attack: risky, dangerous and impossible to ignore.

He narrowed his gaze, a newly constructed wall around him since their altercation. 'Did you come to invite me for that coffee? I've been awake all night,' he continued. 'We had a multiple casualty MVA come in in the early hours, but I'm still jet-lagged, so I could rally myself, I guess. I see The Har-Bar is still there,' he said about their once favourite watering hole, a place where they had kissed, danced, argued and celebrated.

Lauren hadn't been there in years, since she'd last gone with him, in fact. She winced. 'I didn't come to invite you for coffee. I'm working the late shift,' she said, genuine regret stuck in her throat for the way she'd behaved the day before. She wasn't blaming him for her attitude, but Mason had always brought out sides of her personality that no one else could, from the daredevil willing to sit behind him on his deathtrap to the young woman scared to risk building a relationship after losing her mother, who had once nonetheless embarked on something wild and passionate and intense with him.

'Of course you didn't,' he said with a casual shrug that reminded Lauren that not much fazed Mason. 'Don't worry; I heard the message loud and clear yesterday.'

Had he? Lauren had been so thrown by his appearance and the lingering undercurrents of their chemistry she wasn't sure how much sense she'd made. That was why she needed to set the record straight.

'And yet you turned on the charm offensive anyway,' she said, her irritation at his calm, unaffected attitude building. The more reasonable he acted, the snippier she became. Maybe because a perverse part of her craved his flirtatious efforts. It showed he cared a little.

He shrugged. 'What can I say? You're looking good, Laurie. Really good. I hope for your sake it means that you're happy.'

Heat fizzed through her veins at his compliment, only to be dashed by the question in his eyes. What he was actually asking was if she'd found contentment, come to terms at last with the loss of her mother, and for that she had no easy, sanitised answer. But maybe he deserved more than *I'm fine*. After all, he had supported her through the better part of her grief while they'd been together.

'That's why I'm here, actually. I came to apologise for yesterday. I might have overreacted. You caught me totally by surprise, just walking into the ER like that, and I was already having a bad day.'

Concern pinched his eyebrows together in a frown, his stare searching in that way that had always made her feel as if he could read all of her secrets. 'I'm sorry too. I really hadn't intended to ambush you. I only landed in the country on Sunday and time just…got away from me.'

Lauren shook her head, batting away his apology; she understood the pressures of their career. 'I wasn't just unsettled by you. Ben left home last weekend.' She exhaled on a rush, as if the faster she said the words the more used to them she would become. 'I was…missing him.'

She'd had no intention of confiding such a personal matter to Mason of all people, but the words just tumbled out, perhaps because he knew Ben, had taught him to surf and master a skateboard.

'You're still close, huh?' he asked, brow raised over tired eyes. 'Has he gone away to university?'

Lauren nodded, distracted by the sympathy in Mason's stare. She didn't want him seeing her so clearly, but his expression, his understanding seemed to open the floodgates on her confusion and doubt.

'I know it's silly,' she said, 'because he's only in Wellington, but I have to constantly fight the urge to call him, check he's okay, knows what brand of washing powder to buy,' she finished lamely. 'Turns out switching off the caring gene is tougher than I thought it would be.'

She should feel relieved that she'd finally have more time to focus on the promotion she craved now that Ben had left home. A few days ago, she'd even finally moved into the house she'd bought six months ago, which was within walking distance of the hospital.

'I'm sure you've helped to raise a fine young man,' said Mason, his deep voice inexplicably soothing, when with her behaviour so far and what she'd yet to tell him she hadn't earned his compassion. But he'd always been easy to talk to, one of the things she'd missed most about him when they'd split. That and the massive chunk of her heart he'd taken overseas with him.

'Try not to worry. He's probably having the time of his life.' He smiled, doing silly things to her insides. 'He'll be too busy to even care about laundry until his clothes start walking around on their own, or until he spots a girl he fancies and wants to make a good impression. Remember the state of my flat? Four boys sharing a house. Not much housework was done, I can tell you.'

That Mason remembered the bond she had with her brother made her take a fresh look at the man she'd been desperately trying to ignore since he'd walked back into her life. Of all people, Mason had been the one she'd confided in most about losing her mother and its impact on their family dynamics. How she'd lived at home as a student instead of sharing a flat with friends so she could assist her busy grieving father with childcare and school pick-ups, making dinner and homework supervision. She hadn't wanted Ben to miss out, and taking on some of her roles had allowed Lauren to feel close to her mother. Ben had deserved a supported childhood like the one she'd had. And, still grieving herself, Lauren had needed them as much as she'd figured they needed her.

Lauren took a deep breath, torn between holding back from him and laying all of her Ben-related concerns at Mason's feet. She blinked away the burn in her eyes. 'Trying not to worry about my baby brother is like herding cats. Impossible.'

'Well, he's not really a baby now, is he? He's only a year younger than I was when we first got together.' Something dark and seductive glowed in his eyes, like it had in her office yesterday, as if he was remembering again.

'I guess...' This conversation was going down a dead-end path. To steer herself away from that look and what it did to her skittish pulse, she blurted out a confession. 'I'm not sure I can take any credit for raising Ben. I didn't realise it at the time we broke up, but I still had a lot of grieving to do myself.'

He nodded as if he'd already figured that out, but also looked slightly taken aback at her overshare. 'Of course you did,' he said. 'You know, if you want to grab that coffee some'time, we could talk properly. I'd love to hear what Ben is up to and how you've been.'

Lauren avoided his eye contact as she clawed her defences back into place. What was she thinking? No matter how tempting it was to confide in Mason, they couldn't be friends. She shouldn't even be talking to him.

'I'm sorry. That's not a good idea, I'm afraid.' She crossed her arms over her waist, guilt gnawing her stomach that she'd now need to backpedal.

When she met his stare again, she saw confusion and questions, felt their answering doubts tremble through her as the years slipped away. They could have been back on their beach, Lauren's bewilderment gripping her throat as she'd let him down as gently as possible and Mason simply walking away, no questions asked.

It was irrelevant after all these years, but she couldn't seem to stop herself from dredging up the past, from saying, 'It wasn't an easy decision for me, you know, to change our plans and stay behind.'

He stared for long, intense seconds, during which Lauren squirmed and held her breath in foolish, misplaced anticipation.

'I never thought it was,' he said eventually, his eyes clouding over as if he was emotionally withdrawing.

He was right; there was no sense raking over ancient history. They'd each made their decision, gone their separate ways. Him being back now changed nothing. In fact, for her, it made everything way more complicated.

'Anyway—' she checked her phone for the time '—the reason I wanted to talk, aside from to apologise for yesterday, was to explain. There… um…there can't be anything between us now, other than a strictly professional relationship. Coffee dates included, I'm afraid.'

'Why? Just because we work together?' He frowned, his stare flicking over her features as if he considered arguing the point. As if he thought he could convince her, coax her out of herself, the way he had so many times in the past. 'I know we vetoed a wild sexual reunion when we spoke yesterday.' He offered her a playful smile she wanted to return. 'But it's not a crime for a couple of colleagues to spend time together away from work, especially when we used to be friends, didn't we?'

Lauren shrugged, bewildered and unable to concede a thing. They had been friends, but they'd been lovers first. Her body could recall the thrill of his every touch, her resolve tenuous as if being one sexy smile away from disintegration. She couldn't go there with him, of all people. Even a rekindled friendship could put her in an untenable position professionally. And she'd worked too hard.

'Friendship too is out of the question,' she said, her voice emerging unintentionally haughty, likely because part of her mind wanted to imagine exactly how that wild sexual reunion he'd mentioned might go. 'And please, let's try and keep this appropriately respectful.'

His eyes hardened, a frown forming between his eyebrows. 'I am trying, Dr Harvey. You're the one seeking me out in the car park. You're the one who led the conversation down a personal path.' He looked understandably upset.

'I'm not trying to imply that you've done anything wrong. This isn't personal.' She rushed to offer reassurance. 'But there can be no more talk of our past, or sex—' she held up her hand, cutting off his interruption '—no matter who starts it, and I'm aware that yesterday it was me.'

His jaw bunched, his defensive hackles rising. 'So this has nothing to do with distancing yourself from the infamous Murray Ward's son?'

Lauren gaped. 'Don't be ridiculous. I'm hurt that you would even think that of me.' She understood how he might be sensitive to any suggestion of frowned-upon conduct after his father's legacy. But his accusation made her feel as if he hadn't known her at all in the past, that she'd imagined their deep and passionate connection. Perhaps, desperate for solace in her grief, she'd invented his compassion when, in reality, maybe she'd actually meant nothing to him.

Well, she wouldn't fall into that same trap twice. She hardened her defences, rolled her shoulders back. 'This isn't about you. Mason. This is about my career.'

He frowned and Lauren pushed on. 'I'm one of the consultants on the appointment panel for the newest surgical consultant, the position I discovered yesterday that you've applied for.' She stepped closer, her determination rising.

He needed to understand the predicament he'd inadvertently created for her with his return.

Why did he have to come back now, just when everything was finally falling into place for her? She was finally steering her own life on track after years of prioritising her family.

'I've spent years taking care of Ben and working my way up at GHH,' she said. 'I took the appointment committee position because I hope to secure a promotion as permanent Head of ER, a promotion I deserve.' Her eyes watered under his silent observation. 'I have your CV in my in-box, together with all of the other shortlisted candidates. It's a conflict of interest for me to associate with you in any way beyond professionally.'

Couldn't he see that?

'By acting professionally, I'm actually doing you a favour here,' she said, her resentment bubbling to the surface. In keeping Mason at arm's length, she was protecting not only her chances at the promotion she craved, but his too for the position *he* wanted.

'Doing me a favour? And what? I'm acting *un*professionally because I assumed that we could be friends?' Mason shook his head, his snort of incredulous laughter humourless. 'I understand what's going on now. This feels like déjà vu, after all.'

'What do you mean by that?' Lauren clenched her fists as if she could keep tight control of this slippery conversation.

He stepped closer, invaded her personal space so her body heated with more than indignation as his eyes sparked with defiance. 'Come on, Lauren, let's be honest. You've made difficult choices before, despite the way we once felt about each other.'

Lauren's jaw dropped but, before she could ask what his statement implied, he continued.

'Forget about it.' He placed the crash helmet on and tightened the strap under his chin. 'From now on I'll try to stay out of your way as much as is humanly possible. You won't have to compromise your promotion, not for me. We're both focused on career advancement. I just hope that you'll be able to appraise my CV with an unbiased eye, given that the respect and trust we once shared seems to be another casualty of the choices we've made. I hope your shift goes well, Dr Harvey.'

He'd respected and trusted her? He'd experienced conflicted feelings when she'd called it off? Shellshocked, Lauren watched him ride away, her heart in her throat, in no way mollified by their conversation. Her hope for a nice, tidy conclusion to the issue of him being back in her daily life drained away with the shudder of breath she exhaled. The only certainty to come from this interaction was that not only was Mason a constant reminder of what they'd once been to each other, he seemed to be suggesting there had been stronger feelings there on his side than she'd thought. With that in mind, the one thing she'd likely struggle to do was forget.

# CHAPTER FOUR

MASON MADE HIS way down the corridor towards the ER two days later, dread like ice in his veins. Despite what he'd promised Lauren when she'd practically accused him in the car park of acting unprofessionally on his first day at work, contact between them at the hospital was inevitable. Not that he could avoid her away from the hospital either. She filled his thoughts as he relived every word of their three incredibly frustrating conversations. Because he was clearly some sort of glutton for punishment where she was concerned, she even consumed his dreams—hot, sweaty, erotic re-enactments so far removed from the light flirtation she'd found so objectionable the other day he'd laugh if her rejection hadn't been so painful.

Lauren had always been a stickler for the rules, a planner, overthinking every possible eventuality in her mind until she'd figured out the best course of action. And, despite what she thought of him, he had no intention of making her professional life difficult. Of course she couldn't be seen to favour one candidate over another. Nor would he jeopardise his own ambitions, certainly not in *this* particular hospital, by fraternising with one of the appointment panel. Thanks to Murray, his own professional conduct had always been exemplary. He wanted to make a name for himself here, not give anyone an excuse to liken him to his father.

But with Lauren off-limits, even in the friendliest of ways, working at the same hospital could be potentially unbearable. No attraction, no intimate fantasies, no barely controllable temptation to touch her and see if it would feel as good as he remembered.

His pulse raced as he pushed into the department through the double swing doors, his body on high alert, his façade in place, ready to act as if they were complete strangers. The staff roster told him they'd be working the same shift, but so far he'd managed to go all day, almost to the end of the shift, without an interaction.

Resolved to avoid her as best he could, he entered the hectic resuscitation bay a nurse directed him to, braced for the urgent medical scenario beyond, but also braced for the sight of Lauren.

Of course she was there, supervising the controlled chaos of the emergency taking place.

Lauren glanced up as Mason hurried into the action. 'Dr Ward, thanks for coming,' she said, her voice tight, her exhale full of relief that went some way to soothing Mason's ego. Clinically, Lauren was more than capable of managing any case that came through the doors, but her reaction gave him a kick of satisfaction nonetheless. She needed him, if only in this moment of urgency.

'Dr Harvey, what do you need?' he asked, setting aside their personal issues and focusing on their young patient as he snapped on the pair of gloves he'd grabbed the minute he'd entered the bay.

So the sum of their relationship would be polite professional respect. He could live with that, even if the contrast between the expectations and possibilities he'd imagined and the reality left him unexpectedly empty.

Lauren beckoned him to occupy the other side of the stretcher as she listened to the chest of the young woman laid out there. Mason quickly introduced himself to the patient, who was conscious, her wide eyes full of fear, her spine immobilised by a hard collar and backboard, an oxygen mask covering her face and the various monitors reading her vital signs emitting their unique alarms in a jarring symphony.

Lauren tugged the earpieces of her stethoscope from her ears and gave him a succinct history.

'This is Cassie, a twenty-two-year-old, otherwise fit and healthy woman who fell from a second storey balcony. There's a flail chest and pneumothorax on the right. I've completed a bedside ultrasound and there's also a collection in the abdomen from a likely liver contusion, but we'll know more once we can stabilise her and get a CT scan.'

Mason nodded, his hands already completing his own examination of the woman's chest and abdomen, while he noted the patient's tachycardia and low oxygen saturation.

'I think she might be tensioning,' Lauren said as he took the stethoscope from his pocket. 'Grady is setting up the chest drain.' She glanced over her shoulder, where Grady was speedily preparing a sterile tray with the equipment they'd need to save Cassie's life.

When she looked back at him, their eyes met. Mason tried to convey calm assurance in his stare. 'Great. I'll take a quick listen of Cassie's chest.'

Despite their personal friction, they were competent medical professionals. They could handle anything together. Mason listened to Cassie's breath sounds, noting their absence on the right. He placed his fingers at the base of her throat, just above the suprasternal notch, and discovered that her trachea was deviated to the left.

'I agree with your diagnosis,' he said to Lauren, stepping away from the bedside for a few seconds to study the chest X-ray displayed on the overhead monitor, which indeed showed fractured ribs and a collapsed lung.

'Pneumothorax takes precedent over the abdominal injury,' he said, glancing expectantly at Lauren for her nod of assent.

'Agreed. Do you want to do it as you're here?' she asked, concern in her voice.

Like her, Mason was used to triaging patients with multiple serious injuries, albeit in field hospitals and the basements of bombed-out cities. If they didn't treat the tension pneumothorax, a life-threatening condition where air became trapped in the chest cavity with no escape, causing the lung to collapse and the heart and circulation to be compromised, Cassie wouldn't live long enough to make it anywhere near an operating theatre.

'Any head injury, Dr Harvey?' asked Mason, quickly completing his own examination of the woman's rigid abdomen before stepping aside to wash up at the sink.

Lauren shook her head. 'But the neuro team are also on their way down. Spinal X-rays are also clear but we need to stabilise her in order to get her through to Radiology for a proper look.'

While Mason scrubbed at his hands and forearms, Lauren explained the procedure to the patient in a calm and clear manner.

'Dr Ward will be doing the chest drain,' Lauren stated to the gathered staff as Grady wheeled in the treatment trolley containing everything required to insert a chest drain into the patient's chest cavity to relieve the pressure on her lungs and, more importantly, her heart.

Mason dried his hands and put on sterile gloves.

'Has someone done a cross match for blood?' he asked, because if the chest drain didn't stabilise the patient's blood pressure he'd need to whisk her to Theatre to ensure she wasn't haemorrhaging into her abdominal cavity.

'Yes. Grady has organised all of the usual blood work,' Lauren said as she inserted another intravenous cannula into the woman's free arm. 'Anything extra you want while I'm here?'

'No, thank you.' Mason quickly cleaned the skin over the fifth intercostal space, injected local anaesthetic and made a small incision between the ribs. Lauren snapped on a pair of clean sterile gloves and joined him on his side of the stretcher, intuitively assisting him where needed, clamping the tube that would suck the air out of the patient's chest cavity with the proficiency of someone who, like him, had done this emergency lifesaving procedure a thousand times.

They moved in sync, anticipating each other's needs and moves as if they'd worked together for years, as if silently communicating their support and encouragement, all their personal distrust set aside.

The procedure necessitated their closeness. It was like a form of torture. He didn't want to notice the warmth of her body, hear the soft sigh of her breathing or be aware of her proximity with a strange intensity that he'd never experienced before, so he tried to block her out, focusing instead on the job.

No matter how well they'd known each other six years

ago, it hadn't been well enough. No matter how strong the physical attraction, it was irrelevant without trust. She'd stated what she thought of him, made her position clear once more, the same way she had when she'd ended things. Whatever they'd shared in the past, there was clearly nothing left as far as she was concerned.

He would master this physical attraction, ignore it until it passed. Hopefully one day he'd be able to see her around the hospital and not react at all beyond a polite smile of recognition.

Mason adjusted the position of the tube, his gloved hand colliding with Lauren's.

Inside he jumped as if he'd been zapped by an electric fence. He was so attuned to her proximity it was as if they'd touched for the very first time. Her muttered apology, the way she kept her gaze averted, only inflamed the tension.

How could he be so drawn to a woman who'd made it clear she wanted nothing to do with him? A woman who, even when they'd been in a relationship, had been emotionally withdrawn. Conscious of her grief and confused and uncertain of himself after the upheaval of his father's actions and mother's desertion, Mason had retreated too. When she'd broken things off with him without a backwards glance, he'd stuck to his plans and left everything behind when he'd left Auckland.

He hadn't seen it fully at the time, but they'd both chosen the easiest option back then, so it was clear to see now that Lauren was once more prioritising something over a relationship with him, even a friendship.

With steady hands he was acutely grateful for, Mason sutured the chest drain in place so it wouldn't fall out when the patient moved. Lauren unclamped the tube. Bubbles began to escape from the underwater seal immediately, telling them that the tube was correctly positioned and already allowing trapped air to escape. Within seconds, the patient's breathlessness eased, her colour improved and her heart rate approximated normal.

Mason caught Lauren's small sigh of relief. He glanced her way, nodded and, for the split second their stares locked, words passed between them once more. *Well done. We did it. Thanks for your help.*

He ached to be able to voice those things to her. But now he was too unsure of their forbidden situation to say any of that aloud. He didn't know how to act as if she meant nothing to him and refused to repeatedly humiliate himself.

They looked away in unison, the job coming before their personal issues as they continued their efforts to treat and stabilise the patient.

Mason placed his hand on Cassie's shoulder and smiled. 'Well done. That should make you feel a lot more comfortable. We're going to run a few more tests now, to have a look inside your abdomen, okay?'

They finished working on Cassie's care in silence, together but also apart. They'd never worked in the same department together before, training on different teams as medical students. And now, for the sake of their respective careers, they needed to maintain distance, pretend that there wasn't a connection between them, one that as far as Mason was concerned would not be silenced at present.

With the most life-threatening injury resolved, Lauren ordered a repeat chest X-ray and informed the orthopaedic surgeon and neurosurgical registrar of Cassie's status and other injuries. Mason passed on the patient's care to his on-call surgical colleague, happy that the patient's blood pressure and therefore the likely abdominal blood loss had stabilised. This would hopefully save her from an exploratory laparotomy, but with his shift over and other doctors already on the case he was now superfluous to requirements.

Heading out of the resuscitation bay, his feet dragged. He was physically tired, but for some reason the idea of going home to his empty house, alone, left him restless. Even the idea of a surf couldn't provide the usual uplift to his mood.

Hopefully it could be explained by the anticlimax, the plummeting adrenaline levels in his blood now that Cassie was stable. Or the impending funeral. It had been easy to shove his father's cremation from his mind while working, settling into a new department and establishing routines, but with free time on the horizon, free time in which thinking about Lauren was forbidden, his brain would ruminate, dissect his regrets in relation to Murray, ponder the overdue conversations for which it was now too late.

He swallowed the lump in his throat as he acknowledged the likely root of his reluctance to be alone with his thoughts. Lauren. Obviously he'd been more invested in seeing her, in starting up something with her than he'd recognised when he'd known he was returning home, because the hollowness inside him felt reminiscent of the grief he'd felt six years ago as he'd tried to put their relationship behind him and move on.

He spied her seated at the desk in the staff area, typing up her notes on the computer. His first instinct was to take the terminal next to hers to write up his own observations and the chest drain insertion procedure in the patient's hospital record before he left for the night. He could torture himself, prove that they could co-exist quite satisfactorily as colleagues, but he couldn't face the strained silence that would likely sour his day further.

Instead, he headed to the other staff area and took a seat next to Grady.

'Hey,' Grady said in welcome, his stare somewhat wary. 'Cassie has gone for a CT scan. Where's the boss?'

Mason logged into the computer system. 'She's still in Resus, doing what we're doing by the looks of it—writing up notes.' On the one hand he didn't want to talk about Lauren, but on the other she was pretty much his brain and his body's favourite subject at the moment, and Grady knew her better than anyone.

It was like a bad joke.

She was so close and yet a million miles out of reach. There might as well be a barbed wire fence around her adorned with a flashing neon *Entry Forbidden* sign.

'You all respect her a lot, don't you?' he asked.

Grady nodded. 'Her department runs like a well-oiled machine.'

'Unlike many I've worked in,' Mason agreed. In action, in calm, determined life-saving mode, Lauren was the sexiest thing he'd ever seen, not that he could admit that to her or to Grady.

The chasm between them emotionally plunged his mood into darker depths. Their former relationship had always been easy, intuitive, the way it had just been in the resus room when they'd worked side by side. There had been nothing they couldn't fix with a stimulating bicker, a joke around or a well-timed kiss. Until their very last issue, the one that had broken them apart: how neither of them had been ready to commit. How they'd dodged honesty and accepted the inevitable, dumping their relationship into the *too hard* basket and walking away.

Now, older and wiser, Mason would have handled things completely differently. But what about Lauren? Would she make the same choices today as she had then? She'd already admitted that she'd still been grieving for her mother. He'd felt let down by her at the time, but perhaps she'd felt nothing for him. She certainly seemed to be excelling at their current state of enforced avoidance.

She'd clearly done a better job of getting over their split than Mason.

'Is that why you came back? Because of the quality of our ER?' Grady was fishing, and Mason couldn't blame him. He was glad that Lauren had such a good friend in her camp.

'My father died,' he said without inflection. 'I came home to bury him, but it's good to be back at Gulf Harbour, to be honest. You know from your time in the army that there's no place like home.'

'I hadn't heard about your father. Sorry to hear that.' Grady fell silent in that way guys had of saying the bare minimum by stating all that needed to be said. The last thing Mason wanted to do was talk about his father.

'Does Lauren know?' Grady asked.

Mason clenched his jaw, shook his head, biting back the urge to admit that even friendship between him and Lauren was off the table. He'd never had the chance to tell her about Murray. Would she want to know?

Mason finished typing up his notes wordlessly and logged out of the hospital intranet. He and Lauren just weren't meant to be, not then and not now. If he'd developed the discipline to forgo creature comforts and work in some of the most basic places on the planet, surely he could harness the same discipline to forget about Lauren Harvey.

For the second time.

He stood, surprised to find Lauren staring at him from across the room. His pulse thrummed in his throat as he bid Grady goodbye and headed for the exit.

'Thanks for your help earlier, Dr Harvey,' he said as he passed, resigned to the fact that this cold tension would be their new reality.

'I…um… You're welcome, Dr Ward.'

There, he could do it, act unaffected. Only six years ago, the Lauren who was out of sight had been hard enough to forget. But seeing her again every day, unable to speak to her the way he wanted, to tease out her smile or seek out her company would test everything he'd believed about himself: that he'd be able to see her as a colleague and nothing else, that he didn't care what she thought of him, that he'd got over Lauren a long time ago. The truth was she could never be just another doctor, not to Mason. He knew intimate things about her body, her feelings, her dreams.

He exited the department without looking over his shoulder, even though the hairs on the back of his neck pricked up, urging him to look her way once more. But he didn't need to witness her indifference. Not again.

# CHAPTER FIVE

LAUREN SPRINTED DOWN the corridor towards the operating theatres, dodging porters wheeling patients on stretchers and in wheelchairs, ducking in between staff and relatives, her head about to explode with the urgency to catch up with Mason.

She rounded the corner, her heart thunking back into sinus rhythm as she spotted him just ahead. 'Mason, wait!' she called, relief a sweet taste in her mouth.

He spun to face her, the lines and angles of his handsome face wreathed in confusion, questions in his eyes. She stopped in front of him, catching her breath from both the sprint and his presence, close and tall, filling her vision, bathing her senses, corrupting her good intentions the way only a hot man or a slab of chocolate could.

She had no idea where to start; she only knew that, in light of what she'd just learned from Grady, she couldn't leave things with Mason the way they were.

Why hadn't he confided in her? She'd almost sobbed for Mason when she'd heard the news.

Glancing around the busy corridor, she moved to the wall, encouraging Mason to follow her so they'd be out of the stream of human traffic.

'Why didn't you tell me?' She moved closer and dropped her voice. 'About Murray?'

His eyes darkened, stormy and haunted. Before she was even aware of the comforting gesture, she gripped his arm. The warmth of his sun-kissed skin, the strength of the taut muscles beneath her hand and the flare of that familiar but also foreign heat in his stare, that even the way she'd hurt him the other day couldn't diminish, made Lauren drop her hand as if stung and shove it in the pocket of her white coat. 'I'm so sorry.'

For his loss, for the way she must have made him feel with her careless dismissal, and for touching him. Because not only was he regarding her from behind a detached and shuttered expression, something she deserved after she'd upset and insulted him, now her nervous system was lit up like a million stars, just the way it had been when they'd inadvertently touched in the ER while inserting that chest drain.

'Thanks,' he said, his jaw rigid. 'I'm sure that Murray would have valued your sympathy.'

The grim clench of his jaw called to Lauren. She wanted to be there for him the way she'd been when Murray had let Mason down so badly. And, irrationally, she wanted to kiss him, hold him, stay up all night talking to him.

How could she have convinced herself he'd be easy to ignore? How could she be so drawn to him after such a short time? How could all the emotions she'd bottled up after he'd left New Zealand still be there, pressure building, just waiting for something to pop the cork?

'I hadn't heard,' she said, recalling Mason's understandable confusion and anger when he'd learned of Murray's affair. Perhaps a part of him had never overcome the fallout—the break-up of his family. He would certainly have

hated having to return to Gulf Harbour under such circumstances, to bury his father and not on his own terms.

'I wouldn't have expected you to have heard about it,'
Mason said, crossing his arms over his chest, pain and
rejection behind his words. 'It's not like anyone around
here mentions Murray Ward's name. He's been persona
non grata for years. They even renamed the Ward Wing.'

Lauren winced, because *that* she had known. The surgical wing of the hospital had been named after Mason's
grandfather, Professor Isaac Ward, an eminent surgeon and
researcher who had brought in millions of dollars' worth
of funding over his years at Gulf Harbour. Mason had confided to her that he'd been particularly close to his grandfather growing up. With such a prestigious lineage, the Mason
she'd first met had had big shoes to fill and for a while,
before his father's fall from grace and the gossip that followed, he'd embraced the challenge, winning the Hiranga
Cup for Excellence in his third year as a medical student.

Then, after his father had been forced to leave his head
of surgery position after the extramarital affair with a
much younger patient that had shocked the Gulf Harbour
community, Mason had resented his father's hypocritical
weakness, given his previous overbearing expectations. Un-
surprisingly, Mason had grown more and more withdrawn
and restless. Except the naive and emotionally fragile part
of Lauren hadn't expected that withdrawal to extend to
their relationship.

'Apparently,' he continued, a hint of bitterness in his
voice, 'it was nothing personal, just part of a new hospital policy to create uniformity and inclusion. But Murray
never quite overcame the slight. Not that he had any right
to object, of course.'

'I'm sorry about that too.' Awash with so many conflicting regrets, Lauren looked down at her feet, wishing they were somewhere private. She had to fight the temptation to touch him again, to move closer to his warmth and strength and unique Mason scent. To offer him comfort he would probably reject, given the belligerent state of their current relationship.

But this was Mason, a man who'd been there for her, helped her through some of the darkest days of her life. Now that she knew the reason he'd returned, she wouldn't be able to stop thinking about him, grieving and alone. He carried the responsibility of being an only child and, despite his complex relationship with his father, Mason would always do the honourable thing.

'Grady told you, didn't he?' he asked, his stare roaming her features in a way that made her temperature spike uncomfortably.

'Yes,' she admitted, tentatively looking up at him from under her lashes, her gaze drawn to the set of his distracting mouth. 'But you could have told me yourself.' She tried to keep the hurt from her tone. After all, why would he have confided in her after her less than friendly reception, after she'd inadvertently all but accused him of acting unprofessionally? It seemed like a poor excuse now, but she'd been so rattled by his return, so desperate to do the right thing with regard to the appointment panel, she'd ended up being prickly and rude when he'd most needed a friend.

'Could I?' he said, his bold stare forcing her to admit her shortcomings where Mason was concerned. 'I'd planned to tell you, but we didn't stay friends when we broke up and you made it clear that we couldn't start again now.' He shrugged, his apparent nonchalance an irritating itch under her skin. She deserved some rebuke and she couldn't explain why it felt vital that he cared.

'When is the funeral?' she asked, ignoring his reminder of how cold she'd been. Now that she understood the circumstances, she was determined to be there for him, whether he wanted her or not. She too had known Murray Ward. Like most of the Gulf Harbour community, she'd respected him as a surgeon.

'It's Friday,' he said, his jaw tense, looking away over her shoulder.

She swallowed the swell of sympathy that rose up and inched closer into his personal space. 'Can you tell me what happened? How did he die?' Her voice was already a whisper, but the heat rising from his body seemed to steal her air.

Mason pressed his lips together, the emotions in his eyes conflicted, as she knew they would be. No matter how much he despised what Murray had done, no matter that his father had been cold and demanding, the man was someone Mason had once idolised, tried to emulate and impress.

'He collapsed on the golf course,' he said. 'A massive MI. Brought in dead at our neighbouring hospital.'

'I'm so sorry,' she said, her fingers desperate to reach for his hand. Her chest ached for him, for his broken relationships, his solitude. 'When did you last see him?'

When Mason had left Auckland, he and Murray had been practically estranged.

He pursed his lips as if debating how much to confide in her. She winced, recalling a time when the only people they'd been able to talk to were each other.

'I hadn't seen him in person for six years.'

'So you hadn't reconciled at all then?' Her throat clenched

in sadness for Mason and Murray's missed chances. Lauren had at least had time to say goodbye to her mother, not that it had made the grief any easier to bear.

Mason shook his head, his eyes turbulent with contained anguish.

Lauren's eyes stung with unshed tears. Despite holding such high expectations of his only son, Murray had let Mason down so badly through his actions, destroying his own career and their family in the process. Of course Mason had felt the need to get away from it all, to go and work where no one knew the Ward name. Seen in the rational light of time passed, she couldn't blame him. She hadn't blamed him at the time. She'd simply added more grief on top of her existing burden.

Lauren allowed her stare to hold his for long, intense seconds while her heart spasmed in empathy. She had to hope that she was conveying all of the things she was too scared to say, too scared to feel. A part of her knew this man better than she wanted to admit. She still needed to be careful around him for the sake of her equilibrium.

Mason stared back, the sincere non-verbal communication flooding every part of her body with awareness and impatience. Her jumbled thoughts turned selfish. Realistically, how long could Mason tolerate being in Auckland, with the bitter memories and constant reminders? Could Gulf Harbour ever fulfil him after living so long overseas? Would the lure of glory take him away again to a place where he could just be himself?

'Will Sarah be there on Friday?' Lauren asked to distract herself from how the idea of him leaving again racked her body with chills. She had no idea what kind of relationship Mason had with his mother now, but she remembered his devastation when Sarah had left for Australia after his parents' divorce. He'd felt abandoned, rejected, left alone to deal with the fallout of Murray's disgrace. Sarah had moved on, quickly remarrying and, it had seemed at the time, replacing Mason with her new stepson.

Oh, she'd invited Mason to go and live with her, but he'd still had two years left of his degree to finish. Unlike his parents, he wasn't free to up and leave all of the mess behind at that point.

'No,' he said. 'Her new husband has just had his first grandchild. She's moved on, and the last thing she'd want to do is be there for the ex who betrayed and humiliated her.' His voice was carefully devoid of accusation.

So he was truly alone.

Lauren's stomach pinched violently; she wished they were closer, physically and emotionally. But her conflict of interest wasn't the only reason she'd shunned his offer of friendship. Her physical reaction to him after all this time had terrified her. She needed to be vigilant around Mason Ward, to guard her soft spots more than ever.

'I'd have thought that she might want to be there for *you*,' she couldn't help commenting. After all, Sarah was his mother. She lived a three-hour flight away, and she only had one biological son. She didn't blame her for wanting a fresh start after her husband had cheated and created a scandal, but her rejection at the time had made things ten times worse for a confused and disillusioned Mason.

'I'm a big boy.' His voice was cool, his eyes hard, but sparks of determination and what looked like challenge sparked in their depths.

'Everyone needs someone for support.' He needed a friend and she could fill that role. She exhaled, feeling as if this older, more self-assured version of Mason was a total enigma after all. That shouldn't send flutters of excitement through her stomach, but it did.

'Can *I* come to the funeral?' she asked, desperate to ignore the way his proximity, the searching depth of his blue stare, made her feel edgy. 'I'd like to pay my respects. And I think someone should be there for you. Even an... old friend is better than nothing,' she added, stumbling over her words.

'I thought friendship between us was forbidden?' A hint of his mocking smile lifted one corner of his mouth, drawing Lauren's gaze back to his lips. Lips she'd worshipped, kissed a thousand times. Lips whose every uttered word she'd hung on.

'I thought you were accustomed to pushing the envelope?' she countered, because with him sparring came naturally.

He raised one eyebrow. 'I am. I was thinking more about you and *your* career, Laurie.'

Lauren steeled herself against the stupid warmth that spread through her veins at his words and the hint of tenderness that crept into his expression. How did he still know her so well?

She cleared her throat, resolved. 'It's a funeral for a doctor I knew who worked at this hospital. Let me worry about my career.'

Now would be the perfect time to tell him that she'd already spoken with Helen Bridges, Head of Corporate Management Services, and resigned her position on the interview panel. She'd hated to let down the other team members but she'd decided that, in view of her past with Mason, it had been the right thing to do.

Mason regarded her in silence for so long Lauren began to fidget, aware their interaction would appear intimate, aware of the sound of his breathing and the way his pupils dilated when he looked at her.

'Okay. Friends it is.' He nodded decisively, pushed his shoulder off the wall and began walking backwards away from Lauren so that their eye contact remained unbroken. There was no smile on his lips but Lauren could have sworn she spied a flash of triumph in his eyes.

How he managed the manoeuvre without bumping into anyone was quite a feat, but that was Mason. The laws of the universe didn't apply. After a few paces, he spun around and headed for the entrance to the suite of operating theatres.

Lauren stayed inert, her feet seemingly glued to the spot, trapped by the urge to watch him until he disappeared from sight. He swiped his security card over the scanner and pushed the door open and Lauren held her breath, the phrase *be careful* looping through her head.

At the last minute, Mason looked back at Lauren.

Caught staring, she gasped, gripping the handrail attached to the wall for support.

A sexy smile tugged at Mason's mouth. How had he known that she'd stood there watching him instead of returning to the ER?

Mason raised his hand in a salute and disappeared into the department, leaving Lauren bursting at the seams with her belly flutters and her scattered parts and a sense of inevitability that felt oh, so familiar.

# CHAPTER SIX

THE REMAINING FUNERAL GUESTS—a small handful of old university and golfing friends of Murray's and a couple of his distant cousins—still occupied one corner of the function room at the beachside restaurant where they'd gathered after the brief service at the crematorium.

With his duty as host largely over, Mason loosened and removed his black tie, folding it into his jacket pocket. He popped the top button on his shirt as he stepped out onto the deck into the sunshine in search of the one and only person he wanted to be around. Temporarily blinded by the bright sun, he dragged in the first deep breath of the day, relief erupting with his slow exhale as his gaze snagged on Lauren.

She hadn't left yet.

Mason paused, observing her where she sat on a low-slung bough of a pohutukawa tree that hugged the sand in a graceful and convenient arc. In a few weeks' time the entire tree, coined New Zealand's Christmas tree because it bloomed in December, would be dusted with its characteristic red flowers, providing a stunning photo opportunity.

Would they still be *friends* in December?

Would he ever be able to think of her in that way alone?

He shuddered, recalling how Lauren's presence throughout the sombre service that morning and the awkward social gathering that had followed had made the event tolerable. He'd felt strangely removed emotionally, as if he too was merely a funeral guest, his grief deficient from what it should be as Murray's son. Only the sight of Lauren's arrival, her taking a seat behind him as the service began—close enough to offer support, but not too close— had settled the sickening churning of his gut and brought him a sense of peace and homecoming for the first time since he'd set foot back in New Zealand.

Not that the serenity of her presence had lasted. How could it when their past and present were in such a convoluted mess?

Grateful that she'd insisted on attending, he headed Lauren's way, his mind replaying every frustrating detail of their conversations to date. The minute he stepped off the deck, his shoes sinking into the soft sand, he was on another beach at another time...

*'You've changed your mind?' he said, his voice incredulous from the sudden flare of nausea.*

*'Please try and understand,' Lauren pleaded, her eyes huge in the dusk light of their favourite beach.*

*Waves crashed behind them, seagulls screamed, their cries snatched away by the wind. Ice invaded Mason's bones.*

*'Ben needs me,' she said. 'He's only a little boy and Dad's still all over the place.' She looked down at her feet and Mason's stare followed, words deserting him. They'd planned this overseas trip for months, looked forward to it, saved up for the one-way air tickets to Europe. It was supposed to be their reward after graduation. Travel, working*

*in foreign hospitals, adventure in far-flung places where they could be themselves.*

*Only Lauren already knew who she was. It was only Mason who needed to escape the Ward name, to go where no one knew the good and bad of his legacy.*

*'I can't leave.' Lauren's eyes filled with the sheen of tears. 'Mum would have wanted me to be there for Ben, the way she was always there for us.' Her voice broke, her anguish crushing Mason's chest.*

*He tugged her into his arms, pressed his lips to the top of her head and sucked in the comforting scent of her hair. 'Of course he needs you. Don't worry, we'll figure it all out.'*

*He didn't have to know the right thing to say, he just needed to be there for Lauren.*

*A damp patch from her tears soaked through his T-shirt. He'd never seen her cry. They'd talked about her mother's death, about her concerns for her father, who'd started having some counselling. But Lauren had always held something back and, troubled by his own woes, he'd never pushed her too hard. That was why they worked so well; their relationship was easy, fun, and only heavy on the awesome chemistry.*

*Pulling back, Mason lifted her chin. He wiped her tears from her cheeks, kissing the wet paths they'd left behind, and then he pressed his mouth to hers. They'd sort out this blip together.*

*Lauren's lips were cold and tasted of salt. She sighed, her body shuddering as she collapsed her weight against him. Mason moved his mouth over hers in slow, soft seductive swipes. His blood heated, his body reacting as it always did to her closeness, but he kept the kiss PG, wanting to see her beautiful smile more than he wanted to drive* them home as quickly as he could and distract her from her troubles in a different way.

'You should go to Europe anyway,' she said when he'd let her up for air, her stare serious.

His brain, still awash in a fog of arousal, scrambled to concentrate on what she was saying.

She tilted her chin in that determined way of hers. 'It's better for us both if we make a clean break of it now.'

'What?' His stomach started to fight its way into his chest, displacing his wildly panicked heart. He slid his hands from her shoulders and gripped both of her hands, certain that if he literally held onto her, her words would somehow make sense. 'Are you breaking up with me?'

This couldn't be happening.

She tugged her hands from his, wrapped her arms around her waist and turned away to face the sea. 'I have responsibilities here.'

How could her voice sound so cold? He wanted to block his ears.

'Neither of us went into this looking for anything long-term...' she shrugged, and Mason's vision hazed out of focus '...and once we start work that will be all-consuming too...'

Mason cracked a little more inside; he was already bashed about by Murray's infamous affair, his parents' divorce and his mother's move to Australia. She might not have realised it—he hadn't himself until this very moment—but Lauren was all he had. Five minutes ago his exciting future had stretched ahead of him, one Lauren was part of. He'd leave Auckland, a place where, no matter what he did, he would always be compared to other Ward doctors.

*He'd been desperate to get away but hadn't once thought about ending things with Lauren.*

*'Wait...' He scrubbed his hand through his hair. Yes, they'd never talked about being together for ever or confessed deep feelings for each other, but she was just ending it like that, as if he'd meant so little to her all this time? 'Wait...' He didn't have to go to Europe. He paced, confused. Had he done something wrong? Been too wrapped up in his own issues to see her withdrawal? Perhaps she was telling him that she had no time for someone who'd been so tied up in knots over the mess his parents had created.*

*'It's for the best this way, Mason.' Lauren swallowed and he knew her mind was made up. Once she made a decision, she stuck to it. 'I'm sorry that I'm pulling out, but you should still go.'*

*Mason choked on his disbelieving snort. She was breaking up with him and he could either stay and be alone, or leave and be alone.*

*Some choice she was giving him...*

'Hi. How are you doing?' Lauren's enquiry snapped him back into the present.

He blinked a few times, bringing the older Lauren into focus. 'I'll live,' he croaked, his throat dry from reliving her past rejection. 'I thought you might have left already.'

She stood from her perch on the tree, and he shoved his hands into his trouser pockets to stop himself from pushing back the lock of hair the light breeze had lifted onto her cheek. 'I wanted to talk to you before I go.'

Too restless to stand still, Mason slipped off his shoes and socks. 'Okay, in that case, let's go for a walk.'

'Are you sure?' Lauren frowned, her mouth pinched with

worry. 'You're the host. You can't leave before all of the guests have departed.'

He shrugged, in no mood to make small talk. 'I can do what I want.'

If only that were wholly true where Lauren was concerned. They wouldn't be standing here if it were up to him. They'd be on his bike, heading somewhere neutral, somewhere lacking the power to trigger memories he'd rather forget, perhaps making new memories.

'I've done my duty as a son today,' he said. 'And I stopped caring what other people think of me a long time ago.'

Unlike the twenty-five-year-old who'd left New Zealand, the man she'd so easily thrown away, thirty-one-year-old Mason knew himself, understood his worth and his strengths and had his professional life, at least, all figured out.

His personal life still needed some work, though; something that had only become fully apparent when he'd reunited with Lauren.

'Come on.' He tilted his head in the direction of the shore and started walking.

He should tell her to go home. Her conflict of interest hadn't evaporated just because she'd learned about Murray's death. And the last time she'd been forced to make a choice he'd been the one to suffer the greatest consequences. He'd cancelled his ticket to Europe, packed up his ravaged heart and headed for the most inhospitable, isolated job he could find in Australia in an attempt to forget all about Lauren.

Too hot in the afternoon sun, Mason shrugged off his suit jacket, rolled up his shirt sleeves and returned his hands into his trouser pockets as he kept an easy pace, Lauren at his side.

'How are you really feeling?' she asked, her concerned tone brushing away the last lingering cobwebs of his bitter trip down memory lane.

He looked out to sea, focusing for a moment on his convoluted feelings about his father rather than his even more jumbled feelings for Lauren.

'I feel empty,' he admitted. 'Like I'm watching someone else's life unfold today, not my own.' Only now, with her walking next to him on the warm sand, doing something normal, something they'd done a hundred times before, did he feel like himself once more, not Murray's son, not Dr Ward, just Mason.

Of course he couldn't confess that, especially not to Lauren. It would cross some line he'd vowed to keep.

She nodded, empathy warming her stare. 'It's okay to have complex feelings today. There are no rules when it comes to grief, as you know.'

Mason pressed his lips together. 'Complex sums it up perfectly,' he admitted, wishing, for some bizarre reason, he could reach out and hold her hand. For himself, for comfort. Platonic comfort... *Right.*

'I don't know... The service,' he said, 'it forced me to see my father's life as a whole, not just the mistakes he made in the latter years. He was difficult to please, had high expectations for his only son, but he was also a good father in other ways.'

He felt her hand on his bare arm and stopped walking, giving himself time to absorb the intimate heat of her touch. How could he switch off the physical craving, which seemed to only increase in intensity the more time they spent together?

She looked up at him, her eyes piercing him. 'I really do understand.'

'Of course. I know that you do.' He offered her a soft smile that he wanted to follow up by pulling her into his arms and tasting her lips. Instead he curled his fists inside his pockets.

'Thank you for letting me come today,' she said, her voice breathy with emotion in a way that made Mason want to glide his finger over those lips to see if they were as soft as he remembered. Except he'd all but rationalised that the best course of action was for him to make do with her offered friendship.

Instead he looked down to where her hand sat on his forearm. 'Aren't you worried about fraternising with one of the surgical consultant candidates?'

He wanted to rip out his own tongue, so tired was he of pretending he had no desire for this woman whatsoever. If she didn't care about crossing the line, why had he reminded her of it?

'I resigned,' she said, dropping her hand from his arm, crossing her arms over her waist and walking ahead once more.

*What? Had he heard her right?*

'From the appointment panel, you mean?' he asked, striding to catch up while his pulse tripped over itself to try and decipher her motivations.

She nodded, eyes front as if she didn't want to talk about it.

'I hope it wasn't because of me, because you were right. You do deserve that promotion.'

She shot him a sideways glance, her expression unreadable. 'I did it for me. I discussed it through with Corporate Management Services and I decided that our…past relationship was enough to create a professional conflict. If I'm the best candidate for the Head of ER position, it won't matter that I've pulled out of a commitment I'd struggle to handle objectively.' She looked down, kicked at an oyster shell with her toe. 'At least I hope it won't.' She gave a humourless snort and the spaghetti in Mason's head twisted a little more. If he'd thought he hadn't known where he was with the Lauren of six years ago, today's Lauren could tie him into even tighter knots. He'd need to beware, keep his guard up, lock away his feelings.

Then it suddenly occurred to him, as if he'd just dived under the waves out in the bay, the cold shock slapping him to his senses. The ethical barrier to their friendship was gone, like a puff of smoke.

He should feel relief. Excitement was there, but that was pretty constant in Lauren's presence, given their chemistry. But the overriding emotion in him was confusion. Her resignation changed nothing. Only she'd been concerned enough about her past feelings for him to pull out of the interview process.

Did that mean she'd had stronger feelings back then than he'd known about at the time?

He mentally slapped himself. Today was not the day to try and come to important conclusions.

'I haven't said it yet,' he added, 'but I really appreciate you being here today.' He cleared his throat, embracing the vulnerable feeling that he couldn't seem to shake every time they talked.

She frowned, looked down as if ashamed. 'Even though I

inadvertently insulted you and rejected your offer of friendship because I was being a bit uptight about my job?' She gnawed at her lip as she waited for his answer, but there was that hint of a smile in her eyes, a flash of the old Lauren, the one who could give as much as she got when it came to teasing and bickering and goading each other on.

Mason grinned, nodded. 'Even then.' Falling serious, he added, 'Today would have been intolerable without you. Thank you for coming.'

'You're welcome.' Her expression softened, her eyes dancing over his features in the way that told him she had a hundred thoughts in her head. He wished he knew what they were.

'You know, my experiences with Ben have taught me that parenting sometimes feels like an impossible task. Your father was a very intelligent man. I bet he hated knowing he'd let you down by his actions.'

Mason swallowed, torn between keeping things superficial in order to keep her literally at arm's length and confiding his deeper feelings and inadequacies to the only woman he'd ever allowed close, not that it had saved him from pain. Her protective, nurturing role with Ben gave her a mature understanding of relationships, and talking about his father would stop him trying to dissect their current bewildering situation.

He exhaled, content for now to have her friendship. 'I used to feel so angry that he'd abused his position of power. And then I'd feel guilty for judging my own father, a brilliant and diligent surgeon, a man who had done so much good before making one bad choice.'

She nodded in understanding, stepping closer to his side. 'I used to be angry that my mother had left us, even though the rational part of me knew she'd had no choice. Emotions aren't always logical,' she said gently.

'I could have forgiven him,' he carried on, 'if he hadn't continued to be the sanctimonious tyrant he'd always been. Perhaps then his actions wouldn't have been so utterly hypocritical. I grew up hearing how he was continuing my grandfather's legacy, building on the Ward name, but when I said I wanted to follow in both their sets of footsteps and study medicine it seemed that nothing I ever did was good enough. And yet he was the one to throw it all away. He was the one to let himself and others down.'

'It's hard when you realise a man you'd once looked up to is fallible. Flawed.' She shrugged, looked out to sea. 'But we're all human. We all make mistakes.'

She fell quiet, as if putting distance between him and the emotional vulnerability of her confession. Mason wanted to ask if he featured in her regrets, but he didn't want anything to damage their newly found friendship. Instead he said, 'Today must have been difficult for you too. Brought up painful memories of your loss.'

'I'm fine. I've had longer to come to terms with my grief, and at least I got to say goodbye to Mum.' She smiled in reassurance. 'I'm sorry that you didn't have that opportunity with Murray.'

As if in silent agreement, they turned and headed back the way they'd come. Neither spoke, the quiet companionable, so that Mason wondered if perhaps this friendship thing might work.

After a while, Lauren looked him up and down. 'You know, you're different now. You've changed in a positive way. You never used to admit to having any weaknesses or regrets.'

'Maybe that's what age does,' he replied with a smile. 'And you've changed for the better too. You have less barbed wire around you than you used to have.' Not that being close to her wasn't still dangerous.

When they reached the car park next to the restaurant, Lauren dropped her shoes and slipped her feet inside.

'Want a ride home?' Mason did the same and then made his way to his bike and unlocked his helmet. 'I always carry a spare.' He knew she'd arrived by taxi.

She looked at his bike as if it were a double bed, all of her former wariness returning. 'I'm okay, thanks. Look, I don't want to give you the wrong idea. I do want us to be friends, but I'm not looking for a relationship. My priority is still my promotion—'

'And mine is the surgical consultant job,' he interrupted, because they'd covered this ground before and he didn't need a replay of how anything beyond friends was of no interest to her. There were only so many rejections a man could take. 'So, neither of us is in a relationship kind of place.'

She nodded as if appeased; only a small frown pinched her lips. 'Good. That's cleared that up then. Are you going to Grady's birthday drinks tomorrow? He took a lot of persuading that he should mark the occasion for once. Molly, his daughter, is with his ex for the night, so he'll need us to help distract him.'

'In that case, I wouldn't miss it,' Mason said, happy to be included in the invitation.

'It's at the Har-Bar. Seven p.m.' The mention of the bar they'd frequented, playing out much of their former relationship—dates, celebrations, fights and making up—forced a boulder of trepidation into Mason's gut.

'Great,' he said, ignoring the hesitant way Lauren was looking for his reaction. 'I'll see you there.' He jammed on his crash helmet and revved the engine of his bike, climbing aboard and heading for the road. He could do this, keep her at arm's length, be her colleague and her friend.

He could do it, but it would test every atom of his being.

# CHAPTER SEVEN

LAUREN GLANCED AT the door of the Har-Bar, her teeth nibbling at her bottom lip and her nerves jangling with anticipation. Most of the invited guests were already gathered to celebrate Grady's birthday. The bar was packed, the atmosphere buzzing and Lauren couldn't seem to enjoy herself at all.

Grady thrust a glass of wine into her hand and she muttered her thanks.

'Why don't you text him if you're going to watch the door every five seconds?' her friend asked, a small frown tugging at his mouth.

'Text who?' Lauren replied, turning her back to the door and plastering an *I'm having a good time* smile onto her face.

'Mason,' Grady said, smiling a greeting to someone in the far corner of the bar before shooting Lauren a reproachful stare.

'Why would I be waiting for Mason? It's *your* birthday.' Why couldn't she stop thinking about Mason? It was as if since the funeral he'd infected her mind, multiplying exponentially there like a virus.

'Because you've been different since he arrived back,' Grady said in his no-nonsense way. 'I wondered if some of the old feelings have resurfaced.' The sympathy in his voice grated against Lauren's eardrums. Was she that obvious? Had she been moping around the hospital, pining for a glimpse of Mason like a lovesick puppy? She shuddered at the thought.

'Don't be ridiculous. How have I been different?' She took a massive gulp of wine to ease the feeling that she was spinning out of control and everyone was watching.

'Distracted. A bit up and down. I think the new registrar thinks you hate her,' he said, glancing over at Kat Collins, the newest doctor to join Gulf Harbour ER.

Kat paused in her conversation and smiled hesitantly at Lauren and Grady from the other side of the bar. Aware that the younger woman might, quite rightly, assume that they were talking about her, Lauren beamed her friendliest smile.

'She does not,' Lauren hissed at Grady when Kat continued her conversation.

Grady shrugged. 'No, you're probably right. I hardly know her. So,' he said, changing the subject, '*are* you and Mason seeing each other again?'

Lauren sighed; Grady could be like a dog with a bone sometimes. 'Of course not.'

'Nothing going on at all?' Grady pressed.

'We're colleagues and friends. That's it.' Only ever since he'd confided in her about his relationship with Murray, Lauren couldn't help feeling closer to him, and that was without the incendiary attraction she needed to constantly tame with a combination of denial, avoidance and stern self-talk.

The more she saw of him, the hotter he seemed to become. Perhaps because he was so much more self-assured than younger Mason had been, more confident in his own abilities and unconcerned by trivialities. Or perhaps it was because he was respecting their new friendship, following her rules, no more of the flirtation he'd tried on when he'd first returned. No, that couldn't be the reason she wanted to rip his clothes off every time she saw him at the hospital because, truth be told, his cool, collected consideration was driving her crazy with need.

'No. No way, nuh-uh,' she emphasised. 'We've been there, done that. I won't be making the same mistake twice.'

Grady shifted and she flushed, aware that she'd voiced her utter determination not to mistake great sex for a relationship aloud. Not that she wanted a relationship.

She looked up to see his worried expression. 'That's quite a protest.'

'Well, stop asking silly questions then. The only thing causing my distraction, if I have been distracted, is Ben. I'm worried about him. He hasn't called either me or Dad for over a week.'

'He's too busy having a good time.' Grady grinned. 'Surely you remember what it was like to be a student.'

She did, especially once she and Mason had become an item. And she was back to thinking about him again.

'It's okay,' Grady said. 'Completely letting go of an ex is hard, especially when they are part of your daily life, whether you want them to be or not.'

Lauren tilted her head and offered her friend a sympathetic smile. Carol, Molly's mother dipped in and out of their lives when it suited her, leaving Gardy to comfort their daughter when she left, even though they'd been divorced for years and were supposed to have a specific shared custody agreement.

'You're right,' Lauren said. 'It has been hard seeing

Mason every day, especially in the beginning. But we've put the past behind us and moved on as friends. I promise I'm not going to allow myself to get hurt again.' She rested her hand on Grady's forearm to reassure him. 'It took me years to get over him the first time around. I'm not stupid. Now. Can we please talk about something else?'

To her surprise, Grady's complexion turned a little grey. 'I thought you got over him after that first month. That's what you told me.'

Lauren sighed. 'Eighteen months, one month, what's the difference?'

'Quite a big difference, actually.' He dropped his head back and gazed up at the ceiling as if seeking patience from the heavens.

'Don't get your undies in a twist,' Lauren snapped. 'It was my broken heart, not yours.'

When he settled his eyes on her once more, his serious expression gave her chills. 'He called, Lauren, about eight months after he'd left.'

Lauren's stomach twisted with dread. 'What? Called who? What are you talking about?'

'Mason—he called the ER to talk to you. It was the night you'd gone out with Greg, that army buddy of mine, remember? I finally talked you into your first date since you'd split up with Mason.'

Lauren nodded, her head spinning at his bombshell. She'd had a couple of drinks with Greg, which had been enough for her to determine that she wasn't ready, that all she could think about was how Greg wasn't Mason, how it hadn't felt right.

'Why didn't you tell me?' she whispered, the hand hold-ing her wine glass trembling. What did it mean? What had

Mason wanted? Had he called to catch up on the hospital news, or had he called for her, because he hadn't been able to move on either?

Grady winced, shamefaced. 'I wanted to tell you but he asked how you were, and when I told him that you were out on a date he made me swear, man to man, that I wouldn't tell you. He didn't want it to upset you. He said he wasn't ready to come back to New Zealand anyway and he was happy that you were moving on with your life.'

'Grady,' Lauren groaned. She placed her glass on the bar and clutched her hand to her churning stomach. It shouldn't matter. It was in the past. She thought back to that time. She'd just started her registrar job in Emergency Medicine. The hours were long, the stress levels insane. Ben was fifteen and in the full throes of his first teenage rebellion. Their father and he had butted horns regularly and Lauren had somehow ended up with the role of peacekeeper.

It had been a mess. No wonder her first foray into dating after Mason had been a disaster. She hadn't been ready.

But she had moved on eventually and if she'd known about his call at the time it would have changed nothing. She had still been tied to Auckland, and Mason had clearly been happy overseas.

Except she'd never know what it might have meant at the time, and she couldn't for the life of her decipher if it made any difference now. Had Mason had regrets? She'd always assumed that he'd moved on without a backwards glance six years ago, her conscience clear because she might have been the one to call it off in her sensible, rational way, but he hadn't argued or kept in touch.

But now she knew differently…

With exquisite timing, Mason chose that precise moment

to arrive. Lauren was so confused she could barely look at him as he greeted Grady and wished him a happy birthday.

She could smell him though, his sexy spicy aftershave making her dizzy.

Mason handed Grady a small wrapped gift. 'It's an African fertility statue. It represents health, wealth and personal happiness.'

Grady laughed and unwrapped the gift while Lauren sneaked a glance at Mason. He wore a dark T-shirt and black jeans, which were loose and comfortable-looking but hugged all the defined parts of his body like a lover's caress. She wanted to throttle him for the promise he'd extracted from Grady five years ago, then she'd throttle Grady for being stupid enough to keep secrets from her, and if he'd survived the first attack she'd throttle Mason again. Either that or she'd kiss the life out of him until she understood her erratic emotions.

Finally, she met his eyes, a fizzle of arousal spreading along her nerves as she swam in their striking blue depths. He smiled, friendly enough, only with Grady's news colouring everything she thought she knew about the past she searched his stare for answers, an explanation, something, anything to steer her back to a sure footing.

'This place hasn't changed at all,' he said as Grady became swept away into another conversation with his fellow ER nurses.

'The menu has improved,' she said, trying and failing to block out the rush of memories of them here together, a movie-style montage of many of their most memorable moments: the exact table where they'd had their first date, the corner where they'd hissed their first fight, the alcove near the bar where they'd kissed and made up because neither of them had been able to stay angry with the other for long.

'How was your day?' he asked.

'Good. Yours?' Tension pounded at her temples. She wanted to drag him into a quiet corner and demand an explanation. 'Aren't you going to get a drink?' she said before he could reply.

He studied her for a few seconds. 'In a moment. Are you okay?'

No, she wasn't. Everything was shifting under her feet. She didn't know this man; perhaps she'd never fully known him.

'Lauren…?'

She glanced around the bar for a discreet nook where they could talk in private, but the place was packed. Instead, she leaned close, raising her voice over the din.

'What did you mean the other day when you said we'd made a difficult choice, despite the way we once felt about each other?'

Mason frowned. 'Why are you bringing that up? I thought we'd decided on friendship.'

She should let it go and do exactly that, except she'd always assumed that Mason had walked away from their relationship unscathed. That they'd come to an inevitable conclusion after graduation. That he hadn't been ready for commitment anyway and her decision to stay behind had merely brought their split forward by a few months.

Lauren raised her mouth to his ear. 'Grady just told me about you calling the ward to speak to me eight months after you left.' Warmth emanated from his body, the clean spicy scent of him making her legs a little unsteady.

She pulled back and stared, every beat of her heart palpable. He watched her for a few beats and Lauren's patience snapped. 'Why, Mason?'

He sighed, glanced away and then met her stare once more with a shrug. 'I wanted to know you were okay.'

'But why?' This close to him, his eyes deep emotive pools, her confusion amplified. Had there been more than concern? Had he struggled to forget her? Could it be that they'd both had stronger feelings than they'd let on at the time?

'I don't know, Lauren.' He pressed closer so her breasts were only an inch from his chest, blue flames flashing in his irises. 'Maybe because I was homesick. Maybe because I'm a nice guy who cared about you.' He glanced at her mouth and then made eye contact again. 'Maybe because you pushed me away and I hadn't been ready to let you go yet. I missed you, fool that I was.'

She gasped, her pulse raging in her ears. She'd known that she'd let him down, that he'd been disappointed. But she'd understood that he'd needed to leave and she hadn't wanted to hold him back. She hadn't fully realised how she'd felt about *him* until it was too late and he'd left the country, until she was once more abandoned and hating the concept of any emotion that had such power to make her feel as if she had a limb missing.

So she'd blocked her heartache out of her mind, the way she'd blocked out her mother's death. But of course she'd missed him too. She'd grieved for him. She'd assumed a clean break was for the best, but a part of her had wanted, hoped that he'd call or email or come home. She'd almost contacted him a hundred times.

Lauren sighed, emotionally drained.

'Why does it matter now?' Mason asked, his stare trac-

ing her features, landing on her mouth and then returning to search her eyes. She had no answer. Tingles buzzed
over Lauren's skin. The bar was too loud. Too warm. She
couldn't breathe.

'I need some air,' she said, her hand clutching her throat.

Concern replaced the intensity of his expression. 'Let's
go outside.' He took her elbow and steered her to the door,
weaving them between the full tables. They bypassed the
handful of occupied outdoor tables underneath brightly coloured umbrellas. It wasn't until they made it to the pavement just outside the closed tattoo parlour next door that
she managed to take a full breath.

'Do you need to sit down?' he said.

She looked up from where she'd been bent double, hands
braced on her thighs. He appeared lost, uncomfortable, his
hands shoved into the pockets of his jeans, out of the way.

There was no way she could fall apart while he remained
coolly detached. She straightened, dragged in a restorative
breath. 'I'm fine. I'm just trying to make sense of what happened between us six years ago.'

Lauren forced herself to examine those last few weeks
of their relationship. At the time, she'd felt as if they'd both
played a part in their demise.

The changes in Mason the minute his world had im-
ploded when his father's scandal became known and his
mother left the family and New Zealand behind had ini-
tially been understandable and she'd done her best to support him through those tough times. He'd grown more and
more restless, desperate to graduate, desperate to get out of
there, and Lauren had been forced to take a reality check,
to question everything and to finally admit that the writing was on the wall.

'I was a bit all over the place,' she added when he stayed silent and watchful. 'Trying to do the right thing by my mother, who I still missed so much I doubted every decision I made, and by Dad and Ben.'

He'd been going to leave, no matter what, and still confused by divided loyalties, with the depth of her feelings that she just hadn't been in a position to trust and scared that she'd be hurt, Lauren had retreated behind her own defences.

They were so different. They'd never once confessed that they were in love or even serious about one another. Their priorities beyond their careers felt at complete odds. Of course she'd had to look to the future and make a choice. And so had he.

She'd pushed him away before she'd been pushed away by him, protecting herself from heartache.

And now what? Did the fact that he'd called her all that time ago mean that the blame for their split lay solely at her door after all...?

He pressed his lips together in a grim line. 'I know all about your responsibilities. I respected your decision, didn't I? I did exactly what you told me to do.'

'But I let you down?' Lauren asked, because she could see the ghost of his hurt in his stare.

He clenched his jaw, clearly not about to admit a vulnerability. 'Why are you raking over this? I'm trying my best here.' He scrubbed his hand through his hair and turned away. 'Just let it go, Laurie.'

Laughter boomed from a group seated outside the Har-Bar. Mason paced further out of earshot, loitered under the awning of the neighbouring estate agent. Lauren's temperature rose as she strode after him. She touched his arm and he spun to face her.

'Hold on a minute. What are you trying your best to do?' she asked.

His eyes blazed with fire. He dropped his gaze to where her hand still sat on his arm.

She snatched it away. She didn't want to lead him on, but something in her couldn't allow them to wriggle out of this confrontation. She'd resigned from the appointment panel in order to do the right thing. The least he could do was explain himself.

'I'm trying to be your friend, as requested,' he said.

Lauren huffed, indignant. 'Well, don't do me any favours. You're free to abandon this friendship if it doesn't work for you.' Needing to get away from the way he was messing with her resolve, Lauren marched around the corner of the building.

Growing aware of her surroundings, she recognised the familiar alleyway that ran behind the block of eclectic shops surrounding the Har-Bar, which was another part of their history. They'd made out in it too many times to count, too horny to wait until they reached home. They'd even had sex here once, hidden by the shadows of the early morning hours and the neighbouring buildings.

The hairs on the back of her neck prickled and she sensed that Mason had followed her into the alley. She faced him, trying to ignore the way her body incinerated at the sensual memories of this place.

'And how is our friendship working out for *you*?' Mason stepped closer so Lauren had to tilt her chin to keep eye contact. 'Why are you so upset to learn that I still cared about you long after you pushed me away? Long after you yourself had moved on?'

'I didn't have to push that hard, did I?' Her heart pounded so fast she took a step back. 'You agreed to leave pretty readily. So what are you trying to say? That you actually had strong feelings for me or something?'

She laughed, actually laughed, because the idea was so preposterous. She hoped that only she could hear the nervous echo to that laughter. Hoped he couldn't see the excited pulse throbbing in her throat because he was so close she could see flecks of silver in his irises, feel his breath on her lips, almost taste the intoxicating flavour of him.

Their staring match seemed to last an age, neither of them willing to concede defeat. Why could he still get to her this way? She was older, supposedly wiser, more experienced and the stakes were higher. And yet he still had the power to make her feel reckless and unstable, as if she'd do anything for him.

'I'm saying,' he replied after so long that Lauren thought the lust boiling in her veins might have made her deaf, 'that you're the closest I've ever come to a relationship and the only favour I'm doing you is to pretend that we aren't still insanely hot for each other.'

Stunned, she scraped her eyes over his features, willing him to be as conflicted as she felt. She was more than hot; she was incandescent for him. But how dare he throw down some sort of sexual gauntlet? She had been doing just fine since his return, all things considered. Sure, she either hid in her office to avoid him or watched the door of the ER like a possessed fan stalking a celebrity for a glimpse of his confident swagger, but that was just to ensure that she appeared professional. He was her ex after all.

But they weren't at work now. And all she could think about was how good it would feel to admit he was right, to kiss him and finally dispense with all of this distracting sexual tension.

'You are so infuriating,' she said through gritted teeth, trying not to think about sex—sex with Mason and just how good it had been. Yes, their chemistry was as intense as ever, but unlike when they were younger and their differences had driven her so crazy that she'd had to kiss him instead of throttle him, Lauren was now more in control of her emotions, and her urges, and if at thirty-one she was his only relationship, he was clearly as commitment-shy as ever.

A hint of an indulgent smile twitched on his lips, drawing her eyes there. She took a step back towards the wall of the alley.

'And you still overthink everything,' he said, following, step for step, as if they were snarled together in the same net, entangled and helpless and unable to get away from each other.

Surely he couldn't like her worst personality trait—endless future-gazing, the mind-draining consideration of the pitfalls of each and every decision.

'Do you remember this place?' he asked, one eyebrow raised in challenge as if she'd deliberately chosen that location for this conversation.

Her body shuddered, liquid heat in every blood vessel as their eyes remained locked. He was right. The passion still flared between them and she'd been a fool to think she could just deny it and carry on as if he was any other doctor. He knew it, Auckland knew it, this very alleyway knew it, mocking her.

'Of course.' Her voice was a needy whisper that made her cheeks flush. She was practically inviting him to re-enact those erotic scenes she couldn't seem to scrub from her mind.

Torn to the point of utter desperation, Lauren reached out, grabbed at the hem of his T-shirt, not tugging nor re-leasing her grasp. Her gesture confirmed what her eyes and her inertia and her lack of denial blasted. She was too scared to say the words, but powerless to stop her actions.

How could she want him so much? Beyond reason and sense and consequence.

Her breaths had become shallow, rapid. One kiss would likely be enough to destroy all of the memories of how good it had been before, because surely she was inflating the truth? Then they could resume their working relation-ship as if it had never happened.

Lauren's back hit the rough stone wall of the building they'd just left, the air knocked from her lungs in a soft gust of release as Mason closed the distance.

Still gripping his shirt, she abandoned the fight, all ra-tional arguments dissolving in the face of the familiar heat in his eyes and how it seemed to inflame her further until she was burning up.

Slowly Mason braced one hand on the wall beside her head and raised his other hand, his fingertips tracing the curve of her cheekbone and the angle of her jaw, the way he used to when they lay facing each other in bed. He'd once said that he'd never seen anything as perfect as her, that he couldn't believe that she'd chosen him, and then he'd spoiled it, laughed at himself and apologised for being 'soppy'. She'd considered it his most vulnerable moment until he'd talked about his father after the funeral and she'd witnessed all the parts of himself he'd hidden as a younger man.

Mesmerised by his touch, because it felt new, different, enthralling in a way she couldn't untangle, she pressed her cheek against his palm. Perhaps because he was silently staring, no humorous observations to ease the building tension, as if waiting for her permission.

This was so stupid. Just because she knew something would feel so good didn't mean she should do it. But her body seemed to have disconnected from her brain, clearly intent on making its own reckless decisions.

'What are we doing?' she asked on a breathless whisper that sounded worryingly needy as she gripped his T-shirt tighter, pulled him closer.

What was *she* doing? more importantly. She should withdraw from the intense and purposeful look in his eyes, push him away emotionally even if she lacked the strength to do it physically, make some joke as he had back then.

His eyes shone with risk, danger, exhilaration, all the things he represented to Lauren. 'I'm showing you why us being just friends is a pipe dream.' Mason inched closer so that only a few centimetres of space separated their bodies. Lauren looked down and spied the reason; somehow she'd subconsciously hooked her fingers into the belt loops on his jeans the way she'd used to.

The air buzzed with static as Lauren tried to formulate some witty one-liner to remind him that she was a mature woman in charge of her emotions and her hormones, only her body betrayed her. She raised her hands, desperate for the strength to push him away so she could escape the feral look in his eyes, one she'd never seen before. Instead her fingers curled into his shirt over his chest.

It was simply chemistry, its power likely halved the minute they both acknowledged it and then moved on. It would only be one kiss. She could stay detached.

Mason groaned at her touch, his eyelids drooping with arousal, his leg slipping between hers, his thick hard thigh just there, a perfect height for riding.

Still he denied her his mouth, which hovered a hair's breadth from hers. Was this her punishment for throwing up barriers? Would she need to beg? And how did he know she was so close to doing exactly that?

'Laurie...?' His breath gusted over her lips where she'd unconsciously wet them with her tongue. His eyes, which carried the same question as he'd injected into her whispered name, bored into hers so deeply she feared that he'd see her every buried secret thought, see how much she wanted him, how much he'd upended her calm, orderly and responsible life with his return. How the professional grown woman and responsible doctor wanted to lose herself in passion for a second until her mind cleared of the past, where she'd clearly built Mason up to fantastical proportions, and forgot her worries for the future.

Resigned, she couldn't deny herself just one familiar kiss. She raised her chin, tugged at the fistfuls of his shirt and dragged his mouth the final space to hers, her body acting on instinct and her brain turning to mush.

*Nothing* about the kiss that followed was familiar.

As if he needed her to breathe, Mason engulfed her entire being, his hard body pressing her into the wall as their lips met, their mouths consumed.

Lauren moaned, parting her lips, seeking his tongue, diving right back into their former level of intimacy as if they'd never stopped doing this, as if the intervening years—years of loneliness and doubt—had never happened.

Had their connection ever been this passionate? This honest and desperate, as if neither of them could get enough of the other, as if they'd denied themselves for too long and by tasting each other, swallowing up every moan and sigh and grunt, somehow made up for every day of the past six years apart.

Lauren grew dizzy, desperate to take a huge gulp of air, but instead she tangled her fingers in his hair to hold his mouth close, scared to break the bond, scared to come to her senses. She didn't want this one kiss to be over.

Mason's hands gripped her waist, the bump and grind of their hips turning X-rated to any passing observer. But Lauren couldn't find the strength to care. He'd reduced her to a woman willing to take risks, to act like a teenager, snogging in public. She clung to the selfishness of her actions, dragging every scrap of pleasure from her recklessness, soared, free for the first time in years of the compulsion to put other's needs above her own.

But her over-analytical mind refused to wallow in pleasure alone. What if she'd never pushed him away six years ago? What if they'd parted for no reason?

It struck her with the force of a blow to the ribs. No matter how much she'd denied it at the time, how often she'd refused to contemplate the truth after he'd left when the pain finally struck, a part of her had had deep, deep feelings for him back then and she'd been terrified of what might happen. Of what had, in fact, happened. That she'd make herself that vulnerable to another person and he'd leave her anyway.

But this stolen moment of lust had nothing to do with

feelings. She'd made her choices. She'd sacrificed him and any other relationship to focus on family and work, all she could fit into her life. And she would sacrifice this undeniable connection to him yet again for her career and her ongoing peace of mind.

She broke free, tearing her mouth from his. 'This is a bad idea.'

Like the first chunk of chocolate from the bar, his kiss was too good, too addictive, too rewarding, lighting up her brain's poor starved pleasure centres like the fireworks over the Harbour Bridge on New Year's Eve. She couldn't garner the strength to make it stop completely, dragging him back for another kiss, another moment of reckless pleasure.

'I know, I know,' he mumbled against her lips, kissing her again with similar desperation, his hands cupping her face, his fingers tunnelling into her hair as he slanted his mouth over hers and led them both back into irresistible abandon.

For a split second she imagined him inviting her back to his place, heard herself accepting, envisioned them naked and tangled up in sheets, her body fully on board with the fantasy.

Dragged into reality by her keen readiness to take this further than a kiss, Lauren's blood ran cold. He'd been back for five minutes and she was already forgetting about everything else and acting recklessly with Mason in a dark alley. A kiss she could rationalise, mitigate, but living out the fantasy, sleeping with him, would be no casual thing, not now. And, as Grady's earlier revelation had proved, she didn't actually know Mason as well as she'd thought.

Just then, her phone pinged with an incoming text.

Almost reluctantly, Mason broke away, his forehead resting on hers while they caught their breath. She took her phone from her pocket and glanced at the screen, willing the colour to fade from her face and for her legs to start working.

'I need to go. Grady's worrying about where I am.' She wiped at her buzzing lips as if she could erase what had just happened, bucking her hips to free herself from the narrow space between his tempting body and the wall she'd literally backed herself against.

He hadn't fully answered her questions about his feelings, and it really didn't matter how he'd felt back then. He'd walked away, regardless of whether he was pushed or went freely, and, like Lauren, he hadn't had a relationship since. He was as much a danger to her as ever.

What had she been thinking?

Mason Ward might have been the one that got away, but Lauren couldn't allow his words, his kisses or the petrol meets naked flame chemistry they'd just proved was alive and hotter than ever to derail her. Not when, in most of the ways that mattered, he was a virtual stranger.

# CHAPTER EIGHT

By THE END of the week Mason had replayed the kiss over and over in his mind so many times he'd started to believe that he'd hallucinated it. There had been no time to discuss it then—they'd gone back to the bar and Lauren had only stayed for one more drink before slipping away while Mason had been in the bathroom. Since then, they'd either worked different shifts or only seen each other fleetingly in the ER, each of them too busy to do more than cast wary looks at the other person.

Mason sighed, stretching out his back muscles as he took the lift from the theatres to the hospital cafeteria. He was an hour away from the end of his shift. He'd spent most of it operating and what he really needed to see him through the last part of the day, to help focus his mind away from Lauren and how utterly fantastic it had felt to have her back in his arms, was the miracle of coffee.

Entering the cafeteria, he immediately spotted Lauren ahead of him in the queue, his heart giving an excited lurch. He paused behind her, as close as he could without being obvious. It was close enough that the scent of her floral shampoo tickled his nose and reminded him of her breathy moans as they'd kissed as if the world was ending in the alley the night of Grady's birthday.

Mason tucked his hands into his pockets, out of temptation's way. It wouldn't be a good look to tap her on the shoulder and suggest they continue where they'd left off at the weekend, but that was exactly what he wanted to do.

The final hour of his shift would now seem endless.

Lauren reached the front of the queue and ordered her coffee, requesting an extra shot.

'Make that two of those please,' Mason interrupted. 'And I'll pay for both.'

Lauren began to argue, then she blushed to the roots of her hair.

'I insist, Dr Harvey. I've been trying to buy you a coffee since my first day, if you remember?'

'Thank you, Dr Ward.' She glared his way and then moved aside.

The cashier took his money and he and Lauren loitered near the barista, waiting for their take-outs. Mason stood beside her, again at a respectable distance. Like Lauren, he pulled his phone from his pocket and pretended to be engrossed in the screen. With their focus on their phones and the silence shrouding them like a laser field, no one would suspect that there had ever been anything intimate between them. Except Mason itched with the urge to tell her how he hadn't been able to stop thinking about their kiss. His body was so restless to move closer to hers and whisper something in her ear, to see if the heat of his breath would make her shudder, the way she'd shuddered against him a thousand times before in pleasure, that he wasn't sure how he could remain so still.

Lauren too was more affected than she seemed. She'd

been staring at the same three-word text on her phone for the past two minutes.

Was this torture the vibe of things to come? Were they going to try and ignore each other, pretend to be strangers at work, or would their physical needs get the better of them? To Mason's mind, denial was futile. If last weekend's kiss had proved anything, it was that those needs had taken on a life of their own.

Except he hadn't been completely open to her enquiries. He'd shied away from confessing how utterly broken he'd been when she'd called things off. He hadn't wanted her to feel guilty. He'd understood her dilemma, that six years ago she'd made the right choice for her by prioritising her family. He only really blamed himself for walking away without a fight.

If only he'd been in the right headspace himself back then. If only he hadn't needed to get away, to go somewhere where he'd be able to be himself, if only it hadn't taken that separation from everything Auckland represented for him to figure out his own priorities.

The barista delivered their coffees, pushed into the same two-cup cardboard holder, an honest mistake since they'd paid together. Lauren stared at it as if she had no idea what to do. Mason scooped up both drinks, smiled his thanks at the barista and ushered a bewildered Lauren out of the cafeteria.

'How is your shift going, Dr Harvey?' he asked, dragging his stare from the way her ponytail swung as she walked. It had felt like silk between his fingers the other night.

'Busy. How about yours?'

'The same.' They paused together at the lifts and Lauren retrieved her coffee from the holder, taking a long sip with her eyes closed as if in bliss.

Heat pooled in Mason's groin at the sight. He had to look away to stop the rush of blood south. Now that he'd tasted her lips again and relearned every soft curve of her body, it was going to be even harder to ignore how much he wanted her. But even more compelling had been the beginnings of her readiness to talk about their past. He'd refused to tear his heart out and lay it at her feet, but the fact that she'd seemed so shocked to learn that he'd called must mean something. Had she too had regrets for the way they'd parted? Had she felt as bereft as he had in the months after they'd split?

The lift arrived. It was empty. Mason hung back to allow Lauren to precede him inside, his stomach hollow with anticipation at the idea they would soon be alone.

When the doors eventually closed, after what seemed like a year, Lauren released a shaky breath.

'You ran out on the celebrations the other night,' he said. 'I'd hoped we could dissect that astounding kiss, but when I returned from the gents you'd disappeared.' There was no point beating around the bush. There was only one thing they needed to talk about and it wasn't work-appropriate small talk.

She turned her gaze on him, her colour high. 'Astounding?' She looked appalled that he'd raised the subject, but also equally fascinated at his choice of descriptor.

He nodded, answering her question with one of his own, because he remembered how much that had once burrowed under her skin. 'You've had better?'

Mason seriously doubted it. Even their first kiss, his gold standard until the night of Grady's birthday, had been a little awkward at first.

At her dazed expression, Mason continued. 'I'm only so confident because, for starters, I was there, and also because Grady told me that you don't date much.'

She shook her head in disgust. 'Some friend he is...'

Mason chuckled. Grady cared about her and always had. The time for Mason's insecure jealousy had been years ago, first time around, but it had rumbled away anyway, fuelled by the spike in testosterone he always experienced around Lauren.

The lift slowed and stopped. A porter wheeled a patient in a wheelchair inside and Lauren scuttled to the opposite corner from him as if she and Mason had been caught in a repeat of that steamy session in the alley. Mason hadn't even noticed that they'd inched closer, but he wasn't surprised. He was a drone to her queen bee.

The elderly lady in the wheelchair smiled at Mason as if she could feel the sexual undercurrents filling the small space. Everyone was young once.

Mason glanced at Lauren and every second they shared the lift stretched taut. She narrowed her eyes and Mason grinned, enjoying himself so much that he no longer required coffee.

'What are you doing?' she hissed the minute the patient had left the lift and they were once more alone.

'I think we should talk about the kiss, don't you?' He hadn't been fully open with her when she'd questioned him about his feelings six years ago, but those few incredible moments in the alley when they'd finally surrendered to their urges had been a great starting point for ongoing honesty. They needed to keep talking, navigate their renewed relationship with candour and maturity. Not that he was in a position to think about anything long-term. He hadn't had a relationship in six years, since Lauren. Clearly, he'd made a mess of that, and he would never toy with her emotions. He didn't even know if he would be a permanent member of GHH staff yet.

'Maybe I'm tired of thinking about it,' she said, taking another mouthful of coffee. 'I just go round and round in circles, because I still don't want a relationship and you and I have been there, done that.'

So why did she look like he'd just snatched away her brand-new kitten, like she wished that something could happen between them, like she was one step away from ripping his scrubs off in this lift and ravishing him?

'I know exactly what you mean. But that kiss, and the way you're looking at me right now, prove that we're going to struggle to be just friends. Do you really want to get so desperate that we embarrass ourselves at work, have sex in the on-call room or burn down the hospital with the flames we generate?'

'Flames?' she mocked, pressing her lips together playfully.

At least she was embracing their usual banter.

'Don't be too overconfident in your abilities.' She smiled and Mason grinned, elated that he'd finally coaxed her radiant smile free. 'You're not in the operating theatre now, and I'm not a besotted twenty-three-year-old.'

'Besotted…? Now there's something I wish I'd known

at the time. But if we're making confessions you should know that I'm no longer scared of being honest.'

She frowned, her breaths coming faster. 'About the fact that we've always been too different? That we bicker all the time?'

He shook his head, his gaze drawn to her parted lips. 'About the fact that us being friends feels like a consolation prize that neither of us truly wants. That we can try to ignore our chemistry, but eventually we're going to fail. You know it and I know it.'

Eyes wide, she licked her lips, the gesture almost his undoing. Pity that he had no desire to make things difficult for either of them at work. One embarrassment involving the Ward name was more than enough.

Mason was not his father. He wouldn't fall into the same trap, allow his personal life choices to eclipse his work ethic, become the source of hospital gossip.

'Are you goading me again?' She recovered, her eyes narrowing with suspicion, looking so much like his Lauren that he almost had to look away.

Instead he stepped closer. 'I wouldn't dream of it.'

'Yes, you would. Perhaps you should go out and find someone to sleep with if you're having such a hard time,' she said, hurling up another defensive barricade as she backed away.

He cast her a sad smile, turning serious. 'If I thought for one second it would help, I'd take you up on your suggestion in a heartbeat,' he said, unable to recall if he even knew how to seriously flirt with a woman that wasn't *this* woman. He hadn't been a saint overseas, but there were unspoken rules about one-night stands.

'Why don't you, then?' she whispered, her body so still she must have been holding her breath.

He braced his hand on the wall of the lift above her head, bent closer, lowered his voice, wishing they were anywhere but at work.

'Because she won't be you, and right now you're all I can see. All I can think about.'

She gasped, her stare ping-ponging between his eyes.

'What are you doing tonight?' He grinned. 'Wanna go for a surf after work, watch the sunset?'

'Really?' Her voice took on a breathy quality that belied her censorious expression. 'You're using our mutual love of surfing in order to get me into bed. That's low.' She rolled her eyes, as if she had way more control over the demands of her body. But he knew the truth as well as he knew her and the struggle he saw in her eyes every time she looked at him. That night in the dark alleyway, that desperate kiss was the closest she'd come to absolute candour.

He laughed, delighted by how much of Lauren's playful side was reappearing. Maybe there was something to be said for that friendship thing after all, except friends didn't usually want to rip each other's clothes off.

Then her pager sounded, saving them from creating a scandal.

She glanced at the screen as if grateful for the distraction. 'It's the ER.' A small frown pinched her brows together. 'There's been a multi-vehicle accident on the Southern Highway. It's going to be all hands on deck.'

Mason nodded, silencing his own pager, which carried the same alert.

'A rain-check then,' he said as the lift doors opened on the ground floor and they dumped their coffees in a nearby bin. There was no time to think about what would happen next for them, now that they were trapped somewhere between friends and lovers.

Duty called, and that meant that they'd have to put their personal lives aside.

# CHAPTER NINE

TWELVE HOURS LATER, after working a double shift to assist with the extra influx of casualties the major road incident had brought in, Lauren feared that she'd never find the physical strength to leave the hospital. Admitting the accident victims, many of them in a critical condition, had created a knock-on effect whereby the less serious cases already waiting in the ER were triaged as lower priority. It had taken most of the night to process the backlog. She was so tired that her legs might not be able to carry her the short walk home.

But, even exhausted, all she could think about, now that she was free to leave the hospital, was Mason.

They'd seen plenty of each other overnight, which he'd either spent in the ER accepting the steady stream of surgical patients she'd referred, or in Theatre. There hadn't been a spare minute for them to discuss how they were going to navigate the complexities of their inescapable relationship going forward. But what there had been were multiple opportunities for them to show that they were in each other's thoughts.

On several occasions Mason had come to the department with some sort of nutritional offering, placing it wordlessly on the desk next to her before going about his business: a sandwich, a coffee, an apple. Lauren had insisted that he crash for half an hour in between surgeries on the sofa in her office, leaving him a bottle of water and some toast for when he woke up.

Now, she pushed through the doors from Minor Injuries to find Mason waiting at the staff lockers for her with two takeaway coffees and a brown paper bag that smelled delicious. She almost sobbed in gratitude. Like her, Mason was still dressed in hospital scrubs, his hair in disarray and his eyes red-rimmed with fatigue. She doubted that he'd had time for a shower, but he'd made time to fetch her breakfast or dinner or whatever meal it was. She'd lost track of the time hours ago.

She took the proffered bag and inhaled the buttery greasy smell emanating from the contents, some sort of toasted sandwich. She was so hungry she'd have eaten the paper bag alone.

'Sorry—' he passed her one of the coffees with an apologetic smile '—it's probably a bit lukewarm by now.'

She shook her head dismissively, taking a grateful sip. 'It's perfect. Thank you. You really didn't have to bring me more food.'

He shrugged, his tired eyes crinkling in the corners in a way that made Lauren want to hug him. 'I know, but us doctors need to look out for each other, right? We're the only ones who understand what it's like.'

A lump lodged in her throat. He was going out of his way to be her friend, but everything he'd said in the lift last night had been true. It felt as if they were fighting a losing battle, especially after that kiss.

Just being around him, with his thoughtful gestures and his unwavering consideration and his charm-loaded smile, was its own form of torture.

He took a swallow of his own drink and adjusted his bag on his shoulder. 'Have you slept at all?'

'No.' She wiped her mouth with the back of her hand and unwrapped the top of the sandwich. 'But I'm headed home now.' She looked away because exhaustion had stolen her ability to think, but there was one thing she did know: she wanted more than friendship with Mason. His openness and honesty were inspiring, liberating and a little bit terrifying. She wanted to jump on board, explore this new dynamic. Once she'd had a decent night's sleep.

'Me too,' he said with a tired smile. 'I'm going to sleep like the dead.'

Her empty stomach growled loud enough that they both laughed. Lauren opened the bag and took a big bite of cheesy deliciousness. 'Oh, wow...' she said, her eyes rolling closed as flavour assaulted her tastebuds. 'This is delicious. Thank you. I love you.'

The second the words were out she almost choked, wishing she could suck them back into her mouth or that Mason had fallen temporarily deaf.

Covering up, she babbled a stream of verbal incontinence with her mouth half-full. 'Are you...um...staying at Murray's place? I meant to ask you at the funeral if you wanted a hand clearing the house of his things. I have the weekend off so I'm free, and I know how hard that process can be because I helped Dad sort through Mum's belongings.'

Her face was hot so she avoided looking at him, instead slipping into her office and collecting her bag.

Oh, how she wished they were bickering playfully, the way they had in the lift yesterday, but she was too tired and too aware of him to come up with any banter. The old Mason had been hard enough to resist, but this older, self-assured version was ten times hotter—if that were even possible—his diligence and confidence and the way he seemed to look at her as if she was the only woman on the planet a major turn-on.

Mason's stare settled on hers, his eyes serious. Clearly he was too tired to tease her for her slip-up or make some suggestive comment. Part of her half wished he would. Fatigue was a great excuse for making rash decisions and reckless mistakes.

'No. I'm renting in Bushman's Point—great views of the sea, a five-minute walk to the beach. I love it.'

'But that's a thirty-minute drive away.' A stitch of concern pinched Lauren's ribs. He'd had thirty minutes of sleep in the past twenty-four hours. He shouldn't be driving anywhere.

He shrugged. 'I know. The drive helps me switch off from work. By the time I get home I'm ready to head down to the beach for a surf.'

He watched her take a jacket from the hook on the wall and shrug into it. The hood was trapped inside out. Mason stepped close and adjusted it for her.

Lauren swallowed, choked by how cared-for he made her feel. She wanted to kiss him again, to lose herself in the passion she knew would be only one bold move out of reach.

'Thanks,' she said, filling her mouth with warm coffee instead as she flicked off her office lights and headed for the nearest staff exit.

'Where do you live these days?' he asked, the unspoken agreement that they were heading out of the hospital together.

'I've just moved into my own place, a few blocks from

here,' she said, her cheeks warm because she was thirty and had only just vacated her family home. She should invite Mason to crash at her place. Excitement hummed in her veins at that idea, probably not her best, but she liked the alternative—him falling asleep at the wheel and driving off the road—even less.

'Until then,' she continued, 'I was still living with Ben and Dad.' She rolled her eyes. 'I know. Late starter.'

Mason smiled without judgement. 'I'll walk you home then,' he said, eyes front, no innuendo, but also closed-off to any argument.

'There's no need.' Lauren hesitated, not because she didn't appreciate the gesture, although Auckland at five a.m. on a Saturday morning was a relatively safe place, but because she was more worried about him and that long drive.

He shrugged, but his stare was determined. 'I insist.'

Touched by his thoughtfulness, and trying to block out all the times he'd seen her safely home in the past, she cleared her tight throat so her voice wouldn't emerge as a nervous squeak. 'Okay, but only if you crash at my place for a few hours. I'm not having you drive all that way on your bike, on no sleep. It's dangerous.'

He grinned. 'I didn't know you still cared so much.'

She shook her head, a smile twitching on her lips. 'I don't. I just happen to know from the bed co-ordinator that the hospital is full to capacity. We can't take another admission if you fall asleep at the wheel.'

Mason tutted, shook his head in mock disbelief. 'Honestly? You're going to use hospital resource statistics to get me into bed?'

Lauren ignored his chuckle and marched ahead towards

the exit, her heart lighter with the return of their repartee, although at the mention of sex she willed her heart to calm down. The thought of being alone with him, in her house...

She scoffed; she was practically a zombie right now, and likely as alluring.

'I don't have a spare room,' she said, trying to act as nonchalant as possible, 'but my sofa is new and very comfortable.' Then, because she couldn't resist, and she couldn't allow him to have the last word, she shot him a cheeky look. 'And I promise, no funny business.'

His gorgeous grin stretched wide, alarming and enticing. 'Shame, I'm in the mood for some funny business, although I couldn't promise that I wouldn't totally fall asleep on you.'

Lauren almost combusted at the idea of her and Mason naked, tangled up in sheets, hot, sweaty, limbs entwined...

'Good,' She shoved the door open, hoping to find a blast of cooler air to tame her raging internal fires, but Auckland was putting on a show of what promised to be another glorious day, the breeze already warm and slightly humid. 'Then that's settled.'

With the chance of sex dispensed with, Lauren resumed eating her sandwich, despite the rebellion from her fluttering stomach.

'How are the accident victims we admitted?' she asked after they'd walked a short distance in silence.

He scrubbed a hand through his hair. 'They're all stable. One has been transferred to Neurosurgery, a couple to Orthopaedics.'

'And the six-year-old?' she asked about the last casualty they had admitted together in the early hours of the morning. The little girl had been a rear passenger trapped in one of the vehicles for over an hour. The seatbelt had saved her life, but she'd had abdominal injuries and a crushed arm where the car had rolled. She and Mason had worked for an hour together to stabilise her before he'd whisked her to Theatre.

Mason's stare became haunted, the lines around his eyes deepening. 'I had to remove her spleen. Orthopaedics are still observing her arm, but I'm worried that it doesn't look good.'

Lauren swallowed, understanding the implications and Mason's investment in the patient. It was often the cases of the seriously ill children who came through the door that she found difficult to forget. Just because doctors saw all manner of human tragedy didn't mean that they were unaffected.

'That's hard. I'm sorry,' she said, touching his arm, a gesture that now felt second nature, almost necessary to her existence. 'Let's hope that today brings better news.'

He nodded, his fatigued stare searching hers in an exchange of empathy. That they understood each other's work made some of Lauren's doubts settle, but then Mason seemed to understand everything about her, despite the passing of time. He'd seen her at her worst—sobbing with grief for her mother, overwhelmed by her new role nurturing Ben and wishing that her father's grief would lessen so their broken little family could resume some semblance of normal—and he still wasn't put off...

'Still worrying about me, I see,' he said with a smile that would normally reassure her and break the tension but only inflamed her desire to throw herself at him.

'Occupational hazard,' she replied, pressing the pedestrian crossing button to hide her flush. So she cared about him. She cared about many of her friends and colleagues. That was who she was.

Of course she didn't make out with any of them as if the continuation of humanity as a species was dependent on it.

'Don't get me wrong,' he added with smug grin. 'I like it. It's endearing.'

'Do you, now?' Without waiting for his confirmation, and too tired to examine the perilous thud of her heartbeat, she walked across the road.

'That was one of the things that drew me to you in the first place, aside from your smarts and everything else.' He waved his hand in her direction, encompassing her head to toe. 'You always accepted me as I am. I never had to pretend to be anything else with you.'

'That's me—Saint Lauren.' Her head spun at his revelation. Did they really need another confirmation of how good they'd been together? And yet they'd still managed to mess it up.

She couldn't deny that she trusted him, wanted him, and, knowing how he'd always managed to bring out her reckless streak, it seemed inevitable that she would act on her desires, especially if he kept on looking at her in his intense way, as if he was learning new things about her all the time.

Arriving at her town house, she sighed, a tired mess of emotions. She twisted the key in the lock, her hands trembling. It would be so easy to stop fighting, to surrender to their chemistry and sleep with Mason one more time. But she would need to be strong enough to keep her emotions in check. They'd let each other down once before, and neither of them needed the complication of hurt feelings right now when their professional lives were so busy and demanding.

She preceded Mason inside, aware of his proximity,

every brush of air against her skin as if she were already naked. This was the stupidest idea she'd ever had, inviting temptation personified through her front door. The only saving grace, one she intended to remedy before she collapsed into bed, *alone,* was that she hadn't had a chance to clean her teeth or shower since yesterday.

The hairs on the back of her neck prickled to attention as she led Mason into her barely unpacked living room. The house still had that new house smell. She pulled the curtains closed to block out the rising sun. It was weird to go to bed when the rest of the city were just waking up to the start of a stunning weekend, but they were both used to odd hours.

'Couch—' she pointed out the obvious large sectional sofa, wider than a king single bed '—I'll get you some bedding and a pillow.'

Being in an enclosed space with him made her aware of his eyes on her, every beat of her heart, the gentle rhythm of his breathing.

'Looks comfy enough,' said Mason, seeming relaxed where she felt out of her depth. 'I can sleep standing up, so don't worry.'

But then she hadn't ever brought a man home to this house. She hadn't brought a man home to her father's house since Mason. Her last sexual encounter was so long ago she might not actually remember the moves.

One look at a sexily sleepy Mason was all it took to blast that theory to smithereens as heat pooled low in her pelvis and her breasts tingled eagerly.

No, they were both exhausted. Not the time for making momentous, potentially life-altering decisions. Everything would become clear and manageable after sleep. With any luck, Mason would have left by the time she surfaced so she wouldn't have to deal with him all warm and inviting and barely awake.

Lauren marched to the linen cupboard, an insistent throb between her legs. She thrust a pile of blankets and a pillow at him, her eyes darting around the room at the unpacked boxes. Anywhere but at the man who was about to strip his likely still sublime body, probably down to his boxers, in her living room.

'The bathroom is through there,' she croaked. 'Help yourself to a shower. Towels are in the cupboard.'

'Thanks.' He looked as if he was about to say something important or lean in to put a friendly goodnight kiss on her cheek. But she couldn't allow that; she didn't have the strength to fight her urges and she'd likely jump him. The poor man had been operating all night.

Lauren hurried to the kitchen and poured herself a glass of water then shuffled off towards her bedroom. 'Help yourself to anything you want,' she muttered, walking backwards, her hand finding the doorknob. Then she remembered that there was no lock on her bedroom door, no physical barrier to the temptation to ravish him in his sleep.

Her fatigue had reached delirium level now. She let out an almost hysterical laugh. ''Night, Mason.'

His sleepy smile weakened her knees. 'Goodnight, Lauren.'

She closed the bedroom door and rested her forehead against the cool wood while her heart thumped at her breastbone.

Great idea. She'd invited the man she couldn't stop craving, even though it felt foolhardy and dangerous, to sleep naked on her couch. How on earth was she supposed to sleep through that kind of temptation?

Hours later, she awoke to an unfamiliar sound.

Her heart thumped as she sat up in bed, her hearing attuned to the slightest noise from the living room. Mason. Mason had slept in her living room. Naked. Heat zapped through her nervous system so that she became instantly awake. The clock read eleven-sixteen, the bright sun outlining the edge of the blinds. There was no way she'd be able to get back to sleep now, not when the noise had likely been Mason moving around.

Panic gripped her stomach. Was he leaving? Sneaking out without saying goodbye, as she'd hoped he would?

The idea that he might leave when he'd been the first thing to enter her mind when her eyes opened propelled her from her bed. She rushed to her en suite bathroom and cleaned her teeth. She pinched her cheeks and ran her fingers through her sleep-messed hair in the mirror.

She had no idea what game she was playing, but she was done living cautiously and over-thinking. She'd made enough sacrifices over the years and she didn't want the potential of one more passionate encounter with Mason to be yet another loss.

She padded into the lounge, the new carpet soft underfoot. Her pulse thrummed in her throat. Mason sat perched on the edge of the sofa, a glass of water in one hand, his face illuminated by the screen of his phone.

'Sorry,' he said, placing his phone and glass on the coffee table and standing. 'I didn't mean to wake you.' He rubbed a hand over his stubble-covered jaw. 'I couldn't get back to sleep, but I didn't want to leave and risk waking you up with the noise from the front door. Now I've done that anyway...'

He trailed off, his stare moving down her body to her bare legs beneath the hem of one of the oversized T-shirts she liked to sleep in.

Lauren's half-asleep brain blinked on and off like a faulty neon light as she repaid the favour, taking in his attire, or lack thereof. As predicted, he was wearing nothing but black cotton boxers, his lean, muscular body defined in the slant of light from the edge of the closed curtains.

Her mouth dried. Words formed and then evaporated. He was beautiful, strong, more manly than the younger Mason she remembered. Dark hair dusted his tanned arms and legs and chest. She wanted to objectify the hell out of him, stare at his near naked body until her eyes watered, but she also knew him well enough to know that he would never disrespect her that way. That if anything were to happen between them, and it definitely wasn't wise, she would need to instigate it, just like she had with the kiss.

Remembering how he'd almost made her beg for his mouth on hers, she pressed her legs together and shuddered. That he'd respected her stupid, over-cautious rules made him even more attractive, more irresistible. That he'd confessed his struggles in the wake of that amazing kiss, the evidence of his restraint once more etched into his features now, made her want him even more.

Was that even possible?

She met his gaze. Nervous anticipation churned her stomach. She hadn't felt this jumpy and impulsive since their very first time, which had been after the Medic's Ball during their third year.

He'd romantically booked a room for them at the hotel

where the function had taken place. They'd stripped slowly, wordlessly facing each other. 'Are you sure?' he'd whispered against her lips as she'd clawed at him, writhed her body against his, all but begging him to put them both out of their misery.

'Absolutely,' she'd pleaded, kissing him so passionately she'd felt guilty for using every tactic she could to get what she'd wanted: him, inside her, driving them to oblivion.

They'd stayed awake all night, worked their way through a whole box of condoms. It had been the best night of Lauren's life.

'Now that you're awake, I can leave,' Mason said, dragging her mind back to the moment from a past she'd refused to allow herself to recall in too much detail. His voice was gruff from sleep and he looked around for his clothes, sending her pulse into an alarming rhythm.

'It's okay. Once I'm awake, I'm awake. Occupational hazard.' Desperate that he might leave and skittish by how much she was prepared to beg him to stay, she smiled, her cheeks rubbery, trying to calm her nerves and lighten the atmosphere for her own sake.

She needed to pull herself together; she was a mature woman, a sexual sophisticate. She wanted him. She'd agonised over her desires enough. It was time to be honest. No emotions, but also no regrets.

'Don't go.' She stepped closer, her mind blessedly devoid of any noise, warning static or the constant compulsion to do the right thing, be responsible.

But the urge to be reckless, to relive how good they'd been together physically just one more time, clawed at her resolve.

His breath came faster, his stare almost silver in the low

light. 'Lauren,' he whispered, what looked like the agony of uncertainty of a man on the edge reflected on his face.

Wordlessly, Lauren reached out, placed her hand flat on his chest over his heart, her palm absorbing the rapid pounding and the heat of his skin.

'Are you sure this is what you want?' he said, just as he'd done all those years ago, his rigid body stock-still. 'I don't want you to have any regrets, to make things awkward at work.'

'We're not at work,' she said, her focus blurring with the intensity of watching the struggle on his face. 'You were right…about the flames. I'm tired of denying myself. Tired of overthinking.' She stepped closer until her thighs brushed his, her nipples grazing his chest through her T-shirt. 'I want to be reckless again, just one more time.'

She looked up, pausing a hair's breadth from his lips. She wanted to plead, to say *I know this is going to be so good, but if you could be a little bit rubbish it will help me to keep my feelings out of it, help me to walk away afterwards.*

But it didn't matter how much he rocked her world, they weren't meant to be. They'd proved that last time when they'd let each other down. Her priorities still had to be selfish. She owed herself that much after everything she'd given up to get where she was.

Mason cupped her face, that soul-destroying passion shining from his eyes. She'd almost forgotten its potency. To be trapped in its beam once more sent her body swaying in his direction, until she leaned against him from shoulders to hips.

He traced her lips with his thumbs, as if relearning their shape. 'I've thought about the possibility of this every day since I booked my plane ticket to come home.'

She closed her eyes against the decadence of his confession as she slipped her arms around his waist, clung as if he was the only thing keeping her upright. She couldn't hear how he'd thought about her even before they'd met again. Not when he'd hinted that he'd regretted their split, thought about her over the years, called her less than a year after he'd left.

This had to be casual, a one-off. She was too set in her ways, too career-oriented to be emotionally derailed again.

'Shh,' she said, surging up on her tiptoes to close the space between his mouth and hers. She wanted to feel, not to think about what his words meant. She wanted a return to that oblivion she'd only ever felt with Mason.

With a groan, he scooped one arm around her waist and hauled her the last millimetre to crush their mouths together.

She parted her lips under his and kissed him unreservedly, free at last to indulge the way she'd wanted to the minute he'd walked back into her life.

They moved in sync, deepening the kiss, tongues gliding together, lips clinging, breath mingling. It felt as if they'd never been apart, only better: new and familiar and truthful. She tangled her hands in his hair, curled one leg around his, all but climbing his body in order to feel close enough.

But did close enough exist? Now that she'd given in, she doubted she'd ever feel satiated. It seemed impossible, but this kiss surpassed the ones in the alley. Heat, hard planes, tantalising bursts of naked skin against naked skin.

She shook, scared that she might not survive this experience.

Mason tore his mouth from hers and trailed kisses down the side of her neck. 'Are you okay? Cold?'

'No.' She dropped her head to the side on a moan she felt to the tips of her toes, granting him access. She was burning alive, even as she told herself to hold something back.

Mason fisted the hem of her T-shirt and swiped it over her head in one smooth move, dropped it unceremoniously on the floor and allowed his lips to continue their exploration. Her clavicle, her shoulder, her chest.

She slid her hands over his solid warmth, relearning the outline of his broad shoulders under her palms, the contours of his chest, the ridges of his taut abdomen and the silkiness of his skin.

He felt like *her* person, her Mason.

Had it always been this good, an all-consuming drive to touch and stroke and kiss and never stop?

His hands cupped her breasts and her hips jerked. He knew just how to caress her as if they were made for each other, or he'd never forgotten the shape of her body, the places that made her sigh. This man knew her—her weaknesses, her dreams, her body. Surely she could give herself over to this without fear?

She opened her eyes to find him watching her reaction to his touch. Refusing to suffer alone, she stroked him through his boxers. He shuddered under her touch, a sexy groan at the back of his throat. Had he made that sound before? Was she driving him as insane with lust as he was her?

'I want you so badly.' He gripped her hips and shuffled her back towards the brand-new sectional sofa she'd had delivered three days ago.

For a second she wondered if they should move to the bedroom. But she didn't need all of the creature comforts or a fairy tale reunion. She just needed to get past this wonderful, terrible obsession, to prove to herself that them together couldn't possibly be as good as she remembered. With this uncontrollable urge that had taken them both captive managed once more, she could resume her priorities.

She sat on the sofa and he fell to his knees in front of her. Their eyes locked so Lauren felt seen through to her very soul.

'You're so beautiful,' he said, his fingers spearing into her messed-up hair. 'I've thought about this so many times, but my fantasies were rubbish in comparison to the reality of you.'

He raked his stare over her naked body, bold and unapologetic, as if committing every inch of her to memory.

'I wish we'd started this hours ago,' he continued. 'Half the day has already gone. I've wasted hours sleeping.'

She swallowed, overwhelmed by his heartfelt admission, already mentally agreeing that one time probably wasn't going to be enough for either of them, that they could stretch it to one day, the way they had that first time.

His lips trailed over her skin, his words mumbled there, but clear. 'You are so very hard to forget. Believe me, I've spent six years trying.'

Goosebumps erupted over her exposed skin, his confession slicing into her chest. She couldn't hear this now, not when this was supposed to be purely physical, not when he made it sound as if they'd both had undeclared feelings when they'd split.

Was it possible that he'd felt as deeply for her as she'd secretly felt for him?

She gripped his arms and tugged, pulling him up until he crushed her onto the upholstery, naked chest to naked chest, kissing her once more to block out the questions in her head. Lauren combusted, the heat of his skin and the sexy groan he uttered almost melting her into her new sofa.

It was too good. He'd barely touched her and already she hovered close to climax. His hands roamed her skin, his touch warm and sure as if he recalled every contour of the landscape of her body. His scent filled her nostrils, smothering her senses, imprinting into her mind like a fresh and evocative memory.

His mouth trailed south, finding her nipple so that she dug her nails into his shoulders. 'Mason!' The cry was torn from her throat.

'I know, I know,' he said against her skin as he slid off her underwear while she shoved at the waistband of his boxers, as if neither of them could wait a second longer, as if even with him inside of her it wouldn't be close enough.

Could he possibly know how she felt? Was he equally consumed by this compulsion they had no hope of controlling until it had run its course?

He'd hinted as much, teased her about it, but Lauren had always pushed aside pretty words and promises, preferring hard, irrefutable evidence. Even when people swore they'd always be there for her, things changed beyond anyone's control. People left. Disappeared. Died.

He slipped his hand between her legs, observing her reaction to his touch as if he couldn't look away. All she could do was share his kisses and surrender to his inescapable stare until the desire to have him inside her became unbearable.

'There's a condom in the bedroom,' she said between gasps of pleasure, belatedly realising they should have moved to her bed after all.

'I have one.' He reached for his bag and took protection from his wallet.

'Thank goodness.' She smiled in relief.

He smiled too and she cupped his face, familiarity so strong it knocked the air from her lungs. He pressed a quick kiss to her lips, covered himself and settled his hips back between hers, his jaw taut and his heart thumping against her ribs.

Lauren shifted under him, her bottom lip trapped under her teeth in anticipation. Now that she was seconds away from the fulfilment of her wish, she almost wanted to flee. What if it was too much? Too intense? Too dangerous?

As if sensing the vulnerability shredding her, Mason held her face, tunnelled his fingers into her hair, brushed his lips over hers as he slowly pushed inside.

'I've missed you,' he said, his body shuddering with some kind of momentous effort to hold back.

Her stare clung to his, vision swimming, eyes burning. 'Me too,' she confessed, too drunk with lust and awash with their new code of honesty to guard her thoughts. But it was true. Her sexual encounters these past six years had been woefully few and far between and depressingly superficial. She could trust Mason. They knew each other's bodies. They knew each other's pasts, each other's tender spots. She could truly let go with him. Be herself. Be free.

She gripped his arms, which were braced either side of her head as he rocked into her. Their mutual groans collided in a rush of hot breath and unwavering eye contact that felt way too intimate for a one-night stand. But Mason would always be more to her than that. Their shared history meant he would always have a place in her heart, no matter how well she defended that tender organ.

'It's never been like this with anyone else but you,' he admitted, rocking his hips and snatching another moan from her throat. 'I tried to fight it, believe me, I tried.' He closed his eyes on an agonised wince.

Lauren closed her eyes too, as if by doing so she could block out his candour. 'I know. Me too.' But sometimes attraction was too strong for a reason.

No matter how good they were together, this could only be about the here and now. The moment. She'd made enough choices putting others first. This time in her life was for her, and her weakness for him had already come at a professional cost, resigning from the interview panel.

She raised her hips to meet him, tugged his weight fully down on top of her and kissed him, silencing further talk. His declarations, while a serious aphrodisiac, brought her too close to the edge of a terrifying precipice.

They could have this one time. It would put the past to rest and cure them of their all-consuming hunger for each other.

But as she shattered into a million pieces, surrounded by, engulfed by and consumed by Mason, she feared that, this time around, sex, even the best sex ever, just wouldn't be enough.

# CHAPTER TEN

SUNDAY MORNING, MASON abandoned the eastern coastal Road, which featured a dramatic view around every bend, and pulled his bike into a familiar car park at Pinnacle Point. He'd forgotten the perfection of a stunning New Zealand summer's day, or maybe it was more beautiful than he remembered because Lauren was on the back of his bike, just like old times.

He kicked out the bike stand and held the weight of the bike steady, braced for the loss of the heat and closeness of her body as she dismounted. Dread twisted his gut. Just like he could easily recall memories of all their firsts—first touch, first date, first kiss—he was also plagued by their impending lasts. Would today be her last ride on his bike? This trip to the beach their last date? He couldn't bring himself to contemplate that being inside her over and over again since yesterday, watching her disintegrate in his arms, his chest full of forbidden and conflicted emotions, might be the last time they would be truly honest with each other.

Because sex had always been their most vulnerable form of communication.

Mason sighed and removed his helmet.

The minute that first time was over, when she'd come to him all warm and flushed from sleep, wearing nothing but a T-shirt that barely skimmed the tops of her thighs, he'd clung to her, trying to reel his feelings back in, out of sight, in case she'd see the evidence of how he felt about her on his face. In case she was horrified and asked him to leave. He *should* have left, taken the time to put his head on straight. Instead, they'd indulged in a joint shower, eaten brunch on her tiny veranda and then went back to bed until this morning, exhausting their supply of condoms. At one stage, when neither of them had been able to admit the sexual reunion was over, Mason had rushed out to the pharmacy for another box.

This morning, when they'd made love for what felt like the millionth time, he still hadn't been able to bring himself to leave. And as if she too never wanted their weekend to end, she'd suggested a ride, citing the benefits of fresh air to clear the sex haze, and he hadn't thought twice about agreeing.

Stupid, stupid, stupid.

Of course one time with Lauren was never going to be enough. Even one weekend with her hadn't sated him in the slightest. Being with her again physically had felt more like coming home than literally *coming home*.

He was so doomed.

He joined Lauren at the lookout point where she'd paused to admire the view, the screech of cicadas in the trees almost deafening. Mason settled at her side, his forearms braced on the railing as he stared out at the volcanic bush-clad cliffs and the small sandy beach below. Their beach.

'Bit of a cheap shot, don't you think,' she said, casting him a look full of mock reproof from under her raised sunglasses. 'Stopping at our beach, the scene of our first kiss.' She bumped his shoulder with hers playfully, her eyes sparkling and her words coming out a little breathless.

'It seemed appropriate.' He stepped closer until their bodies welded together, shoulder to thigh, the physical draw of her overriding any thought of self-preservation. 'I thought you might enjoy the trip down memory lane.'

He dipped his head, brushed her lips with his, pulling back from actually kissing her. 'And in case today also marks our last kiss, there's a symmetry to it being here too, don't you think?'

She stared up at him, suddenly wide-eyed with an uncertainty that he couldn't allay, no matter how much he might want to. Regardless of how she felt about continuing this fling, he couldn't definitely say he'd be staying in Auckland permanently unless he was successful in his application for the consultant post. And even if he was in that position, Lauren didn't want promises. He hadn't come back to Auckland for her, but things had changed. Like it or not, they'd developed some sort of relationship, even if there was currently no label for what they were to each other. Could he take the consultant job, commit to staying long-term and risk growing closer to her again, risk that she might, yet again, push him away?

'Were you always this romantic?' She kept her face in profile, her hair blowing in the warm breeze, as if she was afraid to acknowledge any of those good times, afraid to see them reflected in his stare. Something inside Mason recoiled. Had she truly had no idea six years ago how he'd felt about her? But then he hadn't recognised it either, until it was too late.

'If you have to ask, then no, I probably wasn't. I guess I had more than one failing as a boyfriend. But, in my defence, you always seemed a little embarrassed by romantic gestures.'

She frowned, glanced his way, quickly returned her eyes to the view. Mason could have kicked himself for killing the mood.

'I wasn't embarrassed,' she said slowly. 'I just struggled to trust my feelings back then, because losing Mum had made me doubt everything. I'm sorry if that's how it came across to you.'

She looked up at him, the face he'd witnessed showing every possible human emotion bar one, perhaps the most profound one—love—shadowed with vulnerability. Mason held his breath, convinced she was about to open up.

'After she died, something in me shut down emotionally,' she confessed, as he'd predicted. He took her hand and she smiled a sad smile. 'We had been so close my whole life and then she was gone. I'd never felt so alone. By the time I met you, I'd already decided that I never wanted to hurt ever again, that pain was directly correlated to deep feelings, to love, and I'd do everything in my power to avoid it.'

Mason drew on a deep well of patience, this moment momentous in its honesty.

'I couldn't articulate all of this at the time,' she continued, her eyes as vulnerable as when she'd come to him yesterday afternoon, 'but I think placing myself in a caregiver role for Ben made me feel as if I was still close to Mum, that she would rest in peace knowing that at least her children had each other. He was so young, and I'd had my childhood with two parents. I was scared that if I left Auckland with you, something terrible would happen and I'd…'

'Be hurt again?' he supplied, his stomach lurching with the realisation that he and Lauren had been destined to fail from the start.

She nodded in confirmation. 'So I stuck with what I knew.'

Mason held her close, his throat thick with emotion and the urge to kiss her until no more doubts existed. Until he'd extinguished the most burning of his questions: Had she loved him?

'I'm sorry if I stifled your romantic gestures because I was messed-up,' she whispered. 'Will you forgive me?'

'There's nothing to forgive. It's like you said, we're only human; we all have regrets and I was messed-up then too.' They'd both made mistakes and let the other one down. Discussing it might be the first step to moving forward, because surely they couldn't just leave things where they were after that weekend...

Seeing her eyes gloss over, he changed the subject. 'Come on, let's walk down to the beach, see if it's as magical as I remember.'

She sighed, a sound of contentment. 'I loved coming here with you,' she said as he tugged her towards the rugged path that zigzagged down the cliff to their beach. 'It was one of the only places I felt carefree. The hours we spent swimming, talking, just the two of us.'

Mason winced, conflicted that one place could hold such dichotomous associations, some of the best and the absolute worst of their moments. 'We also said goodbye here,' he reminded her, his feelings equally forked. Just as she'd been wary of making herself vulnerable to him back then, she'd also had the power to hurt him, a risk that had actually materialised when she'd called it a day.

She chewed her lip, her stare apologetic. 'Yes, we did.'

Mason kissed her hand. He hadn't brought her here to rehash their break-up. He'd wanted to reconnect beyond the intimacies they'd shared, to remind her that there had been, and still could be, more to them than two people who were insanely attracted to each other.

They were good together, good for each other.

But where he felt like a different person from the one that had left Auckland and Lauren behind, he couldn't be sure that she was any more ready to commit to a relationship than she had been first time around. Could he put himself on the line again without any certainty that she too had changed? It had hurt enough last time.

They arrived on the sand to find the small beach deserted. They kicked off their shoes and left them perched on a rock before heading down to the water's edge.

The feel of the cool water around his ankles, the sand softening underfoot, settled the worst of his discord. 'You know,' he said, 'after six years working for Medicine Unlimited, the first thing I did when I hit Auckland was take my board out into the Gulf for a surf. I never realised I could miss the sea so much.'

She leaned into his side, a serene smile on her face. 'Was it everything you dreamed?'

'Better than my dreams and almost as good as *our* times on this beach—picnics, bonfires, that time I persuaded you to go skinny-dipping.'

She laughed, then sobered, a frown tugging at her mouth. 'But you're back now,' she said hesitantly, as if the observation had only just occurred to her. 'You're planning to stay. You're…different.'

He was different. He might make the same choices—he didn't regret his experiences overseas—but a part of him, the part newly intoxicated by Lauren after the two incredible days they'd shared, wished he'd never left at all. But then he might not have learned valuable lessons about himself, he might not have become the man he was proud to be today.

Because she was still staring up at him, her eyes tinged with what looked like wonder, and because he could no more fight the compulsion than he could stop the tide, he leaned close, pressed his lips to hers, moved them slowly and lazily.

'Ben and I love to surf together,' she said, her pensive gaze fixed far off. 'Before, you know, he moved away to Wellington.'

Mason pressed his lips to the top of her head, inhaling the scent of her shampoo as her sigh shuddered through her body.

'He's only an eight-hour drive away,' he said, because he could feel how much she missed her brother and hated to see her sad. 'Or an hour's flight. And they have some good surf in Wellington.'

'Mm-hmm,' she mumbled.

'What will you do if you don't get the Head of Department position?' he asked with bated breath. 'Would you ever consider moving anywhere else?'

Framed in relation to Ben living in Wellington, it wouldn't be too obvious that Mason was asking to satisfy his self-serving curiosity. If he couldn't get a job in Auckland, he'd have to move elsewhere himself. He couldn't locum for ever. He wanted to begin building his own professional network, and for that he needed a consultant job.

She stiffened slightly in his arms. 'I don't know... I've never really thought about it. I've put in years of hard work in Auckland, and I guess I always figured that Ben would move back home again after university.'

She pulled back and looked up at him, her face tipping

up to his. He kissed her, because he couldn't seem to stop touching her, the press of his lips to hers at first relatively chaste, but then turning inevitably heated. The sun warmed his back. Her sighs brushed at his lips, enticing.

The urge to lay her on the sand and forget their past baggage and their future uncertainty was almost overwhelming. But this was a popular spot with families and tourists and it was the middle of a Sunday morning.

Had their previous relationship ever been that intense? Was it just that they were older, more certain of themselves, more honest?

He pulled back, breathing hard, his forehead pressed to hers while he tried to rein in his desire to have sex on the beach, just to make sure it was as good as it had been for the past twenty-four hours.

Startling Lauren, he climbed to his feet. 'I need to cool down or we might end up getting arrested.'

Something so good, so addictive, was always going to be tricky to manage. But with Lauren likely no more ready for a commitment than she had been six years ago, could he really trust his feelings? Should he even try to pursue this? He had a consultant job potentially on the horizon. He needed to take inspiration from Lauren, be a bit more cautious, careful that his eagerness to embrace their new physical relationship didn't end up hurting both of them.

He scooped his shirt over his head and removed his jeans. A dip in the ocean might help him to turn off this fierce craving that had only strengthened now that he'd re-learned every delicious inch of Lauren.

'Are you mad?' Her jaw was slack with disbelief as she gathered his clothes from the sand and automatically folded them into a neat pile.

'Yep, certifiable.' But he had to do something to keep his hands off her, put some distance between their lips, to take his mind off his dangerous thoughts, feelings. He wanted to know where this was going, when she was still predominantly thinking about Ben.

He strode to the edge of the sea, waded out to waist height and then dived under the waves. The shock of the cold slapped him partway to his senses, as he'd hoped. Tomorrow would begin another busy week at the hospital. He had his interview to prepare for and a heap of admin that needed his attention now that his jet lag had finally abated and the funeral was behind him.

He broke the surface of the water, his feet finding shifting sand as he turned to face the beach. He searched out Lauren, expecting to see her where he'd left her, only she wasn't there. She was behind him, wading through thigh-deep water in her underwear.

Mason froze, his heart leaping. She was magnificent. She'd always had the ability to surprise him. He might not know her thoughts, he might not know if they had any more of a future together this time around than they'd had six years ago, but he knew himself. He knew he wasn't ready to walk away from what they'd shared. He owed it to himself to be one hundred percent transparent.

His blood pounded as he watched her dive under the next wave and then emerge soaking wet, her white underwear virtually see-through and her hair slicked back from her face, like something out of a movie.

With a wide grin, she swam to him, wrapping her arms around his shoulders because she wasn't quite tall enough to touch the bottom. Her breasts emerged above the surface, her nipples visible through the wet cotton, the sight decimating every certainty bar one—how much he wanted her.

'I needed to cool down too,' she said, her legs slipping around his hips under the water, her fingers sliding through his wet hair. 'Then I remembered how much fun the skinny-dipping had been. You make me want to be bad, Mason Ward.'

Before his scattered wits could form speech, she kissed him, a salty rush of cold lips and hot tongues that had him bracing his legs against greater forces than the currents. The sea buffeted them, the waves causing their bodies to undulate closer and closer so that all that separated his arousal from the heat between her legs were two flimsy barriers of soaking-wet cotton.

Every cell in Mason's body urged him to be reckless. It would be so easy, so instinctive to push inside her and figure out the future tomorrow. But they had no condom. And that thing buried deep in his chest that wouldn't be ignored clamoured to be set free.

He pulled back, breathing hard, dragging his gaze from Lauren's pupils, which were dilated with desire.

'Are you okay?' she asked, clinging to his shoulders.

'Laurie, I need to tell you something.' He felt her stiffen in his arms and tightened his grip on her waist. Perhaps she wasn't ready for more than one stolen weekend, but if this was the last time they'd spend together as lovers he owed it to himself to be honest about their past, to discuss where they'd gone wrong and acknowledge that they'd let each other down.

'Six years ago, I think I'd been falling in love with you.' The gnawing in his chest intensified at the look of horror on her face.

She gasped, looking down. 'Don't say that,' she whispered, relaxing her thighs around his hips so she could ease away.

'Why? It's true, although I didn't know it at the time.' Mason clenched his jaw, the sickening rumble of rejection accomplishing what the frigid sea hadn't when it came to his ardour for her.

She shook her head, her dark eyes wide, full of fear. 'Mason...' She pressed her forehead to his, her eyes scrunched closed as if she couldn't bear to witness the impact of what she was about to say.

He braced himself, held his breath, gutted that he'd rushed in too soon and made himself so vulnerable.

'Does it matter? We agreed that we are both focused on our promotions right now. This weekend has been amazing. It was even fun being back on the deathtrap,' she said.

She was letting him down gently, retreating to her comfort zone after letting her hair down. Trouble was, he wasn't a pastime. She couldn't dip in and out when she needed a thrill and he couldn't go back to being the man who hadn't known his true self.

Lauren's fear of being vulnerable magnified his own doubts.

He'd been so fixated on trying to make sense of the mess his parents had made back then, so accommodating when she'd dumped him on this very beach, it hadn't even occurred to him to fight for them, to dissect the depth of his feelings, to not give up on the idea of him and Lauren so easily.

Then, like now, he'd obeyed her rules. Aside from that one time he'd called the ER, he hadn't contacted her following the clean break she'd made sound so easy. He'd taken his broken heart, thrown himself into work, joined Medicine Unlimited. One placement had led to another and another, each overseas location easier to exist in because there were no expectations beyond doing his job. He could be himself, be heartbroken Mason and then, after some time, just career-focused Mason. He'd made his own mark—grown into the man he'd always wanted to be.

And that man knew what he would and wouldn't tolerate.

'I understand,' he said, pressing his lips to hers in a chaste kiss before wading them both into the shallows.

He didn't want to hurt her again, or push an agenda that she just wasn't ready for, but he also wanted to be true to himself. She looked up at him warily and he cupped her cold cheeks in his hands. 'The thing is, Laurie, you were right earlier. I have changed. I'm not going to pretend, to take your friendship and the occasional benefit when it's on offer, and I'm not going to sell myself short either. I'm not that man you dumped any more. It matters to me. I know who I am now. I want to be honest with myself, and with you.'

He moved aside and she stopped him with one hand on his arm.

'I'm sorry.' Her stare glistened with emotion. 'Sorry for the cold and logical break-up speech I gave you back then. Of course your feelings mattered. I want you to know that I felt terrible for letting you down, knowing that, either way, I'd have to disappoint someone. And at the time I couldn't bear for it to be Ben.'

He nodded, wanting to state the obvious, that she should always please herself first, but they'd both been dealing with some heavy stuff six years ago. They'd both needed to focus on starting a physically and emotionally demanding job, becoming doctors, building their brand.

'We each had to do what was right for us,' he said, conflicted. Maybe bringing her here hadn't been his best idea. Maybe he'd rushed it, maybe the nostalgia had caused him to mix the past and the present. Maybe they would never be on the same page. 'I guess I just don't want to make another mistake,' he added, shrugging on his T-shirt.

She looked down, gnawed at her lip. 'Of course. Me neither.' She plastered on a brave smile. 'Good thing tomorrow is the start of a new week.'

He'd been referring to the past, the mistake he'd made by letting her go so easily six years ago, where she was clearly talking about this weekend as if she already regretted it.

If that was how she felt it was better he knew it now, before he became too heavily invested. She was doing him a favour and, no matter how heavy the boulder of disappointment that sat in his chest was, it would be nothing compared to how he'd feel if he once more allowed feelings for her to develop, only to have his heart broken again.

Now he just needed to find a way to be okay with them returning to being friends.

# CHAPTER ELEVEN

THE FOLLOWING WEEKEND, the Senior Auckland Health Staff Forum was being held at the Bluewater Bay Winery Estate on Auckland's Waiheke Island, a forty-minute ferry ride from the mainland across the Hauraki Gulf.

Lauren entered the large function room, the venue for the evening's social event, her stomach twisting into knots of desperation to see Mason and to get him alone.

After things had turned rapidly sour that day on the beach, they'd dressed in pensive silence and he'd dropped her at home. Lauren had been so confused, so overwrought by his confession that he'd been falling in love with her when they'd split up, that she hadn't known what to say to him to make things right. Since then, they'd barely seen each other. Mason's week had been filled with extended interviews and social gatherings for the consultant appointment and Lauren had distracted herself from the mess they'd made by succumbing to their physical attraction by finally unpacking all of her moving boxes during her time off.

They'd texted each other, conversed about patients at the hospital, they'd even run into each other in the cafeteria again, but, unlike the time before when they'd flirted so hard she'd almost dragged him into an empty conference room and ravished him, their exchange had been polite and impersonal.

What a difference a week made. After she'd finally admitted how much she wanted him, she'd started to feel as if some missing piece of her had slotted back into place. It made sense. Mason was a huge part of her past, his significance even more marked now that she knew he'd had deep feelings for her back then.

She swallowed hard, choking down her regret. If she'd known at the time would it have made a difference? She stood by her decision to be there for Ben. He was her only brother and she loved him. But what if she'd also been just a little bit selfish six years ago? What if she'd gone with Mason as planned, travelled for a while? What if, instead of breaking things off and then trying to forget him, she'd kept in touch, tried to make a go of a long-distance relationship? What might her life now look like?

Would they have fallen in love? Would they still be together? Married? Have children?

Nausea threatened—she could no longer lie to herself and pretend that she wasn't in serious trouble where Mason was concerned. She frantically searched the room for a friendly face, spying Grady in conversation with Helen Bridges. Desperate for a distraction from her thoughts, she headed in their direction.

Most of the staff attendees, including Helen and Grady, were gathered on the winery's expansive veranda, which boasted a breathtaking vista of the vineyards and olive groves with a backdrop of the distant sea views, in order to take advantage of the last rays of the day's sun.

'I'm sorry again that I had to withdraw from the appointment panel,' Lauren said to Helen with a mental wince. 'I do hope my absence hasn't disrupted the process this week.'

Helen smiled reassuringly. 'Don't worry. My recruitment operations run like clockwork. We missed your youthful enthusiasm, of course—you were the youngest of the group by far—but the rest of us met this afternoon to discuss the shortlisted candidates. One or two of them are head and shoulders above the rest—exactly the right pedigree, if you know what I mean. So unless they botch their final interviews later this week, all that remains is picking the best fit and rubberstamping the appointment.'

Lauren forced her expression to remain politely neutral while curiosity and protectiveness boiled in her blood. Was Mason one of the two in the running, or was he being unfairly judged on the basis of Murray's mistake?

'By pedigree you mean the right aptitude and surgical skills, of course?' Lauren softened her accusatory tone with a smile. Why was she being so confrontational? That wasn't like her at all.

'Of course,' said Helen, slightly taken aback. After a few more minutes of small talk, the woman smiled and made her excuses, heading to another group to network, the main purpose of these forums.

Left alone with Grady and her own thoughts once more, Lauren shivered. What would Mason do if he didn't get the job? Would he leave Auckland again, head back overseas when there was nothing more to keep him there?

And where would that leave Lauren? Would she watch him go before they'd even had a chance to reconnect properly, to see where their relationship could lead? Not that she could call the current frigid state of affairs a relationship, but that was all her fault. She'd been so overwhelmed by the sex, bewildered by how quickly she'd imagined them picking up where they'd left off that she'd frozen at Mason's confession, retreating back into her safe zone like a hermit crab hiding in its shell.

'The talk is that the Scottish guy is the favourite,' said Grady, reminding her of his presence. 'Although Helen can't be left in any doubt who you'd have favoured if you were still on the panel.'

'I don't know what you mean. I'd have been completely professional and impartial, as you well know.' She looked away from his far too perceptive stare, her feelings churning between relief and confusion. If Mason left Auckland there would be a natural break to this thing they'd started, just like last time. Only she'd become horribly invested in him staying around.

'Anyway, it's really not my business any more.' Lauren sighed, wishing she could escape to the room she'd booked on the estate to sort out her feelings in private. She'd survived without Mason for the past six years, so why did the idea of him leaving again, finding a consultant post elsewhere, make her feel as if she'd just been punched in the stomach and couldn't catch her breath?

'You know, there's a bit of a rumour circulating,' Grady said. 'About Mason.'

She levelled her stare on her friend, her defensive hackles once again raised high. 'I hope it's got nothing to do with that ancient scandal involving his father.' She dropped her voice to a hissed whisper. 'It was nothing to do with Mason in the first place. He's perfectly qualified for the consultant position in his own right, more than qualified. I know, I've seen all of the candidates' CV's and...'

She trailed off, finally registering the morbid fascination in Grady's expression. She was busted.

'And you're sleeping with him again,' he stated. 'That's why you had to resign from the interview panel.' There was no judgement in her friend's voice, only concern in his eyes.

Lauren's jaw dropped, face aflame. 'Not that it's any of your business, but I resigned *before* I slept with him. How did you know? Does the whole hospital know? Are people talking about us? It could damage Mason's chances at the surgical consultant post and that's not fair.'

He deserved as decent a shot as the next candidate. In her opinion he was the best man for the job.

Grady looked sheepish. 'I called around to your place Saturday evening after my shift with a Chinese takeaway as my parents had Molly. I thought you could do with a hand unpacking some boxes. I saw his bike parked outside.'

Lauren's veins filled with heat of a different kind as she recalled exactly what she and Mason had been doing Saturday evening. Then she analysed her earlier reaction to the idea that Mason would be unfairly judged to have done something…inappropriate. The same blood burning hot only seconds ago ran cold.

She was way more invested in him than for a colleague she'd had the best sex of her life with. She'd started to develop feelings for him again.

No wonder she'd freaked out after he'd confessed that he'd been falling in love with her. Then, like now, sadness and frustration and grief for the missed opportunities stung the backs of her eyes.

'Actually,' continued Grady, oblivious to her turmoil, 'the gossip has been more speculative than damning. People who remember that you two were once an item are wondering if you're together again, that sort of thing. I'm not the only one who was around when you were med students.'

Lauren rolled her eyes. 'Since when do you take any notice of hospital gossip?'

'Since it involves my friend,' said Grady. 'A friend who hardly ever dates, but is now so heavily involved in a relationship that she's being defensive with colleagues. A friend I'm concerned about being hurt again.'

He was right. Mason had hurt her in the past, but, unbeknown to her, she'd also hurt him. At the time, for self-preservation, she'd shut out the possibility that they'd been way more to each other than either of them had confessed. But, as she'd said to Mason on the beach, that was in the past. He wasn't in love with her now.

Fighting the urge to cry, Lauren met Grady's astute and sympathetic stare.

'You're falling for him, aren't you?' he said.

Lauren blinked, sniffed, tossed her hair over her shoulders. 'Don't be ridiculous. We had one night together and now we're barely on speaking terms.'

Was she falling in love with him? He'd only been back in Auckland a matter of weeks and already her life was almost unrecognisable—motorbike rides, almost having sex on the beach, professional inconsistency.

As if she'd subconsciously always known his location, her gaze darted to Mason on the other side of the room near the buffet table. Her breath hitched at the sight of him, the urge to make things right between them almost overriding every other rational thought. How could he possibly mean so much to her after such a short time? How could she allow him to creep back under her guard, when nothing was certain or planned or decided? She was more exposed, more vulnerable now than she'd been back then. Because the feelings twisting her into knots were momentous compared to the ones she'd fought six years ago in order to be able to let Mason go.

'Why aren't you two speaking?' said Grady, drawing her back from the edge of a terrifying drop. 'You know you can tell me anything.'

She deflated. 'It's complicated, but the gossipmongers are wrong. We're not back together.'

They weren't anything.

'If it's complicated, shouldn't you be over there, untangling it?'

Lauren hated Grady's hesitant smile. It contained too many emotions, the same emotions scrambling her usually rational decision-making processes: a hint of fear, presumably for her being hurt once more, a sprinkle of hope that maybe, this time, she and Mason might make a better go of it and Lauren would finally address the gaping hole in her personal life.

'I don't know any more. I don't have all the answers.' But what if she'd correctly identified her feelings? What if she could work through the fear of losing him from her life once more and meet Mason halfway to this new mature, self-assured and honest relationship?

Didn't she deserve to at least give it some consideration, just like she deserved her professional success?

'I'm no expert,' Grady interjected, 'but what if Mason wants to uncomplicate it too?'

Did he? She had no idea because, stupidly, she'd been so caught up in her own past hurt and her own muddled feelings that hadn't asked him how he felt. She'd just clung to what she'd known, declared it a sound strategy and stuck to her plan.

She shrugged. 'Perhaps it's just better to concentrate on our careers.' Mason's association with her had already put him back at the centre of hospital speculation.

'Translation: you're too scared to even give the possibility a chance,' Grady concluded. 'This is classic you, Lauren. You plan everything, but some things should just be felt, not orchestrated.'

Perhaps realising that he was overstepping a boundary, he softened. 'Well, I'm sorry that it didn't work out. That's a real shame. For a while there, you had... I don't know, a glow about you; something was definitely different. Sorry I brought it up.'

Lauren nodded, choked that she had a good friend in Grady, but scared that the *glow* would be gone for ever if she wasn't brave.

'I think I will explore the buffet,' she stated, raising her chin with a bravado she didn't feel. 'I'm hungry.' Actually, she felt the exact opposite, but she needed to clear the air with Mason.

Grady's gaze flicked in Mason's general direction. 'Good idea.'

Lauren smiled, squeezed Grady's arm and headed inside. Mason had moved to the far side of the buffet table. He was dressed in a casual shirt, which was open at the neck, a place she knew smelled like him and that when she buried her face there, his chest hair tickled her cheek. His dark hair looked damp on the ends as if he'd been for a swim or not long emerged from the shower.

He made her eyes water and her legs wobbly.

Professionally, she'd never faltered in her choices. But

what if her personal decisions had been, and still were, shaped by fear? What if she'd stopped listening to her instincts the day her mother died? Was that truly how she wanted to live the rest of her life? Part of her had never moved on. She'd never given another man a chance after Mason. It was easier to barricade her heart than risk it being damaged again. Didn't she owe it to herself, now more than ever, to be honest about her feelings?

They spoke to her. Yelled. Demanded action.

She headed across the room, her steps growing more sure-footed. Because being too close to him would remind her of the weekend and what it had felt like to be back in his arms, and remind her of how they'd parted Sunday evening, Lauren placed the food-laden table between them.

'How are you finding the forum, Dr Ward?' she asked, picking up a plate and placing a single cucumber-based vegan hors d'oeuvre on top. Her hand shook. She hated cucumber. Now she'd have to carry it around the room pretending to eat it until she could discreetly cast it aside.

'Very informative, Dr Harvey,' he answered, tossing a grape into his mouth, his eyes on hers for a second longer than was appropriate for polite, professional conversation. But, unlike when he'd been inside her, his handsome face and emotive stare an open book, she couldn't read him right now.

Was he angry that she'd been scared enough of their connection to withdraw again? Perhaps he'd already moved on, declared her a lost cause.

Her throat became so tight with regret for the wasted years she feared she might pass out.

She forgot all of the things she wanted to say. All she could think about was how much she wanted to hurl herself at him, to apologise, to spend another night relearning all there was to know about Mason physically and discovering new things about the man he'd become.

A man who'd once loved her.

Mason moseyed around the end of the table in her direction, examining the food selection on offer.

'Are you staying the night at the winery?' she asked, somehow keeping her voice low but casual.

She shouldn't be thinking about the sleeping arrangements, how far away from her room his might be. She was getting ahead of herself.

'No, I brought my bike over,' he said, his stare still on the food as if he found the gourmet vegetarian sausage rolls fascinating. 'I'm leaving soon for the last ferry. You?'

The flood of disappointment reverberated through her bones until she almost crumbled. 'I...have a room booked. I'll be on the first ferry in the morning.'

He raised his head, his stare latching onto hers at last.

Lauren's stomach fluttered. She stepped closer, uncaring that they were in a room full of colleagues. 'Can we talk?'

'Sure.' Mason shrugged, but his penetrating gaze held hers.

'Grady knows about us,' she whispered, toying nervously with the single hors d'oeuvre on her plate. 'He saw your bike parked outside my place last weekend.'

Mason cast her a speculative glance. 'We had sex, Lauren. That doesn't really constitute an us.'

Lauren winced, ignoring his statement. She didn't want this to be over, but what did he want?

'There's more.' She kept her voice low so they wouldn't be overheard. 'There's some gossip going around that my withdrawal from the appointment panel is because we're a couple again.'

His lack of reaction spiked her anxiety. His stare was cool ice-blue, but of course he'd be concerned about hospital tittle-tattle affecting his chances for the consultant job.

'I want you to know,' she said, 'that I'll do everything in my power to assure these rumours don't negatively impact your chances for the post. It's not fair. We haven't done anything wrong.'

'Lauren—' he stepped deliberately closer, so she was bathed in his delicious scent '—I don't care about idle gossip.' He reached for another sausage roll, even though he already had three that were untouched on his plate, his gaze locked on hers. 'If I don't get the job it will be because they have a better candidate. But, more importantly, if my suitability for the post is so precarious that some irrelevant rumour will go against me, then Gulf Harbour isn't the workplace for me.'

Lauren's mouth dried. Why did she suddenly feel naive and unsophisticated, when Mason was all sexy confidence and self-awareness, twice the man he used to be?

He didn't move away, and her heart battered her ribs as if trying to escape the searing, searching look in his eyes. 'Besides, we're not a couple, are we?'

All she could do was shake her head mutely, because she couldn't bring herself to ask if he'd want them to be.

'So, there is no problem.' He shrugged and Lauren wanted to leap up onto the table and announce their innocence to their assembled colleagues for Mason's sake. Only she was guilty of wanting him, she had slept with him when she shouldn't have and she'd do it again in a heartbeat.

'No, except...' She stared at him, blocking out the room, full of hospital bigwigs, as if they were alone on their beach again. 'I don't know what this is, I just know that I don't want it to be over.'

His eyes flicked between hers as if he couldn't trust her words.

'I'm sorry,' she blurted, 'if I dismissed what you told me on the beach last weekend. I was completely taken aback, because you were right. It does matter. It matters to me very much.'

'Does it?' His stare hardened.

Lauren nodded. 'I wish I'd known how you felt back then.'

'Would it have made a difference?' Sparks danced in his eyes and she wanted to touch him so badly, to kiss away the vulnerability she saw there, that she clattered her plate onto the table with a trembling hand.

She swallowed, because the past was gone, but she wanted to believe that she wouldn't have pushed him away if she'd known his feelings. 'Neither of us will ever know, will we?'

She wanted to be honest, as honest as he'd been with her. 'But, whatever this is—friends, more than that—I don't want us to mess it up this time.'

He was quiet for so long Lauren worried it was already too late. Then he stopped a passing waiter and handed over his laden plate. 'I've lost my appetite,' he said. 'I think I'll head down to the ferry, return to Auckland.'

His stare carried so much absolution and heat and promise that she shuddered, too aware of every fibre of her clothes against her skin.

How could he do that? Say one thing aloud and another

thing entirely with his eyes? But she heard every unspoken word.

He checked his watch. 'It leaves in twenty minutes.' He looked up. *Come with me.* 'Goodnight, Dr Harvey.'

He spun away and strode to the exit, never looking back.

Lauren dithered for a split second, hating herself for second-guessing the best relationship of her life, the only relationship she'd ever given half a chance. She worked hard as a professional woman. Why was she selling herself so short when it came to her personal life? Her career, her promotion mattered, but did it have to mean everything?

With her head held high, she strode from the function room, chasing after Mason, chasing the liberating honesty they seemed determined to embrace. In her room, she quickly gathered the few belongings she'd bothered to unpack and headed out into the night, into the reckless unknown.

Mason waited outside the winery's floodlit entrance. His eyes lit up when he saw her emerge and something bold and carefree bloomed inside Lauren.

Wordlessly, Mason fastened the strap of his spare helmet under her chin, pressed a hard kiss that tasted like relief to her mouth and then leaned forwards so she could slide behind him onto his bike.

With the wind snatching at her hair as Mason rode to the ferry terminal, another thought occurred. What would she do if she fell in love with Mason Ward a second time? This time she knew it would be harder, deeper. It would take over her soul. And there was just no plan for that eventuality.

# CHAPTER TWELVE

THE NEXT MORNING, Mason awoke before dawn, reaching for Lauren automatically, as he had every night since their weekend together. Only unlike those intervening nights, when his arms gripped fresh air and his stomach sank that she wasn't there, asleep at his side, this time his hands met warm, soft, fragrant skin.

Half-asleep, she moaned, reached behind her to grip the back of his neck and twist his hair between her fingers. He dragged her close, burying his face in her hair, kissing the side of her neck, cupping her breasts in his palms until he had her full, undivided attention.

'Is it morning already?' she said, turning in his arms. She pressed her lips to his and lifted her thigh over his hip.

'Not yet, but I never want morning to come, because when it does we'll have to leave this bed, shower and go to work.' He dragged his mouth from the corner of hers, down her neck and across her chest, lifting her breast to his lips.

She sighed, her hips moving against his, driving him to distraction. But he wasn't distracted. His head was full of Lauren. His whole being was full of Lauren.

Her scent covered his skin, her voice and her laughter occupied his head and pleasuring her had become his number one priority. For the first time in his life, he feared that he would never be able to stop touching her, that he'd be irresponsible enough to be late for work or even not turn up at all.

He moved his mouth south, kissing her ribs and her stomach and then between her thighs, filling his senses with her in order to make it through a long day of enforced abstinence.

He moved back up to kiss her lips as he reached for a condom. She helped him, the process slowed by the kisses they couldn't seem to stop, even for a second.

Their tongues tangled as he finally pushed inside her. But instead of moving to the rhythm that his body and Lauren's hungry eyes demanded, he stilled, holding himself deep inside her while they kissed and kissed and kissed.

'I'll want to kiss you when I see you later at work,' he said, gazing down at her swollen lips and pleasure-glazed eyes.

'Me too.' She bucked her hips, taunting him, but still he barely moved.

Instead he pushed her wild hair back from her exquisite features and kissed each of them in turn, the tip of her nose, her closed eyelids, her cheekbones and chin.

'I'll want to lure you somewhere private,' he said, peppering her lips with tiny pecks, 'and make you moan until you look at me, just the way you're looking at me now.'

'Me too,' she whispered, her fingers digging into his shoulders while she ran her lips over his jaw and down his neck.

*I'll want to tell you that I'm in love with you again,* he

said, but this time only with his eyes, as he rocked into her and stared down at her and kissed her lips, over and over.

His fertile imagination saw her *me too* in the depths of her stare, heard it in the way she said his name again and again, felt it as she climaxed, clinging so tightly to him with her arms and her legs and her hands that he wondered if they'd actually become one entity with two hearts beating a matching rhythm.

He lay on top of her for long breathless seconds after it was over, the words a lump in his throat. He couldn't just blurt out his feelings and then they'd leave for work. He had no idea how she felt about starting up a relationship again. He understood the fears that had held her back last time. He'd clearly had his own reservations. Why else had it taken him so long to realise how he'd felt about her six years ago?

She'd been open yesterday, showed how much she cared about him by coming to his defence over the gossip she thought might unsettle him, given his father's behaviour in the past. She'd even admitted her confusion and her desire for them to see where this could go. Mason knew these were huge steps for her, given that their previous wreck of a relationship was the most serious one either of them had attempted.

He rolled to lie by her side while they caught their breath. Her hand stroked his chest. His fingers played with her hair. He needed to give her some space, but how would he do that when she felt essential to his existence, like air or water? He certainly couldn't rush to confess his feelings or put her under any pressure. He could be patient. Lauren was worth the wait.

Resolved to reassure her, but also needing to admit his part in the mistakes they'd made, he pulled her close. 'Laurie?'

'Mm-hmm?' she answered, still groggy and replete from pleasure.

'What I didn't say last night at the function was thank you for looking out for me.' He pressed a kiss to her neck and she snuggled closer.

'You're welcome. It's like you said, we need to look out for each other.'

'But you don't need to worry.' She had enough going on with Ben and her promotion. 'I meant what I said about not caring if people can't see the real me.'

'Okay.' She turned to face him and pressed a kiss to his lips, one he could easily become lost in, if only there were more hours in the day.

He stroked her hair back from her flushed cheeks. 'I wasn't blameless in messing up what we had, you know. After everything that happened with my father, I was sick of being Mason Ward, sick of the expectations and everyone watching me, waiting for me to slip up too. When my mother left, it was easier for me to go where no one knew me, where I could start again, be myself and focus on being the kind of surgeon I wanted to be. Not some guy from surgical royalty perched on a wobbly pedestal. I watched my mother run away, start over, and I thought, why not? Of course I hadn't planned on staying away so long, but then one job led to another and I became increasingly removed from this place, from you, from the idea that you'd moved on and I'd let you go so…easily.' He sighed. 'Until

I felt comfortable in my own skin, certain of my own abilities and who I was… I couldn't face coming back, only to be rejected again, so, like my mother, I too took the safer route and stayed away.'

And although she'd been the most constant person to believe in him back then, and that should have been enough for him to take a risk, she hadn't believed in *them*. But surely if he gave her time, if he showed her his feelings, she'd find her way there? Part of him didn't want to be patient. He wanted to shout his feelings from the rooftops. They'd already missed out on the past six years because they'd both been too wrapped up in other stuff to be honest about the way they'd felt, not that she'd ever admitted she'd been in love with him. But he didn't care about the past any more. He only cared about the present and his future with Lauren.

'How are you feeling about how your interview went?' she asked.

'It will be what it will be,' he said, holding her tighter. He hadn't yet told her that he'd received a different job offer via email last week. He'd been head-hunted for a consultant job in his old Australian stomping ground. He planned to tell her once he knew about the Gulf Harbour position, a part of him scared that she might use the news as an excuse to withdraw from him again, encourage him to take it without giving them a chance.

Doubts pounded in his temples. He wanted her to trust him with the important things: her feelings, her private life, her heart, but then he hadn't completely trusted her with his news either.

'What will you do if the job goes to someone else?' she asked, her body stiffening the slightest fraction.

He didn't want his answer to freak her out, so he hedged. 'I don't know. Keep locuming. Look for another job. I haven't really given it too much thought.'

Lauren chewed at her lip.

'What if they're stupid enough to pass you over for the Head of ER?' he asked in return. 'Would you go for a promotion elsewhere?'

'I don't know,' she whispered. 'It's not as easy for me to just up and leave for greener pastures. I have Ben, Dad. Whereas you're free to work wherever you want.'

Mason heard what she didn't add, that she still had the same responsibilities she'd had six years ago, the ones she'd chosen over him.

But there was no way he wanted her thoughts going down that track.

Changing the subject, he said, 'Let's go away for the weekend, somewhere romantic. We can take the bike, find somewhere to risk skinny-dipping again.' If his plan materialised perhaps by then she'd be ready to hear his feelings for her, ready to admit her own.

She laughed, her eyes alight with satisfying excitement. 'Where will we go?'

He nuzzled her neck, drawing out another of her contented sighs. 'You just leave all of the logistics to me. I've checked the roster. We both have next weekend off. Do you have plans?'

She shook her head, gazing up at him with dreamy eyes that settled most of his doubts.

'Good. Then I'll whisk you away from it all.'

That was what they needed. To spend time together away from work, to fall in love all over again, only this time they could hopefully both enter into a brave new relationship without fear.

# CHAPTER THIRTEEN

THE FOLLOWING FRIDAY, after a satisfying week of work, where she'd discovered that she'd been awarded the Head of Department promotion, and five blissful nights of falling asleep entwined with Mason, Lauren had been looking forward to celebrating on their romantic weekend away. Instead, her stomach writhed into a tight knot of trepidation as she heard Mason turn the key she'd given him in the lock of her front door.

Now she had to tell him that she couldn't go away with him this weekend.

She folded a T-shirt and tucked it into her weekend bag, dread dragging at her posture. Mason was going to be disappointed. She was disappointed. But surely he'd understand? After all, they were both fully aware of how life sometimes just happened.

Mason appeared in the bedroom doorway, his slow and sexy smile ripping Lauren to shreds so all she could do for a second was stand frozen to the spot and stare. He'd changed from work clothes into jeans and T-shirt. He looked delicious. Everything inside Lauren clenched. He was so handsome, a brilliant surgeon, a good, kind and caring man.

Because she couldn't stay away from him for a moment longer, she rushed over to him, met him halfway across the room. Their lips collided, their kiss a storm of passion and the desperation of two people who hadn't touched for twelve hours too many.

'I've wanted to do that all day,' he breathed against her lips, his glazed stare zigzagging between her eyes. 'How can I miss you when I see you every day?' Without waiting for an answer, he cupped her breast through her shirt as he backed her up towards the bed where they fell into each other's arms. His thumb teased her nipple and she forgot that she'd had a bad day at work, forgot that she'd need to let Mason down about their trip, almost forgot her worry for Ben and her impending departure for Wellington.

'I missed you too, so much,' Lauren managed as Mason groaned and trailed kisses down her neck. He covered her body with his, his hips fitting between her legs, his hands in her hair, tilting her face to his kiss.

Lauren's head swam with arousal. Oh, how she wanted to block out the world, her responsibilities, block out reality for a couple of days and immerse herself in the two of them: Lauren and Mason. It didn't matter where, she'd be happy to stay in this bed all weekend if it meant she had a hope of quenching her insatiable need for him. Her flight wasn't for another two hours; there was time for this, but if they ended up naked she'd become sidetracked.

Reluctantly, she pulled her lips from his. 'Wait. Wait,' she said as his hand delved inside her top, curling around her ribs and heading for the clasp of her bra. 'I need to talk to you.'

Her shove at his shoulders was pathetically weak, her hips still writhing against the hard length of him. But then he sobered, looked down at her with such tenderness and devotion she almost sobbed.

'I heard about the patient you lost,' he said, stroking her hair back from her face. 'I saw Grady. I'm sorry.'

She nodded, too grateful for his support and understanding to do more than blink away the sting in her eyes and shuffle away from him so she could think straight.

He lay on the bed next to her, his head propped on one hand while the other hand caressed her hip. 'You don't have to shoulder everything alone, you know. I understand what it's like. I'm here for you.'

She nodded, squeezed his hand, showing him that she agreed. 'I know. It's not that.'

Lauren, as much as the next person, understood how life carried no guarantees. How it could be brutal. People died, like her mother; or they made mistakes, like Mason's father, or they let other people down, the way she and Mason had done in the past.

'What is it?' He sat up, his stare full of concern.

She stood, paced her bedroom to the wardrobe and tugged a sweater from a hanger, nerves stalling her breath. 'I can't go wherever it is you had planned this weekend.' She kept her eyes downcast while she folded the jumper, only looking up once she'd placed it in her bag. 'I'm sorry.'

His brow crinkled in confusion. 'Why not? Do you need to work?'

Lauren shook her head, regret gripping her throat. 'No, it's not that. Ben called earlier. He's sick.'

Mason stood, moved to her side and took both of her hands in his. 'Seriously sick? Is he okay? What is it?'

She looked away, his worry for her brother pressing down on her chest. 'No, just some horrible virus that's going around his hall of residence.'

'Oh, that's good.' Mason breathed a sigh of relief and

then added, 'Well, you know what I mean—it's good that it's nothing serious.'

Lauren nodded, refusing to contemplate the kind of panic she'd be in if Ben had been seriously ill. 'I'm flying to Wellington. My plane leaves in just under two hours.' Lauren couldn't bear to witness any dejection he might feel, so she fussed with the zip on her bag. 'I'm sorry about this weekend. Can we…reschedule?'

Mason frowned, walked to the window in silence.

Lauren chewed at her lip, awash with guilt and frustration. After their busy week, she'd been looking forward to spending time alone with Mason. But Ben needed her. Their father was in Australia on a work conference. There was no one else. She and Mason could go away the next time their rosters coincided in a weekend off, whenever that would be…

'Does Ben want you there?' Mason's voice was quiet, careful, his back to her so she couldn't read the expression behind his tone.

'He didn't ask me to come.' Lauren stiffened, slightly defensive, because Mason knew her situation. 'But he'll need me. I always take care of him when he's ill. I can take him some fever medication and make him soup when he's feeling hungry.'

It was one of the things their mother had done, one of the roles Lauren had adopted.

'Lauren…' said Mason, gently, 'he's twenty years old. Don't you think he's capable of caring for himself?'

She flushed, aware that where Ben was concerned she had the tendency to be overprotective.

'Of course he is,' she huffed, 'but we all need someone sometimes.' She would do the same for Mason if he was sick.

Mason nodded, but looked unconvinced. 'Maybe he has friends who will check in with him, someone from the university? A girlfriend who's crazy enough about him that she'd risk catching whatever he has just to stroke his fevered brow.'

She winced, recalling the times when Mason had been ill and she'd gone around to his place anyway, just to see him and be there for him, and he'd done the same for her in return.

Lauren frowned, her heart thumping with uncertainty. 'He'd tell me if he had a girlfriend.' They were close. Ben confided in her...

'Would he?' asked Mason dubiously. 'It took me a long time to tell my parents about you, and that wasn't because I wasn't serious about you. I was, head over heels. It was because they were my parents, and it felt like none of their business.'

'Well, I'm not Ben's mother, so—'

'So stop acting like you are,' Mason implored. 'Call him, send him a care parcel, but don't change your plans for the entire weekend just because Ben has a cold.'

She shot him a look full of the indignation she felt. 'I don't know what you're saying.'

'I'm saying be what he needs, Laurie. Be his big sister.' He came to her, took both of her hands in his. 'But think about yourself too. Do what you want and need. Stop putting yourself last and making sacrifices that no one wants you to make.'

Lauren shook her head, trying to dislodge the irrational feeling that she'd done something wrong. 'I don't expect you to understand. Ben and I have a special bond. A unique relationship…'

Mason lifted her hands to his mouth and kissed the backs, one and then the other. 'And I love that you have each other to rely on and share things with, believe me.' His expression softened and he cupped her cheek. 'But don't you think rushing down to Wellington to hold Ben's hand is…a bit over the top? We'd made plans for this weekend. I was looking forward to spoiling you.'

A twinge of doubt pinched her ribs. 'I know and I'm sorry that I'm letting you down, but my family is important to me and—'

'And I'm not.' It wasn't a question. He stared, his only movement the slight tightening of his jaw.

'Of course I care about you, Mason. I just have other priorities too. I don't expect you to understand because you're an only child, but my mother would have wanted me to take care of my brother and that's what I've always done. You knew that about me when we met.'

If she'd thought he looked disappointed about the weekend, the defeat in his eyes then was hard to witness. 'We all have other priorities, Lauren, and I understand yours. I'd support you all the way, you know that. I'd even come with you to Wellington, just for the chance of spending a few minutes of this weekend with you in between your commitments to your brother. But relationships work both ways. You're giving me nothing in return and it feels awfully reminiscent of the last time you pulled away from us.'

She gasped, horrified that he'd throw up the past when they'd both confessed to making mistakes. 'We agreed that we both played a part in our break-up. You can't just blame me for everything.' Now, when she was one step away from loving him, and placing herself in the most vulnerable position of her adult life, he was changing the rules of the game.

He dropped her hands, turned away, snorted as if in disbelief. 'You know, I can't believe that I've done this again...'

'Done what?' Lauren's temples throbbed in confusion. Was what he'd said true? Lauren could admit that she probably had overreacted by rushing to buy a plane ticket, but were there deeper motives behind her actions? Was she spooked by how fast this was happening, by the force of her feelings for Mason this time around?

But he couldn't blame her for her caution. What did either of them know about making a serious relationship work?

'I might have been the one who left the country six years ago, but you're the one who ran away, from us, from what we could have had. You pushed me away, just like you're doing now.'

She shook her head as if she could shake the truth of his words from her consciousness, but he was right. She had pushed him away then, but she'd explained why, confessed her grief-driven doubts. Deep down, she'd known that he'd leave her anyway. People left. Her mother, Ben, Mason. What else was she supposed to do but protect herself?

'I'm not pushing you away.'

Her phone pinged; the ride share she'd ordered was outside.

She collected her bag from the bed and threw it over her shoulder, torn in so many directions she thought she might collapse into pieces on the ground.

He continued as if she hadn't spoken. 'Do you realise that you haven't even asked me if I got the consultant job?'

Lauren covered her mouth with her hand. 'Oh, I completely forgot. I'm so sorry. I got distracted.' She swallowed down her self-disgust, needing to get away from the way he was looking at her, but she had to ask.

'Did you get the job?'

He shook his head in disbelief, as if it was irrelevant. 'No.'

'I'm sorry,' she whispered, even more scared of what this meant for them.

'I don't want your apology, Lauren.' His expression grew tortured and a piece of her shrivelled. She didn't want to cause him pain, but she needed to be certain because last time she'd loved him they'd messed up, and another part of her had withered and died with grief.

She couldn't lose any more of herself to that emotion.

Numbness tingled in her fingers and toes. 'I don't know what else to say.' She was seconds away from crying, from spilling all of her past pain, her doubts and fears all over the front of his shirt in great heaving sobs.

The doorbell rang. They stared at each other for a few more seconds and then Lauren fired off a text to the driver. 'That's my ride.' She tried to swallow but her throat was too dry. 'I know I've made a big mess of things today, but I do want to make it right. Can I call you later? We can talk properly. Once I know that Ben is okay.'

He nodded, his expression resigned. 'Of course. I hope Ben recovers soon.'

She pressed her lips to his cheek and fled to the taxi. She needed time to deal with her family stuff and then figure out how she felt. Because Mason deserved more than she'd been giving him and the last thing she wanted to do was hurt him again.

* * *

Slamming her front door behind him, Mason chased after Lauren, reaching her just as she opened the rear door of the taxi.

'Lauren!' he yelled, aware that he might be making the biggest mistake of his life, but driven by the urgency of letting her go once before without telling her exactly how he felt.

She turned, her wide eyes alarmed and red-rimmed.

He gripped her shoulders, hugged her close for a second and then held her at arm's length. 'I can't let you go without telling you this. I'm in love with you. There. I couldn't hold it in any longer.'

She looked up at him, overwhelmed, silent, and dread flushed his veins with ice.

'I know you're not ready to hear it,' he rushed on, 'but I didn't want us to part without you knowing how I feel. I planned a whole elaborate weekend so I could tell you properly this time, so you'd know and be in no doubt and perhaps then you'd be brave enough to tell me how you feel about me in return.'

Lauren clutched one hand to her chest as if in pain. 'Mason...' She shook her head and looked down at her feet. 'I have to go... My flight.'

He felt winded, shook his head in disbelief. 'I tell you I love you and you say nothing.'

Her eyes shone with unshed emotion. 'My head is full of worry for Ben. I need time to think.'

Deflated, his hands slid from her shoulders. 'Do you even care if there's an us, Lauren? You can't even give me that much of yourself, can you, not even this time around?'

'Of course I care. I've given you more of myself than

I've ever given anyone else,' she whispered, hating how inadequate that sounded when spoken aloud. 'I'm sorry that I've let you down this weekend, I truly am, but—'

'But you're leaving anyway, just like that?' His heart sank at how far apart they still were emotionally. He loved her and she couldn't get away from him quick enough. History was repeating itself and yet again he would be the one to end up with a broken heart.

The driver muttered something over his shoulder and Lauren tossed her bag on the back seat. 'I have to go. I'm sorry.'

'I don't want your apology. I want you to want me as much as I want you. I want more of you than you were willing to give me last time, but this—' he threw his arm out wide '—it feels like you're willing to give me even less, and I deserve more.'

Lauren nodded, tears filling her eyes. 'You do deserve more, Mason. You always have.'

Regardless of what he deserved, she left him anyway, speeding away, protecting her feelings once again. Only this time Mason was done.

# CHAPTER FOURTEEN

HOURS LATER, LAUREN EMERGED from the domestic terminal of Auckland Airport. Grady waved from the driver's seat of his car, which he'd pulled into the drop-off zone. Lauren sagged with relief and then sprinted towards the car, muttering an apology to the disgruntled-looking parking warden, who pointed at the *No Waiting* sign with an accusatory finger.

'I'm sorry. I'm here. Let's go,' she said, diving into the passenger seat and shoving her bag over her shoulder.

The minute she'd clicked her seatbelt into place, Grady pulled out. 'What's going on, Lauren?'

Lauren gripped her temples, her head hung low. 'I don't even know where to start. I'm a mess.' She couldn't cry again. She already had a headache from the tears she'd shed since the car had pulled away from Mason earlier.

Remembering her manners, she turned to her friend. 'Thanks so much for picking me up. I really appreciate it. You're a lifesaver.'

'No problem.' Grady frowned. 'You can pay me back by babysitting Molly some time.'

Lauren nodded and Grady wordlessly navigated the traffic for a few minutes. She fought the urge to consult her phone again for what felt like the millionth time, desperate to make the last ferry of the day to Waiheke Island.

'I'm confused,' he started up again when they were on the motorway heading into the city. 'First you fly to Wellington on a whim and then you turn straight around and fly back again, without even leaving the airport. Are you trying to use up all of your frequent flyer miles or something?'

She knew Grady was being kind, making light of her behaviour. But she only had one explanation for her erratic decision-making.

'Mason said he's in love with me,' she blurted. *And I love him too...*

The sickening words swirled in her head, because she'd been so confused by the intensity of her feelings for Mason, so terrified by the speed at which she'd fallen effortlessly back in love with him, that she'd overreacted to Ben's news, bungled their plans for the weekend and hurt Mason badly, the very last thing she'd wanted to do.

'So you ran away to Wellington?' Grady frowned but kept his eyes on the road.

'Yes. No. Kind of.' She covered her face with her hands, slowing down her panicked breathing. She had time to fix this. And she would, because she couldn't lose Mason a second time.

'I know... I messed up, big time,' she muttered, too scared to look at Grady's expression for confirmation that it was too late, that she'd already had too many chances. 'You have to help me make it right.' She gripped his arm and gave him a brief summary of the events of her morning, including her conversation with Mason and her whistlestop trip to Wellington Airport.

She hadn't even bothered telling Ben that she was in his city. Mason was right. He was a grown man. If he needed his big sister, he'd ask for her help. She'd really only freaked out, retreated to her comfort zone because she'd already been feeling out of control and overwhelmed by her feelings for Mason.

'I'll do what I can, but what's your plan?' Grady asked when they stopped at a set of traffic lights.

She groaned, banging her fist on the dashboard. 'I'm sick of plans. Overthinking, worrying about what might happen. That's what landed me in this mess in the first place.' She'd had three hours to come up with some fail-safe strategy to win Mason back while she'd sat in Wellington waiting for a return flight, finally concluding that plans were grossly overrated.

'So for once in your life you don't have it all figured out?' Grady's voice bordered on incredulous.

'No,' she said, panic a hot ball in her chest. 'Can you drive any faster?'

'Nope,' Grady said. 'I'm not speeding and getting a ticket just because you've finally fallen in love.'

Lauren bit her fist in frustration. She'd always loved Mason. She'd probably never stopped loving him the first time around. She'd simply buried her pain alongside her grief for her mother and tried to live without him. But that wasn't living; that was hiding.

'Please can you just save the lecture and drop me at the ferry terminal? I'm going to Waiheke.'

'I hope that's where Mason is, because you need to tell him how you feel this time.'

'I will.' Lauren's legs began jiggling. 'At least I hope that's where he is and that he's not already halfway across the Tasman.'

She'd called every hotel on the island, asking if they had a reservation for Mr Ward, until she'd tracked down his booking. He hadn't checked in yet, but his phone was switched off so this was her best shot. She couldn't just sit at home and wait; that would drive her crazy.

Now was definitely the time for action.

'I can't believe how badly I messed up,' she whispered, more hot achy tears finally spilling free.

Grady tilted a sympathetic smile her way. 'He'll understand if you explain how you feel about him. How do you feel? You do love him back, right?'

She nodded, searching his glove box for a tissue. 'I'm not sure that I ever stopped loving him, to be honest, not that he knows that. I was just so scared to feel anything that strong and intense after Mum died that instead I've spent most of my adult life pretending not to feel at all when it comes to my own life.'

'So what will you do when you find him?' Grady said. The fear in his voice shot panic through Lauren's veins.

'Beg him to give me another chance.' She gave up searching for a tissue and wiped her face on her sleeve. 'Follow him around until he can look at me with something other than disappointment. Pray that I haven't missed my opportunity.' She sniffed, her eyes stinging.

'Well, if he's disappointed, that's a good thing,' said Grady with the wisdom of an old soul. 'It means that he still cares.'

She dropped her head onto Grady's shoulder, grateful to have such a good friend.

Grady pressed his lips together in a grim line. 'Why didn't you tell me that you loved him then? If I'd known how you felt about each other I would have told you he'd called that time, broken my promise to him, encouraged you to go and find him.' He glanced sideways, regret haunting his stare.

'Please don't feel responsible in any way. If I'd realised how I felt about him at the time, I'd have hunted him down myself, don't worry. Instead I blocked him out. I'd already had years of practice, blocking out thoughts and happy memories of Mum, that by the time I pushed Mason away I'd one hundred percent convinced myself that it was for the best, that we would never have lasted, that I was saving myself from heartache down the road, when in reality all I was doing was drawing out the heartache over six long years.'

Her voice wobbled but she pushed on, finally certain of how she felt. 'To be honest, I'll probably always be an expert at hiding my deepest emotions, but reconnecting with Mason has shown me that there's more to fear from shielding my heart than there is from exposing it, being vulnerable. I don't want a hollow personal life. I want more. I want it all, with him, if he'll forgive me.'

She wanted to ride pillion on Mason's bike, feel the wind in her hair and his heat at her front. She wanted to skinny-dip with him and make out in public places and sleep in his arms on her wide-enough-for-two sofa. She wanted his love, even when she was terrified to lose it.

'Well, that's definitely worth getting a speeding fine for,' said Grady and he put his foot down.

# CHAPTER FIFTEEN

AFTER DRIVING HIS bike around Waiheke Island for most of the afternoon while he ruminated on what had transpired with Lauren, Mason pulled into the hotel he'd booked for their romantic getaway—a secluded boutique luxury lodge perched on the coast and boasting its own private beach.

The receptionist greeted him with a welcoming smile he struggled to return. He'd wanted to bring Lauren here. He'd planned to finally lay his feelings bare, to ask her to give them a second chance at a real committed relationship. He'd wanted to be upfront and honest with her, but she hadn't even given him the time of day, cutting him off, pushing him away and running, just like she'd done six years ago.

'Mason Ward. I have a reservation,' he said, wondering if Lauren had made it safely to Wellington. He should forget about her, not that that was a posibility. He hadn't managed it for the past six years so what made him think he could achieve it now?

The receptionist hesitated.

'The booking was for two people, but now it's just me.' He shrugged, sick to his stomach.

He'd told Lauren that he was in love with her, for goodness' sake, but even that hadn't made any difference. He'd even chased after her, this time determined not to give up as easily and always live with the regret. He was stronger than that.

The receptionist nodded and glanced over his shoulder. 'Yes. We're expecting you, Mr Ward, but there's…um… someone here to see you. She's been waiting a while.'

He turned around to find Lauren sitting near the fireplace. His heart lurched, part elation, part dread. Was she here to let him down again? To calmly rationalise all the reasons why they just wouldn't work out?

She stood, wordlessly twisting her hands in front of her, looking pale but still breathtakingly beautiful. Would he ever be free of loving her? He doubted it, but that didn't mean he'd continue to lay himself at her feet, only to be trampled on.

Mason absently accepted the room key from the receptionist and crossed the foyer towards Lauren, his mind racing. How had she found him? Why wasn't she in Wellington? Was Ben okay?

He paused far enough away that he wouldn't be tempted to touch a single hair on her head, his natural inclination to take her in his arms and kiss her until she loved him the way he loved her.

'How did you know where to find me?' he said, pressure building in his head.

Lauren swallowed, her eyes dark pools of uncertainty. 'I called every hotel on the island until I got a hit. I didn't know that you'd be here for sure; I was just praying that you hadn't already gone back to Australia.'

He looked down at his feet in case the seed of hope that could germinate any second was clearly displayed on his face. 'No, not yet. I came here to consider my options.' He met her stare once more, recalling the promises he'd made to himself on the beach just thirty minutes ago. To walk away, whether it was going to Australia or another consultant position in New Zealand. Only now that she was standing in front of him, now that his heart recalled what was at stake, he couldn't seem to find one tenth of the resolve.

'What are you doing here Lauren?' he asked bluntly, overwhelmed by her appearance and what it meant. He'd allowed her to hurt him once before, but he wasn't a fool.

'I wanted to apologise. I was crazy for leaving you earlier. I stupidly wasted several hours flying to Wellington and simply waiting in the airport for the next available return flight home.' She shook her head and rolled her eyes. 'I didn't even leave the airport.'

'Is Ben okay?' he asked.

'I don't know. I'm sure he's fine. I didn't tell him I was there. Look, can we talk?' She waved in the direction of the rear exit. 'There's a garden.'

He nodded, following her outside. They found a bench large enough that they wouldn't touch each other when they sat side by side in the landscaped garden beyond the hotel's restaurant. Mason wanted to reach across the divide that separated them so much that his hands shook. But he wanted to hear what she'd come all this way to say even more.

'I can't believe how badly I let you down this morning,' she whispered. 'I'm so sorry.'

Mason dragged his eyes away from the way her lips moved, forced himself to focus on the lamps that lit the walkway leading down to the hotel's private beach instead. 'I should have saved my grand declaration of love. You clearly needed space to visit your brother.' All he'd done was expose himself to more pain and rejection.

She shook her head. 'No. You've given me enough space. Six years of space. And I'm actually sorrier for myself, how I've let myself down.' She sat on the edge of the bench, impassioned. 'You told me that you loved me, Mason, something I've wanted to hear since our very first kiss that night on our beach, and I ruined that for myself and for you. Why?'

It was a rhetorical question because she gave him no time to answer.

'Because, all those years ago, I convinced myself that I wasn't ready. But I was just scared to love you, scared to have you love me in return, because I didn't want to lose you. But it happened anyway. I pushed you away before you could hurt me. I was a coward. And today I did it again.'

She stood, pacing a few feet away, her hands on her hips, anger and passion and fight rolling off her in waves. 'I don't think I fully realised how much we'd hurt each other last time until you showed up again. Nor did I fully acknowledge how in love with you I'd been then. All these years I've been pretending that I was okay, keeping busy, focusing on my work and my family in order to ignore what a mess my private life was. But I don't want to hide from it any more.'

She returned to stand before him, her eyes shining with unshed tears. 'I loved you six years ago, Mason, but what I feel now is bigger, stronger, un-survivable.' She placed her hand on her chest, her breath catching. 'I love you so much that it crushed me with terror. I felt that if we were to mess up again, to let each other down again…that I'd be broken beyond repair. So I panicked. I became all caught up in my own head. It felt easier to focus on Ben than on myself, on my own feelings for you—feelings I've been denying for weeks.'

She dragged in a breath as if collecting herself and he couldn't help the pride that stole his ability to speak. He'd always known she'd held back from fear; her mother's death had robbed her of the security to trust her feelings. But she was right. This time they had more power to hurt each other. They had to get it right.

'I'm going to book a room here. I'll give you all the time you need,' she said. 'But please give me a chance to make things right.' She backed up a pace, putting distance between them. 'Please know that the last thing I want this time is to push you away.' Another pace, so that she stepped onto the path that led back inside. 'Please don't leave us behind until you're certain of my love, even if you no longer want it.'

And then she was gone, leaving him with a decision to make and another hole punched in his chest.

Lauren was in the middle of a dream when she was jolted awake. Her neck cricked and she sat up in the armchair next to the fireplace, pain shooting to the base of her skull.

'Lauren, I've had enough time to think.' Mason loomed over her, dressed in the same clothes he'd worn when they'd walked in the garden.

'What time is it?' she asked, rubbing sleep from her gritty eyes.

'Two-fifteen. I thought you said you'd booked a room?' He straightened, his face etched with fatigue and his expression unreadable.

'There were no rooms available, so...' She'd decided to spend the night waiting in the foyer, only the heat from the huge fire in the hearth must have lured her into a fitful doze.

'We can't talk here. Come with me.' He collected Lauren's overnight bag from the floor, the one she'd packed to go to Wellington, and marched ahead along one of the guest corridors. Lauren hurried after him, her stomach a riot of fear and longing.

At the furthest door, he swiped a keycard and pushed inside the room, holding the door open for her.

'I'm sorry that I woke you, but I didn't want you to wait another six years for my decision.' He placed her bag on the floor just inside the room and Lauren had to grip the door handle at her back to stop herself from collapsing in a heap.

'I see.'

'Do you?' he asked, his burning eyes boring into hers. 'Because I don't think I've seen anything clearly since the first time I saw you at that lab where you stabbed at me as if I were a pincushion.'

In two strides he was in front of her, filling her vision, eclipsing any other consideration, being her everything.

'Mason…' she whispered, tears spilling free.

'No, Lauren. It's my turn to talk.' He cupped her face, his thumbs wiping at her tear tracks. 'I've wasted hours doing what you asked, thinking about what you said, and it's all irrelevant because I love you and I always have.'

'I love you too,' she snuffled against his chest, wetting his T-shirt.

'I know you do.' He stroked her hair, tilted up her chin, smiled indulgently. 'I've known all along. I was just too stupid, too scared to push the issue and make you admit it in case that backfired.' He placed his hand over hers on his chest, trapping it there over his thudding heart. 'But I felt it. You always showed me, even if you didn't say the words.'

He scooped a hand around the back of her neck and tucked her head against his steady but rapid heartbeat. 'When we were together last time, I was young, a bit messed-up, unsure of myself.' He pressed a kiss to the top of her head and Lauren squeezed his waist in case he changed his mind and disappeared.

'But I don't need the words. I just need you to feel my love and to trust it. Because I'll never give up on us again. I won't let you down. I won't walk away when things get tough, and they will. We're realists. We know every relationship has struggles. But you'll never have to fear my love ending, because I'll still love you from the grave. I'll love you eternally. And I'll show you every day for the rest of my life the truth of that.'

Fresh tears spilled onto her cheeks as she tried to drag in a full breath. He loved her. He believed she loved him.

Before she could draw another breath he cupped her face, brought her lips to his and kissed her and kissed her until her tears dried and her heart was so full she thought she might explode.

'Mason…' She pulled away, her eyes dry but puffy, her lips swollen from his kisses. 'I don't want to make another mistake. I want you to stay in Auckland or I'm coming with you to Australia. I want us to be together, see each other every day, fall asleep together every night.'

She lifted her face to his, looped her arms around his neck as their lips and tongues met in a passionate rush.

Mason gripped her waist and tumbled them backwards onto the bed. She sprawled on top of him, shoving at his

T-shirt so she could press kisses over his chest, his neck, his jaw.

'I'm not going to Australia,' he said, his fingers gliding through her hair. 'I'm staying wherever you are.'

She grinned, her heart soaring. 'Good. Move into my house. Your rental is too far away from work, anyway.'

He grinned. 'Okay. Don't be bossy and demanding,' he teased.

'Why not?' she sighed, collapsing on top of him and nuzzling kisses up his neck. She wanted him now, naked, hers, for ever. 'I know what I want, and I've denied myself long enough. I want you. I want us. And I always have the last word.' She pressed her lips to his once more to silence any verbal retaliation.

Things turned purposeful, the bickering unnecessary as they showed each other the love they'd both finally declared.

# EPILOGUE

LAUREN STARED SO hard into Mason's eyes that her own stung. She didn't want to miss one second of his reaction as they made their vows to love each other for ever.

As was their way, they hadn't agreed on much when it had come to organising a wedding. Despite what Mason thought she should have, Lauren had wanted a quiet ceremony with just a handful of witnesses. Mason had vetoed a tux for beach casual attire and Lauren insisted on a band rather than a DJ. But one thing they had agreed on was that they would become man and wife on their beach, the site of all of their important moments: their first kiss, their first and only break-up, and Mason's proposal.

'Lauren and Mason,' their female celebrant said, 'you are now husband and wife.'

The small crowd gathered on the beach behind them cheered and clapped as Mason cupped Lauren's cheeks and she raised her face to his.

'I love you,' he said, looking down at her with his words also displayed in his stare.

'I love you too,' Lauren managed just before he closed the distance and sealed their union with a kiss.

Lauren clung to her new husband as if she'd never let him go. She sighed into their kiss. He looked so handsome in his white linen shirt and casual trousers. Lauren had chosen a simple ivory shift dress with spaghetti straps and flowers in her hair. Their feet were bare so they could feel the sand between their toes as they made a lifelong commitment to each other.

They finally broke apart, both of them unrepentant for the lengthy duration of their first kiss as a married couple. There would be plenty of time for hugs and congratulations from friends and family, but this time, these few precious seconds of celebration, was for them.

'Allow my sister up for air,' laughed Ben, slapping Mason on the shoulder so he could embrace Lauren in a six-foot-three bear hug. As her man of honour, he too looked handsome enough to bring tears to Lauren's eyes. Her father was next with hugs and congratulations, followed by Grady, her second man of honour.

Champagne corks popped and glasses were passed around to the guests. The photographer appeared but, before they could become too caught up in the celebrations, Lauren took Mason's hand and led him along the water's edge, away from the wedding party.

'Are you okay, Mrs Ward?' he asked when they were alone, raising her hand to his lips and pressing a kiss over her shiny new gold band.

'That's Dr Ward to you, and I'm better than okay. I just wanted a few minutes alone with my husband.' She paused, pulled him close for a kiss and sighed. 'I don't think I'll ever take those two words for granted: my husband.'

'I feel the same about *my wife.*'

Lauren smiled, her chest tight with happiness. She clung to his hand and rested her head against his shoulder as they walked a little further. 'I can't wait for our honeymoon. I hope you had a hearty breakfast, because you're going to need the stamina. I might not let you out of our hotel room for a month.'

Mason chuckled. 'But what about Europe? We have all that sightseeing to do.'

They'd booked a month-long tour of Europe's main cities and tourist spots, followed by a six-month working sabbatical in London, Mason in the surgical department and Lauren in Accident and Emergency.

'Sightseeing is overrated,' said Lauren in all seriousness. 'I have everything I'll ever need right here.' She looked down at their clasped hands, their entwined fingers, and then lifted his other hand to her lips, kissing his wedding band in a repeat of his gesture.

'Are you saying you've changed your mind about our sabbatical?' he asked with a wink. 'Because there are going to be two very disgruntled departments in London if we don't show up for work next month.'

'I suppose I can muddle through, as long as you're by my side.'

'You'll always have that.' He gripped her hips and pressed her body flush with his.

'Yeah? Promise?' She wrapped her arms around his waist and held him close.

'Absolutely.'

'Promise me one more thing…' she said.

'Anything.' He pulled back, kissed the end of her nose and then her lips. 'Anything at all.'

'Later, when the reception is over and that lot have gone home—' she tilted her head towards their friends and family '—promise me that we can jump on the bike, come back here and go for a midnight swim.'

'Brilliant plan,' he said, his eyes heating. 'As long as we can go skinny-dipping.'

Lauren grinned, already wishing away the rest of her wedding day so she could be alone with Mason.

They sealed the deal with a kiss.

* * * * *

# BREAKING THE SINGLE MUM'S RULES

## JC HARROWAY

MILLS & BOON

To my sister, Lucy,
an inspirational woman and a wonderful mother.

# CHAPTER ONE

Dr Kat Collins liked nothing better than a good to-do list and the accompanying sense of achievement when she crossed off each completed item. Sadly, when it came to patients, reaching the end of that list was impossible, as her first day in the emergency department at Gulf Harbour Hospital was proving.

Thanks to a boating accident out in Auckland's Waitematā Harbour, where many of the occupants hadn't been wearing life jackets, the ER had admitted three near-drowning victims. In addition, the city's largest sports stadium was host to an international rugby final, which brought in a constant stream of buoyant and boisterous casualties, many of them highly inebriated, loud and obnoxious. And, of course, neither of those events interrupted the everyday flow of people suffering from broken bones, chest pain or respiratory illnesses.

For Kat, dealing with the extensive backlog of patients in both the resuscitation room and the minor injuries clinic helped to take her mind off her daughter, Lucy, who was currently partway through her first day at school. Heading for her next patient—a seventy-seven-year-old woman who had taken a fall at home that morning—Kat calculated that the new entrants' class of five-year-olds would be having morning tea right about then. A twinge of maternal worry tightened her chest. She loved her job, found the diversity and challenge of Accident and Emergency work varied and rewarding, but as a single parent working full-time she couldn't be in two places at once and was rarely free of parental guilt.

Would Lucy have made any friends? Did she like her lovely teacher, Mrs Alder? Would Kat need to answer the dreaded question about why Lucy's family only had a mum and no dad?

Swallowing down that pang of inadequacy that always accompanied thoughts of how she'd chosen the wrong man to father her beloved little girl, and that she not only carried all of the parental responsibility for Lucy but the financial responsibility too, Kat scanned her next patient's ambulance summary as she left the minor injuries area in search of Mrs Gibbs.

As she passed she smiled at one or two of the other staff, including her new boss and Head of Department, Lauren Harvey. Her colleagues were so friendly and welcoming, making Kat feel like a valued member of the team.

For several minutes Kat scoured the department for her patient. Every corner of the chaotic ER was overflowing with people. Less urgent patients on stretchers even lined the corridors outside the ER's main treatment rooms, which was where Kat finally located Mrs Gibbs.

Kat approached the frail woman, noting that her eyes were closed, marvelling that she'd managed to nod off on a hard stretcher amid all of the noise and activity. Someone had covered her with a blanket, so all that was visible was her pale and gaunt face.

Kat checked the time on the admissions slip before waking the elderly woman, her frustration mounting to discover the poor lady had been waiting for over four hours to be seen. Kat winced, hating the unsatisfactory parts of her job. In an ideal world there would be enough beds and staff for all of the patients. But in reality limited staff and an unknown, ever-changing and potentially infinite waiting list of patients meant that delays were inevitable.

Gently resting a hand on Mrs Gibbs' shoulder, Kat woke her from a light snooze.

'Mrs Gibbs, sorry to startle you. I'm Dr Collins, one of the ER doctors.' She smiled her most reassuring smile, the one usually reserved for Lucy when she cried over a scraped knee or asked tricky questions about her father.

'Oh, that's okay, Doctor,' said Mrs Gibbs. 'I just closed my eyes for a second.' The woman struggled to sit upright.

Kat stilled her. 'Just relax for a few minutes while I ask you some questions.' Of course Kat would need to examine the patient, but she couldn't do that in a draughty corridor with no privacy.

'Thank you, dear.' Mrs Gibbs patted Kat's hand.

Her fingers were cold. Kat tucked the blanket up to the woman's chin, concealing her dissatisfaction with the system. She understood that no hospital was perfect, that accidents happened, placing enormous strain on already stretched resources, but she hated seeing vulnerable patients languishing in corridors. The sooner she could assess Mrs Gibbs and either admit her or send her home, the better.

'Tell me what's brought you in to see us today,' said Kat, taking the woman's radial pulse and reviewing the observations the paramedics had charted during the ambulance ride.

'Well, it's like I told that other lovely doctor,' Mrs Gibbs said. 'My feet got tangled around my neighbour's cat, you see, dear. He always comes to me first thing in the morning for breakfast, and I tripped over him and fell. Such a silly thing to do.'

Kat sympathised. As a cat owner herself, she could clearly envision the scene. But something about the story snagged her attention.

'What other doctor?' asked Kat, scrolling through the notes in case Mrs Gibbs had already been assessed by one of her ER colleagues.

'That one.' Mrs Gibbs pointed at someone over Kat's shoulder, her smile turning ever so slightly adoring.

Kat turned and spied Nash Grady, the department's clinical nurse specialist, who was currently taking blood from another patient further down the corridor.

'Oh, he's not a doctor,' Kat explained, relieved to clear up the simple mistake. 'That's Nash. He's our clinical nurse specialist.'

She'd met him briefly at the start of her shift, his easy-going, friendly smile causing a flood of unprecedented curiosity she'd assumed was long ago deceased, not for re-suscitation, another casualty of her last relationship with Lucy's father, Henry. She just hoped that the smile she'd offered Nash in return had been less obvious than the one currently worn by Mrs Gibbs.

With a master's degree in nursing, Nash could assess patients and even prescribe treatment. And as most of the ER staff wore scrubs it was no surprise that patients sometimes struggled to distinguish who was who, especially when their eyesight prevented them from clearly reading name badges. And with his tall and broad-chested physique and dark hair, Nash certainly carried off the scrubs spectacularly.

'That's the one.' Mrs Gibbs nodded, her expression dreamy. 'Lovely man. Very kind. He reminds me of my son.'

Observing the man who'd inspired Mrs Gibbs' devotion, Kat's rusty, battle-scarred libido stuttered to life. In that second, with both women staring his way, Nash looked up and locked eyes with Kat. A small smile twitched his lips, his expression tinged with a warmth and charm that made Kat suspicious. Closing her mouth, she hurriedly turned away.

'Let's move you somewhere private so I can examine you,' Kat said, mildly flustered from ogling the sexy nurse, who seemed to be friendly with everyone.

With her life full to the brim with her job, her daughter and the gratitude she owed to her parents, Kat had neither the time nor the inclination for work friends, especially when they came packaged as the department's charismatic, laid-back hottie.

She'd been fool enough to fall for Henry's lure—the biggest mistake of her life. Not that she regretted the wonderful gift that was her darling Lucy, but for her daughter's sake she wished that she'd chosen a partner with a little more care, one interested in being more than a sperm donor.

Ignoring the sensation of heat on the back of her neck as she unlocked the wheels of the stretcher and pushed Mrs Gibbs past Nash, Kat reaffirmed that relationships and love were for the naive and deluded. And if her personal life lacked a certain sizzle, that was why romance novels and battery-operated toys existed.

She wheeled the cumbersome stretcher to the nearest freed-up examination cubicle, locking the wheels and drawing the privacy curtains. The medication chart showed that Nash had indeed seen Mrs Gibbs and prescribed some analgesia.

'I need to have a look at this sore leg of yours, Mrs Gibbs,' Kat said. 'Are you feeling comfortable enough for me to move you a little?'

Mrs Gibbs nodded. 'Yes, Doctor. The pain's not too bad now.'

'I'll examine your hip, and order an X-ray, just to be safe, although there might be a bit more of a wait, I'm afraid.'

Kat was about to raise the blanket from the patient's legs to begin her examination, when a hospital porter poked his head through the curtains.

'Is this Mrs Gibbs?' he said with a cheery smile that seemed to be the number one job requirement. 'I'm here to take you to the orthopaedic ward.'

Kat frowned. 'Hold on,' she said, confused. 'I haven't referred Mrs Gibbs to Orthopaedics. I haven't even examined her. She needs an X-ray and—'

The curtains swished aside once more and Nash appeared, flicking his bright reassuring smile Mrs Gibbs' way.

'Are you causing more trouble?' Nash asked the patient with a wink, clearly joking around in a way that made Mrs Gibbs giggle and Kat want to fan her face.

He moved to the patient's side opposite Kat and adjusted her pillows so she appeared more comfortable, his small considerations second nature in the way of all great nurses.

She'd bet he was universally adored by the patients.

'There seems to be some sort of mix-up,' Kat said, her stare swooping from Nash to the hospital porter, who was already raising the side of Mrs Gibbs' stretcher in preparation for wheeling her from the ER and up to Orthopaedics. A niggle of irritation sent prickles down Kat's spine. She was losing control of this consultation before it had even properly begun.

'Mix-up?' Nash asked, smiling down at Mrs Gibbs before levelling his gaze on Kat.

Her heart began to gallop now that she was trapped in the focus of the man responsible for the first pulse of attraction she'd experienced in over five years.

But her job was the only area in her life where she felt in

control. The rest—being so thoroughly betrayed by Henry, being forced to raise Lucy alone, watching the consequences of her mistake unfold and affect the people she loved most—were circumstances that had been thrust upon her and therefore only added to her sense that she was doing things badly.

Swallowing the irrelevant thrill of excitement coursing through her body, she gripped the rail of the stretcher. 'I know it's my first day—' she directed her comments to Nash '—but I'm confused. The notes indicate that I'm the only doctor to see Mrs Gibbs.'

Nash shrugged, unlocking the wheel brakes and pushing the foot of the stretcher away from the wall. 'You *are* the only doctor to see Mrs Gibbs, but she's one of the lucky ones.' He gave Mrs Gibbs another wide smile. 'She'll be spending the night as a VIP guest in Orthopaedics.'

Kat scrabbled around for the missing punchline, her patience wearing thin. 'I haven't referred her to Orthopaedics.' Offering Nash a tight smile, she folded her arms. A mistake, because now she'd lost the game of stretcher tug-of-war.

'I know,' Nash said with a casual shrug and then addressed Mrs Gibbs as if the matter was decided. 'We've laid on Graham, the best porter in the whole hospital, to take you to Ward Twenty-Five, where they'll look after you like a queen or they'll have me to answer to, okay?'

'Thanks, dear.' Mrs Gibbs beamed, both her and Nash oblivious to the tension coiled around Kat like razor wire.

She strived to be good at her job, liked to do things by the book. If there was a different protocol to follow at this hospital she wanted to be informed. His laid-back charm, his rapport with the patients was all very well, but procedures and regulations helped to avoid mistakes.

With a stifled sigh of defeat, Kat watched the porter wheel the patient towards the lifts, throwing a 'Cheers,

Grady' over his shoulder. Nash swished the curtains fully open and wiped Mrs Gibbs' name from the whiteboard on the wall, freeing the bay for the next patient.

'Hold on a second,' Kat said, following his rapid footfall down the corridor. She refused to be dismissed. 'We need to talk.'

What on earth was going on? What sort of a place had she come to work in? Were there no rules at all?

'Can't it wait?' Nash said without glancing her way. 'It's pretty crazy today and we all have lives we want to get home to at the end of our shifts.' He logged into the nearest computer and began flicking through some notes.

Kat was certain there would be steam coming out of her ears. 'I know how busy it is. I work here too, remember. Which is why I'd appreciate an explanation. I was about to examine that patient and send her to X-ray, if needed. I don't enjoy being professionally undermined.'

'She'll have her X-ray from the ward,' he said, his fingers rapidly typing. 'And she'll be much more comfortable there while she waits. I wasn't undermining you, just thinking about the patient.'

Because he still hadn't looked up from the screen, because he was acting as if it was okay to throw protocol out of the window as long as he flashed his dazzling smile, she employed her frostiest tone. 'So, who authorised her admission to Orthopaedics?'

Logging off the computer, he finally turned to face her, sparing her thirty seconds of his undivided attention.

'*I* authorised her admission, Dr Collins,' he said, his tone cool and clipped.

Momentarily distracted by his eyes, which were the colour of chestnuts flecked with gold, Kat reacted to the fact that his relaxed attitude seemed to be slipping.

'I realise that,' she said, annoyance now her overriding driver, 'but—'

He held up a hand, cutting her off. 'We have two more elderly ladies like Mrs Gibbs who have been waiting just as long, so can I suggest that, for now, we set aside our differences and do our jobs?'

Kat's jaw dropped. Insufferable man. She'd been trying to do her job when he'd muscled in and done things his own way.

Before she could argue further, he grabbed a stethoscope from the desk. 'If you still have a problem with my methods, once things have calmed down,' he said, backing away, leaving Kat in a scented cloud of his delicious aftershave, 'feel free to take it up with me later.'

Kat most definitely had a problem, but it was too late. He'd already turned his back on her.

'Welcome to Gulf Harbour, Dr Collins,' he threw over his shoulder.

All Kat could do was silently fume.

# CHAPTER TWO

AT THE FIRST lull in the organised chaos that filled the ER that day, Nash Grady—or Grady as he was widely known since his army days—looked up from the notes he was making, unsurprised to find that the new registrar had come to settle their unfinished business.

'Dr Collins,' he said, acknowledging her presence while he typed up the suturing procedure he'd just completed on a drunken footy fan who'd fallen over and smacked his head on the pavement. All he wanted to do today was get through this horrendous shift, go home and hear all about his daughter Molly's first day at school.

But first he'd have to deal with Kat Collins.

'What can I do for you?' he went on, spinning his chair to face her. Dealing with her meant reining in the flare of attraction he'd experienced the minute she'd walked into the ER that morning.

Even gunning for him, her full mouth pinched with annoyance, those big blue eyes of hers narrowed, she was gorgeous. Not that it mattered. She could be the woman of his dreams and he still wouldn't be interested. He was a veteran of a failed marriage, a practically full-time single parent. That rarely left time to notice attractive women.

'I'd like to finish our conversation,' she said, jutting out her chin in confrontation. Showing him that she had no intention of being fobbed off a second time, she crossed her arms over her chest, a move that cinched in the waist of her scrub top and made the appealing outline of her figure more noticeable.

Grady sighed, mentally reviewing their earlier inter-action. Yes, she was prickly and uptight and had already formed a pretty low opinion of him if the way she'd ques-tioned his methods earlier was any indication. But perhaps he'd been a little short in return. He'd normally make a new member of staff feel welcome: give them a tour of the department, take them to the hospital cafeteria, chat about their previous experience and their expectations for their new position. But not only had it been a crazy morning, Kat Collins was far too distracting for his usual warm and welcoming meet and greet. She was an absolute bombshell. Tall, blonde, intelligent. And, from the dressing-down he expected he was about to receive, she also took no nonsense.

'Okay, let's talk,' he said, standing. They were in the cen-tre of the busy staff hub, a workspace away from patients dedicated to computer stations and the large whiteboard they used to list each patient in the department.

Kat Collins and her agenda was the last thing he needed when his day had already begun with his ex-wife, Carol, dropping in before breakfast. Her unannounced visits usu-ally disrupted the calm he tried to maintain, but today there had also been an uncharacteristic flood of tears from Molly, who would only be appeased if Mummy joined them for the trip to school.

'Just so I'm clear on how you do things here,' Kat said, resuming their disagreement. 'You admitted Mrs Gibbs *without* a diagnosis and before she'd been seen by a doc-tor, is that right?'

'I did,' Grady said, trying his best to ignore the withering contempt in her voice. He prided himself on his integrity, always tried to do the right thing. That was how he'd ended up in a rushed marriage, one doomed to failure. He and Carol hadn't really known each other, nor had Carol been particularly interested in rectifying that situation.

But the reminder was timely. No matter how many positive attributes this new doctor had, Molly was his number one priority.

'Why?' Kat asked, fisting her hands on her hips.

'Because I diagnosed what is most likely a fractured neck of femur. Because she'd been sitting in the cold corridor waiting to be seen for hours. Because I knew she'd be more comfortable waiting for an X-ray on the ward and I don't like to see patients suffering.'

He'd spent enough time in the ER with Molly as a patient to know how intolerable those wait times could be.

Thinking about his five-year-old daughter's health, his protective urges rose to the surface, the concern that he'd had to force down while he managed the morning's unexpected influx of patients reawakening. What if her upset this morning triggered an asthma attack at school? Would Carol's insistence that she be the one to pick Molly up that afternoon create more distress for their daughter, especially when Carol would once more disappear for an unknown period of time?

The only stability in Molly's life came from the calm routines he tried to maintain during his ex's prolonged and unpredictable absences, but Carol rarely thought about anyone other than herself, oblivious to the trail of drama she left behind.

'How do you know that your diagnosis was correct, Nash?' Kat asked, drawing his thoughts back to a matter that, as far as he was concerned, was resolved.

Her accusing tone needled him like a bee sting. He wasn't reckless. The army had taught him that sometimes you had to act on instinct, even if it deviated from the rulebook.

'I'm good at my job,' he stated simply. Although he'd learned during his marriage that trying your best, doing everything right, wasn't always enough.

'As the admitting doctor,' she continued, 'I'd planned to take a complete history, examine the patient and then order the relevant tests.'

Grady nodded, searching for the patience he was well known for. Hopefully Kat wasn't one of those doctors who believed that some roles could only be performed by members of her profession. A nurse's job wasn't confined to changing bed pans and taking temperatures, especially nurses with his qualifications.

'And had you done all of those things,' he said, keeping his voice even, fighting the urge to check his watch, 'I'm sure you'd have come to the same diagnosis as I did.'

Because he still had a list of jobs the length of his arm to do before he could meet Carol and Molly back at his house, he headed for the treatment room, fully expecting Kat to follow.

'By the way—' he took a key from a collection worn around his neck on a lanyard and unlocked the treatment cupboard where all of the medications were stored '—most people around here call me Grady.'

It had been a long time since anyone had called him Nash. Even Carol had adopted Grady. He hated to admit that his first name sounded way too good on Kat's lips.

Kat huffed. 'Well, I dislike nicknames.'

'Fair enough.' He grinned to himself as he selected two vials of intravenous antibiotics from the cupboard before relocking it. 'Although it's not a nickname. It's a hangover from my army medic days that just stuck.'

Sometimes he missed the camaraderie of the army, not that he regretted leaving to be more of a family man. Being Molly's father was more fulfilling than any job in the world. He'd wanted stability for his daughter, to be there for dinner and bedtime, to read stories and provide cuddles. And given Carol's general dissatisfaction with parenthood, his decision had worked out for the best.

Focused on what he was doing, he injected sterile saline into a vial of antibiotics and shook it to dissolve the powder into a solution, all the while conscious of Kat's warm scent—whimsical floral accents and woman. Not that he'd ever met a woman less whimsical than Kat Collins. She was practically ironing board straight, the biro, pen torch and notebook neatly regimented in the top pocket of her scrubs. Her golden hair was pulled back into a tight ponytail, not one single strand out of place. Even the pale freckles dotting her nose and cheeks were uniform and symmetrical. He'd bet his life's savings that she used hospital corners to make her bed at home.

'Well, I don't know how they do things in the army,' she said, tossing her hair over one shoulder, 'but there are protocols in hospitals—protocols *I* prefer to follow.'

Smiling because his nonchalance seemed to ruffle her feathers, Grady nodded. 'You are absolutely right, there are protocols. I know because I helped to write them, despite only being a nurse.'

Was she for real, throwing the rulebook in his face? He wasn't some inexperienced student. He'd worked in the medical field longer than her, earned his master's degree. He'd been deployed overseas as an army medic, treated wounded colleagues and civilians before taking the position at Gulf Harbour when Carol had discovered she was pregnant.

Kat sighed as if she were dealing with a small, misbehaving child. 'I wasn't implying that you're not qualified. But in my experience patient referrals are made by medical staff, *after* a diagnosis is made and all relevant tests have been ordered.'

She tilted her chin triumphantly.

He reached past her to dispose of the needle in the sharps bin, caught her quick inhale of breath when the move brought them closer than before. Was she attracted to him too? Well, wouldn't that be highly inconvenient for a woman who probably made lists for fun.

'And in an ideal world,' he said, shoving the irrelevant thought aside, 'with ample time and resources, every case would be perfectly managed according to the rules and protocols, but sometimes it's better to be flexible.'

'Flexible?' She gaped as if he'd suggested handing each patient a textbook so they could treat themselves.

'That's right, it means adaptable,' Grady said, pointing out the obvious and noting how the flare of challenge lit her pretty eyes. 'Here at Gulf Harbour we occasionally use our intelligence and initiative and extensive clinical experience to dispense with strict protocol, especially at times of stress to the system and when we have elderly and frail patients waiting unacceptable lengths of time to be seen by busy doctors.'

Kat spluttered, actually spluttered with indignation.

Looking away from her full mouth, he breathed through his inclination to be unusually obstructive. Who was this doctor telling him how to do his job, how to run his department on her first day? Even if her reprimand was justified, he had a patient waiting for the antibiotics he'd just prepared and a meeting to attend before he could leave for the day. As it was, he'd be lucky if he had a chance to eat the apple he'd grabbed from home that morning, let alone to take a proper break.

As if sensing his imminent departure, Kat positioned herself in his path, literally blocking his escape. 'No disrespect, but—'

'Most disrespect begins with that disclaimer,' Grady said, interrupting. 'Just so you know.'

She ignored him. 'But aren't you, with your flexible methods and disregard for protocol, scared of missing something? Of making a mistake? You can't possibly know that your diagnosis is correct without an X-ray.'

He sighed, momentarily closing his eyes and dragging in a calming breath that was maddeningly laced with her scent. He'd chosen nursing as a career in order to help people. Sometimes that meant bending the rules in order to minimise suffering and keep the entire system working. Now this woman was more or less suggesting that he was deliberately putting patient safety at risk.

'She's probably had her X-ray by now,' he said, 'along with a nice warm, comfortable bed and some attention from the ward nurses, rather than occupying a hard ER stretcher in a draughty corridor, where no one really has time to chat to her about her grandkids.'

Hesitation flickered across Kat's face. It gave him pause. Like him, she was fighting for the best patient outcome. They just had different ways of doing things.

Then, as if deciding the argument was still worth winning regardless of logic, she narrowed her stare. 'Yes, but rules are not bendable. You should have waited for me to confirm the diagnosis.'

Grady stepped closer, still trapped by her stubborn presence in the doorway, still distracted by the way she looked at him while she tore off a few strips, still determined that her attractiveness and what was clearly the most chemistry he'd experienced in a long time could be ignored.

'Rules can be bendable if you know what you're doing.' He stared, refusing to acknowledge how her breasts rose into his line of vision with her rapid breaths. 'And, as per the remit of my role, I took clinical history. That's how I found out that Mrs Gibbs has osteoporosis, a risk factor for fractures.'

She opened her mouth to argue but he ploughed on, frustratingly more aware of her femininity than ever. 'I also examined her and guess what? Her right leg was shortened and externally rotated, indicating a likely fractured neck of femur.'

Grady could almost see steam coming out of her ears, she was so wound up. But if she thought she could swan into the ER and start waving her rulebook around or make him jump through her hoops she could think again. It didn't matter how stunning she was or how much she stirred his libido, or how fascinating and energising he found her challenge.

He'd once tried everything in his power to please Carol, but nothing he'd done had been good enough. He'd vowed to never make the same error again. He had nothing to prove to this woman.

'So, as you can see, Dr Collins, I made a diagnosis and ordered an X-ray for confirmation. I know from my extensive past experience seeing hundreds of similar cases that my diagnosis was likely correct—by the way, she's the fourth patient this week alone with the same presentation. But as it's your first day here I'll let your slightly patronising lecture on following the rules as you see them slide, just this once.'

But Kat wasn't ready to back down.

'So doing the right thing is for the rest of us, not you?' she volleyed. 'You can just do what you like, regardless of how it might affect others.'

'Well, that's not at all insulting,' he said. 'Look, I'm here to do my job to the best of my abilities.' Keeping his anger at bay, he held his ground. 'That includes doing everything in my power to keep patients like Mrs Gibbs comfortable and moving through the department.'

He agreed with Kat in principle, but sometimes there wasn't a nice clean-cut solution. He'd learned that the hard way during his rocky marriage, was still learning the lesson every time Carol threw him a curveball, just like today, irrespective of what might be best for Molly.

Aware that he'd allowed this woman to rile him up until his pulse was throbbing at his temples, he took a calming breath. 'Your concern for my methods is noted. Thank you for bringing your opinions to my attention. Now, if you'll excuse me, I have other patients to help, and I'm sure you do too. Any further comments on my performance can be directed to our departmental head, your boss, Dr Lauren Harvey.'

He smiled. 'Enjoy the rest of your first day, Dr Collins.'

Shoving down the emotions, good and bad and downright inconvenient, that she'd roused in him, Grady left the treatment room. First thing tomorrow he'd rearrange his shifts so he and Kat spent as little time as possible working together. She might be beautiful, but clearly they had nothing in common.

No, Kat Collins was a complication Grady in no way needed in his life.

## CHAPTER THREE

RELIEVED TO FIND a parking space, Kat parked her car on a residential side street a short walk from Harbour View Primary School. She couldn't be late for pick-up on Lucy's first day. Nor could she turn up still horribly distracted by her frustrating altercation with Nash Grady.

Bendable rules... Huh! Who did he think he was?

Realising that a large part of her animosity was aimed at Henry, another man who thought he could do whatever he liked without a care for the consequences, Kat tried to take a few calming breaths before she left the car.

Most of her woes circled back to Henry. Just like he was currently missing his daughter's first day at school, her ex had also missed out on every other important milestone of Lucy's life: her birth, first tooth, five consecutive birthdays and Christmases. Hurt and humiliated by his rejection, at first Kat had tried to think of his choice not to be in his daughter's life *his* loss. Except around the time Lucy was old enough to understand the difference between a mummy and a daddy, Kat had begun to resent Henry anew. His selfish rejection, his continued absence impacted not only Kat, who was raising Lucy alone, but also Kat's parents, who regularly stepped up to help out with childcare so Kat could work, despite her father's stroke. And, most importantly of all, his desertion affected Lucy and would for the rest of her life.

With her stomach wound in a familiar knot of anger and self-recrimination, Kat grabbed her bag and locked up the car, hurrying along the street. Her fears that her beautiful daughter had been somehow irretrievably disadvantaged by Kat's disastrous taste in men were a constant niggle in the back of her mind, one of the reasons she'd been so off-kilter today.

Six years ago, blinded by what she'd thought was love but what she now considered naiveté, she'd chosen the wrong man. A man who, when she'd told him she was pregnant, had casually informed her that fatherhood was *not for him*, as if creating a life was like a jar of tart marmalade he'd tried once but wouldn't buy again, and that he wanted no part in Kat's life or the life of his child.

No wonder she'd allowed Nash and his laid-back charm and winning good looks to burrow so far under her skin. Thanks to Henry, Kat had an enduring distrust of ridiculously attractive men, and Nash Grady fitted the description like a hand in a latex surgical glove.

Pushing through the school gate, Kat forced a smile onto her face and tried not to ruminate on what she considered her biggest mistake.

Bad enough that she'd fallen in love with the most unreliable man on the planet, her penance hadn't ended with Henry's rejection. Foolishly grieving his loss and ashamed that she'd been stupid enough to fall for his superficial veneer in the first place, Kat had returned to New Zealand, her overseas working holiday in the UK cut short. She'd been forced to move back in with her supportive parents. Her pregnancy had been complicated by hyperemesis gravidarum, the severe form of morning sickness, in the first trimester, and she'd developed pre-eclampsia in the third trimester. Kat was still convinced that the stress of having her home, of watching his only daughter go through such a difficult pregnancy had contributed to her father's stroke.

Checking her phone, Kat fired him a quick text, asking how he was going with the daily crossword they'd begun to do together as part of his rehabilitation after his stroke. It helped with his memory and language skills and boosted his confidence.

If only it could ease a fraction of her guilt.

Kat arrived outside Lucy's classroom just as the school bell sounded. She loitered with a group of other nervous-looking parents, all eyes focused on the classroom door in anticipation. Seconds later, accompanied by their teacher, a steady stream of cute five-year-olds appeared, their new uniforms baggy with growing room and their backpacks dwarfing their small frames.

'Mummy!' Lucy cried, trotting towards Kat with an enormous grin on her angelic face.

Kat exhaled a relieved breath at the sight of her daughter's cheery smile.

She wanted to call Henry right now and yell, *See? Despite you carelessly throwing me away like rubbish, calling me irresponsible and selfish, there's nothing wrong with me. I'm a good mother and your daughter is happy and well-adjusted.*

Not that he deserved to know anything about the amazing child they'd made together.

Lucy held what looked like a first reading book in one hand and a fellow classmate—a freckled little girl with skewwhiff pigtails and huge dark eyes—by the other hand.

Kat caught the eye of Mrs Alder, who was speaking to

one of the other parents nearby. The teacher logged Kat's presence with an efficient nod.

Kat crouched down, accepting the book Lucy thrust her way.

'That's my reading book,' her daughter said, full of importance. 'Molly got one too. Molly is my new friend. We're reading partners.'

The girls looked at each other and giggled as if they'd been friends since birth, their tightly clasped hands swinging between them.

A lump of gratitude the size of a watermelon lodged in Kat's throat. Lucy hadn't spent her first day sobbing or sitting alone in the corner or being teased for not having a father. Her brave, beautiful girl had made a lovely friend.

'Hello, Molly. It's nice to meet you.' Despite all of Kat's reservations that by giving her a father like Henry she'd ruined Lucy's life, surely this wonderful first day success meant that her daughter was going to be okay.

Kat eyed the nearby parents in search of one who might belong to Molly, hoping to foster the friendship and perhaps make a new friend herself, although she had little time for socialising. She'd spent every minute of the past five years working, helping out her parents or being a mother to the best of her abilities, which some days she feared were at best a B minus.

But not today. Today was an A plus day.

Today, she could shake off the doubts Henry's cruel rejection had embedded in her psyche.

Kat stood, tucking the reading book into the pocket of Lucy's backpack, in no hurry to leave since Molly was still unclaimed. Hating that her ex still had the potential to taint a brilliant moment of mother and daughter triumph, Kat busied her mind with imagined play dates and future sleepovers with Lucy's new-found friend. Trips to the beach and joint birthday parties. With a best friend at her side, maybe Lucy wouldn't notice that her family was different.

While the girls chatted and laughed, Kat checked the text from her father, her spirits lighter.

Everything felt better now that her worries for Lucy's first day had lessened. She could even reflect on her disagreement with Nash, acknowledge that he'd acted within his job description, even if she'd have handled things entirely differently.

Clearly, they had nothing in common. But perhaps next time they shared a shift she should apologise, clear the air.

Flushed with a new sense of achievement, Kat watched both girls perform some kind of funky dance to which only they knew the moves.

A glimpse of Henry in their daughter's facial expression caught Kat off-guard, as it often did. How could a person not want anything to do with their own flesh and blood? Rejecting her she could handle, but his rejection of their child she'd never understand or forgive.

'Mummy…' Lucy said, drawing Kat away from the return of her dark thoughts. 'Molly says there's a park near here and she's going there with her mum after school. Can we go too?'

'Um…maybe,' Kat hedged, not wanting to commit to a firm *yes* until she'd met Molly's mother. 'Can you see your mum, Molly?' Kat asked now that the group of parents and kids left in the playground had thinned to a few stragglers.

Kat couldn't wait for ever. It was a school night. Her hectic first day had left her craving a home-cooked meal that she hadn't planned, a hot bath that would probably end up tepid once Lucy's ablutions had used up most of the hot water and an early night she had no chance of achieving because she still had study to do once she'd settled Lucy into bed.

But maybe she could bend the rules just this once in celebration of Lucy's momentous first day success.

Molly's smile switched to a small frown as she glanced around the playground. It was as if she'd forgotten to seek out her own parent in all the excitement of leaving class with her new friend. Her eyes rounded with uncertainty, her lip trembling.

Kat's stomach dropped. The last thing she wanted to do was to make someone else's child cry because she'd pointed out that their mother was late for pick-up. It happened. It could just as easily have been Kat if her boss, Lauren, hadn't found her five minutes before her shift ended and insisted on taking over the assessment of Kat's patient.

Despite Lauren's high expectations for her ER, despite not having a family of her own, Kat's boss was fair and supportive. Her only flaw seemed to be her longstanding friendship with Nash but, as Lucy and Molly had proved, everyone deserved a friend.

'Don't worry,' said Kat with an overly bright smile. 'She'll be here soon.' She didn't want the girls' first day to end in tears.

Molly's eyes shone. Not even Lucy could coax a smile. Kat was about to interrupt the teacher for support when Molly squealed excitedly and ran off.

Relieved, Kat grabbed Lucy's hand to stop her daughter chasing after her new best friend. Perhaps a trip to the park wasn't such a good idea. The five-year-olds had had a long day. Emotions were bound to be fragile. Better to end on a high.

Hoping to manoeuvre Lucy to the car without too much fuss or begging, Kat pocketed her phone and turned away from the classroom. She wasn't looking where she was going, which was how she ended up colliding with a hard, delicious-smelling male chest.

'Oh, sorry,' she muttered, disentangling herself and shuffling aside.

'My fault, sorry,' the man said, one hand gripping Kat's arm as if to stop her falling to the ground and the other wrapped around Molly.

Kat's brain blinked off and on as she tried to compute what, or rather who, she was seeing.

Nash Grady was the owner of the deliciously buff chest. Nash Grady's aftershave was filling her senses and making her want to close her eyes on a dreamy sigh. Nash Grady was touching her arm, the tingles zapping along her nerve-endings reminding her that this was the most intimate touch she'd experienced in almost six long and sexually barren years.

Kat swallowed, her body ignoring every first impression she'd formed of her disagreeable colleague.

Seeing she was steady on her feet, Nash dropped his hand.

Kat rebounded from the loss of his warm touch. Her legs felt insubstantial, her head swimming from the lingering scent of him: citrus and spice and the ocean breeze. Her breasts tingled where they'd briefly made contact with his muscular chest.

He was ignoring her now, instead soothing a sobbing Molly.

A sharp spike of envy all but swept Kat's feet from under her as she watched him stroke Molly's hair back from her tear-soaked face. He whispered reassurances into the little girl's temple, all of his focus on Molly, as if nothing else existed.

Pulling herself together as best she could with her raging lust hormones let loose, Kat tried to close her mouth, tried not to stare, to make her feet move. She didn't want him to witness the effect his touch had on her.

But before she could make the appropriate brain synapses fire Nash shot her an apologetic look, as if finally remembering his manners now that Molly's tears were mostly over.

'Are you okay?' he asked.

She must have bumped her head when she'd collided with him because the flicker of heat, an awareness that hadn't been there before, lingering in his stare couldn't be real.

Kat cleared her throat. 'Um…yes… Sorry, I didn't see you.' Oh, good, she'd not only body-slammed the only man in six years to jumpstart her libido, she'd also temporarily lost the power of intelligent speech. 'What are you doing here?'

As if recognising her for the first time, as if recalling their difference of opinion and how she'd as good as accused him of mismanaging a patient, his eyes hardened. 'I'm collecting Molly from school,' he said with perfect reasoning.

From her position snuggled into his chest, Molly turned red-rimmed eyes on Kat and Lucy. Kat took a second look at those eyes: the colour of chestnuts flecked with gold.

That was when Kat's brain began to work once more. Time stopped as reality dawned.

No, no, no. It couldn't be true. Fate wouldn't be that cruel to Lucy, even if it had no such compunctions for Kat's emotional welfare.

'Where's Mummy?' Molly asked, her lip trembling anew so Kat's heart lurched with empathy for Lucy's new friend.

Nash placed Molly on the ground as if she were a priceless work of art and gently cupped her face. 'I'm sorry, darling. She had to work. But that's lucky for me because I get to take my best girl to the park, right?'

Kat watched in wonder as Molly smile turned from hesitant to beaming. She threw her little arms around his neck. 'I love you, Daddy.' Even her eyes were closed in relieved bliss.

'I love you too.'

Accepting that the universe clearly hated her, Kat looked down at her feet, away from the sight of the kind of father-daughter moment that Lucy would never know. Typical that Molly's *daddy* was the one and only laid-back, rule-bending Nash Grady. Out of all the kids in Auckland, Lucy had chosen Molly Grady—the cute-as-a-button daughter of Kat's new work nemesis—as a friend.

And worse, despite the fact that she and Nash were destined never to see eye-to-eye, her body seemed to be having some sort of revolt, as if watching a man parent was the ultimate turn-on.

'You're Molly's dad,' she said, stating the obvious, her voice as flat as a week-old helium balloon. She owed it to Lucy to at least be polite. But there was no chance of the parental friendship she'd envisioned. Not with him.

'I am,' he confirmed, standing and taking Molly by the hand. His gaze sought Mrs Alder over Kat's shoulder and he mouthed the word *sorry*.

Now his lateness made sense. No doubt Nash applied the same flexibility to time as to protocol and rules.

'And who is this?' he asked, smiling down at Lucy. To his credit, his expression showed no sign of ill-will following their earlier disagreement.

'It seems our daughters are reading buddies,' Kat said, introducing her daughter, secretly fascinated by the attention he lavished on Molly. He might be casual about his timekeeping, but he and Molly obviously had a very close relationship. Lucy's closest male role model was Kat's father, where Molly had the real thing—an apparently doting father. Even if that father was the man who had ruined Kat's first day at Gulf Harbour, she couldn't deny that his attentiveness towards Molly made him twice as hot in Kat's book.

Good thing there was a wife in the picture.

'Hi, Lucy.' He smiled broadly at her daughter in a way that spoke directly to Kat's ovaries. She glanced at his left hand for a wedding ring, hoping its presence would kill what now appeared to be the first serious man crush she'd had since Henry.

There wasn't one. But it didn't matter. Her hormones would soon get the message that her life was full to the brim as it was, without a man, without sex. A couple more clashes of opinion with Nash would likely do the trick in killing the unwanted urges.

'Thanks for waiting with Molly,' Nash said, his eyes meeting Kat's once more. 'You didn't need to.'

For the first time since they'd literally bumped into each other, Kat identified annoyance in his expression. They might have shared a second of physical awareness, they might have daughters the same age and in the same class, but they were still very much adversaries.

'No problem,' Kat said, meeting his gaze with defiance and giving free rein to the immaturity she might have been able to fight if she hadn't had such a strong physical reaction to the hateful man. 'We were happy to be *flexible* as you were clearly held up.'

She threw his words from that morning back at him, her smile falsely sweet.

So she played by the book—there were times when her

planning and checklists and reliability came in very handy, like it had today.

Reading her dig loud and clear, Nash narrowed his eyes. 'I wasn't held up.' He'd lowered his voice in a way that told Kat he didn't want Molly to overhear, but she was once more giggling with Lucy, oblivious to the tension between the adults.

'I called the school, informed them there'd been a last-minute change of Molly's mother's plans. I don't owe you any explanation, but if I'd been scheduled to pick her up I'd have been here on time.'

As if reminded of her mother's absence once more, Molly glanced at the adults, her laughter fading. Kat backed down. Before Nash had arrived she'd been careful not to judge Molly's mother for being five minutes late. She didn't want the return of Molly's tears. Nor did she want the girls to witness a continuation of her previous standoff with Nash, not when their daughters were so obviously enamoured of one another.

'Well, you're here now and I'm actually glad. The girls had me trapped in the middle of a tricky negotiation involving the park where I was outnumbered.' She offered him a hesitant smile, hoping for the girls' sake they could put their spat behind them.

'Daddy, can Lucy come to the park with us?' Molly asked, her eyes pleading.

Nash looked as cornered as Kat felt.

'I think it's time we headed home, actually,' she said. The last thing she wanted was to spend any more time with him than was absolutely necessary given her body's absurd physical attraction to him.

'It looks like Lucy's mum is too busy for the park,' Nash

said, smiling down at his daughter before flicking a triumphant look Kat's way.

Seeing the challenge for what it was, Kat held his stare. No way would she play the bad cop to his good cop. He'd already made her appear uptight and rigid once today because they had different ways of doing things. But Kat could be fun and spontaneous. If he thought throwing down the gauntlet would scare her off, he was wrong. She could tolerate his insufferable company for ten more minutes for the sake of their daughters.

'Actually, we'd love to see the park, wouldn't we, Luce?' Kat said, her chin raised in defiance.

It wasn't until she was forced to walk beside him in awkward silence while the girls ran ahead that she fully appreciated the enormity of her error.

Their ridiculous game of one-upmanship meant there was no escaping him or the way he made her feel both antagonistic and helplessly aroused.

# CHAPTER FOUR

GRADY WALKED AT Kat's side behind their girls, willing away the last of his annoyance with Carol for being so utterly unreliable. The minute he'd arrived at school to see the distress and uncertainty on his daughter's face, he'd had only one goal: getting to her as soon as possible, engulfing her in a soothing hug and hoping that it would be enough to take away her pain and confusion.

Why had he given Carol the opportunity to let Molly down once more, today of all days? He should have known from past experience that her selfishness wouldn't make her think twice about picking up an extra shift at work at the last minute and leaving him scrambling to make it to the school on time. She pulled stunts like this all the time.

He should never have capitulated to Carol in the first place. If he'd stuck to the arrangements that had been in place for months he'd have been at school before the bell rang.

Aware of the light floral scent of Kat at his side, close enough that the hairs on his arms stood to attention, Grady silently cursed his luck that Kat had been there to witness the upset Carol had caused. She already had a pretty low opinion of him. But worse, because of his own pig-headedness and the way he'd allowed her to rattle him, he now had to spend even more time in her company.

Seeing Molly laugh with her friend after the inevitable tears of earlier was all the reward he needed for his self-inflicted torture. He'd give Molly the moon if he could. Being stuck with the most infuriating woman he'd ever been attracted to was a small price to pay for his daughter's smile.

'You know—' Kat spoke over the excited chatter coming from their daughters '—if you or Molly's mum are ever stuck at work or running late, Lucy and I would be happy to wait with Molly until you get here. They obviously get on like two peas in a pod.'

He glanced her way, caught the indulgent smile on her face as she watched their daughters giggle together, Lucy's blonde head next to Molly's brown. Was she having another dig at him because he'd been five minutes late to collect Molly?

He shouldn't care what she thought of him. When it came to parenting his daughter, Grady was his own severest critic. The only person he cared about being answerable to was Molly. That was why he kept on giving Carol the benefit of the doubt, always hoping that she'd step up and be the mother that Molly deserved. He never wanted his daughter to one day blame him that she and Carol had no relationship.

Sometimes, just like during his marriage, he couldn't win no matter what he did.

'Is that your idea of an apology?' he asked, trying to forget the way she'd felt pressed up against his chest for the split second they'd collided. He could still feel the soft mounds of her breasts, still see the way her pupils had dilated when their eyes had met, still hear the sexy little sound of her shocked gasp.

No wonder he was being paranoid. His brain was poisoned by testosterone.

'No,' she said. 'I just thought, as you're probably as relaxed about time-keeping as you are for the rules, that I'd offer.'

Acknowledging that some of his testiness was aimed at Carol not Kat, he scrubbed a hand over his face, biting back a retort.

'As I said,' he replied, because a part of him, the part he'd assumed was as good as done with women, couldn't have Kat thinking that he was blasé when it came to parenting, 'I wasn't late or held up. Molly's mother was supposed to pick her up, but couldn't at the last minute.'

Despite them having a shared custody arrangement, Carol's job as a flight attendant, and the way she seemed to find parenting mundane, meant that Molly lived practically full-time with Grady. For himself, he couldn't be happier with the arrangement, but even while keen to foster Molly's relationship with Carol, he wished it could be different for Molly's sake. But he should have known that Carol being a part Molly's first day at school would end in tears. Twice.

'Of course,' Kat said, surprising him with her understanding, although it was probably aimed at Carol, not him. 'Things come up.'

Uninterested in Kat's opinion of his fathering skills, he walked in silence for a few minutes. He might tolerate her criticisms at work, but since the moment he'd heard about Carol's pregnancy he'd moved mountains to be the best father he could be.

He didn't want the mistakes he and Carol had made to affect their little girl, even though at times, like today, he was doomed to fail one way or another.

'Is your…um…wife in medicine too?' Kat asked when they reached the playground.

'Ex-wife,' he said with emphasis. He and Carol had been

long over even before the divorce. 'No, she isn't. She's a flight attendant.'

'Oh… I see.' Kat fell quiet.

'Let me guess,' he said. 'You don't approve of divorce.' The part of him struggling with the chemistry he felt every time they were together, whether she was confronting him or not, couldn't resist the opportunity to point out their differences.

'Why would you say that?' she asked, shocked.

He shrugged, keeping his eyes on the girls as they ran ahead towards the swings. 'Because you're a stickler for the rules type of person.'

Not for the first time, he wondered what her story was. She didn't wear a wedding ring, but a husband, fiancé or even a boyfriend would be really convenient in helping him to forget his attraction and see her as nothing more than a work colleague.

When he turned to face her, she was gaping. It made him aware of her soft-looking lips and the pink of her tongue.

Kat fisted her hands on her hips. 'For your information, I've never been married. It's just me and Lucy.'

Grady's pulse kicked up. 'So, Lucy's father isn't part of the picture?'

His body's enthusiastic response to the news that she was single made no difference. Just because he found her attractive didn't mean he intended to act on it. Beyond their marital status and their daughters, and their jobs, they had zero in common.

'No.' Kat shook her head and looked away, but not before he'd seen the flash of vulnerability in her eyes. 'He lives in the UK.' She immediately frowned as if regretting her candour.

Gobsmacked, Grady allowed his curiosity for the woman

he'd vowed to avoid to bloom. Was this ex the reason she was so prickly, so defensive? Had he hurt her? He wanted to ask who'd left who. Kat certainly didn't seem the type to deliberately flout convention.

Then he checked himself. He wasn't interested in the answers. He was only tolerating her company because she made him uncharacteristically confrontational.

Except that flash of pain in her eyes, the way her chin had tilted when she'd said *'It's just me and Lucy...'* It called to the nurse in him.

'Being a single parent is hard,' he said, empathetic towards her in a way he'd have sworn was impossible half an hour ago. 'Especially when you work full-time in a stressful field, the way we do.'

She eyed him grudgingly, her wary expression back. Then she conceded with a small nod.

For a few minutes they watched in silence as the girls took turns on a blue plastic slide. Despite her story, despite them being complete opposites personality-wise, Kat was clearly a good mother. Lucy seemed delightful. Her job was demanding, and he knew from Lauren that she was also studying for her professional emergency medicine exams.

If only Carol was as constant in Molly's life.

Before he could once more ruminate how his marital failure continued to have consequences for his little girl, Kat spoke.

'Look, about this morning—I feel like I owe you an apology.'

Grady couldn't believe his ears. He forced himself to meet her stare, to ignore the uncertainty he saw there. It would be easier to dismiss his attraction if she stayed neatly inside the box he'd assigned her to after their difference of opinion: not a team player. But they still had to find a way to work together.

Seeing his doubtful expression, she ploughed on. 'I was intent on making a good impression on my first day. I hate mistakes, but I'm not too uptight to admit that I probably overcompensated.'

Probably?

'Okay,' he said, stalling for time. The last thing he wanted was to complicate his life with another tricky relationship, even if it was only at work. Carol provided all the turmoil and disruption he would ever need.

But Kat wasn't done with her speech.

'It's obvious that Lucy and Molly get along.' She smiled over to where their daughters were contemplating the monkey bars.

A twinge of regret lodged under his ribs. His frustration with his ex meant that he too had played his part in the battleground of Kat's first day at Gulf Harbour. That wasn't him.

'I'm happy to put our difference of opinion behind us for the sake of their friendship,' she said, then nibbled at her lush lower lip in a totally distracting way. 'What do you say?' She held out her hand for him to shake, her smile stretching into the open version he'd found so attractive when they were first introduced that morning.

Then, like now, it left Grady disconcerted. He didn't want to find her appealing. He enjoyed his job, the only area of his life Carol couldn't upset, unlike Kat. The potential for misunderstandings and differences of opinion should steer him back to his original plan to manipulate the staff rota so they saw as little of each other as possible.

But there was something about Kat Collins, beyond the chemistry, that made him want to grasp the proffered olive branch. Who knew, perhaps they'd end up friends. Lauren, Grady's oldest friend at the hospital, had certainly sung Kat's praises today.

'Sure.' He took her hand in a brief shake that wasn't brief enough, because it sparked his keen awareness of her once more: the softness of her skin, the quirky, lopsided slant to her smile, the allure of her intelligence and strength of character.

'Great. That's sorted,' she said, laughter in her eyes as she headed over to the swings, pushing Lucy and then Molly higher and higher until they squealed.

As he watched her uninhibited delight transform her face from beautiful to breathtaking, he realised that he'd have his work cut out for him managing his attraction to Gulf Harbour's newest doctor. Just because their daughters were going to be friends didn't mean Grady needed to personally ensnare himself with another woman who was on a different wavelength and found him lacking.

All he had to do was wait for his body to get the message. Easy.

# CHAPTER FIVE

TWO DAYS LATER, in response to an urgent call, Kat pushed through the doors of the resuscitation room. One of the ER house officers was alone with an elderly patient who was clearly having a grand mal seizure, his arms and legs jerking violently.

No sooner had Kat joined the overwhelmed-looking young doctor at the head of the unresponsive patient than Nash arrived.

Quickly assessing the situation, Kat and Nash manoeuvred the patient onto his side to protect his airway. Kat reached for a nearby nasopharyngeal tube and oxygen mask. Nash connected the patient to the monitors that recorded his vital signs, each of them anticipating the other's moves as they worked quickly with practised moves to stabilise the patient.

'What is the history?' Kat asked the house officer. The woman recited the brief clinical presentation that she'd managed to glean, while Nash drew some blood for the lab. The man, who had no known history of epilepsy, had presented in the ER with confusion and other non-specific symptoms of headache and fatigue. The house officer had been about to examine him when he collapsed and the seizure began.

'Can you please get me four milligrams of Lorazepam?'

she asked Nash, who nodded and retrieved the drugs from the locked cupboard on the wall.

Returning to the bedside, Nash grunted with frustration. 'The cannula has tissued,' he said to Kat, reaching for a new one.

'We can use intramuscular midazolam instead,' Kat said, although they both knew that IV was better.

Nash shook his head and applied a tourniquet around the patient's other arm. 'If I can't gain venous access on the first try, we'll switch to midazolam.'

Kat bit her tongue, torn because IV would enter the bloodstream quicker, but in the time it might take Nash to insert another cannula they could have already administered the intramuscular injection.

He quickly set about inserting a new cannula into the other arm, expertly achieving it on the first go; no mean feat considering the continuing seizure.

But Kat had no time to be impressed.

With the IV treatment administered, Nash took over airway maintenance while Kat examined the patient for signs of head trauma and then scanned the notes for any clue that might explain the patient's seizure.

'That's four minutes with no change,' Nash said, his gaze meeting Kat's loaded with meaning.

Kat nodded. 'Thanks for keeping count.' The longer the patient remained unconscious the greater the chance of serious complications like brain damage.

Staving off the instinctive panic the adrenaline coursing through her blood was causing, Kat took a few seconds to mentally work through the emergency protocol for status epilepticus, a prolonged, life-threatening seizure. She felt Nash looking to her for a decision, aware that he most likely would have his own way of handling the emergency, but a niggle in the back of her mind made her stick to her protocol.

'Have you checked a blood glucose?' she asked the junior doctor as she administered the second dose of intravenous drugs in an attempt to stop the seizure.

'Um…not yet, no.'

'That's five minutes, Kat. Do you want to intubate?' Nash reached for an endotracheal tube and glanced her way expectantly.

Newly aware of their fragile truce and their disagreement on her first day, Kat hesitated. He'd called her a stickler for the rules. She didn't see that as a flaw. She'd once lost control of her life, a situation that had caused a lot of pain to a lot of people, not just her. Rules and routines gave her control back, along with a modicum of peace. She should trust her instincts.

Injecting her voice with certainty, she answered Nash. 'No. Keep bagging him; his sats are good.'

Kat ignored Nash's small frown, which told her he'd have done things differently, and spoke to the other doctor. 'Do the glucose now, please. We need to know if there's something treatable causing this fit.'

'Don't you want to consider a second line treatment?' Nash said, casting Kat a look that told her he disagreed with her management of the case. Yes, they needed to treat the seizure, but if there was an underlying and easily treatable cause it needed to be excluded.

'Protocol is to concurrently exclude a reversible cause,' she said, sticking to the flowchart she knew by heart, even though his confidence and gut instinct to try for venous access had been the right one.

But, just like she hadn't questioned him pushing for the second IV, he didn't question her insisting on the blood test.

Within seconds of performing the finger prick test for blood glucose, the sheepish-looking house officer returned. 'Blood sugar is less than two. I'm sorry.'

'You were right—hypoglycaemia,' Nash said as he attached an intravenous glucose infusion to the cannula he'd inserted and gave Kat a nod of respect.

Tense seconds followed while they watched and waited.

Kat was about to ask for the second line anticonvulsive drugs when the seizure stopped.

All three of them breathed a collective sigh of relief.

'Always check blood glucose,' Kat instructed the house officer. 'And check all of his blood work—electrolytes, toxicology, blood gases. Also, see if you can get a better history from a relative or his GP. Is he on any medications that might be causing hypoglycaemia, or does he have a history of alcohol abuse?'

The doctor nodded, spurred into action now that the emergency had eased.

Kat spoke to the medical registrar, who had just arrived, handing over the patient's care.

She drew aside the curtains, preparing to leave, to return to the patient she'd been seeing prior to the emergency call. Some inexplicable drive made her look back at Nash.

Their eyes met, silent communication passing between them. They were different in every way. They would likely always have different methods, approach the same situation from different angles, but at the end of the day they'd just proved that when required they could work as a team.

'Thanks,' she said.

'Good call,' he replied.

Kat left, buoyed up not only by a sense of job satisfaction that she'd managed to help the patient, but worryingly also by Nash's unexpected praise.

\* \* \*

Later that week, Kat emerged from the ED's minor injuries clinic to find Nash talking with Lauren. Loitering near one of the workstations, Kat surreptitiously watched them chatting, her attention drawn to Nash as if he were a specimen under a microscope. The friends laughed about something, and a prickle of absurd jealousy made Kat's temperature rise.

Nash's broad, relaxed smile mesmerised her; she couldn't look away. Just like she'd been fascinated when he'd unselfconsciously goofed around in the playground with both girls on their first day. Or when his smile crinkled the corners of his eyes when he laughed with a patient. And most distracting of all was how well he wore hospital scrubs, as if the baggy functional garments that made everyone else look sickly were specifically created with his physique and colouring in mind.

The easygoing version of Nash laughing with Lauren seemed to be the one that everyone else saw. Since her first day, Kat had quickly discovered that the man capable of pressing her buttons more effectively than anyone else had a reputation throughout the hospital as a straight up nice guy. He was universally adored by the patients. Nothing about the day-to-day running of the department was too much trouble for him, but neither was he a pushover. He just got things done, quietly and efficiently, always patient-focused.

Flushed from how much more attractive his reliability made him, and frustrated by the persistence of her silly hormonal urges, Kat dragged her gaze away from the pair.

Despite their truce and the way they'd compromised on the management of the seizure patient, there was still a brick wall of wariness between him and Kat. She sighed, wishing the tension would just evaporate because Lucy and Molly's friendship was going from strength to strength.

Keeping her head down, she tried to slink past Nash and Lauren unnoticed.

Just as Kat was almost home free and around the corner out of sight, Lauren called her name. 'Kat!'

Kat froze, plastered a breezy smile on her face and joined her boss and Nash.

'How are you settling in?' Lauren asked, her sharply intelligent eyes searching Kat's stare as if the woman were a human lie detector. Would Lauren sense the awkwardness between her and Nash? Had he spoken to the departmental head about their clashes?

'Um…good, I think.' Kat shot Nash a sideways glance, her heart thudding excitedly behind her sternum.

Why couldn't she just dismiss his charm, exaggerate his negatives, switch off her body's animal responses? It would make life so much easier if she wasn't attracted to him.

Because Nash and Lauren were both still looking at her expectantly, as if she'd walked into the middle of a conversation where she was the main topic, Kat added, 'Everyone has been extremely welcoming and helpful, and I seem to have a handle on how things work here now.'

Now that she'd settled in, Gulf Harbour ER seemed like a great department in which to work.

'Well,' Lauren said, shooting Nash a pointed stare, 'as Grady here seems to have temporarily forgotten his manners, *I'll* do the honours. Come and join us at The Har-Bar tomorrow night.'

Kat opened her mouth to mumble some excuse, but was cut off.

'It's Grady's birthday,' the other woman added. 'I've just this minute persuaded him that it's something worth celebrating, so you're officially invited. You're not rostered on this weekend, are you?'

Kat tried not to squirm in discomfort, her cheeks warming as her back hit the proverbial wall. She couldn't refuse her boss. Nor could she decline without it appearing like she was still harbouring a grudge against Nash.

'Um…no…no, I'm not.' Kat looked anywhere other than at Nash. She didn't want to witness his irritation or resignation now that he'd had his hand forced to invite her along.

This was awkward enough. It was obvious that Nash hadn't planned on inviting Kat himself. And why would he? They had nothing in common and she'd been avoiding him as much as she could since her first day, hoping to minimise further differences of opinion and still embarrassed by her physical crush.

Perhaps six years and counting of celibacy wasn't such a bright idea after all.

'Great, that's settled,' Lauren said with a self-satisfied smile. 'See you tomorrow.' Leaving Kat alone with Nash, Lauren strode away.

Now she'd have the added embarrassment of extricating herself from the invitation without letting him think she was offended that he hadn't wanted her along. The last thing she needed to be was the unwelcome guest at his birthday bash. Clearly, despite what they'd agreed in the park, they weren't going to be friends.

'Look—'

'Are you free now?' Nash interrupted and then apologised. 'I could do with a second opinion on a patient.'

Kat breathed a sigh of relief, grateful for the distraction of work.

'Of course, lead the way.' She followed him over to the

workstation, where he logged in to the computer and brought up a patient's record.

'What's the case?' Kat asked, stepping close enough to see the screen while trying to ignore the heat of his body and the subtle scent of his aftershave that she remembered all too well from their playground collision.

'There's an eight-year-old in bay six,' he said, glancing her way so their eyes met.

Kat swallowed, praying her attraction wasn't transparent.

'He presented with general malaise, fever and coryzal symptoms, but I think he might have Koplik spots inside his mouth. I've only seen them in textbooks, so I wanted another pair of eyes.'

Why had he asked her and not Lauren for a second opinion?

'Any rash?' Kat asked, because Koplik spots were associated with measles, but could often appear first.

'No, not yet, but of relevance is that the child hasn't been vaccinated.' He turned to face her, crossed his arms over his chest, looked down, waiting.

A fresh wave of lust body-slammed her. She could still feel that strong arm preventing her from taking a tumble outside the classroom. For a second, before he'd focused all of his attention on his daughter, Kat had imagined her attraction was reciprocated. But she must have invented his interest.

'Okay,' Kat said, reaching for a face mask. 'Let's take a look.'

They entered the bay together. Kat introduced herself to the boy and his mother and performed a quick examination to exclude other common childhood infections that might be responsible for his symptoms. When she shone a torch into the boy's mouth, she instantly saw what had Nash concerned—small white spots lining the cheeks.

'I think you're right, Nash,' she said when they were once more out of earshot. 'Good spotting, excuse the pun.'

She laughed nervously. How could he make her feel giddy? Perhaps avoiding him wasn't the best plan. Perhaps she needed to flood her system with contact until she became immune.

'I've only seen Koplik spots a few times.' She removed her mask and tossed it into the bin, then washed her hands in the sink beside the one he was using. 'We can run measles serology and if it's positive we have to notify Public Health. Are you happy to tell the parents the diagnosis?'

Nash nodded, switching off the water at the other sink and drying his own hands with a paper towel. 'Thanks, Kat.'

For a second she froze, her stare locked to his, trapped. She should say something—anything—to break the tension. By doing her best to avoid him she'd only fuelled the flames of her attraction.

'Listen, don't feel like you have to come to The Har-Bar tomorrow,' he said, as if sensing her discomfort, 'just because Lauren invited you.'

Kat busied herself with the paper towel dispenser on the wall while she willed her expression to stay neutral and not give away any hint of her inner deflation.

'Of course not,' she said, flashing him an overly bright smile that hopefully concealed the sting of rejection.

He was giving her a gentle escape route because he didn't want her there. It was the reminder she needed that her infatuation was one-sided.

'Kat...' Rather than move away and resume his duties, Nash stepped closer. The scent of clean laundry and spicy aftershave made her head a little woozy as her pulse throbbed in her throat.

She looked up, the pressure of meeting his searching stare making her eyes water.

A flashback of the way he'd doted on Molly and included Lucy in a game of tag sent another sharp pang of longing through her ribs. What would it feel like to be held in those strong arms? To be the focus of his desire? To feel those distracting lips brush hers?

Her throat was so dry she dared not speak.

'Just to be clear,' Nash said, dragging Kat's mind away from her wildly inappropriate and probably one-sided thoughts. 'If Lauren had given me the chance, I'd planned on issuing a department-wide invitation for tomorrow night, which, of course, includes you.'

His gaze dipped from her eyes to her mouth.

For an exhilarating second Kat thought he might kiss her. Insane. They were at work and he'd shown no sign that he harboured the same attraction.

'But it's late notice.' His lips moved, killing Kat's wild flight of fancy. 'You'd need to find a babysitter. So don't stress if you can't make it.'

Babysitter...?

She shook her head, so distracted by the chemistry she just couldn't shake off that she'd almost forgotten about Lucy.

Lucy. Her child. Her responsibility.

No matter how much her body wanted to explore a flirtation with the first man she'd fancied in so long, Lucy would always come first.

'Yes, of course you're right.' Kat's voice was an embarrassing croak.

As if he'd overstepped some imaginary line, Nash moved back and her stomach dropped with disappointment.

'I would need to find a sitter,' she said, now horribly conflicted.

Whether Nash was interested in her was irrelevant. The often lonely and seriously neglected woman in her deserved a night out, a harmless drink with work colleagues. Her parents would probably be overjoyed to have Lucy for the night if it meant Kat being social; she just tried not to ask them for childcare favours too often as they'd already done so much for Kat after she'd returned from the UK.

Backing away, she cleared her throat. 'Well, thanks for the invite—I'll try and be there if I can.'

Hating his relaxed shrug, she turned away.

Henry's cold and cruel dismissal had robbed Kat of a vital chunk of self-esteem. Now, that damaged part of her wanted Nash to be disappointed if she couldn't make it.

She sighed. She was tying herself up like a bow with all her doubts and justifications, over-thinking a simple invitation. But, no matter how harmless the social event seemed, the past five minutes in his company had shown her one thing. When it came to Nash Grady, Kat's thoughts were still far from innocent. And that was proving to be a big problem.

# CHAPTER SIX

GRADY TURNED FROM the bar, where he'd just bought Lauren a glass of wine, and almost spilled it down the front of his shirt. Kat had made it at last, just when he'd given up hope that she'd appear.

After all, she'd looked horrified by Lauren's invitation yesterday. When he'd tried to repair some of the damage by insisting that he'd always intended on including her in the invitation, she couldn't seem to run away quick enough, just like she'd been avoiding him all week, her head ducking when she assumed he hadn't spotted her around the department.

So much for friends…

Heading back to Lauren, who was having some relationship drama of her own tonight with her ex, Gulf Harbour's newest locum surgeon, Mason Ward, Grady stole another glance Kat's way.

She looked spectacular in her civvie clothes—skinny black jeans, heels and a silky top that exposed one tanned and freckled shoulder—her hair loose in a wavy cascade and her eyes bright and animated as she laughed with a group of the ER staff.

He couldn't seem to stop staring.

While he chatted with Lauren, who was constantly watching the door for Mason, Grady tried to ignore the rumble of arousal Kat's arrival caused. He wanted to speak to her, to thank her for coming along to celebrate his birthday when he knew that meant she'd organised childcare. He knew how hard it was to juggle everything.

Every time he moved in her direction he kept being drawn into other conversations—people wishing him Happy Birthday, enquiring after Molly or making a joke about his advanced age.

When he finally made it to Kat's group and thanked everyone for coming, she was too far away, opposite him in the small huddle of people, her stare only meeting his for a fraction of a second.

He went through the motions of contributing to the conversation while restless energy coiled inside him. All he really wanted to do was speak to Kat one-on-one. Every time he looked at her, she blinked, smiled, looked away. It was driving him nuts. One minute he was certain that she was as into him as he was to her and the next convinced it was all in his head.

He felt sixteen again, in the throes of a desperate crush but clueless as to the recipient's feelings.

Clearly, no matter what he tried, it wasn't going to be easy to get his attraction to Kat out of his system. And it was no wonder. Not only was she sexy and smart and a great mother but, despite their differences, despite their first day disagreement, they also somehow just clicked professionally. His respect for her had gone through the roof as they'd collaborated on the seizure patient. The dauntless look in her eyes and the determined tilt of her chin had told him that she'd disagreed with his suggestions on more than one occasion. But they'd made it through together, worked out their differences when it counted to treat the patient.

Kat excused herself from the group and headed for the

bathrooms. Grady chatted to a few more people while he waited for her to return. Noticing that Lauren and Mason had disappeared, Grady texted his friend, concerned.

Somewhere between bidding farewell to a handful of guests and watching the door for Lauren's return, he realised that Kat seemed to have disappeared.

The taste of disappointment soured what should have been an enjoyable evening so that ten minutes later, with most of the guests departed, Grady too left The Har-Bar, frustrated that Kat had left without saying goodbye.

He kicked a stray pebble along the pavement and headed for the car park behind the bar. It was a lost cause. Clearly she wanted nothing to do with him outside of work and that suited him just fine. His life was complicated enough. He'd barely made it to his own birthday drinks, because Carol had tried to talk to him about them getting back together when he'd dropped Molly off at her place. It was a stunt she tried every six months or so, even though he always gave her the same answer: a resounding no.

At his car and before he could open the door, his thoughts were interrupted by the unmistakable sound of an engine turning over, an exercise in futility. Someone was having trouble starting their car.

Weary but unable to ignore a person in need, he approached the vehicle and tapped on the passenger window, his heart lurching when Kat looked up.

Her shock turned to relief as she recognised him in the dark.

'Are you okay?' Grady smiled, glad now that he hadn't minded his own business and thanking his lucky stars. Not that he wished a breakdown on her. But this was the chance he'd craved all evening—him and Kat alone. No children, no patients, no colleagues.

She opened the car door. 'Hi—it won't start for some reason.' She gave the ignition another go, as if to prove the point.

They both winced at the dull clicking sound.

'I don't understand why,' she said. 'The battery is only six months old, and I definitely didn't leave the lights on.'

She exited the car with a deep sigh of frustration, looking to him for a suggestion.

'I could offer to look under the bonnet, but with modern cars it's most likely something electrical that I won't have a clue how to fix.'

'No, don't worry. Thanks anyway.' She reached inside for her bag and took out her phone, closing the car door with more force than needed.

Perhaps she didn't want his help.

'Do you have roadside assistance?' he said anyway.

Kat was an intelligent, independent woman who could organise her own rescue, but he didn't like the idea of her waiting alone in that car park, not with the bars emptying soon. He indicated his own car, parked several spaces away. 'You can wait in my car if you want.'

'I do, but I don't fancy waiting around for them now. I'll call them in the morning, ask my mum to give me a lift back here.'

Grady nodded. 'Do you want a lift home? I've been on soft drinks all night.' Even though he was the birthday boy and Molly was spending a rare night at Carol's house, he'd begun the habit after Molly's diagnosis of asthma, because he just never knew when he might need to drive her to the hospital in an emergency. 'You probably need to get back to relieve your sitter,' he added, conscious of holding her up.

And driving her home would give them a chance to talk.

'Um…' She blinked up at him, looking a little flustered

while she debated her response. 'I don't have to worry about that—Lucy is staying the night with my parents.' She glanced at her phone, chewing on her lip. 'I'd call them now, but they've probably already gone to bed. Lucy tends to wear them out when she stays over.'

'Thanks though,' she said, her voice ever so slightly breathless. 'I appreciate the offer.' She smiled that crooked smile of hers and the current of awareness, the connection he might have imagined pulsed anew.

Grady hesitated. He couldn't leave until he knew she was safe, but he wouldn't force his offer of a lift onto her either.

'Okay...' He stepped back a pace. 'Well... I just wanted to thank you for coming tonight. I know it's not easy when you have to organise childcare. I really appreciate it.'

Saying what he'd hoped to say gave him no sense of satisfaction. Probably because close up she looked even prettier than she had from afar.

'You're welcome,' she said, staring up at him with uncertainty. Then she started, as if remembering something, touched his arm. 'Oh, wait.'

Grady's nervous system ignited like a lit box of fireworks after that single touch of her hand. Her perfume tickled his nose, reminding him of the sunset from his deck on a sultry summer night, the scent of jasmine carried on the warm air.

Looking embarrassed, she pulled a slightly battered card from the back pocket of her jeans and thrust it his way. 'Happy Birthday.'

'Thanks.' He couldn't help his grin as he tore into the envelope, which was still warm from her body heat. The spark of excitement in her eyes felt like the best birthday gift he'd ever received.

The card depicted a cartoon girl flying through the air on

a swing, the caption *Life's Short, Swing High* underneath. Inside it was simply signed *from Kat and Lucy*.

It reminded him of their trip to the park when he'd seen Kat's fun side as she'd taken a turn on the swings alongside Lucy and Molly, making who could go the highest into a game. He'd been forced to take a second look at Kat and adjust his first impressions.

Except that had only left him hungry for more information.

'I completely forget to give it to you earlier. Sorry that it's a bit bent,' Kat said with a shrug, as if justifying her gesture.

'Thank you, Kat,' he said, strangely touched. 'It's a great sentiment.' He forced his stare away from her lush lips, from her satisfied little smile.

Their eyes locked.

Grady's pulse kicked up, his body urging him to test his theory that Kat Collins shared the sexual chemistry he could no longer deny. But something held him back, some hangover of his bad marriage. He no longer rushed into things, not since his divorce. And even if he was right that she shared his attraction, that didn't mean he should act on it, nor that Kat would want to.

'Look,' he said, tucking the card and envelope into his shirt pocket, 'I'm not going to be able to leave until I know you're safe, so you can wait in my car for your ride, or you can accept my lift home. It's really no big deal, in fact you'd be doing me a favour. I don't want to worry until our next shift together that you fell victim to some kind of foul play.'

'Foul play?' She laughed, her head tipping up, exposing her neck.

He nodded, totally distracted by her soft-looking skin, wondering if it would feel as good against his lips, if she'd smell as fantastic close up as she did from a polite distance.

'It's true what everyone says about you, isn't it?' With her eyes still dancing with humour, her gaze traced his face, assessing him on what felt like a whole new level. 'You're just a really nice guy.'

Grady shrugged, his head full of the more than nice things he'd like to do with her. 'I can be sometimes.'

She pressed her lips together as if she too might be thinking dirty thoughts. Then she came to a decision 'Okay. I'd love a lift. Thanks, Nash.'

Grady swallowed hard as he headed for his car. She was sticking to the first name thing and from the way *Nash* sounded on her lips he couldn't say he minded one little bit. Unlocking his car, he opened the passenger side door for Kat before rounding the bonnet and climbing into the driver's seat.

'So, where is Molly tonight?' Kat asked as she clicked her seatbelt into place and looked over at him.

The interior of the car was dark, her face illuminated by the streetlight outside. She was inspecting him in a way that left him hot under the collar.

He cleared his tight throat. 'She's at her mum's place tonight, although she often stays with my parents at weekends, especially if I have to cover a night shift.'

He left the car park, pulled onto the road and headed for Kat's suburb.

'Do your parents help out with Lucy a lot?' he asked, because he had first-hand experience of the childcare struggles faced by most single working parents.

Kat nodded. 'I'm so lucky to have them, otherwise my job would be a lot harder. So, do you and your ex share custody?'

'Carol,' he clarified with a shrug. 'Kind of.'

The last thing he wanted to discuss with this woman who

had driven him to distraction all night, while her birthday card was burning a hole through his shirt, was the mess of his post-divorce *relationship* with his ex-wife, which largely consisted of disagreements over Molly, or Carol just doing whatever the hell she pleased and then trying to persuade him that they should be a proper family again.

Kat frowned at his cryptic response. 'Oh… That sounds… complicated.'

'Yeah,' Grady admitted, a stab of familiar guilt jabbing between his ribs at his betrayal of the woman he'd once loved enough to make Molly with, to marry, to quit the army and put their family first with. The ashamed part of him, the part that had rushed into that relationship, the part that felt he hadn't truly known Carol until things had started to go wrong, wanted to hide from Kat and what was an easy, light flirtation.

'We do have a shared custody agreement,' he said, trying to keep the pointless bitterness from his voice, 'but I'm essentially Molly's parent full-time. Carol travels a lot with her job.'

That was generous of him. Carol's career in the airline industry was another choice she'd made after the divorce, almost as if she needed an excuse to abandon the parts of parenthood she found monotonous.

'That must be hard on you and Molly,' Kat said. 'That's what happened on the first day of school, right? She had to work?'

Grady felt her inquisitive stare burn the side of his face as he kept his eyes on the road. He fought the urge to overshare. He didn't want to badmouth Carol but, for some inexplicable reason, he also didn't feel comfortable lying to Kat.

'Yes, she did. I just wish she'd given me a little more warning so I could have managed Molly's disappointment.

Do you mind if we change the subject?' He glanced her way, catching her wince of embarrassment.

'Of course. Sorry. I'm being nosy.'

'It's okay. I'm curious about your situation too, for the record. I'm just…conscious that she'll always be Molly's mother, and for Molly's sake I want them to have a good relationship.' Although he had his work cut out for him with Carol's erratic and unreliable attitude to parenting.

He stopped at the lights and glanced at Kat.

Her bottom lip trapped under her teeth, she was looking him over as if he were a fascinating new species she'd discovered. 'I have to say I'm impressed. I can spout an unending stream of vitriol regarding Lucy's father.' She laughed, but then clarified. 'Never in front of her, of course.'

'He really hurt you, huh?' Grady said, his eyes on the road once more. His instincts had been right; Kat had been badly let down by this British guy.

'You could say that,' she admitted flatly. 'But at least I get Lucy all to myself. One of the perks of making a baby with the wrong man.'

Grady nodded, unable to imagine the precise, rule-abiding Kat ever making something as human as a mistake. Nash's money was on her ex, who'd obviously monumentally messed up.

'Does Lucy ever see her father?' he asked. Although he sometimes despaired at Carol's broken promises, cursed her for letting their daughter down, Molly's first day of school being a prime example, Molly at least had some contact with her mother.

But perhaps a total absence would hurt Molly less.

'No, he doesn't, and before you suggest that I deliberately moved home to New Zealand to make it hard for him, you should know that the minute I told him I was pregnant he bailed on the two of us and never looked back.'

If he'd thought he'd heard her angry the day he'd admitted her patient to the orthopaedic ward, now she was all but spitting nails. No wonder. Kat was a smart, driven woman. It would really sting to be discarded, to have Lucy treated that way too.

'Just for the record, I'd never suggest you capable of such a thing,' he said, his voice tight with genuine regret for her situation. 'I'm sorry to hear that you and Lucy were so badly let down.'

Grady knew exactly how it felt to be disappointed by someone you'd once loved. How the rejection would be compounded tenfold if it also included your child.

'The guy sounds like an idiot,' he said, trying to lighten the atmosphere.

'I agree.' Kat laughed, her eyes dancing with flickers from the streetlights.

'What?' he asked at her continued enigmatic smile.

She shrugged. 'Who knew that a stickler for protocol and a rule-bender would agree on anything?'

'Not me.' He laughed, warmed inside to see her opening up, playful, flirtatious even. But along with their daughters and their work, they also had one more thing in common: their messy past relationships. No matter how much he wanted to kiss her and see if the chemistry was imagined or real, instinct told him to keep things friendly.

Trouble was, he couldn't deny that he was wildly attracted to Kat Collins.

With an internal sigh, he silently recited the words his wise five-year-old said when something went wrong: *Not good...not good at all.*

# CHAPTER SEVEN

KAT HELD HER breath as the last rock-solid misconception she held of Nash crumbled to dust, unearthing more and more of his undeniably attractive facets.

She knew from the trip to the park that he was a great father, despite what sounded like a tricky situation with Molly's mother. He was even driving goodness knew how far out of his way to drop her home. And just like he was an outstanding and experienced nurse but demonstrated enough humility to ask for her help, like he had with the measles case, Kat could admit that thanks to Henry and the intuition and trust she could no longer rely upon, she'd grossly misjudged Nash's character.

Glancing over at her from the driver's seat, he smiled, the sexy crinkle around his eyes flipping her stomach. Her stare traced his strong profile and the subtle wave in his glossy dark hair. If only she could trust her libido and take what was becoming increasingly clear was a mutual attraction to the next level. Except the last person she'd slept with was Henry. The Kat who'd come back to New Zealand, alone and pregnant and forced to move back in with her parents, had vowed to be a better judge of the male character.

And then motherhood and work and being there for her parents after her father's stroke had consumed all of her time and energy. Now she was so rusty at flirtation it was a joke.

Wishing she'd scraped a razor over her legs in the shower earlier, just in case she found some unmined well of liberating bravery, Kat shelved her dithering for the time being.

'So,' she said, 'how long have you been divorced, and do you date much?'

*Oh, real subtle.* Perhaps she should ask him to switch on the car's air conditioning to cool herself down.

He took her probing questions in his stride, his deep laugh a comforting sound. 'I've been divorced for coming up to five years and dating isn't a priority for me at the moment, not when Molly is so little. How about you?'

Kat swallowed hard, nerves gripping her throat in a stranglehold. But she wasn't marrying him, only considering sleeping with him.

'I'm a single mother who works forty-eight hours a week—what do you think?' She rolled her eyes, the sarcasm in her voice preferable to the self-pity she tried to keep at bay every time she considered her barren personal life. She was twenty-nine, not eighty-nine. Until she'd met Nash, she'd managed to convince herself that she no longer had any use for the opposite sex. But she owed it to herself to explore this chemistry. She wasn't imagining his interest, her body's reaction every time their eyes met telling her the attraction was mutual.

But was she ready to take the plunge after so long? She might as well be about to do a bungee jump for all the activity going on inside her abdomen.

Nash smiled, his gaze lingering a little too long. 'I know what you mean. Being a single parent is tough when it comes to dating.'

Kat nodded, relieved that she could share some of her feelings on the subject. Although sympathetic, none of her married friends understood. 'It's hard enough sneaking the time for a haircut or to take some exercise. Considering that side of your life just feels…somehow selfish.' Just as Henry had once accused her of being because she'd made the choice to have their baby.

'I know what you mean.' He nodded in agreement. 'As it is there just doesn't seem to be enough hours in the day.'

'And the last thing you need is to use up energy you don't have to develop or maintain any sort of relationship, even a casual one.' She pressed her lips together, scared she might have over-shared in her enthusiasm to talk to someone who understood. It was easier to ignore her sexual side, and until Nash she'd been doing a great job.

'I agree, most of the time,' he said, pensive.

Kat watched him pull into her street, curious now if he ever experienced loneliness, like her. Her heart rate accelerated so high she thought she might pass out.

'Most of the time?' she asked as, following her directions, he parked next to her driveway. Her weatherboard villa sat on a rear section, set back from the street behind another house.

He turned off the ignition and faced her, his expression hidden in shadow but his eyes mesmerising. 'I try to remember that we're human beings. We have biological needs that it's healthy to occasionally address.'

Kat nodded, not trusting her voice, her own biological needs clamouring to be heard after she'd shoved them aside for so long.

'My house is down that driveway,' she finally croaked when the pressure of meeting his gaze burned her eyes. It was decision time. Invite him in or say goodnight.

'I'll walk you to the door,' he said, exiting the car before she could protest.

The doubts rooted by Henry's rejection returned. It had

been so long since she'd done this. No matter how much she wanted to be seen as a sophisticated professional woman who navigated her own destiny, inside she was a quivering mess.

Postponing the decision for a few more seconds, Kat walked at his side down the long, dark driveway, every step knotting her stomach a little tighter. It wasn't until they'd walked halfway down the drive that the motion sensor security light activated, flooding the property, and her and Nash, in its bright halogen beam.

He smiled, and her panic eased until the awkward moment on the doorstep. Kat hadn't trusted her instincts for over six years. But perhaps that was the biggest reason of all that she should stop over-thinking and just act on their chemistry.

Nash was a mature, responsible man with his own baggage. They had way more in common than she'd originally assumed. He was no more looking for a relationship than Kat. They could just have one night and then pretend it hadn't happened.

'Thanks for the lift,' she said, pushing her key into the lock while she tried to get her heart rate under control.

'You're welcome,' he said, looking up at her from the step below. 'Thanks again for joining us tonight. I'm glad you made it.'

Sick of her fear and hesitations, she leaned forward and brushed his cheek with her lips. 'Happy Birthday, Nash.'

She pulled back, her head swimming from lack of oxygen, her hand staying on his shoulder. Her lips tingled where his stubble had grazed them, his scent a disorienting cloud, filling her mind with the erotic possibilities she'd denied herself for so long. He smelled so good.

Instead of leaving, Nash regarded her intently, as if aware that her peck on the cheek was more than platonic.

Kat's overwrought brain made one last-ditch attempt to apply the brakes, her thoughts turning to the unopened box of condoms in her bathroom cabinet that had been there for years—a *time to get back in the saddle* joke gift from a friend. For all she knew, they had long since expired.

But she was done with denial. Henry had once decimated her self-esteem, made her feel unattractive and worthless. She deserved something for herself, didn't she?

Laying herself open, she curled her fingers into the fabric of his shirt, hoping he'd be left in no doubt of her desire.

As the feel of her lips on his cheek faded, her fingers gripping his shirt, Grady surrendered to the chemical attraction he'd been fighting since the first day he'd met Kat.

Before she changed her mind, he chased her lips with his, capturing her sensual mouth in a kiss that raised the stakes from the friendly peck on the cheek from which he might have walked away. But ignoring Kat's feminine sexuality was like ignoring a hurricane warning, something only a fool would do.

As his lips moved against hers, she shuddered, her body collapsing onto his chest as he held her close. Now that they'd surrendered to the first inevitable kiss, their mouths connected, as if magnetic.

Grady shut out all of the dismissals and justifications, the mental gymnastics he'd endured on the drive to Kat's place. It made no sense to fool around with a work colleague— his life was already complicated enough—but the minute she'd flexed her fingers against his shoulder, her vulnerable stare holding him captive, there was no reasoning with his desires.

Helpless to their connection, which as their conversation in the car proved went beyond animal attraction, Grady allowed Kat to take everything she wanted from their kiss. Her fingers anchored in his hair, her breasts crushed up against his pecs and her soft moans urged him to part her lips and meet her tongue with his own, the surge and retreat a carnal exploration, each kiss more potent than the one before.

He'd known it would be this good from that collision in the playground, although he'd done his best to fight his instincts. Somewhere in his subconscious, the niggle of warning clamoured to be heard. She'd shared things with him tonight, intimate clues to her past and her struggles as a solo parent. He didn't want to lead her on, or complicate their working situation, but her lips tasted so good. She was making it so hard for him to think straight.

As if intent on torturing him further, Kat released a sexy little whimper against his lips, her hands sliding under the hem of his shirt to caress his back.

He growled, cupping her face, spearing his fingers into her hair and pushing her back against the door jamb so he could pin her there with his hips.

Any minute now he would put a stop to the kissing. Anything more required careful thought, a serious conversation, managed expectations in order to avoid misunderstanding or hurt feelings.

When Kat began to ride one of his thighs, which had somehow ended up between her legs, the last rational part of his brain shut down. He reciprocated, grinding his hardness into her stomach while he explored her mouth in slow but demanding swipes of his tongue that freed more of her sexy little moans.

Finally, maybe because he needed to breathe, he paused

to gulp air. He looked down, lost for words at how quickly one kiss on the doorstep had escalated. Kat's lips were swollen, her stare pleasure drunk, her eyelids heavy.

She looked even more beautiful. He closed his eyes to block out the tempting sight.

'Don't stop,' she whispered, tugging his mouth back to hers.

His body hummed with desperation. He was done denying that he wanted her. But some kernel of doubt germinated. He needed to be sure that she wanted the same thing.

It almost killed him, but he pulled away once more. 'Kat...' Her lips followed his, her kisses swallowing the words he tried to speak. 'Are you sure this is a good idea?'

He wanted to do the right thing but she'd made him so worked up he was no longer sure what the right thing was.

She looked up at him, her expression dazed. 'Don't tell me you've decided to stop going with the flow. I thought I was the one who needed rules.'

At her continued tugging of his waist, Grady sighed and rested his forehead against hers. 'You are the one who needs rules. I just don't want there to be any misguided expectations.'

Kat's lips found his earlobe, the side of his neck. His eyes rolled back in his head as he fought for control over his libido.

'I want you, Nash, and I'm tired of fighting it. That doesn't mean I want more than sex, more than just one night. Consider those my rules if you want.'

Despite the fact that her lips and hands seemed to be everywhere at once, Grady forced himself to demand her attention. 'I want you too. But we work together and our situations are similar. I don't have any spare energy for a relationship.'

'Which is why you won't bend my rules: one night and then we pretend it didn't happen.' With a spark of challenge in her eyes, she turned the key in the lock and stepped over the threshold.

'It's like you said, Nash—we have biological needs.' She held out her hand, inviting him inside.

He took her hand in his, still hesitating on the other side of the front door. He cursed his own words from their conversation in the car. He'd been caught up in the moment, humbled that Kat felt comfortable enough with him to share some of her feelings. A part of him had wanted her to know that she deserved to consider her own needs, beyond her role as a doctor and a mother.

Wasn't that exactly what she was doing now?

He'd dallied for so long hesitation flickered across her face. 'I mean, I don't want to force you. I just thought—'

Before she could finish that sentence or doubt how much he wanted to follow her rules, he stepped into the hallway, closed the front door and hauled her into his arms for another kiss.

'Of course you're not forcing me,' he said when they parted for air. 'I'm only too happy to abide by your rules.'

Her smile dazzled him. 'Good. As long as you're not going to go off script and become all clingy on me.'

'I promise.' Because he felt ravenous without her mouth on his, he kissed her again, only pausing when she took his hand and guided him the few metres along the dark hallway to her bedroom.

Inside the room, Kat paused. They both glanced at the bed.

'I'm sorry,' she said, her teeth tugging at her bottom lip with sudden hesitation. 'I haven't done this for a while. Do you want a drink or something?'

Grady shook his head, tugging her into his arms and tilting her chin up so their stares locked. He traced the lip she'd chewed with his thumb. 'How long? I need to know if I should bring out my A game.' He smiled, trying to put her at ease.

Because he was still cupping her jaw, he felt her swallow. 'Six years,' she whispered.

*Six years?*

Grady tried not to gape at her shocking confession. That meant she hadn't slept with anyone since before Lucy was born, since the idiot who obviously broke her heart.

Her body tensed in his arms. Cupping her face, he gently caressed her lips with his, focused on how good her kisses felt, hoping that Kat would feel as good.

'In that case,' he said, sliding his hands under the hem of her top to stroke her waist, 'I'll aim for A plus with an excellence distinction.'

Her laugh banished the last of his doubts. Kat was an intelligent and beautiful woman who could have anyone. That she'd chosen to break such a long dry spell with him was incredibly flattering. And no one, especially not Kat, deserved to have their sexuality neglected for so long.

'Can we get naked now that we've set the parameters?' Amusement danced in her eyes.

'Absolutely.' He slid his hands up her ribs, bunching up her blouse and lifting it over her head.

In return, Kat urged his arms up, helping him to yank off his shirt. When she hummed appreciatively and pressed a kiss to his bare chest, he had to force himself to take things slow.

His body was primed for action, his stare was drawn to the curve of her breasts above the lace of her bra. But he was determined to worship every neglected inch of her body, make her feel as beautiful as she was physically.

Then on Monday they'd go back to being just colleagues. Neither of them needed the complication of a relationship. They could dispense with their powerful chemistry and move on, no regrets.

As if his brain had finally conceded power to his body, Grady dragged her closer, his elbows at her back and his hands tilting her face up to his kiss. Her breasts pressed against his chest, her hands roaming over his skin.

He walked her backwards towards the bed, where they stripped off their remaining clothes.

'There are condoms in the bathroom cabinet,' she said at the next chance he gave her to speak. 'Although,' she added with a nervous chuckle, 'we'll need to check the expiry date. They've been there a while, were a joke from one of my girlfriends.'

'I have one,' he reassured her, retrieving the protection from his wallet.

When he joined her back on the bed she slipped into his arms, her mouth back on his, their tongues once more duelling for satiation. He pressed her into the mattress, determined to take things slow, to make it good for Kat, who had waited a long time to trust her body with another man.

'You smell so good,' he groaned against her skin as he kissed a path down her neck and chest to her breast, taking the nipple into his mouth and lavishing the bud with swipes of his tongue.

Kat cried out, her nails digging into his shoulders.

'I have to taste all of you,' he said, scooting lower, his gaze roaming the curves of her astounding body, kissing her stomach and the silvery streak of her Caesarean section scar, her hipbones and finally in between her legs.

Kat gripped the sheets in her fists, her gasps of delight music to Grady's ears. They might only have this one night, but he'd make it count, make up for each year of her long abstinence. Take her trust in him and deliver on his promise.

Her orgasm, when it came, shook her like a rag doll, her cries echoing in the darkness as she gripped his hair as if for dear life and rode out every last spasm.

He gave her a few minutes to recover, kissing his way back up her body, her skin so sensitive she giggled more than once. Then he covered himself with a condom and lay beside her, self-satisfied warmth pounding through his veins.

'You're beautiful,' he said, cupping her face and drawing her mouth back to his, making sure that he'd kissed and caressed every part of her before he finally pushed inside her.

Grady had experienced lots of good sex, but there was something deeper about the connection between two pleasure-focused people sharing an honest and open connection. When he'd first met Kat he couldn't have predicted they'd have a single thing in common but as he drove them over the edge, his stare locked with hers, finishing with a hoarse cry of her name when she tumbled with him once more into blissful release, he knew for certain that his own love life had been severely short-changed.

Fortunately, Kat's box of condoms had still been in date.

'One last time,' Nash said, slipping inside her from behind.

'Yes,' Kat cried, curling her fingers into his hair and holding on tight. Needing more contact, she entwined her other hand with his where it lay flat against her stomach, her back melded to his front as they rocked together, desperate to make the pleasure of their one night last.

Nash too seemed reluctant to stop. It was as if, having set the rules, they were both determined to stretch out the experience beyond the realms of the space time continuum.

'Nash…' She'd said his name so many times in the past three hours she was almost hoarse from yelling it, screaming it, pleading for what, she didn't know. She'd never known anything like the passion they'd shared. He'd taken her in positions she'd never heard of, his thorough and inexhaustible form of sex the best she could have hoped for after six years of denial.

And she saw now that she'd forgone an essential part of her femininity after her heartbreak at the hands of Henry. Why had she waited so long? Except instinct told her that there was nothing common about this experience. Unlike his laid-back work persona, Nash was a perfectionist when it came to pleasure.

He cupped her breast, his thumb lazily swiping her now tender nipple. 'Don't leave it another six years, Kat.' His stubble grazed her neck, sending shivers down her spine. 'You deserve to be loved.'

She knew he meant physically, not emotionally. He couldn't possibly know that her deepest fear was that she was somehow unlovable because of Henry's rejection. But her eyes stung with the threat of tears all the same, a confusing mix of gratitude that she'd made the right decision in choosing Nash as a lover for the night, in trusting him with her body, and apprehension, because sex this good was going to be so hard to forget.

But forget it she must. Because trusting him with her body was one thing. Beyond that, even if they wanted more, which they didn't, she'd forgotten how to extend that trust to relationship-building.

Instead of second-guessing the guard she'd placed around

her heart six years ago, Kat imagined exactly how she would face Nash the next time they had a shift together, knowing that, among all of his other strengths, he was an enthusiastic and considerate lover. A part of her already regretted crossing the line, inviting him into her bed, because she was one hundred percent certain, now that she'd experienced a night in Nash's arms, that the one night on which she'd insisted was not going to be enough.

Except it had to be. They'd agreed. She'd made the rules and he'd made certain she understood he was no more looking for a relationship than she was.

As if he sensed her distraction, he moved on top of her. His hands cupped her face as he pushed inside her once more, his lips coaxing hers in a soft, sensual kiss.

'Stop over-thinking,' he whispered, as if he knew the exact contents of her head. But that was insane. He couldn't know her fears and doubts. He'd simply learned almost all there was to know about her body in one single night, that was all.

'Just feel,' he said, driving her higher and higher, helping her to be free of her own head, making this one night so perfect a part of her wanted to never let him go.

Ignoring the dangerous inclination, she stared into his eyes, certain that she'd exhausted her body's supply of climaxes. But as sure as the morning sun was peeking over the horizon outside, Nash kissed her and stroked her and drove into her until he'd dragged one more from her spent body, himself surrendering seconds later.

After he collapsed, Kat rolled onto her side, buried her face against his neck, swallowing the ridiculous urge to cry. She wasn't a crier. She was just overwhelmed on endorphins, high on too much good sex and not enough sleep.

A trickle of fear for Monday morning crawled over her

skin. She would have to work extra hard to ignore him now, to treat him like any other colleague, to act as if everything was back to normal, as if she hadn't learned what turned him on and what he looked like naked.

'I'm going to go,' he said after a few minutes of holding her close.

'Sure.' She nodded, reluctantly slipping her hands from around his waist.

Time to get her game face on.

He pressed a kiss to her temple, stood and disappeared into the bathroom. When he emerged he was fully dressed. His hair was sex-rumpled and his stare sleepy. He looked hotter than ever and, worse, he'd shown her his vulnerable side tonight, confided in her about his marriage and his hopes for Molly, shown her that there was way more to him than the irresponsible charmer she'd first assumed. She wanted to drag this new-found version of him back to bed and suggest that he stay until morning, that they talk some more, get to know each other better, but that wasn't part of one-night stand protocol.

He bent over her, a knowing smile making him look more boyish. But he was one hundred percent man. She knew that now.

In an absurd display of belated modesty, because he'd seen and tasted every part of her, Kat clutched the sheet to her chest and his smile widened.

'That was the best birthday I've ever had,' he said, brushing his lips against hers, feather-soft.

It left her wanting more.

To hide the fact, she laughed, grateful to him for making light of the situation.

'Bye, Kat.' He pressed his lips to hers in a final kiss that was way too brief and left the room and then the house.

Deflated, her skin crawling with trepidation, Kat lay still for the longest time after she'd listened to his car pulling away, her overriding emotion in the face of such an overwhelming success perversely that of failure.

The younger Kat, newly graduated from medical school, who had travelled overseas on a big life adventure, the way most young New Zealanders did, had been full of optimism and hope. She'd fallen hard for Henry, had loved him deeply. But why, when he'd proved himself to be so unworthy of her love, unworthy of his beautiful and funny daughter, had she allowed him to tear down her confidence so completely?

Nash was right. Her personal life didn't have to be over just because of one mistaken choice, one sour relationship. Kat might have reached that conclusion earlier if her mistake hadn't also had long-reaching consequences for both Lucy's emotional wellbeing and her father's health.

Maybe if her error in judgement had only affected Kat, if *her* broken heart had been the only casualty, she might have overcome the betrayal more easily.

She rolled over and tugged the duvet up to her chin, for the first time since Henry considering that one day she might be able to move on. Of course, a relationship involved a lot more than one incredible night. But if she was brave enough to sleep with Nash, to listen to her body and admit that she had needs beyond work and motherhood, maybe she could be brave enough to start dating again, when the time was right.

She fell asleep, thanks to Nash her dreams full of possibilities.

# CHAPTER EIGHT

THREE DAYS LATER, the first shift he and Kat shared since they'd slept together, Grady pushed open the door to the multi-bedded resuscitation bay to find her busy at one of the computer workstations. His blood surged at the sight of her—those lips that had tasted so addictive on Saturday night pursed in concentration, her expressive eyes down-turned when in pleasure they'd glowed with golden embers as she'd clung to him, her hair tamed into a practical po-nytail when he could still recall its scent and lush silkiness between his fingers and trailing over his skin.

He clenched his jaw. This obsession had to end. He was breaking the rules, exactly what she'd accused him of that first day they'd met. She'd been adamant it was for one night and he'd insisted on clear expectations.

So why was he so eager to have her look at him the way she had when he'd kissed her goodbye, as if he'd taken her to heaven and back? Was it just ego on his part? If so, he could get over that.

When she'd said they should pretend like it hadn't hap-pened, he didn't realise she meant to act as if they were strangers, or the adversaries from her first day. But beyond her brief *Good morning* they hadn't spoken a word.

He should have felt relieved that she was *business as usual* at work, so much so that no one would suspect they were anything other than barely acquainted colleagues. Instead, he'd tied himself into knots considering what he truly wanted. Walking away from such great sex was, of course, difficult. But did he truly want his often perplexing personal life further stretched by a fling with a work colleague?

Molly took up all of his spare energy. She was his priority. And managing Carol also sapped his time and energy. Only yesterday she'd turned up on his doorstep unannounced, demanding to see Molly because she had an unexpected shift cancellation, when they were supposed to stick to their appointed custody days.

Irked that he was so emotionally labile when Kat—who had barely given him the time of day all morning—seemed to have reverted easily to their pre-sex distance, he cleared his throat.

'Your suspected meningitis case is almost here, Dr Collins.' His voice emerged a little gruffer than he would have liked. He didn't want Kat to know that he was having second thoughts about the one-night rule but the fact that she'd hardly registered his presence left him itchy with frustration, as if he'd been...used.

'Thanks,' Kat muttered, clearly focused on what she was doing. She seemed to be going out of her way to avoid any interaction with him, even professional courtesy.

Because he'd yet to move from the doorway, Kat looked up.

A flash of what looked like fear passed over her expression. 'Sorry, I'll be right with you.'

Her voice was clipped in a busy doctor-like fashion. Her attention returned to the monitor, making him aware he'd been effectively dismissed.

The hair at the back of his neck prickled.

Kat's behaviour reminded him of Carol. She'd walked all

over his feelings during their short marriage, inconsiderate and focused on her own needs, her own agenda. And she was still trying to pull those kinds of stunts, even though she no longer had any claim to him.

He wasn't asking for much from Kat, just some eye contact would do. A small smile. Any sign that let him know that what they'd shared meant more to her than an item ticked off a to-do list.

*Start new job—check*
*Socialise with work colleagues—check*
*Sleep with available man to break overly prolonged dry spell—check*

Resentful that he should have listened to his doubts and never have slept with her, Grady locked open the double doors that separated Resus from the ambulance bay and made his way outside to receive their next patient.

As he watched the ambulance backing up he became aware of Kat arriving at his side. 'I think you can call me Kat, don't you?'

He glanced her way but she kept her eyes on the reversing vehicle.

She appeared breathless. Was she reacting to his proximity the way he couldn't help but react to hers? His arms could still feel her, the unique scent of her soft skin imprinted on his brain, her passionate moans as she'd called his name over and over looping through his head.

Had she any idea how hard it had been for him to leave her warm bed when his overriding desire had been to curl his body around hers and drift off to sleep with the beat of her heart thumping against his chest?

'Okay.' He clenched his jaw, desperate to get her alone and clear the air. 'Kat it is.'

He didn't play games. He didn't want tension at work. Better to talk about it, discuss how they felt, and then move on.

Only part of him was stuck. The last thing he'd been expecting when he'd found her in the car park behind The Har-Bar was that they'd end up in bed together. But despite the current ice queen vibe she was channelling for reasons only known to Kat, she'd not only opened up about Lucy's father, she'd been as insatiable for him as he'd been for her, one time leading to another and another until he'd been certain from the look of vulnerability in her eyes that she'd ask him to stay the night.

Shaking off the unsettling thought that he would have happily held Kat until it had been time to collect Molly from Carol's house, Grady jolted into action as the rear doors of the ambulance swung open.

Two paramedics wheeled out a stretcher carrying a little girl around Molly's age, her features pale underneath the oxygen mask on her face.

Work-focused, he guided the foot of the stretcher into Resus, aware of Kat's rapid stride at his side. The girl's concerned parents followed and Grady cast them what he hoped was a reassuring look. The girl was now in the best place, and hopefully he and Kat could assess and treat her quickly so that she was out of danger.

'This is Hannah Roberts,' the paramedic said as Kat and he transferred Hannah easily to the resus stretcher.

'She's a normally well six-year-old girl who's been ill with a fever for two days. This morning she became increasingly lethargic, with a worsening headache and vomiting,' the paramedic continued. 'Mum and Dad report what sounds like a seizure, with loss of consciousness lasting approximately two minutes.'

With his handover complete, the paramedic smiled reassuringly at Hannah and her parents and then left the family in their care.

Kat met Grady's stare, concern clear in her eyes.

Any confusion or regret fell away as they silently communicated. Meningitis, if not treated quickly, could be life-threatening. They both had daughters Hannah's age. They were obviously concerned about the worst-case scenario for this little girl. They could empathise with Hannah's parents, who must be terrified to see their daughter so seriously unwell.

Sadly, Grady recognised the helplessness from his personal experience during Molly's admissions for acute exacerbations of the asthma she'd had since she was three years old.

With a swallow Grady was certain only he witnessed, Kat prepared herself. She spoke to Hannah's parents in a calm, reassuring voice. While she took a more detailed history of events, Grady connected Hannah to various monitors that immediately began recording her vital signs. Relieved to see that the paramedic had applied local anaesthetic cream to the antecubital fossa of both arms, he set about obtaining venous access and extracted several vials of blood for the lab. Then, thinking ahead, he applied some more local anaesthetic cream to the little girl's lower back.

Kat would probably want to do a lumbar puncture.

Seeing his forethought, she nodded gratefully as she quickly examined Hannah.

The presentation was indeed worrying for meningitis. The sooner they could start some antibiotics, the sooner they could eliminate a life-threatening infection.

Grady brought up Hannah's hospital record on the computer and ordered the most likely blood tests he figured Kat would want, including blood cultures.

A few minutes later Kat joined him at the workstation, worry evident in her expression.

'What do you think?' he asked, his voice low so their conversation wouldn't be overheard. He had to fight the bizarre urge to smooth the frown creases between Kat's eyebrows with his fingertip. Instead, he concentrated on labelling each vial of blood for the lab.

'There's no rash,' said Kat, her voice betraying the tension she wore around her mouth, 'but she has photophobia and neck stiffness.'

That told Nash that Kat suspected the GP's diagnosis of meningitis was correct. The sooner they could administer the correct intravenous antibiotic, the better Hannah's chances were of fighting the infection.

'She needs a CT scan and an urgent lumbar puncture,' Kat said, sharing her concerns, their personal issues set aside while they focused on their patient.

He nodded. 'That's protocol in cases with this presentation.'

Her frown eased, as if she'd been waiting for his corroboration. 'Have you called the paediatrician? She'll need to be admitted.'

Grady winced, glancing over at where Hannah lay, still and worryingly uncomplaining, on the stretcher. He had no good news on that score.

He stepped closer, dropped his voice further. 'I informed the paeds team that we might have a meningitis case coming in as soon as I knew Hannah was on her way, but they're currently dealing with a SIDS case and Lauren is next door inserting a temporary pacemaker on a patient with symptomatic complete heart block.'

They stared at each other, the implications sinking in. For now, he and Kat were Team Hannah until the paediatrician was free. The emergency department often operated in a feast or famine way, one doctor or specialist needing to be in two places at once.

'You're experienced at lumbar punctures, right?' he asked, his expression as reassuring as he could make it. What he really wanted to do was hold her in his arms, feel her weight sink into him the way it had on Saturday, when she'd been open to him, trusting that he'd catch her when she fell apart.

She nodded, looking uncertain.

'Do you want me to talk to Lauren?' he offered. The department was busy as usual, but their acting head consultant would get Kat the supervision she needed, if required.

Kat nibbled at her lip. Then the doubt cleared. 'No, I've done it lots of times before.' She moved closer, her arm brushing his. 'It's just that…she's so little, you know.'

Nash nodded, compassion and concern a lump in his throat. He knew exactly what she was feeling. 'You're thinking of our girls?'

She nodded.

'Me too, for the record.' He gripped her arm above the elbow, giving her a light squeeze of encouragement. 'You can do this, Kat.'

Nash had watched her in action since her first day. He'd seen her dedication to patient care and her humility. She wasn't scared to ask for help when she needed it. If she said she could perform the lumbar puncture unsupervised he had complete faith in her.

As an ER doctor, she would have done the procedure

many times before. Her second's wobble of confidence was solely down to maternal empathy.

Kat's eyes shone with gratitude. 'Yes, I can. Thanks, Nash.'

He nodded, dropping his hand from her arm and missing the contact immediately. 'I'll be right here to help if you need me. Do you want to prescribe some antibiotics so I can organise an IV infusion?'

She nodded and released a controlled sigh as she added her signature to the prescription. The smile she gave him spoke a thousand words. At work they could still operate as a team, even if they'd complicated their professional relationship by acting on their attraction and sleeping together.

Kat ordered the urgent CT scan and then spoke to Hannah and her parents, informing them that she needed to exclude meningitis with a lumbar puncture test.

Grady readied the equipment she'd need for the procedure. She didn't need him to hold her hand but he wanted to offer support in the same way he'd always mentored the junior doctors. That was how he and Lauren had become friends.

Except while they washed their hands side by side at the double sink Grady struggled to ignore the protective urges he felt towards Kat, aware that this felt more personal because they'd spent the night together. He should have known that sex was never just sex, especially when two people shared this kind of connection. Hopefully, there'd be time to talk about Saturday later.

Kat dried her hands and glanced over at Hannah once more. Their patient's age was understandably making her draw comparisons.

'You know,' he said as they put on sterile gloves, trying to ease their apprehension, 'Molly has asthma.'

Kat looked up, her shock turning to empathy.

'I've spent one or two nights here with her as an inpatient—longest nights of my life. But we both know that kids can be flat one minute and running around the ward chattering away the next.'

'I'm sorry to hear that about Molly,' she said, looking at him as if she wanted to touch him in a comforting way. Instead, she drew local anaesthetic into a syringe. 'You're right, children are resilient. Hopefully those antibiotics will work soon.'

The lumbar puncture procedure went smoothly. As Grady cleared away the used equipment, Kat's pager sounded, a call to assist one of the house officers with another case.

'I'll be back shortly,' she said, peeling off her gloves.

He nodded, glad that when it counted they could remain professional.

'I really appreciate your support.' A small smile twitched her mouth, one he recognised from Saturday when she'd looked at him as if he was the man of her dreams. Only he didn't want that. He just wanted more than the frosty distance of this morning.

'Any time,' he said, faking the easygoing vibe that before Kat had always come naturally. Now, his stomach was tight with anticipation, his reasoning conflicted, his precious certainties, the convictions he'd lived by since his divorce, rattled.

He watched her leave, his confusion proof that he was in danger where Kat was concerned.

# CHAPTER NINE

FORTY MINUTES LATER, with a stable Hannah transferred to the neighbouring X-ray department for a CT scan, Kat entered the deserted staffroom, dragging in her first deep breath of the day.

Despite the reviving oxygen in her system, her hands trembled as she prepared a cup of coffee, the adrenaline only partly due to treating a seriously ill little girl the same age as Lucy.

Her remaining tremors were entirely related to Nash. The minute she'd seen him that morning every stern lecture she'd given herself over the weekend since they'd slept together might as well have been in a foreign language for all the sense it made to her shaky resolve. She'd insisted on their one-night rule for a reason: she neither wanted nor was ready for more.

Her long physical recovery from a difficult pregnancy and birth had been compounded by the emotional impact of Henry's cruel rejection. Her subsequent guilt over her father's stroke, helping to care for him while raising Lucy, meant that by the time she'd met Nash she'd almost forgotten how to interact with a man she found attractive.

Only despite the rules she'd laid down one night with Nash had unleashed a torrent of emotions. Kat had spent most of the weekend following her routines—walking on the beach with her parents and Lucy, visiting the farmers' market and shopping for groceries, tackling the week's laundry—trying to keep a lid on the way he'd made her feel beautiful, desired, more than just a mum.

No wonder it was taking all of her energy to walk that fine line between acting *normal* at work and wanting to drag him somewhere private, kiss him again and beg him to throw her rulebook out of the window so they could prolong their fling.

Aware of how erratic her emotions were, she sighed as she took a seat. Could Nash see how conflicted she was? Her cool as a cucumber act was probably convincing no one. But Nash was a reasonable man. Surely he could see that the sooner they returned to business as usual and dispensed with all the uncomfortable silences and stilted interactions the better for them both. They had jobs to do and busy personal lives. If they could get past the awkwardness they'd be fine.

Gulping her coffee in the hope that the caffeine would straighten out her convoluted thoughts, Kat chided herself for her silly hormonal angst and forced her thoughts back to Hannah. The distress on the faces of her poor parents as Kat had put a needle into Hannah's lower spine to retrieve a sample of cerebrospinal fluid for testing haunted Kat.

She was so highly strung that without Nash's calming presence she might have embarrassed herself with the tears that threatened if she envisioned Lucy lying on a stretcher with a potentially life-threatening infection.

Nash's stoicism, given Molly's asthma, was humbling. Her respect for him had doubled.

Her body flooded with heat. No matter how hard she tried to wipe Saturday from her mind, all roads led back to Nash.

The staffroom door opened at Kat's back. Aware that

she was no longer alone, she slapped a bright smile on her face and turned.

It was Nash.

'Oh…hi,' she said, her cheeks flushing, the frozen smile on her face more of an embarrassed grimace. Would he know that she'd spent the past three days fantasising about him? Could he sense the loneliness gnawing away inside her like a toothache, made stronger by his attention and compliments, which she'd soaked up like a sponge? She should never have slept with him in the first place. Because, just like it was impossible to stuff a champagne cork back inside the bottle, forgetting his touch, his kisses, his whispered words after such a long drought was impossible.

'Hi,' Nash said, his expression telling her that this morning's awkwardness was back.

He moved to the sink and Kat's brain turned to mush, all the things she wanted to say to him, things she'd spent the weekend practising and perfecting, vanished, the way they had when he'd walked into the resus room looking sexier than ever. The only thing left in her mind was, *I know we agreed it was a one-time thing, but you seem to have awoken the sex maniac in me. Want to do it again?*

Of course he didn't. He could barely look at her.

Kat blinked away the sting in her eyes, hoping that by selfishly sleeping with him she hadn't ruined their already fragile working relationship. She held her breath while Nash kept his back to her, preparing a drink. What she wouldn't give for the return of easygoing, rule-bending Nash. But without the buffer of a patient, or unless it was physical, they seemed to have forgotten how to interact with each other.

Nash glanced over his shoulder, their stares colliding.

'Would you like to be alone?' he asked, his voice infuriatingly relaxed as if this was one of their pre-sex conversations. 'I can sit in the corner and pretend that we haven't seen each other, if you want.'

Kat bristled, annoyed that he was calm enough to make jokes and that he seemed to be implying the issue lay solely with her.

'Don't be ridiculous. We don't have to ignore each other.' Although it might help her hormonal imbalance if he promised to forget how she looked naked. Lord help her…even now she was still trying to scrub his gloriously male physique from her mind.

'Don't we?' he said, his stare seeming to probe every last one of the scars Henry had inflicted on her ability to trust both her own judgement and romantic relationships in general. 'Apart from when we've had to set our issues aside for the sake of our patients, it seems to me that you'd prefer to pretend that I didn't exist. I know we said we'd ignore the fact that we had sex, but ignoring each other is taking it too far.'

Kat's indignation soared along with her body temperature at his casual mention of the sex. Her eyes darted around the staffroom, checking they were still alone. 'I wasn't ignoring you; I was just trying to follow the rules,' she hissed, 'trying to behave professionally at work.'

Of course he wouldn't appreciate her efforts. Of course he would be the first one to disregard the guidelines they'd both put in place in order to move on from the best sex Kat had ever had.

'I'd expect nothing less,' he muttered, stirring his coffee and clattering the teaspoon into the sink.

'I suppose you'd rather we discuss it blow by blow, would you?' she asked, determined to act as casually as him.

Oh, please let him decline. A detailed post-mortem of the experience might tip her over the edge.

'And to think,' she said, 'that I'd been about to thank you for being such a gentleman by not mentioning it.' To stop the bubble of hysterical laughter that threatened to erupt, she took another scalding sip of coffee. They were acting worse than their five-year-olds.

As if he too saw the ridiculous in their squabbling, Nash grinned, added a splash of milk to his coffee and then took the seat next to hers.

Kat wanted to squirm at the chaos his closeness was causing in both her head and her pelvis. How could he simultaneously turn her on and rile her up?

Leaning into her personal space, he stage-whispered, 'Who said I was a gentleman?'

His gaze held her captive, every second he stared, his eyes full of intimate knowledge of the night they'd shared, pulsing through her weak body.

She ignored his question. His integrity was part of the reason she'd trusted him with her body in the first place.

'See,' he continued, his deep voice low and conspiratorial in a way that made her pulse skyrocket, 'you don't know the real me at all.'

Was that what bothered him? Was he offended that she'd tried—and failed, although she wouldn't be confessing that—to forget their one-night stand? Of course she wanted to get to know Nash better, beyond his skills as a lover. But even though Henry and Nash couldn't be more different, she was still struggling to trust her judgement when it came to the opposite sex.

'I may not know everything about you,' she said, hoping he couldn't hear the longing in her voice, 'but I know that for some reason you're trying to get a rise out of me.'

And she was taking the bait.

Infuriating man. Why couldn't they just move on from the fact they'd slept together and go back to being colleagues?

Because she still wanted to rip his clothes off, that was why. He shifted in his seat, getting comfortable, the move bringing them so close their arms brushed, heightened physical awareness prickling her skin as if she was allergic to her scrubs. Kat tried to scoot as far away from him as the chair would allow, but it was too late. The memories of his weight on top of her, his stubble grazing her neck, the mindless passion of his kisses rushed her mind.

'And I know that you're most likely prickly out of fear,' he replied, casually sipping his drink.

'Fear?' she huffed.

Confident, Nash nodded slowly. 'Yes, you're scared to get to know me because you've spent years being closed-off.'

'I'm not closed-off.' Kat gaped, outraged because he could see through her so effortlessly. Ever since that night she seemed to be entirely composed of emotions. Just like the sex, it had been six years since she'd trusted anyone enough to show them her softer side. 'Just because I made the mistake of thinking you'd respect my rules, that we could move on from what happened on Saturday.'

If only she could move on.

Her body was desperate for more, although it would have to go back to surviving without regular sex. She stood a small chance of forgetting one time, if only Nash would stop looking at her as if he'd taken mental photographs. But indulging more than once meant getting to know him, opening up, being vulnerable—exactly what she feared the most.

How did he know?

'Well, one of us had to raise the topic.' He pursed his lips to blow the surface of his coffee.

Kat swallowed hard, reminded of his kisses, of all the

places those lips had explored. Was he enjoying making her feel hot and bothered in good ways and bad?

'Why do we have to talk about it at all?' she implored. 'Can't we just forget it happened, as agreed?'

His eyes flashed with sympathy, his stare dipping to her mouth. 'I don't really want to forget the best birthday I've ever had.'

Kat opened her mouth, words failing her as she remembered how he'd held her with such tenderness, how he'd whispered things he hadn't needed to say.

Why was he changing the rules, and why was a part of her tempted to do the same?

'Look, Kat,' he said, his voice gentle, 'I guess I am technically breaking one of the rules by raising the subject, but I guess I'd hoped you might be interested in getting to know me better, at least at work.'

She wanted that. Why hadn't she suggested it first?

'I'll be honest,' Nash continued. 'This morning I couldn't help but feel that you used me for sex, only to put me back on the shelf like some sort of toy.'

Kat gasped, appalled. 'That's not true.'

Was it? Had her attempt to put the best sex of her life behind her, as promised, made him feel used? When it came to men, she'd had her guard up for so long she wore it like a second skin. Could it be that made her appear cold and egotistical, uncaring of how Nash might feel?

'It feels true from where I'm standing.' He placed his half-drunk coffee on the table. 'If I'd had your number I'd have called you on Sunday to clear the air, make sure you were okay. I've waited all morning for this opportunity to get you alone. But when I walked in just now you looked like you wanted to run.'

Kat flushed, shame burning her cheeks, because a part

of her had wanted to flee. She was so confused over her expectations—having one night of pleasure and putting it behind her—and reality, waking up on Sunday morning flooded with feelings she hadn't experienced in years, with the yearning for more of Nash gnawing in the pit of her stomach, that she'd totally freaked out.

'I… I just…' Dropping her head, she groaned silently. He was right. She was inflexible and closed-off and afraid.

She'd set aside her own needs when she'd limped away from Henry, focused on motherhood, her job, repaying her parents for their support. It was easier to set that part of herself aside than to probe the way that her ex had made her feel not good enough.

Reeling, she blurted the truth. 'I'm sorry that you feel used. I'm just not used to putting my needs first the way I did on Saturday and, if I'm brutally honest, I wasn't expecting it to be that good. I became completely overwhelmed.' She looked away from the compassion that filled his stare, embarrassed by her sad admission. She didn't want to be so transparent.

'I'm struggling to forget it myself,' he said, that sexy smile of his making a reappearance.

Kat nodded, looked away, forced herself to lower her guard. 'But I'm not looking for a relationship. Lucy's father threw me away like rubbish and for a long time I felt like there must be something wrong with me.'

'There isn't,' he said emphatically.

'I know, but just because we had sex doesn't mean trust comes automatically. I'm processing a lot, so I'm sorry if I handled it badly. I told you that I was rusty.'

A small frown settled between his brows. 'I'm sorry that you were so badly let down, but I'm not interested in hurting you, Kat. I'm not that guy. That's why I made certain our expectations aligned before we slept together. I'm not looking for a relationship either.'

'I know.' Kat nodded, her cheeks hot. 'You're considerate and understanding and honourable. I'm not used to that.' He wasn't Henry, she understood that on an intellectual level, but her subconscious fears clearly had no such insight, maybe because it wasn't just her happiness at stake any more. There was Lucy to consider.

On Saturday night he'd made her feel cared for—ensuring she was safe when he'd discovered her stranded in the car park, escorting her to her dark front door, telling her she was beautiful and catching her as she'd fallen apart.

Peeking at him from under her lashes, she smiled, feeling raw and exposed. 'I guess I practised the rules too diligently, overdid the casualness.'

'It's okay.' He shrugged. 'I probably overreacted, a side-effect of the divorce.'

Kat nodded, curious for more but emotionally wrung-out. 'So what now?'

They still had the same priorities: their girls and work. As he'd just reminded her, he was no more interested in a relationship than she was.

He tilted his head, a hint of regret in his eyes. 'We go back to your rules.'

Kat nodded, while her stomach sank. She'd voiced the rules to keep herself from getting hurt again, but she couldn't help her stab of disappointment that neither of them was willing to risk more than one night, when it had been Nash's rule-bending that had first brought him to her attention.

'Good plan,' Kat croaked, staring at her hands in her lap.

'If it helps, we should get to know each other better,' he said, as if in consolation. 'As you pointed out that day in the playground, it makes sense for us to be friends, because Molly is smitten with Lucy.'

Kat's heart lurched at the vulnerability in his stare when he mentioned his daughter, just like when he'd shared Molly's medical history earlier.

'That's exactly what I want too.' She forced a bright smile. Friends was okay as consolation prizes went, although him being a complete jerk would help her to dismiss the sex her body still craved.

The last thing she needed was a sexy male friend/colleague she couldn't look at without being assaulted by erotic memories, especially when, despite all of the fears he'd recognised in her, he'd also awoken some long-buried emotional vault she owed it to herself to explore.

'Good,' he said, sounding far from convinced as he scanned her expression.

'That's sorted then,' she replied, unable to break the eye contact that had somehow gone on way too long for people negotiating a mere friendship.

'Perfect,' Nash said, his gaze sliding to her lips, settling there, searching as if he were testing the credibility of her resolve.

Kat held her breath. He couldn't be. He'd just confirmed that he was happy with the rules. Except when his eyes met hers once more they carried the flare of heat she'd seen time and time again on Saturday night.

Was he going to kiss her again?

Her pulse flew. He was going to kiss her again.

Her bones started to melt, the taste of his lips already on hers as if they'd been kissing nonstop since their first time on her doorstep.

His pager bleeped. He scanned the screen and stood, his

expression clear, so that Kat wondered if she'd imagined the sexual tension. 'Hannah is back from her CT scan.'

Kat's endorphin high plummeted as he placed his mug in the dishwasher, seemingly unaffected by the past few seconds.

Kat nodded, dumbfounded by how quickly he could veer from heated looks that seemed to speak louder than actual words to work-focused and how easily led her body had proved.

'I'll…um speak to Paediatrics,' she said, her voice husky with arousal, 'see how long before we can get her admitted.'

Forget friends. Her body wanted to stride across the staffroom, tug the neck of his scrubs and finish what he'd started with his eyes moments ago.

Instead, she cleared her dry throat. 'Let me know when the lumbar puncture results come through.'

'Will do.'

He left the staffroom, where Kat tried to reassemble the pieces of her scattered wits, slipping easily back into old patterns of self-denial.

# CHAPTER TEN

THE FOLLOWING SATURDAY Grady knocked at the red front door where the six-year-old's party was being held, a big smile at the ready so he didn't display any of his uncertainties to Molly. He glanced down at his daughter, relieved to see her happy and so excited that she couldn't keep still.

Despite the positive signs, his stomach pinched with nerves. She looked adorable dressed as a princess, but he couldn't stave off the trepidation that he'd somehow messed up Molly's outfit.

After all, what did a six-foot-three ex-soldier like him know about princesses?

Not for the first time, he questioned that his efforts as a solo dad were enough for his daughter. He'd left the army before Molly was born, as soon as Carol had begun making noises about pursuing a new career in the airline industry. Sometimes he missed the camaraderie and varied work of his old career. Although at the time he'd consoled himself that Molly had needed stability and consistency.

He still feared that she might need a more dependable female influence, especially on days like today.

Interrupting his pity party that, through the choices he and Carol had made, they were letting down their beautiful girl, the front door swung open and the host mum appeared, surrounded by a parade of similarly dressed princesses all craning their necks to assess the new arrival.

'Hi,' Grady said to the woman, gripping Molly's hand tighter. 'This is Molly and I'm Nash Grady, her dad.'

He was so out of his depth that his palms were sweating.

Molly smiled sweetly and handed over their wrapped gift to another princess that Grady presumed was the birthday girl. Squeals of excitement ensued among the princesses.

To his utter relief, Lucy appeared, immediately taking Molly's free hand.

As if attuned to her presence, he glanced into the hallway, instantly spying Kat, who was looking down, manoeuvring her way out through the animated throng.

The sight of her triggered a cascade of testosterone in his blood. His heart jerked an erratic rhythm in his chest the way it had when he'd almost caved and kissed her in the staffroom after they'd both admitted that one time hadn't been enough.

He'd been so tempted to suggest another hook-up but he didn't want to hurt her the way she'd been hurt before, so instead they'd decided on friendship.

As if hearing his internal groan of frustration, Kat looked up. Their eyes met. Static buzzed in Grady's head, the chatter of children and words of the host fading.

Damn, she looked good, her face relaxed and her hair free of its practical work ponytail. She smiled, the hesitant but intimate smile he both loved and dreaded. He could be her friend. It made sense for both of them to avoid further complications.

Nope, sense was overrated. He just wanted to barge past the five and six-year-olds and kiss Kat again until he'd reminded her how good they'd been together.

Aware that he was staring, he looked away as Kat finally managed to exit the front door to join him on the doorstep.

'Have a fun time, okay?' he said to Molly, stooping to her level for a final check that she was a happy little princess.

She barely acknowledged her hovering father, clearly desperate to get inside and hurl herself into the party action. But just as she stepped over the threshold, side by side with Lucy, her tiara slipped from her head onto the ground.

Grady bent to retrieve it at the exact same moment as Kat. Their hands collided, hers a fraction of a second ahead of his.

'Oops, here you go,' she said, holding her prize out to Molly, who simply stood dutifully in front of Kat, her face regally upturned as if she wore a crown every day and was used to the attention of ladies-in-waiting.

Before he could step in and fix it—although he'd been the one responsible for precariously fitting the slippery apparel in the first place—Kat replaced the tiara on Molly's head, expertly fastening it in place with the stabby little side combs that had almost given Grady an aneurysm.

He exhaled a sigh of relief as the girls trotted inside, followed by an already slightly frazzled-looking host. He was overreacting. Molly looked like all the other little girls, the outfit he'd sweated over appropriate. She even appeared none the worse for having been dressed by a man who'd spent way too long on the internet researching tiaras versus crowns. He'd almost called Kat several times for dress-up advice.

That was the kind of things friends did, right?

The door closed, leaving them alone on the doorstep. He swallowed, recalling another doorstep, passionate kisses, a night he'd never wanted to end.

'Thanks,' he said, 'for fixing the tiara. It took me ages

to put it on. Clearly there's a knack I need to master.' And master it he would. He wouldn't have Molly feeling different because her mother was rarely in the picture.

'They fall off all the time.' Kat smiled, her tinkle of laughter boosting his confidence that, despite knowing his way around an assault rifle, he wasn't as terrible as he feared when it came to princess costumes.

'I'm sure they are going to have lots of fun,' Kat said, glancing back at the closed door.

'I hope so. She's so excited; she's been awake since six this morning,' Grady said, grateful that Lucy and Molly's friendship seemed unwavering. At first he'd wondered if Molly's obsession with Lucy would be a flash in the pan, but all he heard when she was at home was *Lucy does this* and *Lucy said that*.

'Lucy too.' Kat laughed as they walked back to the pavement together.

Did he imagine her checking him out?

His own thoughts were seriously un-platonic.

*Want to book into a motel for an hour and see if last Saturday was a fluke? How about an amendment to the former rule—just friends at work, lovers in our own time?*

At his car, which was parked on the street, Kat hesitated. 'Do you have plans...?' she said, all trace of the awkwardness from the other day gone. 'I was going to grab some coffee. There's a place nearby.' She pointed in the direction of the beach, which was a few streets' walk away.

'If by plans you mean going home to tackle the week's laundry, I'd love some coffee.'

With the exception of Molly, he couldn't think of anyone else he'd rather spend time with at the moment.

See, he could do friends.

They set off walking. The day was warm. Kat wore a

loose short-sleeved shirt, through which he spied distracting glimpses of bra, and cut-off denim shorts that made her backside and tanned legs look so amazing he almost walked into a lamppost.

'So, I've been thinking…' She glanced his way, her expressive eyes concealed by her sunglasses, her sensual mouth set in that determined line he'd come to recognise.

For the millionth time since their conversation in the staffroom he wondered why he hadn't just come out and told her that any time she needed to scratch an itch she could use him as much as she liked.

'Oh?' Insanely attracted to Kat, he'd been so wary of rushing into a fling after that spectacular night, hung up on past resentment that Carol hadn't really known him, otherwise she wouldn't have found him constantly lacking during their marriage, that he'd not only hammered home his message on keeping things casual, he'd also insisted on the *friends* thing. When all he really wanted was to put that satiated look on her face over and over again.

Kat snorted. 'You were right about getting to know each other so, in that spirit, I'd like to know something new about you every time we speak. What do you think?' She flicked a triumphant smile his way, shoving her sunglasses on top of her head.

That in this moment he'd quite happily be her plaything. Was it too late to ask if the rules he'd agreed to uphold were negotiable?

'It doesn't have to be personal,' she said, assuming he needed convincing. 'I'm just trying to redress the balance of what I know about…you…you know…physically.'

Man, she was adorable when she blushed.

The trouble was that his desire for her hadn't abated one little bit. If anything, it was growing stronger the more time they spent working together. Since they'd cleared the air, Kat had often sought him out with a work-related question, joking around with him the way she did with the other nurses. It was as if, slowly but surely, day by day, she was letting a little more of her guard slip.

He'd taken to leaving doors open every time they were alone to stop himself from suggesting they pick up where they'd left off the night of his birthday.

No, this was better. They had too much in common to ruin it with sex.

'So, what do you think?' she asked as they crossed the road.

Realising that she was waiting for an answer and that what he truly thought was in no way fit for admitting aloud, he cleared his throat. 'I think it's a great idea.'

'Good.' She nodded, looking pleased. 'It's obvious that our girls are determined to be best friends. So we're probably going to be seeing a lot more of each other outside of work.'

He smiled, held the door open and followed her into the café. He should have been more careful about his wishes. She was enough of a temptation at the hospital with people around and no hope of anything physical taking place. But spending more time outside of work, focused on getting to know each other... He'd need to invest in a straitjacket to keep his hands to himself.

They ordered drinks and sat outside, his rejuvenated libido imagining play dates between Molly and Lucy as an excuse to see Kat.

'Are you okay?' she asked. 'You seemed stressed earlier.'

Grady rubbed his hand over his chin and the days' worth of stubble there, nodding. 'I just had a dad/daughter freak-out about the party. I don't want Molly to feel different because her father doesn't know one end of a fairy wand from the other.'

'Oh, stop.' She narrowed her eyes with mock censure. 'You're a great dad and you know it.'

Her compliment shifted something inside his chest. Did he know that? He certainly tried his best to give Molly as good an upbringing as his single mother had given him, but most days he felt as if he was running around extinguishing fires armed only with a water pistol.

He sighed, lamenting how little he could rely on Carol for help. 'You have no idea how relieved I was to see all the other girls dressed similarly to Molly.'

'Didn't Carol help?' she asked, and he realised that this was what friends did. They chatted, confided, shared, just like he'd inadvertently forced Kat to open up about her trust issues.

Sighing, he shook his head. 'It's officially her weekend to have Molly, but I haven't heard from her.' Not unusual when his ex had a new man in her life or if work took her somewhere exotic for days on end.

'Does she do that a lot? Let you and Molly down?' Kat asked, frowning.

He shrugged in answer. 'I couldn't care less for myself. I love every minute I spend with Molly.' He parented alone just fine, as did Kat.

'But you love Molly enough that you want her to have a relationship with her mother.' Her eyes brimmed with understanding.

'Even when it sometimes means I'm literally giving her chance after chance to let Molly down. I know. I can't win.'

'Do you mind me asking what happened with you two to cause the divorce?' Her teeth scraped her bottom lip and Grady once more thought of her passionate kisses and the way she'd cast aside all of her barriers when they'd been intimate.

If only she showed that side of herself more often, but then he couldn't blame her for being cautious. He was himself after rushing into marriage, giving up his career, watching it all crumble.

He owed it to Molly, if to no one else, to keep his relationships casual.

'Carol and I were never right for each other,' he said, exhaling the tension this subject caused. If Kat could open up, he could too. 'We met while I was still an army medic. I think Carol hoped for an exciting life of overseas postings in exotic places, but we'd only known each other a few months when she fell pregnant.' He shrugged, an indulgent smile twitching his mouth at the memory of holding his newborn little girl for the first time, how he'd marvelled at her minuscule fingernails and the sooty length of her eyelashes.

'Failed birth control,' he clarified, although a part of him had suspected Carol had planned the *oops* to encourage a proposal, as it indeed had. Not that he was free from responsibility—it took two to make a baby and what an adorable one he and Carol had created together. Grady had been instantly and eternally smitten.

'So you proposed,' Kat said, a look of fascination in her eyes.

He shrugged just as the waitress appeared with their drinks. He took a grateful sip before continuing. 'Yeah. It felt like the right thing to do at the time. I was excited about becoming a dad. So we got married, I left the army and took a job at Gulf Harbour and Molly was born. For a while I felt as if I'd won the lottery. Then everything began turning sour.'

'In what way?' Kat asked, her sympathetic stare encouraging him to continue.

'I don't think Carol really wanted her single life to be changed by parenthood. Even before Molly was born she announced plans to retrain as a flight attendant. Nothing I did was good enough—I didn't earn enough money, or I worked too hard, or we never did anything exciting.'

He grimaced, surprised anew by the familiar taste of defeat that had been a constant during their marriage. 'I was raised by a single parent. My mother did her hardest to make sure I didn't feel disadvantaged, but I was determined that my child would have the best of everything, including two parents in a committed relationship. But that's not how it turned out.'

'I'm sorry that it didn't work out, but don't take all of the blame on yourself.'

Grady shrugged, his heart thudding faster when she seemed to see things about him it had taken years for him to see himself. 'I did blame myself for a while. But I don't think my ex really wanted me specifically, rather she wanted someone committed to her and I fit the bill. But where I was content to spend the weekends doing family stuff—walks in the park, fixing up the house, cooking—Carol became increasingly restless, always out for drinks or celebrating something with her new work friends, or planning girls' holidays with the staff discounted air tickets.'

Kat waited patiently, her barely touched coffee cooling in front of her.

'Once resentment sets into a marriage it's like rot,' he said. 'It spreads, and no amount of glue can hold it together. I didn't want our wonderful daughter to be that glue, so I suggested a trial separation in the hope that Carol would realise what she had and rush back to us with fresh perspective. But the opposite happened.'

He'd failed to create a happy family of his own. He'd let Molly down.

'Did she meet someone else?' Kat asked, her voice quiet, her eyes full of compassion.

He shrugged. 'She started dating a series of pilots as if Molly and I didn't exist. Rather than feel betrayed, I realised that I was happier without her, that just like she'd seen something in me that wasn't there—some macho tough-guy solider who would sweep her off her feet and provide a life of thrills with none of the mundane moments—I hadn't really known her either. I'd just rushed to do the right thing as I saw it by proposing.'

He shrugged again, taking a mouthful of coffee so he didn't say any more.

'You know,' she said, leaning forward so her elbows rested on the table, 'Molly is a lovely little girl. You should be very proud of her. You're doing a great job, and I can say that because I know how hard it is raising a child alone. She still has two parents and it's probably better for her to know you both happy on your own than together but full of resentment.' She held his stare, her understanding dissolving some of his worries for Molly.

Single parents faced extra challenges, but that didn't mean they weren't doing their best to be everything a child needed. Kat pursued her career, studied for her professional exams and made sure she was always there for Lucy.

Grady nodded, now almost desperate with curiosity about the man who had abandoned a woman like Kat. 'What about you? Tell me about Lucy's father.'

It was Kat's turn to shrug, to shift in her seat as if mildly uncomfortable. 'I think of him as a sperm donor actually, because being a father is what you do for Molly, not just donating genes.'

To try and banish the sadness in her eyes, Grady reached across the table and took her hand, squeezed her fingers. 'I'm sorry. You don't have to talk about it. Forget I asked.'

Kat shook her head, determination in her stare. She held his hand, silent communication passing between them so he felt her trust like a hesitant caress.

'It's okay. I met him on my OE,' she said about the overseas experience, a working holiday considered a rite of passage by most young New Zealanders. 'I was so full of optimism, a qualified doctor, living in London. I felt invincible.'

Grady smiled, imagining a younger Kat taking on the world.

'Stupidly, I fell in love, swept off my feet by a charmer, as it turned out.' She fiddled with her teaspoon, swirling it idly through the foam on her coffee, disrupting what was left of the barista's artwork. 'Lucy's father had that X-factor, you know, had this way of making you feel like you were the only person on the planet.' She huffed. 'And I fell for it...'

'I see.' He waited, his sympathy pulsing with each beat of his heart. Her pain made him want to book the first flight to London and hunt this guy down.

'He made all these promises,' she continued, 'all the things we'd do together, all the places we'd travel and the amazing life we'd have. I was working every minute that I didn't spend with him, surviving on little or no sleep. I must have inadvertently missed a couple of pills because, the next thing I knew, I was expecting Lucy.'

When she looked up the love he saw shining in her eyes almost stole his breath.

'He was a mistake, but my darling girl is a wonderful gift.'

Grady nodded in understanding. Their core values were so similar. How had he ever considered them opposites?

'I was so excited,' she said. 'I loved my career, but I also hoped to have a family one day. When I told Henry that I was having our baby, at first he was shocked but support-ive. Then, quite literally overnight, he changed, became distracted and less attentive. As the weeks went by, he was increasingly hard to pin down, avoiding my calls and mak-ing excuses for why he was too busy to see me.'

Her expression hardened. 'I'm not stupid. I heard the mes-sage. When I confronted him, told him that our baby was coming whether he wanted to face it or not, said we needed a grown-up conversation about becoming parents, he showed his true colours. He informed me that I was being irrespon-sible, selfish, that I'd made the decision to have our baby alone so I could raise it alone, and he left, just like that.'

Grady stiffened, stunned. 'I can't believe it.' He tried to hide the worst of his shock for Kat's sake.

She nodded, the humiliation in her eyes confirmation. 'He's never met Lucy, despite me leaving him my New Zea-land contact info before I left London.'

Grady stroked his thumb over the back of her hand, des-perate to hold her until the vulnerability in her voice faded.

'The worst part,' she said, glancing away, 'is that my mis-take…it affects other people, just like he said.'

Grady frowned, drawing her eyes back to his with a small tug on her hand. 'Who? Lucy? I hate that this guy let both of you down so casually, but she's better off without a fa-ther like that.'

Kat inhaled a shuddering breath. 'Not just her,' she whis-pered.

He waited, hoping that she'd tell him more so he could con-tradict the guilt she'd clearly heaped on her own shoulders.

'When I returned from the UK I moved back in with my parents. I don't think I'd have made it without them. I had a miserable pregnancy, complicated by pre-eclampsia and an emergency Caesarean section.'

Grady sighed. 'That's an awful lot to go through alone, Kat.'

She didn't acknowledge his comment, only gnawed at her lip and continued. 'To complicate matters, my father had a stroke shortly after Lucy was born. I'm glad I was there to help out with his rehabilitation, but I can't help but think the stress of having his single pregnant daughter back home, what with all of my complications, must have contributed to Dad's stroke.'

Words failed him. He shook his head automatically. 'You're being hard on yourself. It sounds like a terrible time for all of you. You can't take responsibility for everything.'

No wonder her ex's rejection had created deep-seated trust issues. Kat was intelligent and caring. She'd hate to think that a choice she'd made had impacted on others.

Kat peered up at him from beneath her lashes. 'I hate that he might have been right, that I was irresponsible.'

'By doing the right thing for you?' Grady asked. 'By being a great mother and an amazing doctor? He just didn't want to accept his share of the responsibility so he heaped it all on you and walked away.'

He hated that she looked uncertain.

'After that, I felt as if it took me the first two years of Lucy's life to recover, both physically and emotionally.' She shot him a tentative smile. 'And, of course, I was also trying to find a new job that would employ a frazzled single mother who often wasn't sure what day of the week it was.'

As if spent, she took a long swallow of coffee. 'Do you

think you'll ever give marriage another try?' she asked from behind her coffee cup.

Dazed from everything he'd learned about her, Grady frowned. 'I don't know, to be honest. Molly has been let down enough. You saw on the first day of school that she's old enough to understand people coming and going from her life.' The handful of casual dates he'd had since his divorce had been nothing special. Sex was one thing, but making another woman a part of his and Molly's lives, the potential for disruption and disaster... She would need to be an exceptional woman to warrant the risk.

Kat nodded in agreement, finally releasing his hand to place her cup carefully back on the saucer. 'That's why I've totally neglected that side of my life too.' She flushed.

Was she remembering their night? It was never far from his mind.

They finished their coffees, talk turning to easier topics: their girls, the school programme for the term, the upcoming swimming lessons. Baffled by what he'd learned, his attraction to Kat stronger than ever, he half participated in the conversation, half grappled with his shifting feelings.

He respected Kat, he wanted to obey her rules and be her friend, but she deserved so much more than she'd been dealt by Lucy's father. Any man would be lucky to have her. She was hard on herself when all she'd done was fall for the wrong man—his problem, not hers. Surely that justified one little bend of the rules?

'Thanks for suggesting coffee,' he said, pausing in the shade of a tree outside the café. 'I'm glad we had that talk.' Glad, but more conflicted than ever.

Kat looked up at him, her lips parted distractingly. 'You're welcome.'

His pulse pounded in his head. He didn't want to ruin

what they had, but nor could he seem to fight their chemistry. 'I know what my thing is,' he said, catching the way her breathing sped up.

It was still there, the pull, the mutual consciousness, the compatibility.

She frowned, her lips pursed in confusion.

'The new thing that you don't already know,' he added, hoping to fill her head with something other than the worthless ex who'd hurt her so badly she hadn't gone near another man for six years.

'Oh. What?' She looked as if she were holding her breath.

He stepped closer, couldn't help himself. 'I want you to know that if this were a date, which it isn't, because dating isn't a priority for either of us—'

Kat licked her lips, her pupils dilating as she gave an impatient nod.

'And if I'd chosen a better place for this conversation than this spot next to the bins…' He paused, his gaze tracing the curve of her mouth. 'I would very much want to break your rules and kiss you again right now.'

She swallowed, her shocked speechlessness lasting the entire walk back to the party.

# CHAPTER ELEVEN

BY THE FOLLOWING FRIDAY, after a busy week where she'd shared at least part of every shift with Nash, Kat knew quite the collection of new facts about him, admittedly none as thrilling or rebellious as his first admission. He'd once taken salsa classes, his party trick was juggling raw eggs and when he was seventeen he'd been a witness to a road accident, an event that had spurred his interest in medicine.

Only the most important thing she'd learned was that she hated her own rules with a vengeance. Kat was addicted, obsessed, convinced that the biggest mistake of her life was in fact insisting that their fling last only one night.

Apart from that single deviation, where he'd confessed that he wanted to kiss her again, Nash had frustratingly controlled his impulses, throwing Kat into a spin of conflicted emotions: one minute certain that friends was better, the next minute convinced his kiss was the only thing between her and insanity.

Leaving her latest patient and telling herself to get a grip and focus on her most pressing issue—that of childcare—Kat headed for the staff area in search of Nash.

She needed a favour and, to her surprise, he'd been her first choice of rescuer. Refusing to analyse at what point she'd progressed from thinking the worst of him to relying on him to help her out of a tricky school pick-up dilemma, Kat pulled her phone from her pocket and sent him a quick text.

Her heart thumped as she recognised just how much more she'd come to trust him since the night of his birthday when she'd trusted him with her body. But seeing his human struggles with solo parenting and hearing how he couldn't rely on his ex, how he'd been disregarded and betrayed, Kat felt more connected to him than ever, a state that was both exhausting and exhilarating.

While she awaited his reply, she typed up her observations on her current patient—a twenty-seven-year-old primip—a woman pregnant for the first time—with signs of pre-eclampsia. Henry had done such a good job of convincing Kat that there'd been something wrong with her for wanting Lucy she had to fight the urge to overanalyse if her plea for help was emotional dependence on Nash. But of course she wasn't reliant on him. They were friends and aside from her parents, who already did so much for Kat, it felt good to know she could ask him for help, that Nash would never let her down if it was in his power to assist.

As if sensing him nearby, the hairs on her arms prickled to attention.

'Yes, I can collect Lucy from school,' he said from right behind her, his voice low so no one else would hear. 'No problem at all.'

Instantly breathless, Kat spun around and smiled, her relief and gratitude all tangled up with lust. He was dressed in his own clothes, his blue shirt one of her favourites and his worn jeans moulded to his muscular legs and butt in all the right places. Oh, how she wished she could leave with him, suggest they take the girls to the beach for a stroll, watch them frolic in the waves, grab ice-creams and kiss on the sand...

Whoa, talk about taking a fantasy too far.

'Are you sure?' she asked. 'Because of course I'd planned to be out of here in time. This is a one-off request.' She'd do the same thing for him in a heartbeat, of course, but probably because Henry had criticised her choice, called her selfish, she was hesitant to rely too heavily on others.

He nodded, his eyes flicking over her face, settling briefly on her mouth. 'Positive.'

Kat exhaled a shaky breath, ignoring this lingering look the way she'd ignored all of the others this week. Even if he intended to make good on his admission and kiss her again, even if she was ready to turn their one night into a fling, there had been no opportunity. Their schedules were insane. One or other or both of them were either at work or after hours had commitments to their girls.

'Thanks, Nash.' His proximity was dangerous, as if the rest of the department, the patients and staff might disappear at any second. 'My…um…patient is twenty-six weeks pregnant and has pre-eclampsia. She needs to be admitted, but I won't be very long.' Even though her shift had ended fifteen minutes ago, medical staff often wanted to see a case through to admission.

His eyes softened, showing her that he understood that some cases were more personal than others, especially since she'd shared her own medical history with him.

'Kat, don't stress. You focus on your case, and I'll take the girls back to my house and give them a snack. You can swing by on your way home to pick Lucy up. Okay? Just call the school and explain.'

'I will. You are a lifesaver.'

*In more ways than one.*

Sometimes she couldn't shake the feeling that he'd brought her back to life, although the emotionally guarded and intimacy-starved woman he'd first met would have sworn there was nothing lacking in her life.

But to Kat, Nash's helpful gesture was a big deal. In the few weeks she'd known him, he'd shown Lucy more attention and kindness than her biological father ever had. Henry and Nash were as different as night and day. Nash praised her parenting, the compliment worth more coming from someone so dedicated to his own daughter, where Henry had seen her choice as selfish and reckless. His accusations wouldn't have carried half the weight if her pregnancy had been smoother, or if the timing of her father's debilitating stroke hadn't added to her guilt.

Forcing her thoughts back to her patient, she first called the on-call obstetrician to refer the woman and then the school, informing them that today Lucy was being collected by Nash. Such a momentous leap of faith gave her momentary jitters. She'd never thought she'd count on another man after Henry, but he was Lucy's father and she wouldn't trust him as far as she could throw him, let alone allow him to care for her precious girl.

The degree of faith she had in Nash was unprecedented, the comparisons between her worthless ex and the man showing her that some men could be relied upon feeding her growing feelings towards Nash.

Perhaps if she could trust him with her daughter she could trust herself to sleep with him again, to give her terrifying feelings a physical outlet, and trust him when he said that he wouldn't hurt her. Was she strong enough to share the kind of physical intimacy she knew him capable of and keep her heart out of harm's way?

An hour later as she drove to Nash's house from the hospital, her stomach flutters doubling with each passing minute, she tried to contain her excitement. Following the directions Nash had sent, she parked outside his neat weatherboard villa, her hands literally trembling. His front garden was well-maintained, and she spied a trampoline over the fence at the side of the house, the very thing Lucy wanted for Christmas. Kat would struggle to ignore her daughter's pleas now that Molly had the very thing Lucy coveted.

When Nash opened the door, his body language relaxed and his feet bare, Kat's mouth dried to ash. Why did she find his chill, everyday charm so sexy when it had been the first thing about him she'd also found annoying? But caring for the girls, reliable and trustworthy, and don't forget his skills between the sheets. Kat had to bite her lip to stop herself from dragging him close for a kiss right there and then.

'Hi,' she croaked feebly, her body practically melting into a puddle on his doorstep.

'Come in. They're on the trampoline,' he said, his easy yet somehow also knowing smile encouraging her pulse rate to triple.

'Of course they are.' She laughed in defeat. 'You do realise that I'll be tormented between now and December—a trampoline is the only thing on Lucy's Christmas list.'

'In that case,' he said, leading her through the house until they came to a sunny living area, 'we can let them enjoy it for a while longer. Would you like a drink?'

'Sure,' Kat said as they headed for the kitchen. 'Tea would be great.'

The sliding doors were open and Kat ducked out onto the deck to wave hello at Lucy and Molly. Her daughter, too busy bouncing, barely registered her mother's presence.

'There you go,' Nash said, placing a mug of tea on the bench in front of her, his gaze sliding up her body to her eyes in a slow and obvious perusal that left Kat doubting the wisdom of entering his home.

Their eyes met. All pretence seemed to slip away. All that remained were two people ridiculously attracted to one another who'd agreed to be just friends.

Giddy and breathless, Kat looked away first. 'Thanks,' she said, pulling out a bar stool and taking a perch. Even with their daughters a few metres away, when there was absolutely no chance of anything physical happening between them, he was tempting enough that she required the physical barrier of the kitchen island to stop herself from taking that kiss she hadn't been able to stop thinking about since he'd casually mentioned it.

She took a scalding sip of tea, desperate to do something, anything, with her mouth other than snog him or tell him about her fling idea.

'I'll give you fair warning,' Nash said, resting his forearms on the bench in a way that meant she could lean forward for that kiss, meet him halfway, 'they're planning to beg for a sleepover. I heard them plotting. Who knew five-year-olds could be so devious?'

'We did,' Kat said, laughing to hide her own request for a sleepover in Nash's bed. If only it was that simple...

'Lucy's never had a sleepover with a friend,' Kat said, trying to keep his eye contact instead of staring at the way his mouth moved.

'Neither has Molly. I think they're a bit too young, but they've clearly heard of the concept at school.'

'I agree. I'd worry that she'd change her mind in the middle of the night and wake you up.' Kat swallowed the lump in her throat, in awe of how wonderful a father Nash was.

Because Kat was close with her own father, she knew that Molly was a very lucky little girl. Poor Lucy would never know that kind of male role model bond.

'If you have tomorrow off,' Nash said, looking at her with

that intense focus again, 'I wondered if you'd like to come with us to the aquarium. I promised I'd take Molly—she's obsessed with the penguins.'

Kat eyed him as he slowly stepped around the end of the kitchen island, her tea forgotten.

'That sounds good.' Her voice croaked. Her temperature soared at the thought of spending all day with Nash away from work, even with the girls as a barrier. Perhaps she could hurl herself into the water with the fish to cool down.

'Although…' she said, trying not to moan at the clean manly scent of him.

He frowned. 'Although…?'

Kat hesitated, her stare searching his. She was out of her comfort zone when it came to being open and vulnerable with a man she found so addictive. But Nash wouldn't judge her for her caution. He shared her reservations about bringing a new person into Molly's life.

'Do you think it might confuse them?' she said, longing gripping her throat while the old protective urges knotted her stomach. 'Us spending time together, I mean.'

She and Nash being friends along with their daughters was one thing, but they had to take care not to act like one big happy family.

She blinked away the vision, blocking out the dying excitement she saw in Nash's eyes.

She couldn't allow her libido to drive the bus unsupervised. Nash was a great guy, but relationships were tricky and time-consuming. That was why she had rules. Nash must have faults; everyone did. He was divorced, so obviously lacked something as a husband, even if he and his ex had been mutually responsible for the marital breakdown.

Kat glanced into the garden to stop herself from imagining Nash as a husband. The girls were still laughing on the trampoline.

'I think we're responsible parents, both wary of hurtful attachments,' he said, his voice calm and reassuring as he pulled out the stool next to hers. 'I understand your concerns, for Lucy and for yourself.' His expression brimmed full of compassion.

He saw through her thinly veiled attempt at keeping distance for her own sake too. If he could tell what she was thinking, did he also know how much she wanted him still?

She nodded, too turned-on and emotionally conflicted to speak.

'You're worried that if we spend too much time together Lucy might become attached to me, mistake me for a father figure?' Nash tilted his head in that way he had when he was listening to a patient. 'I have the same concerns for Molly. I've seen the way she relates to you.'

Kat felt see-through, as if she were made of glass. She certainly felt as fragile. This thing with Nash was dangerous. It reminded her how it felt to be emotionally vulnerable, to risk rejection, not just for herself but also for Lucy, who was old enough to grow attached to any man in Kat's life, but especially this man, as the wonderful father of her best friend.

They needed to tread so carefully.

'I'm probably being overprotective,' she said, trying to stave off stupid tears, because Lucy would be as lucky as Molly to have a father figure like Nash. Even the idea of it made her stomach twist. It was best not to think about such an impossible and risky scenario.

'If you are, I am too,' Nash said in his reasonable way. 'Look, if you think the aquarium is a good idea we'll just tell them the truth, that we're friends who work together.'

'Good idea.' Kat nodded, captive to the way he looked at her.

She should feel relieved that he was mature and responsible enough to consider her and Lucy's feelings as well as his own and Molly's. Instead, she wanted to selfishly hurl herself at him, to kiss him the way she had on her doorstep that night, regardless of the consequences. To remind him that friends didn't know how to pleasure each other's bodies to the point of exhaustion, didn't look at each other as if they were seconds from doing it all over again.

Only they had become friends, something she valued as much as him ending her sexual drought.

'Thanks for bailing me out today,' she said as he took a seat, his knee bumping her thigh.

'Stop thanking me. I'm certain you'll be able to repay the favour some time. It's no big deal.'

'It's a big deal for me.' Her voice emerged as a choked whisper.

Their eyes met. As if he knew her thoughts, as if he could read every one of her insecurities and doubts, Nash placed his hand on hers where it rested on the bench top. 'You don't have to do everything alone, Kat. Just because we chose to be parents, it's okay to ask for help. If I can be the one to help you, I will.'

She nodded, overcome by his touch, his thoughtfulness, his steadfast presence. She turned her hand over until their palms connected, fingers entwined, tiny jolts of electricity zapping along her nerves, his stare dancing between her eyes and her mouth. Her entire body shuddered.

Oh, please let him be about to kiss her...

'Are you ready for today's Nash fact?' he asked, his thumb tracing a lazy circle in the centre of her palm, flooding her blood with hormones so she was seconds away from ripping his shirt off.

She laughed, nodded, deaf to the sounds of their daughters playing in the garden. Immune to the fears and guilt that had held her back for six lonely years.

Desire this strong was too hard to fight.

He smiled, a slowly stretching upward curve of his tantalising lips that Kat watched with almost obsessive concentration.

As if he was thinking about how their kisses had tasted, he licked his lips. 'I like that you call me Nash when everyone else calls me Grady.'

'It's your name.' Kat's voice was the pathetic feeble whisper of a woman so turned-on that she might actually combust.

'It is, but it feels intimate when you say it. My favourite time was when I was inside you and you moaned it against my shoulder.'

'Nash...' Kat's eyes rolled closed. His words, his reminders, the feel of her hand in his—it was all too much.

She wanted him ten times more than she'd wanted him the night of his birthday. She deserved something casual and fun with a man she could trust in the bedroom but, like her, had no interest in commitment. As long as she was careful to keep her feelings out of it and hide it from Lucy, it was perfect.

He took her face in both of his hands. She opened her eyes.

'I can't stop wanting you,' he said, his stare locked with hers.

She nodded her agreement, too spellbound for speech.

'I know I'm breaking the rules.' His fingers tunnelled into her hair. 'If you want me to stop, I will.'

Her hands found his hips and she leaned closer. 'Kiss me.'

His lips grazed hers in a tease, one brush, two. Then he sealed their mouths together.

The breath stuttered out of Kat's lungs as she kissed him back, her fingers finding the belt loops of his jeans so she could pull him between her legs. He groaned as she parted her lips, his tongue sliding against hers, his hands tilting her head for better access.

Kat allowed desire to take her, the usual doubts silenced. All that remained was Nash, his kiss making her feel cherished and wanted and strong, his arms there to catch her if she slid from the stool, his passion the reward she'd craved since she'd watched him walk away the night they'd slept together.

He pulled back, breathing hard and looking down into her eyes with such intensity he almost looked angry or confused, but then he was kissing a path along her jaw and down her neck, his hand under her top caressing her breast.

Kat had a fleeting thought that she should stop, but instead she exposed her neck to his mouth, her own hands exploring the warm smooth skin of his back under his T-shirt. His muscles bunched and flexed under her palms and she recalled the way he'd scooped one strong arm around her and rolled them when they'd been naked and tangled in her sheets.

As if he was recalling the exact same memory, Nash's thumb worked over her nipple, coaxing the sensitive peak to harden as he watched her reaction through hooded eyes.

'Dad, there's a butterfly in the garden,' Molly yelled from outside.

Kat and Nash were dragged to their senses.

They sprang apart as a thunder of footsteps echoed across the wooden deck. By the time the girls came hurtling into the kitchen, Kat and Nash were once more on either side of the island, their clothes righted but their breaths still coming in pants.

Willing her frantic heart to settle, Kat stood and turned to face her daughter, praying like crazy that she didn't look as guilty and caught-out as Nash.

Lucy's excited chatter about monarch butterflies and the wonders of trampolining sharpened Kat's guilt for behaving so recklessly. What had she been thinking? How would she have explained that to Lucy if they'd been discovered necking and feeling each other up? Nash's *friends who work together* description certainly wouldn't have convinced her beady-eyed five-year-old.

'Can Lucy stay for a sleepover, Dad? Can she, please?' Molly drew out the last word for at least five seconds so show her commitment to pleading.

Kat shot Nash a grateful look, relieved to see humour and residual desire in his eyes. When it came to parenting, forewarned was definitely forearmed.

'Um…not tonight,' he said. 'But why don't you invite Lucy to come to the aquarium tomorrow instead?'

Molly didn't bother to issue the invitation. The girls just squealed and bounced up and down, as if it was all settled.

'If that's okay with Lucy's mum, of course,' Nash said, looking at her in their private, grown-up way.

Kat gave a shaky exhale, her mind stuck on playing mummies and daddies with him rather than on organising a play date.

Reaching for her bag, she clutched it to her chest. The last thing she needed was to spend the day with temptation personified under the watchful gaze of two impressionable young minds. But who knew when she and Nash would next have a weekend off together? Disappointing Lucy also meant disappointing herself.

'I think that sounds like fun,' she said, wondering how on earth she would keep her hands off Nash while imagining all the things they could do if they ever had another chance to be alone...

Nope, *fun* was the wrong word for that kind of torture.

# CHAPTER TWELVE

GRADY POPPED THE boot of his car and reached inside for Lucy's backpack while Kat freed her daughter from her car seat. Waving a cheerful goodbye to Molly, Lucy ran ahead into the house. Kat placed the booster seat back into her own vehicle.

He'd argued that they had to virtually pass Kat's place to travel to the aquarium, but really he'd just wanted to spend the extra twenty minutes with her in his passenger seat so they could share secret glances and stolen smiles throughout the too short journey. He'd lost count of the number of times he'd almost reached for her hand while driving, and the number of times she'd grinned and winked as if she knew exactly what he was thinking.

Except she'd probably be shocked by how badly he wanted her still and how hard he'd fought to keep his hands off her all day.

Kat met him at the back of his car, taking Lucy's backpack, which she clutched to her chest like a shield. 'Thanks for a lovely day. Hopefully we've worn them out and we'll be able to bring forward bedtime tonight.'

Their eyes met, all kinds of grown-up communication passing between them, none of which could be voiced in front of their girls. He knew she wanted to touch him, saw it in the way she shifted her weight from foot to foot, her eyes darting to the back of the car every few seconds.

'You're welcome.' Grady smiled, his body wound tight like a spring because he too wanted nothing more than to haul her into his arms and kiss her goodbye. He wouldn't change a thing about today apart from this moment, wishing he and Kat could climb inside a bubble of invisibility for a few stolen seconds.

Not that it would be enough. He'd want Kat to come over once Molly was asleep, to share a glass of wine or a beer with her out on the deck, watching the sunset, to hear her dreams and her laughter and know that he was responsible for the beautiful smile on her face.

'Thanks for joining us,' he said, prolonging the moment.

'You're welcome,' she replied, playing along.

He stepped closer, checking that they weren't being observed over the top of the still-open boot. 'I wondered if you're free tomorrow,' he asked, subtly reaching out to tangle his fingers with hers at her hip. 'I want to take you on a date, just the two of us.'

Her pupils dilated. He tugged her hand, bringing her closer still, his reward a wave of her scent.

'Oh…what did you have in mind?' She looked up at him, playfulness and excitement in her eyes.

Being unable to touch her when he wanted, sneaking around behind their daughters' backs was torture. But he loved that he could put that relaxed and dreamy look on her face, that he could take away her wariness, that she'd seemed carefree all day in his company.

He shrugged in answer, his grin wide. 'Anywhere you like.' As long as they were alone, holding hands, free to touch while getting to know more and more about each other.

'We could see a movie,' he suggested, 'or take a walk

on the beach. Coffee? Molly's spending the day with her grandparents so whatever works best for you.' He wanted to hog her to himself all day, but he understood the pressures of organising childcare.

She nodded, that now familiar longing in her eyes. 'Okay, I'll see what I can do. How about brunch?' Her stare dipped to his mouth.

He was going to have to kiss her, otherwise he'd regret it for the rest of the day and all of the night until he saw her again tomorrow.

'Sounds good.' Bolder now because Molly was engrossed in a book, his free hand settled on her hip so he could draw her lower body flush with his. 'I'll book somewhere.'

She licked her lips, distractingly beautiful, and slowly shook her head. 'Let me organise something.' She lowered the backpack and placed her other palm flat on his chest, over his galloping heart.

Kat glanced down the empty driveway for Lucy, but they were as alone as they could be.

'Great minds think alike,' he said, scooping his arms around her waist and hauling her up to his kiss.

The thud of the backpack hitting the driveway made him smile. Kat speared her fingers through his hair, her body languid in his arms. He caressed her mouth with his, their lips moulded together as if carved from the same piece of marble. He sighed, his breath mingling with hers as she parted her lips, their tongues touching, teasing, tangling, a goodbye kiss he hoped ended all goodbye kisses.

His groin tightened and he spared a fleeting thought for Kat's neighbours. If he didn't stop soon, they might get more of a show than he'd anticipated.

Why was it so hard to resist Kat Collins, and how could

he slow down the train, because it felt as if there was grease on the tracks?

'You are so sexy,' he murmured against her lips. 'I couldn't tell you what the penguins looked like because I was watching you the whole day, wondering how long I'd have to wait to do this.'

He kissed her again, enjoying the feel of her hands gripping his biceps and her breasts crushed to his chest as she exhaled a soft whimper that made him almost forget that he had parental responsibilities.

But their daughters were the number one priority for each of them. That didn't mean he wasn't already looking forward to tomorrow.

She pulled away. 'Right,' she said, tugging down the hem of her T-shirt. 'Enough of that.'

A pink glow suffused her face and neck and she was breathing hard. Grady's feet were like concrete as he tried to catch his own breath. It was going to be so hard to walk away. But no matter how much they wanted each other, the girls came first.

'I'll see you tomorrow.' She retrieved the backpack and stepped back out of arm's reach, her expression stern, as if willing him not to follow. 'Brunch—it's a date.'

'Text me when and where and I'll be there.' Grady grinned, already keen to get home and fall asleep so he could wake up in the morning.

'I'll pick you up,' she said, laughing and backing up towards her front door.

The last thing he saw before she disappeared inside was her excited eyes and seductive smile, full of promise.

How was he so lucky to have met a woman like Kat? The more he got to know her, the more there was to like. She was warm and compassionate and had a great sense of humour. He could tell her anything.

He drove home, half his attention on Molly's chatter about penguins and Lucy and Kat and the other half on the woman who was now barely recognisable compared to the Kat he'd first met. She was so much more open than the prickly perfectionist of her first shift at Gulf Harbour. That she'd started to trust him, coming to him for advice at work and even asking for his help with Lucy, made him want to always be there for her, to never let her down.

He gripped the wheel, aware that he hadn't thought about the future in relation to a woman since Carol. Was he becoming serious about Kat and, if so, how would that even work?

They saw each other almost every day at work, spent a lot of time together at the hospital. Could they also have a personal relationship without taking each other for granted, allowing resentment to grow because they'd spent too much time in each other's company? He had enough grief from the upheaval Carol still caused. And he owed it to Molly to provide a stable home life.

'Dad, can we see Lucy and Kat tomorrow?' Molly said, dragging Grady from his ruminations. 'They can come to Nana and Granddad's house with me.'

Grady's stomach sank a little at the perfect timing of his daughter's request. Was Molly already becoming attached to Kat, as they feared? What if he made space in his life for a relationship with Kat and it didn't work out and Molly was hurt again? Kat's longest relationship had been with Lucy's father, before it turned sour, and he was a divorcee. Relationships ended. He wouldn't risk Molly being abandoned by another woman in her life because he'd rushed into something that wasn't right.

'Not tomorrow, gorgeous. Nana and Granddad want to have you all to themselves.' And, besides, he had his own plans for Kat, plans that he'd have to ensure included keeping things between them light and easy, proceeding with caution, controlling how much time Molly spent with Kat for as long as it lasted.

A hollowness settled in his gut. They'd barely started and he was already seeing their demise. Now he was the one being overprotective. Kat had been adamant that she wasn't interested in anything long-term.

He drove the rest of the way home, his buoyant mood dampened, and he couldn't for the life of him figure out why.

At eleven precisely the next morning Kat knocked at Nash's door, her stomach a riot of nervous anticipation. She was so worked-up she couldn't imagine eating one mouthful of the delicious brunch she'd prepared.

Just as well she had other plans for Nash.

After a minute or so he opened the door, his smile wide, his eyes sparking with the same excitement, making her hands tremble.

She swept her gaze over him, appreciation warming her blood. He was casually dressed for their date, the ends of his hair still damp from a shower.

'Hi,' he said, opening the door wider and inviting her inside.

'I brought brunch.' Kat presented the platter of bagels and various DIY toppings his way and stepped over the threshold, the idea of having him all to herself forcing her pulse so high she might actually pass out.

'Has Molly been picked up?' she asked as she followed him to the kitchen.

'Um...yeah, an hour ago. My parents are taking her for

the day.' Nash looked confused as Kat took the platter from him, placed it in his fridge and slipped off her cardigan.

'Well, I only have a couple of hours,' she said, edging closer, slipping her hands around his waist, her intent obvious. 'My parents can only have Lucy for the morning.'

She tilted her face up to his, desperate to kiss him again after the torture she'd had to endure all day yesterday. 'Kiss me,' she said, looping her arms around his neck to bring his mouth down to cover hers.

He obliged with that sexy smile of his, catching on to her plan to skip the outing, backing her up against the kitchen bench so he could thoroughly ravage her mouth.

Kat moaned, loud and long. This kiss was the one she'd kept inside since that evening they'd been interrupted by the girls. Kat had fantasised about a different ending, her wild imagination spiralling out of control until she'd almost snogged him in the penguin enclosure.

Now, free from little prying eyes, her hands roamed his taut body, the muscles of his back, his broad shoulders and corded arms.

She'd spent hours getting ready to see him today, lathering her body in her favourite body lotion after her shower, wearing the only sexy underwear she owned, dressing for him in the blouse he'd once complimented her on.

Kat slipped off her shoes and hopped up on his bench, tugging him between her spread legs. She pushed his T-shirt up, broke free for a second from his lips so she could raise the garment from over his head, but then their mouths connected once more and Kat collapsed forward into his arms.

She was so turned-on she'd probably agree to kitchen sex, uncaring if his neighbours had a bird's eye view. Aware of the seconds passing, Kat reached for the button of his jeans.

'Whoa…wait,' Nash said, clasping her wrists. 'I wanted to take you on a proper date.'

'I appreciate that, but time is precious.' And she didn't want to waste one second by leaving the house. 'Yesterday was torture, not being able to touch you, to do this.' Her hands tangled in his hair and she kissed a path down his neck.

'You don't play fair,' he groaned, his hands flexing on her hips. Then, with a grunt of defeat that made her heart sing, he scooped her up into his arms and strode towards his bedroom.

The rest of their clothes came off in record time, to Kat's utter relief. They stumbled onto the bed, collapsing in a tangle of arms and legs, moans and giggles until Nash ended up on top.

He looked down, pushed her hair back from her face with both hands and stared deep into her eyes, slowing the pace.

'You are so beautiful. I haven't been able to stop thinking about you, about this, since the night of my birthday. You're always in my head. All of the time.' He pressed a chaste kiss to her lips, cupping her face with such tenderness her vision blurred.

Nash was the whole package and she didn't want to think about how dangerous that made him. She didn't want to think at all.

'You're in my head too,' Kat whispered, her heart thumping against his warm wide chest. She pressed her lips together in case she said more—that she'd imagined them being a couple, eventually moving in together, those fantasies so tangible she'd had to shut them down and remind herself what had happened the last time she'd been invincible and reached for the stars.

To focus on the pleasure to be had in his arms alone, she

spread her thighs, welcoming him into the cradle of her hips, crying out when he took one nipple inside his mouth, laving the peak with slow flicks of his tongue.

She could allow this physical indulgence, but more than that terrified her. How could they navigate a relationship when they could barely touch each other without serious implications? How would he and Molly fit into her already full life? Nash also had an ex-wife to deal with. There were so many variables. He'd been adamant that he wasn't looking for anything serious. She'd be a fool to ruin such a good thing with feelings.

'How are we going to do this again?' she asked in between gasps of delight as he teased first one breast and then the other. 'I already know that I'll want you tomorrow and the day after.' And she needed the next time to look forward to before this time was even over.

But Kat was an obsessive scheduler, the only way she could juggle everything successfully, so she knew for certain how precious and rare her free time was. It seemed impossible, the cruellest form of deprivation. They spent so much time together, but never alone.

'We'll figure something out,' Nash said, kissing a path back up to her mouth, his confidence and the intense look in his eyes appeasing her for now.

'Nash…' she pleaded, stroking her nails up and down his back because she'd learned that it made his hips flex as if involuntarily and his eyes darken with desire.

Was she imagining that she saw something more there? Was her own longing clouding her judgement, the way it had been way off before, with Henry? How could a grown woman be so wrong about a relationship? She was older and wiser now, knew what she wanted physically. But emotionally? She'd spent so many years shutting down those needs, focused instead on the needs of her daughter, that she still couldn't trust her feelings.

When Nash reached over to the night stand for a condom Kat almost fled, so deep was the emotional chasm at her feet. But then he was back on top of her, his strength surrounding her and his eyes communicating his wants and desires as he pushed his way inside her.

For the longest time he stilled, the only movement the matching beats of their hearts, chest-to-chest, stare-to-stare. Kat held her breath, her eyes swimming out of focus as she held him tight and tried her hardest to just be in the moment, that perfect moment.

But she'd always struggled to separate physical and emotional intimacy. That was why she'd waited so long before selecting a new sexual partner. She couldn't help the feelings she had for this man, who'd shown her that she was worthy of care and attention, who welcomed her daughter too, treating her the same as his own when they spent time together.

As if he saw her doubts and dreams in her eyes, Nash tilted his head, his intense stare softening.

'Kat...' He stroked her hair away from her face and brushed the softest whisper of a kiss on her lips. 'It's okay. We'll figure it out together.'

Kat nodded. She had no idea what *it* was. He could have still been talking about how to solve their privacy issue, to ring-fence some alone time for the intimate moments neither of them seemed able to resist. But Kat heard more than that. Right or wrong, she trusted this man, a decent man. He'd once told her he had no interest in hurting her and she believed him. Whatever the outcome of their relationship, she knew they had the same priority: their daughters. She would trust the rest to fate.

Dragging her mind back to pleasure, Nash moved inside

her, finding a rhythm that left them both gasping, clinging to each other as if this might be the last time. The tempo built and built until the frenzy of their coupling reached fever-point and they climaxed together, their cries mingling.

After, Kat lay in his arms, her face pressed to the comfort of his heartbeat, where his chest hair tickled her cheek. His fingers traced long strokes down her arm and back as their breathing slowed and their sweat cooled.

'Are you okay?' he asked, pressing his lips to the top of her head.

She nodded, so many conflicting wants clamouring inside her that there didn't seem to be any space for air. Physically, she was more than okay, but meeting Nash, becoming his lover, it had shown the gaping holes in her life, holes she'd ignored and neglected for far too long.

How many moments of contentment had she missed out on over the years because she'd abandoned her search for this intimate closeness? Not that what she had with Nash was commonplace, of that she was certain.

'I'm just happy,' she said, holding Nash tighter, as if afraid to let him go. Because the type of connection they shared was rare. Something to be cherished, for as long as it lasted. Something to always remember. Something she was so lucky to have found.

'Me too.' His arms held her a little closer and Kat sighed, content for now, but still thinking of the dreams she'd had as an optimistic younger woman, dreams of finding a soul mate, getting married, having a family.

'How much time do you have?' he asked, rolling her on top of him so her hair fell around her face in a tumble.

Kat's gaze flicked to his alarm clock for the time, although she knew exactly how many more minutes she had him all to herself, as if the countdown ticked aloud in her head. 'An hour.'

He nodded, his stare unreadable. 'I start night shifts this week. Do you have a day off?'

Kat swallowed her sigh. 'Wednesday.' That felt like a year away.

'Want to meet for *brunch* after school drop-off?' he asked with that sexy smile that she'd travel miles to see. Already he was growing hard again between her legs. Would there ever be enough hours in the day to quench this craving for his touch, his kisses, the way he looked at her and made her feel as if she was the only woman in the world?

'Absolutely,' she said, leaning forward to brush her lips over his. 'But won't you need to sleep?'

The idea of him coming over while the girls were at school filled her stomach with flutters, but she didn't want to wear him out.

'I'd happily sacrifice sleep to be with you.' He stroked her hair back and brought her mouth down to his, his hips jerking up from the bed.

The second time was less frantic, but as Kat crested another climax she knew without a shadow of doubt that she was totally addicted to Nash Grady, and couldn't escape the alarming feeling that it was like trying to hold water in your bare hands.

# CHAPTER THIRTEEN

THE PRINTER SPEWED out the prescription and Kat added her signature, her thoughts lost in a delicious daydream of Nash. Due to his stint of night shifts, she hadn't seen him at work or at school since the weekend when they'd stolen a few hours together, her brunch abandoned in the fridge while they'd gorged their fill of each other instead.

The days felt like years.

But tomorrow was Wednesday, her day off. Her stomach somersaulted in anticipation. They had another *brunch* date, if you could call spending as long as possible in bed before they had to collect Lucy and Molly from school a date.

Kat smiled to herself, already planning what she would wear under her jeans and T-shirt. If he was going to strip her, to marvel at her body as if he was unwrapping a gift, she wanted to wow him.

Something brushed her exposed neck, a soft almost incidental glide of fingertips under her hairline. She turned, her shock morphing into delight as she took in Nash standing behind her.

'What are you doing here?' she asked, glancing around the staff area to check that they were alone. They weren't doing anything wrong by seeing each other, but they hadn't discussed going public as an official couple and Kat liked that their relationship felt like a decadent secret only they knew.

'I just called in to resolve some work matters,' Nash said, his manner a little distant. 'Do you have a second?'

Dispirited that he seemed distracted, Kat nodded.

'Good. We can talk in my office.' His walk was businesslike. Kat followed him into the tiny room he only used when conducting a meeting or if he needed to reprimand one of the nursing staff.

Her pulse accelerated as he closed the door, her confusion turning to a shudder of relief when he pressed her up against the wood and kissed the living daylights out of her. Kat responded, kissing him back with pent-up desperation, her guilt at behaving inappropriately at work heavily outweighed by her constant need for Nash.

The old adage was true; absence did make the heart grow fonder or, in the case of Kat's heart, grow more and more terrified that she was becoming so dependent on him for her happiness that she'd started to see a future, hear wedding bells, imagine another baby with Nash's dark colouring and her big eyes.

Eventually and way too soon for Kat's liking, he pulled away, rested his forehead against hers while they both caught their breath.

'I missed you,' he said, his eyes closed, his heart still thundering under her palm.

He'd called into the department when he should be asleep, just to kiss her.

'I missed you too. I can't wait for tomorrow.' She swallowed hard, forcing down the feelings that were becoming impossible to ignore. But a few snatched minutes in their work environment wasn't the time or the place to ask him how he felt about her and confess that she wouldn't be averse to them having a proper relationship.

His phone pinged and he pulled it from his pocket, his face slashed in a harsh frown as he read the screen.

Kat's stomach swooped, anticipating the blow. 'What's wrong?'

For a minute he didn't answer, only straightened, moved away, muttering under his breath so she knew it was bad news.

'Is it serious?' she asked, imagining every possible scenario.

He shook his head. 'I don't know. I hope not.' When he looked up from his phone, his stare was bleak with worry. 'Carol,' was all he said. He rubbed a hand over his tired face.

Kat wanted to go to him, to hold him, but he still hadn't fully explained. 'Is Molly okay?'

He shook his head. 'She's fine. I just got Carol's invitation to mediation at family court. She wants to discuss changing our custody arrangement.'

Kat stifled a shocked gasp, appalled on his behalf. She touched his arm. 'That sounds scary.'

Nash pressed his lips together, distracted, perhaps deciding how much to share.

She looked away from the hesitation on his face, embarrassed for prying. They weren't a couple. His private life was none of her business. Just because her trust for him deepened day by day didn't mean that he owed her any explanation or loyalty. That the realisation stung told Kat just how emotionally invested she'd become in this man.

'I'm sorry. I need to go,' he said with a sigh. 'I need to speak to my lawyer.'

'Of course. Is there anything I can do to help?'

He must be worried. Molly was happy and settled with their current custody arrangement. Surely there would have to be a very good reason to alter it. Nash was supportive of Carol's relationship with their daughter, but he wouldn't want to sacrifice any more of his time with his daughter.

He shook his head, his eyes filled with sadness. 'No. Thank you. I'm afraid I'll have to cancel our plans for tomorrow.'

Kat ducked her head, ashamed of her disappointment, which left her calculating how long they'd have to wait for another opportunity to be alone. 'Of course, no problem.'

The ache in her chest was evidence of her investment. She had no role in this situation, regardless of her feelings for Nash and Molly. Their daughter's welfare was between him and Carol. Kat wasn't even Nash's girlfriend, and if he wanted her there he would have asked.

Redundant and deflated, Kat focused on the big picture. Molly was his priority. That he was such a dedicated father was one of the things she loved about him.

She froze, the 'L' word buzzing in her head like a wasp. She didn't love Nash, did she? She couldn't. It was way too soon. Surely she was simply heavily in lust, cared about him as a person and valued his friendship.

That didn't make it love.

But would she even know? She'd thought that she'd loved Henry but that had felt totally different.

Easily dismissing her mini freak-out, she glanced back at Nash, who was collecting his bag from the ground. 'Hopefully her request will come to nothing, but I have to be seen to go through the motions of mediation.'

Kat nodded.

'I hate letting you down,' he said, pacing to his desk, obviously preoccupied.

She shrugged, desperate to feel as unaffected as she

acted. 'Molly is more important. We can reschedule any time.' She meant it, but the words also left a bad taste in her mouth. Nash wasn't hers. Regardless of her feelings and fantasies, nothing had changed. Molly already occupied the place at the centre of his world and she wouldn't have it any other way.

He nodded, rearranging some papers on his desk. 'She does this, Carol. Flits in and out of Molly's life, causing maximum disruption. She's just messing with me.'

'Why would she do that?' Kat asked, genuinely puzzled. Just like Molly was the most important person in Nash's life, Lucy was the centre of Kat's. That was what happened when you became a parent; you put your child's welfare above your own.

Nash snorted. 'Because she can.'

She'd never seen him so bitter. Of course he felt threatened. Kat would fight to her dying breath to keep custody of Lucy. Clearly Nash had some serious issues to deal with. Their cancelled date was irrelevant.

'You should go, do what you have to and then try to get some sleep,' she said, ignoring her selfish yearnings, her jilted dreams.

'Thanks for being so understanding,' he said, stepping close once more.

Cupping her face, he brought their lips back together, this kiss tender and full of regret.

For a second Kat surrendered, trying to ignore the niggles of doubt taking root. Irrespective of how good it felt to be with him, irrespective of her wild imaginings of a shared future, they both had other responsibilities beyond their own needs and wishes. The part of her that had spent hours looking forward to their precious time together couldn't help but feel cheated. But it was a timely reminder that starting a new relationship was a pretty low priority for Nash. Kat needed to protect herself and, in doing so, protect Lucy. She didn't want to be the victim of a one-sided love affair again.

But when the kiss came to an end and she saw the tension in Nash's expression her concern for both him and Molly expanded. It was too late to pretend that she didn't care.

'I'll let you get back to work,' he said, effectively leaving Kat out in the cold.

He didn't want to share his feelings. He didn't need her right now.

Her pager vibrated in her pocket, telling her she was needed in Resus, a prompt that duty called. 'I need to go,' she said after reading the digital display. She swallowed the lump of hollow loneliness, the fear that she could no more rely on Nash to always be there for her than she could Henry.

When it came to the crunch she was still alone.

'Good luck for tomorrow.' She stuffed her hands in her pockets to stop herself from touching him again, dusting off the guard she'd mistakenly thought she no longer required. Experience had taught her how it felt to be second best, rejected, discarded. She had no desire to expose herself and Lucy to that kind of hurt once more.

'Thanks. I'll let you know the outcome,' Nash said, once more focused on his phone.

She opened the door and backed out of the room, stealing one last look at his worried face. Compassion squeezed her heart. How, in all her enthusiasm for what she'd found with him, had she missed the glaring reality that Nash had a lot to deal with and clearly wasn't in the right space for a new relationship? Pushing for more than the snatched scraps they had now would only lead to more heartache. She couldn't allow those crazy dreams of the future, her feelings and especially the scary 'L' word to take hold.

She just couldn't risk it.

# CHAPTER FOURTEEN

THE NEXT DAY Grady pressed Kat's doorbell, the need to see her so strong he was worried he might rip the door from its hinges with impatience. He exhaled, trying to find calm after his incredibly frustrating morning. The meeting with Carol and the lawyers had been the typical waste of time he'd expected.

The door opened and Grady sagged with relief. The sight of Kat was like a ray of sunshine on a cold spring morning, raising his spirits and clearing his mind of all the extraneous chatter.

'Can I come in?' he asked, because Kat was smiling as if pleased to see him but also shocked.

'Of course.' She reached for his hand and drew him inside.

Acting purely on instinct, he pulled her into his arms, held her close, just breathed. The warmth of her body comforted him like a blanket, her scent now so familiar he loved that it clung to his shirt long after they'd spent time together. For a few seconds, with the thud of his heart slowing against hers, nothing else mattered.

'Are you okay?' she whispered finally.

He nodded, pulled back, his lips seeking hers in a kiss that was soft and desperate, his emotions spilling over, jumbled and startling in their intensity. She had no idea what she meant to him. How much he craved her or how a simple smile, a touch, a glance from her soothed his soul.

Breaking the connection of their lips at last, he rested his forehead against hers. 'I'm sorry. I just really needed to do that. I really needed you.' All of the tension of the day, his fears that he'd lose Molly, shuddered out of him as she smiled, pressed her lips to his once more, her hands stroking up and down his arms.

'Come in,' she said when she pulled back. She took his hand and led him into the lounge.

They sat on the sofa together, hand in hand. Grady wanted to pull her into his arms, to selfishly hold her for ever until all was right in the world. He swallowed, panic that his need for Kat had become so violent gripping his throat. When had that happened? How had she burrowed so deeply into his soul that she was his first thought when he opened his eyes in the morning, the person he wanted to share all of his daily trials and tribulations with?

Not that Kat needed his dramas. Her life was full with work, Lucy, her parents.

'What happened?' she asked, squeezing his fingers.

'Nothing major, just a lot of talk.'

'So nothing's changed for you and Molly?'

He shook his head. That she cared about him, cared about Molly, left him speechless. He'd spent the day wishing she was at his side, her calming presence and reassuring smile making sense of the crazy in his life.

Kat exhaled, her relief for him palpable.

Emotion compressed his lungs. He was falling for this wonderful woman in a way he couldn't be certain he'd ever fallen for anyone before. It reminded him of the terror of his very first parachute jump.

'I don't want to download my drama onto you.' He

gripped her hand tighter, his frustration with Carol and worry for Molly already eased after a few minutes in her company.

In the same way they worked as an efficient and effective team at the hospital, Grady had the sense that together they could conquer any obstacle. But that was wishful thinking. He'd let Kat down today. He couldn't bombard her with his emotions, especially when he was too scared to tease them out for closer examination.

What if she didn't feel the same way about him?

'I don't mind listening,' she said softly, her gaze full of concern.

Grady sighed. His personal life was a mess and all he really wanted to do was hold Kat, lose himself in their passion, forget about the emotional wringer his ex continued to put him through.

'Carol likes to play games,' he said, wincing at the idea that his ex could potentially ruin what he had with Kat as she had interrupted their date today. 'She claims that she wants more time with Molly, which is crazy. She hardly ever uses the days she's supposed to take Molly. She just comes and goes as she pleases, regardless of what's best for Molly and usually when it's most inconvenient for me, like today.'

Kat nodded, her gaze flitting away. 'Does Carol know about me…about us?'

Grady froze, noticing Kat's distraction for the first time. 'I haven't told her.' His love life was none of Carol's business. The only access she had to his life was when it concerned their daughter. 'But she's been fishing, questioning Molly.' Sensing something about Grady had changed, Carol had figured out there was a new woman in his life. 'I think today was about making me jump through her hoops.'

'Why would she waste everyone's time like that?' Kat asked, frowning.

'Because she's upset that she can't call the shots with me any longer. She grabbed me after the mediation, said she wanted to talk about getting back together.'

Kat stiffened, her tension transmitted to him through their hands.

'She's done that before. Several times. My answer is always the same: no.' He understood Carol's desperation. Kat was the closest Grady had come to a relationship since their divorce. She could clearly sense the depth of his feelings for Kat and wanted to let him know that as Molly's mother she was still part of the picture.

Feeling as if Kat was slipping away, as if she didn't believe his assurances, he touched her chin, tilted her face up so their eyes met. 'I'm sorry that I let you down today. I promise that I'll make it up to you.'

'I was just a little disappointed, that's all.' She looked down, but not before he witnessed the doubt and uncertainty in her eyes. 'I don't want to make things difficult for you, Nash,' she said. 'It's understandable that Carol wouldn't want a random woman interacting with her daughter. I'd feel the same.'

'You're not some random woman, Kat.' He scrubbed a hand through his hair in frustration. 'I don't care how Carol feels about my private life.'

His ex never told him about the men she saw. Of course he would have told Carol about Kat eventually, but he'd wanted Kat to feel comfortable with him and Molly before he exposed her to his ex. His circumstances would put many women off, and he wasn't even sure if Kat had changed her mind about taking their relationship forward.

Perhaps she wasn't ready. Casual and fun was one thing.

It was a whole lot more serious to take on not only him and Molly but a meddling ex-wife too. Maybe he was rushing it. He'd made that mistake once before. Perhaps Kat just needed more time.

'Okay,' she said, looking unconvinced, making him question her feelings. 'But we always said we'd put the girls first, so if you need for us to cool things down, that's fine.'

It might be fine with her but it rankled him that, through their daughter, his ex was still trying to exert some sort of hold over his life.

'Our joint responsibility for Molly doesn't give Carol any rights over my life, Kat.' Frustration twisted in his belly. Yes, his daughter came first, but that didn't mean he'd given up on his own search for happiness. He'd realised that yesterday when he'd received Carol's message, wishing that Kat was a serious part of his life so he wouldn't have to choose between his responsibilities and being with her. She'd be a part of his life, all areas of his life.

A trickle of apprehension snaked down his spine. Unless that idea filled her with horror.

He cupped her cheek, lured her eyes back to his. 'Is that what you want? For this to be over?'

Perhaps, for Kat, him and his complications were a risk not worth taking. His stomach churned. But he'd rather know now, before she became any more indispensable for his happiness.

'Of course not.' Sparks danced in the depths of her irises.

Grady exhaled, relief shunting his heart back into a steady rhythm.

'But Molly is the most important thing in your world, just as Lucy is in mine,' Kat continued. 'If our…fling is putting her happiness and yours at risk then…'

He gripped her face. He didn't want to hear how that

sentence ended. He didn't want this to be over. He pressed his lips to hers, willing things to be the way they'd been at the weekend when, for him, it had moved beyond a fling.

'We haven't talked since we broke all of the rules...' he hedged, needing to know if she saw any future for them.

'No.' Kat's eyes widened, like a deer trapped in the headlights, forcing his pulse dangerously high. 'I guess that's what I'm trying to say. I want you, but I understand that you have other priorities.'

Grady nodded, his stomach plummeting. She wanted *him*. But what about Molly?

Was it still just about their physical connection for her? Even if she wanted a relationship, would she tolerate Carol trying to pull his strings, robbing them of their precious time, the way she had today?

Perhaps they should do the responsible thing, call things off before anyone's feelings became hurt. Except he was already way too invested to emerge from this unscathed.

Accepting defeat for now, he nodded. 'You're right. I do have other priorities, and I always will. That doesn't mean that I don't want you too.'

He winced at his hypocrisy and selfishness. Kat deserved more than a fraction of his attention. After the rejection she'd been through in the past, she deserved to be adored unreservedly. If he let her go, she could find someone without his baggage.

With impeccable timing, a text alert sounded on his phone. It was Carol, informing him she'd decided to collect Molly from school.

He sighed. 'I need to go. Carol has just turned up at the school.'

Kat nodded, standing. 'My parents are collecting Lucy today.' She walked him to the door.

Grady hesitated. Nothing was resolved.

The urge to pour out his feelings and beg her to keep giving them a chance gripped him as if by the throat. Maybe, with time, if they managed to carve out some space to allow their relationship to blossom, she'd come to feel the same way.

'Do you want to know today's revelation?' he asked, aware that he was rushing off and had no right to ask any more of Kat.

'Sure,' she said, her smile tinged with sadness, as if there was nothing he could tell her that mattered more than what they'd already said.

He prayed that wasn't true. That she'd learn to trust him enough to give another relationship a chance.

'I think you are a terrific mother, Kat,' he said. 'Lucy is a very lucky little girl to have you.'

Her eyes grew glassy, her stare raking his. 'I'm lucky to have her too, just like Molly is lucky to have you.' She took his hand, squeezed his fingers. 'You always put her first, Nash, and I wouldn't want it any other way.'

Of course she wouldn't, because she was wonderful and she'd been badly treated, had watched her lovely Lucy be badly treated.

He pressed a kiss to her cheek, walking away on heavy feet.

They shared the same dedication to their daughters. They shared a career and a sense of humour and incredible intimacy. The question was: would that be enough?

# CHAPTER FIFTEEN

IT WAS UNUSUAL for the night shift to be quiet. In Kat's experience, night-time in the ER was often just as busy as the daytime, and she preferred it that way. Keeping busy left no time for thoughts, and in her current conflicted state there was only one topic on her mind: Nash.

She was no longer in any doubt that she'd fallen in love with him. His text was the first thing she looked for when she opened her eyes in the morning, their late-night phone call the last thing she wanted to do before she fell asleep, where, invariably, he filled her dreams.

And if she needed any more proof, her reaction when he'd told her that his ex had suggested they get back together, the seething hot jealousy, the nausea, had been the icing on the cake.

But just because she fallen didn't mean that their situation wasn't complicated. Perhaps sometimes love wasn't enough.

Kat's admiration for Nash and the way he handled the various expectations placed on him in a calm, reasonable, considerate way was unwavering. If she had her choice of any man in the world she'd want a partner with whom she could weather any storm. A mature and compassionate man who put others first, even when it was hard and took personal sacrifice.

So why was she terrified of the many factors that might derail them from being more than friends and lovers?

Not that Nash had asked for more.

For a brief second, when he'd mentioned how badly they'd broken her rules, her heart had surged with hope. But every time she tried to picture the future that had been crystal-clear for a fleeting second, all she saw were barriers: Carol, the girls, even time seemed to be against them. It seemed impossible.

She couldn't fight the feeling that she was being selfish by bringing a man into Lucy's life, that it might fail and hurt them all—Kat, Lucy, Nash and Molly.

Frustrated that she'd spent the last ten minutes trying to see a way forward when she should have been revising for her trauma exams, Kat turned the page on her textbook and began reading the same paragraph on spinal immobilisation for the third time.

A sudden commotion, raised voices, had her rushing towards the reception area and patient waiting room. Before she could get there the double doors swung open and Nash backed into the ER carrying Molly in his arms. She was dressed in her pyjamas and seemed to be struggling for breath.

'She's having an attack,' he said, his voice more urgent than Kat had ever heard.

Kat's heart lodged in her throat, panic pounding adrenaline through her blood.

'Tell me when it started.' Kat rushed after him as he strode into a nearby bay. She would need to set aside what the little girl meant to her and focus on her training. She couldn't allow the emotions she felt for Nash and his daughter to cloud her clinical judgement.

Nash placed a limp and docile Molly onto the bed, reaching for an oxygen mask, uncaring that he wasn't on duty and technically his role was that of a family member. 'She's got a cold at the moment, but I hoped we'd get away with it.'

Kat could hear Molly's pronounced wheeze from her position at the side of the bed.

'She's been coughing all night,' Nash continued, the distress in his voice urging Kat to comfort him. But Molly needed her more.

'Her oxygen sats dropped half an hour ago,' he said in full-on nurse mode. 'I have a monitor at home.' He tenderly placed the mask over Molly's face and turned on the flow of oxygen.

Kat understood his automatic actions; he was doing what needed to be done, as always. If it were Lucy lying there, she'd do the same. But he was also a parent and he needed to let Kat do her job.

Kat turned to the nurse on duty.

'Get me nebulised salbutamol and prednisolone, please.' Her gaze flicked to the digital monitor, which showed Molly's oxygen saturation to be an alarming ninety-one percent.

'I need to have a quick listen, Molly.' Kat kept her voice calm, even though her stomach knotted with worry. She loved this man. She loved his little girl, but she needed to be strong for them both, to keep her own panic well concealed. Showing Molly her distress would only make things worse.

She took her stethoscope from around her neck. 'It won't hurt, just might be a little bit cold.'

Nash unbuttoned Molly's pyjama top and Kat pressed the bell of her stethoscope over Molly's chest on each side, noting that the little girl was using her accessory muscles of respiration, a sign that the asthma attack was severe. Molly was working very hard to make her lungs function. She stared over at Nash while she listened to the lung fields, trying to show him with her eyes that she was there for him and Molly, that she'd do everything in her power to help. The helplessness in his eyes was hard to witness, but Nash knew the implications of a severe asthma attack as well as Kat.

Medical staff often treated the emotional needs of the entire family when a loved one was sick. Only Kat had never been so heavily invested. It was as if it were Lucy lying there struggling to breathe.

'No pneumothorax,' she said, looping her stethoscope back around her neck.

'Don't worry, sweetheart.' She smiled, took Molly's small hand and felt her feeble grip. The last thing she wanted to do was transmit any of her concern to Molly. 'We're going to make you feel all better, okay? I'm glad Daddy brought you in to see me tonight.'

The nurse returned with the medications and set up the nebuliser in place of the oxygen mask alone over Molly's mouth and nose. Kat and Nash stood on opposite sides of the bed, each holding Molly's hand. Her chest ached for him. Each time he looked at her his stare implored Kat to do something—anything. But he knew she was doing everything she could.

'Give me the rest of Molly's history,' Kat said while they waited for the drugs to work.

Nash answered Kat's enquiries about Molly's general health, the frequency of her asthma attacks and her regular medications. Kat fought the urge to reach out across the bed and take his free hand so they formed a tight little circle of comfort, but not only was she conscious of crossing professional boundaries, she also needed the physical distance to give her enough emotional distance that she remained objective.

More than ever, she needed to protect herself too. She

wasn't Molly's mother. She and Nash were still technically casual. Any possible future for them would be complicated. He'd stated that he didn't want to get back together with Carol, but Kat couldn't help the insecurities that made her doubt his word.

Shoving her fears aside, Kat watched Molly breathe in the drugs, which formed an aerosolised mist in the mask. Each of Molly's inhalations and laboured exhalations added to the panic she was trying to keep at bay. The seconds seemed endless as she kept one eye on Molly and the other on the monitors, observing her respiratory rate and oxygen saturations, willing the numbers to move in the right direction. Willing Molly to recover.

Finally, the oxygen saturation reading improved to ninety four percent. Kat breathed a shaky sigh of relief, her stare taking in Nash's haggard features.

He looked to her, a glimmer of hope in his eyes.

Kat nodded, almost overcome by her love for both of them. It was a good sign that Molly might be out of danger.

Nash visibly crumpled a little. He silently mouthed the words *thank you*, his gratitude, his vulnerability, his trust, almost buckling Kat's knees.

Because her emotions were so close to the surface Kat feared he'd see them on her face, she looked down, blinking away the sting of tears. If only she could hold him, confess her feelings aloud, tell him that she loved both him and Molly and that together they'd make everything okay.

When had Nash and his daughter snuck under her guard and wormed their way so deeply into her heart? If she'd thought she loved him before tonight, she was even more certain now, his happiness and Molly's vital to her own.

Deciding that she owed it to herself to tell him her feelings, to ask him to give their relationship a chance, she would wait until Molly was out of danger and then find the right moment.

The curtains around the bed swished open and a woman rushed in. She was tall and slender, her blonde hair cut short in a sophisticated style, which looked good even though she'd clearly rushed there in the middle of the night.

Kat's stomach churned with nausea. This must be Carol.

'Darling, Mummy's here,' she said to Molly, standing at Nash's side, so close that their shoulders touched. Obviously concerned, Carol looked to Nash for an explanation.

'She's doing really well,' he said to his ex, his eyes flicking to Kat and then back to Molly.

Kat swallowed down the hot ball of tangled emotions in her throat.

Her envy was pointless. Nash and Carol had made a baby together, loved each other enough to get married. Of course he'd informed Molly's mother that he was taking her to the ER. They were co-parenting. In an emergency they were still a family. United.

Nash would always do the right thing and she loved his integrity.

So why did it feel like rejection?

Returning her attention to Molly, Carol placed her hand over Nash's so that they were both holding their daughter's hand.

'I'm her mother,' Carol said, her eyes darting between Nash and Kat as if she'd noticed the look they'd shared. 'Is she going to be okay?'

Kat was still holding Molly's other hand. The other woman noticed this, her lips pursing with disapproval.

'I'm Dr Collins, one of the ER doctors,' Kat said, introducing herself to Nash's ex, the woman from whom Molly had clearly inherited her heart-shaped face. Kat refused to release Molly's hand. The little girl's previously feeble grip was growing stronger, a good barometer of her recovery.

'We're treating Molly with some nebulised medication and oxygen,' she explained, her voice reassuring. 'And it seems to be working.' Kat smiled at Molly, aware that being unable to breathe must be terrifying.

Carol spoke to Nash in a hushed voice, asking him for more details of the attack.

Excluded, Kat's isolation flared anew. She was an outsider. She wasn't part of Molly's family. Even if she and Nash committed to building a relationship, Carol wouldn't want to share her daughter with Kat, as she'd already proved with her request for more custody. No matter how deep Kat's feelings were, any relationship would struggle under the pressure of such enormous potential for conflict.

She looked away, tried to give them some privacy, busied herself by checking the monitors, re-examining Molly's chest.

'How are you feeling now, sweetheart?' She smiled down at Molly, the term of endearment just slipping out because she'd used it so many times before when Molly and Lucy were together.

'Where's Lucy?' Molly asked, speaking for the first time since she'd arrived in her father's arms.

Kat smiled, breathing easy for the first time. 'Lucy is at home asleep. But if you're feeling better, and if it's okay with Mum and Dad, maybe she can come visit you.'

She glanced at Nash, her relieved smile matching his. Her promise was probably unwise given the complexity of their situation. But Kat didn't have the heart to disappoint Molly, not after what she'd been through.

'Who's Lucy?' Carol asked, scrutinising Kat.

'My best friend,' Molly replied.

Reluctantly releasing Molly's hand, Kat moved to the work station and logged on to the computer. She ordered a chest X-ray for Molly and made some notes. She tried to give the family some privacy, but it was hard not to notice that while Carol comforted Molly, Nash remained quiet.

'I'm going to speak to the paediatric team,' Kat said, addressing Nash and Carol. 'We might just keep Molly in tonight for observation.'

They both nodded, their focus returning to their girl.

She left them alone, her heart heavy. It wasn't her place to explain her role in Nash's life to his ex-wife. Perhaps he'd never had any intention of telling Carol about Kat because his feelings for her weren't serious.

As she spoke to the on-call paediatrician her loneliness intensified.

Carol might not always be around, but she was still Molly's mother. Kat was happy that Lucy's friend had two parents to love her. She was even grateful that Nash could share the worries of parenting with someone. She knew how hard it was doing it alone.

But where did that leave her and Lucy?

A serious relationship with Kat would mean he'd also need to make room for Lucy. Would he consider it worth the effort, when his life was already complicated enough?

Returning to Molly's bay, she was about to open the curtains, to tell the family that Molly would soon be transferred upstairs to Paediatrics, when she heard the hushed and urgent voices of Nash and Carol.

She froze, aware that she shouldn't listen but desperate to make sense of tonight, her feelings, the implications of it all for her and Nash.

'I'm sorry I didn't answer as soon as you first called,'

Carol said. 'I'd gone out for a drink with the crew after work. That doesn't mean I don't care.'

'I know you care about Molly,' Nash said, his voice flat. 'I'm just tired of picking up the pieces after you let her down.'

Kat ached for him, for the toll tonight had taken.

'Well, if you would just listen… If we were a family again we'd all be under one roof, so you wouldn't need to call me.'

Kat shuddered, placed her hand over her mouth, Carol's plea for a reconciliation making her stomach churn with nausea. She should leave. She was invading their privacy. But her feet wouldn't move. Would Nash agree?

'You should think about Molly,' Carol continued, 'about what she wants.'

Part of Kat agreed with Carol's logic. After all, a complete family was what she'd wanted for Lucy. But a child wasn't enough glue to hold two people together and it was selfish to even place them in that position.

'You and I are a separate issue,' Nash said. 'I've told you before. I've moved on. Molly is all the family I need. I don't want to discuss this again.'

Kat heard the scrape of a chair on the floor, her heart jumping into her throat. She scurried away before she was discovered eavesdropping.

It took her a solid five minutes to calm down, to perfect a convincing enough mask to face them again.

Chilled to the bone by her realisations and by what she'd overheard, Kat had never felt more alone. Despite the rules she'd put in place to protect herself, she'd not only fallen in love, she'd started to make future plans that involved Nash and Molly, as if they were already a blended family, before knowing Nash's feelings.

But Nash didn't want the same things. He was content

as he was, just him and Molly. Kat was more vulnerable now than when she'd boarded a plane back to New Zealand, pregnant and heartbroken. Because she hadn't loved Henry as deeply as she loved Nash. Nash was the real deal, everything any woman would be lucky to have in a partner.

Only she was still very much alone, and loving him might turn out to be her biggest mistake ever.

# CHAPTER SIXTEEN

LATER THAT MORNING Grady strode into the ER in search of Kat. Emotionally drained, his adrenaline spiked so high his hands trembled, every cell in his body clamoured for one glimpse of her before she went home after her night shift.

Last night had been one of the longest of his life, Molly's attack the worst one yet. He'd almost collapsed with relief the minute he'd seen Kat, the panic coursing through his veins easing. When she'd gripped Molly's hand, her reassuring gaze locking with his, he'd known in an instant that his feelings were undeniable.

He loved her.

Glancing around the department, he tried to slow his breathing, the sense of panic returning, as if Kat was slipping through his fingers like sand.

The timing of his eureka moment couldn't have been any worse. There'd been no time to talk to Kat, no time to touch her, no time for anything but using every scrap of his energy to will Molly well.

Spying Kat at last, he tried to get his emotions under control. She was talking to one of the male orthopaedic registrars, her smile wide and easy, the tinkle of her laughter causing Grady's skin to prickle hot with jealousy.

His muscles tensed in frustration. Kat deserved a straightforward relationship, one that put that carefree look on her face every day.

But what did he have to offer? A few snatched kisses and the mess of his complex personal life.

He dragged in a steadying breath. The emergency with Molly had rattled him to his bones. He needed a shower, a good night's sleep, some food. Until his daughter was home, no longer an inpatient on the paediatric ward, he'd need to shelve the urge to approach Kat and confess his feelings.

As if she sensed him behind her, Kat turned. Their stares locked, silent communication passing between them the way it did when they worked on the same case, when they smiled over something cute one of the girls said, when they were intimate.

But could that connection translate into a committed relationship? He knew how much work that took. Would Kat want to take that risk for him when he was currently able to give her so little in return?

Ending her conversation, she came to him, a small frown of concern on her face.

'How is she doing?' she asked, her compassionate gaze a balm for his weary soul.

Disappointed that she'd put her hands in the pockets of her lab coat, Grady fought the urge to drag her into his arms, to know she was his, that they'd work out the rest together. He didn't care if the whole department knew that they were more than friends and colleagues.

'Better. Thanks to you,' he said, trying not to sigh at the respectable distance she kept. Clearly she did care.

Gratitude swelled up inside him, threatening to block his throat. No matter what happened between him and Kat in the future, he'd always be indebted to her for helping Molly.

Kat shook her head, dismissing his compliment. 'You

look exhausted. Do you want to grab a coffee from the canteen? I've just finished my shift and was about to head home so I'm free if you need to talk.'

She was so strong and kind and smart, and he loved her so deeply. He'd probably loved her from the minute she'd fixed that troublesome tiara.

He shook his head, regret like a stone in the pit of his stomach. 'I can't be away for too long.'

He did need to talk, to tell her he loved her, but it would have to wait. 'I've left Molly with Carol.'

The minute Molly was out of danger, thanks to Kat, he'd realised that he'd been holding himself back, scared to confess his feelings, scared he'd fail to be what Kat needed, scared he'd be rejected. Because more people than just he and Kat would be hurt if it didn't work out. Molly had been too young to remember Carol leaving. But as he'd watched Kat and Molly's connection last night he'd realised that his little girl was truly attached to Kat, a fact that hadn't escaped Carol's notice.

'Can you come to my office for a second?' Unease at Kat's continued distance gripped him. Had she planned to leave without checking on them? Something was definitely off with her, aside from her concern for Molly.

'Of course,' she said, ducking her head.

He strode to his office with Kat in tow. If he could get her alone, speak with her in private, he'd not only have some sense of how she felt about him, he could also ask her to give him some time to get things sorted.

Once inside, he shut the door, his heart pulsing in his throat with all that he wanted to say but needed to postpone.

Because he couldn't stand the distance, he took both of her hands in his. 'I'm so grateful to you, Kat. I know it happens every day around here, but you saved Molly's life. I can't tell you what that means to me.'

Kat nodded, blinked as if heading off tears. 'I know what she means to you,' she whispered and then cleared her throat as if brushing off the emotion. 'I was only doing my job.'

She sounded so reserved. He hadn't slept for thirty-six hours, but it wasn't just his imagination.

'I know it's your job—' he frowned '—but when you're on this side, as a worried parent...' Words failed him. They seemed to be making everything worse anyway. She looked even more withdrawn.

'You don't have to thank me.' She looked down at her feet. 'I'm sorry if Molly asking for Lucy created an issue for you with Carol.'

'Is that what's wrong? You're worried about Carol because she put two and two together about us?'

Of course his ex had volleyed a string of personal questions his way the minute Molly had fallen asleep. She'd noticed the bond between Kat and their daughter, witnessed the way he'd looked at Kat, not that his love life was any of Carol's business. She'd even used his vulnerability to push her agenda that they get back together again.

Kat winced, extricated her hands from his grip. 'She's Molly's mother, Nash. She always will be. She has every right to ask questions about the people in her daughter's life. I'd do the same.'

'I agree,' he said, feeling as if he was losing control of his train of thought. 'And I answered her questions, explained that Lucy is your daughter.' But that was where his loyalty to Carol ended. Until he and Kat had discussed moving their relationship from casual to serious, until he asked her to make them official, told her of his feelings, he had no obligation to inform Carol. And right now, exhausted, worried and confused by Kat's apparent withdrawal, his sense of where he stood with her was rapidly disappearing.

In that moment his phone rang. Seeing that it was Carol, he answered, speaking to her for a few seconds to confirm he was heading back to the ward as soon as possible.

'I'm sorry, I have to go,' he said to Kat after he'd hung up. 'The team are there for a ward round.' He needed to focus all of his energy on Molly's recovery so he could take her home, invite Kat and Lucy over to cheer her up, smother her with love and care until there was space in his head for his own needs. 'They are talking about discharging Molly later today.'

Kat stepped back. 'Of course. You should go.' She opened the door to his office and loitered on the threshold as if she couldn't wait to get away.

Part of him couldn't blame her. He had no idea if she wanted more, but he currently had nothing to offer her anyway, beyond vague promises. He wouldn't risk letting her down. Better to wait until they could talk it all through.

'I'm going to take the rest of the week off,' he said, hoping that they would find an opportunity to discuss their relationship. 'Obviously Molly and I will have to cancel the plans we made with you and Lucy for tomorrow.' They'd organised to share a barbecue at his house after school. Now he just wanted to take Molly home and wrap her up in cotton wool until she was once more her usual energetic self.

'I'd offer to help,' Kat said, looking down, avoiding his stare, 'but you and Carol will have everything covered, I'm sure.'

Nash opened his mouth to protest and then closed it again. He wanted to reassure her that for him, personally, he'd rather have Kat's help than Carol's. But it wasn't about *him*. It was about Molly, and Carol was her mother. If Molly wanted Carol around then that was what she'd have if it was in his power.

'I should go home, get some sleep,' she said, inching further away.

Unable to hold her, kiss her, reassure her, Grady curled his fingers into fists, wishing he could ask Kat to stay with him on the ward, but she'd been up all night too. Night shifts messed with your circadian rhythm. He should let her go, but he couldn't help the sickening feeling that this felt like a goodbye.

'Wait.' He scrubbed his hand through his hair, dread making him desperate to make things between him and Kat right. 'I know my timing is off, because I really do have to go, but I've been thinking about us for a while now—'

'It's okay, Nash,' she interrupted, holding up her hand to ward off his words. 'You don't have to explain. We always said it was temporary.'

She shoved her hands in the pockets of her white coat, her guard up. He was reminded of that prickly, rule-loving version of Kat that he'd encountered on her first day at Gulf Harbour. He'd assumed they'd moved past all of their differences, but maybe not.

He tried to think, his fatigued brain sluggish. 'I'm not calling it off if that's what you're thinking.' The idea spiked his adrenaline, panic leaving a metallic taste in his mouth.

He'd been about to tell Kat that he had feelings for her, that he wanted them to be an item, that they could take things at her pace, take it slow for the sake of their girls, but he wanted a proper relationship, not just the fling they'd squeezed in between work and their family commitments.

But she was already halfway out of the door, literally and figuratively had already begun shutting down from him and what they'd shared, reverting to the immovable Kat.

Had he totally misjudged her feelings for him and Molly? It wouldn't be the first time he'd rushed into a relationship.

Kat shook her head, looking like a cornered animal. 'It's okay if you are ending things. It's probably for the best. You have a lot going on, Nash—Molly, Carol—and the last thing I want—*or need*—is to get in the way.'

He stepped closer, willing her to hear him and not just run scared because she'd been hurt in the past. 'You're not in the way, Kat.' He'd had a bad experience with love too, but he was willing to make this work, put in the effort required and see how far it could go.

'Look,' he said, lowering his voice. 'This has moved past a fling for me—I...care about you.' The fearful look in her eyes made him shy away from confessing his true feelings. She was already looking at him as if she couldn't get away quickly enough. The L-bomb might scare her away for good.

'I care about you too, Nash.' She clenched her jaw as if her words were hard to get out. 'I also care about Molly. But she has everything she needs in you and Carol. I have to remember that Lucy only has me. *She* has to be my priority, irrespective of my feelings. I don't want us to let this go on longer and end up hurting the ones we love the most.'

Grady's blood turned to ice. 'So you're ending it, just like that?'

Obviously his feelings were very much one-sided. He'd rushed into this, despite lecturing himself on keeping things casual. He'd fallen for her and she still couldn't trust him, was unwilling to take a chance on him, preferring to keep herself closed-off, the way she'd done for six years after the last time she'd risked her heart. While he'd given his all, Kat might never be in a relationship place, not for him, anyway.

He sighed, the urge to beg rising up in his chest. 'I thought we were building something special here, Kat. I thought we might have a future together…you, me and our girls. Molly is already attached to you; I saw that last night.'

She nodded, her eyes bright with the sheen of tears. 'Just as Lucy feels the same way for you.' Her expression was desolate.

Guilt shredded him; he was torn in so many directions.

'Don't you think that I've dreamed of a future with you?' she said, her voice strangled. 'But be honest—do you really see it working? The timing isn't right for either of us. There are so many things to consider, so many people's feelings at stake in order for us to be together.'

As if she'd made up her mind, she jutted out her chin with determination. 'I don't want to be hurt again, and I won't put Lucy through an emotional upheaval when it could all be for nothing. Molly has you *and* Carol to fall back on if it all went wrong. Lucy only has me. I have to be selfish for her sake.'

She was making it sound as if he and Carol were getting back together, one big happy family. Grady scrubbed a hand through his hair in confusion, aware that the clock was ticking and he needed to be on the ward five minutes ago.

'I told you I won't hurt you. I'm not your ex.' It was Kat he wanted. He understood that she was scared. He'd give her some space, and when Molly was recovered they could talk it all through.

Her face crumpled, her lip trembling. 'I know you would never intentionally hurt anyone, Nash. You're a good man. But you and Carol and Molly—you'll always have each other, even if you and Carol aren't together, and I'm glad for you all. But if you and I didn't work out, and let's face it we can barely find time to conduct a fling, let alone anything more serious, I'd be alone again.'

Unable to argue with her logic, he faltered. He wanted to

hold her and tell her it would all be okay, but she was right; his loyalties were as divided as his time. He needed to go upstairs to Molly. He couldn't even give Kat the time this conversation deserved.

As if sensing that she'd won her argument, Kat stiffened, stood taller, composed herself while he tensed for the blow he sensed was coming. 'I can't do that to Lucy. It's a risk I'm not willing to take. I'm sorry.'

She left his office and didn't look back.

# CHAPTER SEVENTEEN

BY THE THIRD day after she'd ended things with Nash, Kat's soul-searching had peaked. Heartsore and listless like a wrung-out dishcloth, she fought the urge to call him on an hourly basis. But she wanted to give him space; his priority would be Molly, who was home from hospital.

And a call would only confirm that it was over, something Kat's heart already knew.

Nash hadn't contacted her, despite the fact that Molly was back at school, according to a delighted Lucy. There had been no sign of him at the hospital, his name blanked off the staff roster for the rest of the week.

The distance had given Kat plenty of time to think about the decision she'd made. He was done with her, and she only had herself to blame.

She'd been an utter coward, running scared when she'd seen Nash and Carol and Molly together, when she'd heard him state that he didn't want Carol back, the old doubts that she must be unworthy or unlovable because of Henry's rejection resurfacing with freshly sharpened claws. But what if she'd got it all wrong? What if, one day, he might want the same thing Kat dreamed of—their own family of four? Despite her feelings, she hadn't been able to trust him enough to overcome her fears, and she'd seen how that knowledge had hurt him.

To stave off the tears that hovered perilously close to the surface, Kat sipped her coffee, the ever-present lump of regret in her throat making it difficult to swallow.

*I thought we might have a future together...you, me and our girls.*

His brave and wonderful words from that fateful morning haunted her, threatening to set off the waterworks once more. But Kat refused to cry in front of Lucy, and she'd spent enough time this week locked in the bathroom with red and swollen eyes.

Of course his statement had given her hope. But when she'd tried to visualise the dream, to picture them happily living together under one roof, the sacrifices and complications—managing Carol's expectations, preparing their daughters to be sisters and stepdaughters, carving out enough 'them' time to make their relationship work—had overwhelmed her, blurring the vision like a swirl of paint in a jar of water.

Fear had taken hold. All Kat could see was the broken version of herself, the one hurt by another man.

How could *that* damaged and scared woman be everything Nash and Molly and Lucy needed?

'Mum, do you like my picture?' Lucy asked, startling Kat from her daunting ruminations. Lucy held up her drawing of what looked like a house and a family with two kids and a mum and dad.

A fresh wave of guilt slammed into the centre of Kat's chest. Perhaps, as Lucy grew older, a father figure, a whole family, would become increasingly important to her. Perhaps Kat had just been lucky up to that point, the questions about her daughter's missing parent few and far between.

Lucy's needs weren't reason enough for Kat to find a relationship, but in pushing Nash away she'd realised her biggest mistake yet—that *she* deserved to find happiness, to be a role model for her daughter, one who didn't give up on her dreams just because the journey was terrifying and hard.

'It's a lovely picture, darling,' she said, trying to avoid the panic that told her that this time she'd made the wrong choice in walking away.

Kat was so much more than the woman Henry had cast aside—alone and embittered, with no confidence in her own judgement. Kat and Lucy were as lovable as anyone else. Henry was the one with the problem. For his own messed-up reasons, he'd missed out on knowing his amazing little girl, more fool him.

'Tell me about your picture,' Kat said, pausing her reflections.

'That's the unquarium,' Lucy said with a smile, adorably mispronouncing the tricky word, 'and these are the penguins.' She pointed at some black blobs Kat had assumed were scribbles.

'And that's Nash and that's Molly next to you and me, Mum.'

Kat nodded, her eyes brimming that Lucy's version of a happy family included Nash and Molly. Kat wanted that too.

This time, she'd chosen a winner in Nash. She was brave enough to fall for a man worthy of her love. Just because she and Nash had each failed at relationships in the past didn't mean that they shouldn't give theirs a chance. What kind of a wimp would she be to allow fear of the unknown to dictate her happiness?

If she overcame that fear, the only thing stopping Kat from having her dream was the minor adjustments they would all need to make. Reaching for her phone, Kat fired off a text to her babysitter.

She should have told him how she felt the last time she

saw him, confessed that she was in love with him and agreed to do whatever it took to be together. She wasn't going to allow the sun to set on another day where she was too afraid to tell Nash how she felt.

'Come, on,' she said, placing the lids back on the marker pens Lucy had been using. 'Time for your bath and story and bed.'

Maybe she and Nash would work out, maybe they wouldn't, but there was only one way to find out, and the new fearless Kat deserved to know.

Grady locked his locker and tossed his scrubs into the used linen bin outside the staff changing rooms. Today had been his first shift back at work since Molly's discharge from hospital. Not only had he wanted to be around at home to ensure she'd fully recovered, a part of him had also been avoiding Kat. He'd deliberately put himself down for the late shift, knowing that she would have left Gulf Harbour by the time he started work.

It was a spineless thing to do, but until he'd fully processed their last conversation he didn't want to confront her and end up saying the wrong thing.

*It's a risk I'm not willing to take.*

Of course when she'd said that she'd meant that *he* was a risk not worth taking. Her words had winded him like a punch in the stomach. It was as if she didn't know him, didn't trust him at all, as if they were still those two strangers arguing over his rule-bending tendencies. But he was no longer the man who'd fancied her the minute she'd walked into the ER. That guy had been closed off to what he'd found with Kat since, and what he'd found was something real and rare. Something neither of them could afford to ignore, even though facing it was the harder option.

Just because circumstances had made him and Carol rush into marriage didn't mean he couldn't try again, nor did it mean that failure was inevitable, the way Kat seemed to suggest. Yes, there'd be hiccups along the way—there was in any relationship. Except Kat should realise by now that he'd do everything in his power for the women he loved—Molly, Kat and Lucy.

'Oh, you're still here—good.' Lauren stood in the doorway, snatching him away from a trip into fantasyland. 'I hoped I'd catch you.'

His friend's stare softened with sympathy. 'Is Molly still well?'

Grady nodded, smiled. 'She's all back to normal, running around, bossing her old man as usual.'

If only he could say that he was anywhere close to normal. He felt like a soft toy minus the stuffing. Because his normal would always be associated with Kat.

But he hadn't fought hard enough for her.

'So, what's up?' he said, hoping Lauren wasn't about to ask him to work late. He was tired, needed to call his parents and check on Molly.

'Nothing, really,' Lauren said. 'I just wondered when we can expect you back at work properly—I was hoping now that Molly's well you could resume your day shifts.'

He'd known Lauren a long time. They'd worked together for years. Her subtext was loud and clear: *You can't avoid Kat for ever.*

It wasn't a sustainable plan, mainly because if he didn't see her soon, tell her how he felt, he was going to explode.

She needed to know that he loved her and had everything all figured out. That last bit was a stretch, but he couldn't go on without her so they'd just have to make it work.

Frustrated, he shrugged into his jacket. 'As of today, I'm available for any shift you want.'

'Great.' Lauren grinned as if she could read the determination to win Kat over that was currently making his mind spin too fast.

Why had he allowed Kat's fear to trigger his own? So they were both scared to commit, scared to be hurt and resolved to protect their daughters. He'd show her that they could still do that and be together.

Eager to text Kat to meet him for breakfast tomorrow, he rushed past a smug Lauren. Then he paused, gripped her arms and placed a friendly kiss on her cheek.

'Thanks for the pep talk,' he said.

Forget breakfast tomorrow. He couldn't wait that long. He'd rush home, have a shower and call round to Kat's place tonight.

Bewildered but clearly delighted to see that he'd pulled himself together and come to his senses, Lauren laughed. 'You're welcome. Now, go get her, and don't come back to work until you've convinced her that you're the man of her dreams.'

Taking her sound advice, Grady sprinted to the hospital car park.

# CHAPTER EIGHTEEN

KAT'S STOMACH TOOK another tumble as she stood on Nash's doorstep and sheltered from the rain. Inside, the house was dark, no sign that anyone was home. She should have called first, but the minute she'd acknowledged she'd made the wrong decision she'd wanted to see him, to say all of the things she'd bottled up inside since she'd started to develop feelings for him, which was some time after that very first kiss on his birthday.

Desperate, she pressed the doorbell once more, her teeth chattering, her feet soggy from running through the puddles on Nash's path and her sweater clinging to her damp skin. She pushed her wet hair back from her face; she must look a state. But none of that mattered.

She was about to dash around to the side of the house and peek through the windows when the front door flew open.

'Oh, you're home,' she said, her throat tight with longing because Nash was naked but for the towel around his hips, his skin covered in water droplets like a sweating ice lolly on a scorching summer's day.

Kat licked her parched lips.

'I was in the shower,' he said, swinging the door wide, his shock fading. 'Come in. You're drenched.'

'It's raining,' she said, stating the obvious.

When Nash closed the door and faced her she almost lost

her nerve. He was so gorgeous she wanted to throw herself into his arms. But she'd messed up, succumbed to her fear, hurt both him and herself in the process.

'Am I disturbing you?' she said, feeling sick with anticipation. Perhaps he was on his way out. Perhaps he had a date.

No matter. She'd come here to say her piece and say it she would.

'I was on my way to your place, actually. I just jumped in the shower after my shift.' His gaze traced her face, swept over her body, dousing Kat's chills in welcome heat. Perhaps it wasn't too late.

'Oh, good, because I think we should talk,' Kat said before she became too distracted by his bare chest. He was too far away. She wanted him all over her, but she wanted to tell him her feelings more.

'I agree.' He nodded, crossed his arms, looking far too relaxed and in command of his emotions whereas she was a trembling wreck.

'I've been thinking,' she continued, determined to be brave this time, 'and I've decided that you need to know how I feel. About us, about you.'

'I agree,' he said, his eyes burning bright into hers, stealing her breath.

'Is that all you're going to say?' she whispered because he was looking at her with such intensity it was hard to think. Or maybe there wasn't enough oxygen supplying her brain.

'No.' He dropped his arms and stepped closer, forcing Kat to look up at him. 'There's something new you should know about me.'

'There is?' She couldn't help but smile, even though her heart was in her mouth and they were yet to resolve a thing.

She loved him. She loved every one of his revelations. Just standing here with him dripping was a precious gift.

'What is it?' she managed, her head spinning and knees weak.

'I love you, Kat,' he said, a triumphant smile on his face.

Kat gaped, her own declaration of love forgotten in the face of those amazing three little words.

'Wait...' She held up her palms, trying to control the rush of her emotions, which threatened to bowl her over.

'I'll wait as long as you need,' he said. 'But you have to know this.' He gripped her upper arms, grabbing her attention, although there was no need. Kat was engrossed in every word that came from his mouth. 'I wasn't thinking straight the last time we talked and now I am.'

She nodded, feeling the same, willing him to continue because she was so choked speech was impossible.

'I know you're scared.' His gaze softened. 'I am too. We've both been hurt and we're both protective of our girls. But I love you and I'm begging you to give us a chance.'

He loved her? Kat opened her mouth to speak, but still nothing.

'It doesn't have to happen overnight.' His hands slid to hers, gripping her fingers as if he'd never let her go. 'And obviously there will be lots of hurdles, but we can make this work. We have so much in common. We understand the pressures of each other's work. We're both family-orientated, and I love you. I might have already mentioned that.'

His vulnerable smile was her undoing. She nodded, tears pricking the backs of her eyes.

Misinterpreting her continued muteness, he stepped closer and cupped her face. 'Please give us a chance at a relationship, Kat. You and I deserve happiness as much as our girls. If we're content, they can only benefit. We can take it slow... I promise. Date properly for a while, and when we think the time is right, when we think they might be ready, we can explain it to the girls, prepare them for us to become a family, living together.'

Kat snapped out of her daze. Her joy was too much. He was describing every one of the dreams she'd dared to believe possible. 'Nash...'

But he seemed to be caught up in his enthusiasm, his speech still persuasive, emerging in a rush. 'I've already told Carol that I'm in love with you, not that it's anything to do with her, but we're all going to have to get along for Molly's sake. But I swear that you and our girls are my priority. We'll always do what's right for the four of us. Just please say you'll give us a chance to do it together.'

Impatient, Kat tugged on his hands. 'Nash, can you let me get a word in, please, before you make up all of the rules on your own?'

He swallowed, contrite and nervous-looking. 'Of course, sorry. I've just had all of that bottled inside for so long. Okay, you go.'

'Thank you.' She sighed, expelling her relief and elation in one big shudder. Before he could list ten more reasons why she should give them a chance, she stood on tiptoes and kissed him, pulling back quickly to reassure him that she'd heard every word he'd said and felt the same.

'I love you too, Nash. I came over to tell you because I didn't want you to give up on us, the way I stupidly did the day Molly was discharged. You're right, I was scared. I overheard you and Carol talking and I freaked out. But meeting you, knowing you, has made me strong enough to be open to love again. You're the best man I've ever met.' She stepped into the circle of his arms and gripped his face in both hands. 'You're a wonderful father, a brilliant nurse and don't even get me started on your prowess as a lover.'

He smiled, his arms around her waist a little tighter.

'I was overwhelmed when I realised how much you and Molly mean to me,' she said, needing to explain why she'd messed up, that it had nothing to do with her feelings for the two of them. 'I didn't mean what I said. You *are* worth the risk. You're worth any risk. I know that there are no guarantees in life, but I don't need them, Nash. I just need you and Molly and me and Lucy. I just need us.'

With a groan, Nash hauled her close and brought his mouth down on top of hers, his kiss hard and passionate and full of the love they'd just declared.

In the frantic embrace that followed, where they kissed and laughed and kissed some more, his towel slipped from his hips and fell to the floor.

'I love you so much,' he said, staring deep into her eyes. 'I want so many things for us, but I mean it; we can take it slow. I won't bombard you with proposals here and now, especially as I'm completely naked.'

Kat laughed, part of her wanting to hear those proposals. But he was right. They needed to consider what was best for all four of them before they rushed ahead, carried away by the emotions that for so long Kat had cast aside.

She slid her hands up his back, nuzzled her face against his chest. 'I should probably get out of these wet things myself.' He was hard against her stomach. She surrendered to the temptation she'd fought since the minute he'd opened the door and licked a stray water droplet from his skin.

'It would be a shame to waste such a golden opportunity...' she raised her eyes to his '...don't you think?'

Nash grinned, scooped her up in his arms and strode towards the bedroom.

'Whatever you say.' He kissed her, laying her down on the bed. 'You make the rules and I'll follow.'

'Oh, I like the sound of that,' she said, laughing as Nash stripped away her clothes.

Soon, with his every touch reverent, his kisses showing Kat the truth of all his declarations, there was no space for anything other than the love they both deserved.

# EPILOGUE

KAT SIFTED THE warm golden sand through the sieve of her fingers, one eye on Lucy and Molly frolicking in the sea a short distance away. The low, late afternoon sun glinted off the water, temporarily blinding her, but she wasn't concerned. She knew that Nash too would be watching their girls play, ensuring that they didn't wander out too deep.

He shifted, adjusting her head where she lay on his lap, his fingers stroking through the strands of her hair as if he needed to ensure she was real, to constantly touch her, to connect.

The feeling was mutual.

In the two months that they'd been an official couple the four of them had been virtually inseparable. A blended family. Complete.

Kat's rules and schedules had helped to keep everyone on track at all times—appointments kept, deadlines met, childcare juggled—and Nash's easygoing patience meant that even at the most hectic moments there was always time for a giggle, a hug or a passionate kiss.

'Am I squashing you?' she asked, turning her face away from the water's edge to look up at her gorgeous man with a smug grin.

'No.' He took her hand and raised it to his lips, kissing her knuckles. 'And even if you were I wouldn't care.'

Kat smiled, so content she almost felt guilty. She had a wonderful partner, their daughters were still the best of friends, and she'd even just passed her trauma exams.

Life was perfect.

'I've been thinking,' Nash said, his gaze flitting from her to Lucy and Molly and then back again, 'about Christmas presents. Why don't the girls just share a trampoline? They're pretty much always together anyway.'

Confused, Kat sat up. 'But Molly already has a trampoline... Why would you buy her another one?'

Nash tilted his head, his grin wide and his stare indulgent as if waiting for her to catch up.

'I'm asking you and Lucy to move in with us, Kat.'

Kat froze, her mind tripping over itself in her haste to comprehend. But there was no time for her usual overthinking, a wave of love rushing in to obliterate everything in its path.

'Do you think they're ready?' Her *yes* hovered on her lips, no deliberation required.

Lucy and Molly were at the centre of every decision they made, whether it was a trip to the beach or the *sleepovers* they'd tentatively trialled for the past two weekends, where the girls had shared the bunk beds in Molly's room and Kat had ostensibly stayed in the spare room for appearance's sake, only sneaking into Nash's bed when the girls were out for the count.

'I think they'll take it in their stride,' Nash said, once more checking on the girls. 'Just like they accepted that sometimes Lucy's mum and Molly's dad kiss each other.'

Kat's blood heated at the expression on his face. 'Well, Lucy's mum fancies the pants off Molly's dad.' She leaned into his side, shoulder to shoulder, tilting her face up for a relatively chaste kiss.

She couldn't ravage him on a public beach, but later, when the girls were asleep, all bets were off.

'So is that a yes?' he whispered against her lips when she reluctantly pulled back. 'Will you move in with us? I want to wake up with you in my arms. I want to be lulled asleep by your heartbeat against my chest. I want to live with you for the rest of my life.'

The prickle of tears threatened. Kat pressed her mouth once more to his, awash with love for the man who'd made her and Lucy's life complete. 'Yes.'

His smile widened. 'Good. In that case, it's time for today's new Nash fact. Now that we're going to be living together, it will make much more sense.'

Kat laughed, giving him a playful shove. 'You're not going to tell me that you leave the toilet seat up are you, because that I already know.'

Nash's expression grew serious, his eyes brimming with the love that wrapped around Kat like a safety net.

'Are you ready?'

She nodded, captivated by the intensity in his eyes.

He gripped her fingers, his thumb swiping across the back of her hand. 'I'll love you for ever, Kat.'

She was about to say he'd told her that last week and the week before, but he shushed her, placed his fingertips against her lips.

'Which is why, in about ten seconds,' he said, dragging out the suspense, 'I'm going to ask you to marry me.'

She wasn't sure how he'd managed to render her utterly speechless again, but it didn't matter. Sometimes actions spoke louder than words, and Nash had been showing her that he was a man she could rely on from the first day they'd met.

She leaned into him, kissed him, clung to him, determined to never let him go for as long as they lived.

'So will you?' he said, laughing when she let him up for air.

'Yes, yes, I will,' she said, laughing too, tears in her eyes. Spying the girls running up from the sea towards them in her peripheral vision, she stole one last kiss.

'Good decision,' he said, falling back against the sand good-naturedly as he was attacked by two giggling five-year-olds.

*Yes, perfect decision,* thought Kat, joining the tumble.

\* \* \* \* \*

# COMING SOON!

We really hope you enjoyed reading this book. If you're looking for more romance be sure to head to the shops when new books are available on

## Thursday 13th April

To see which titles are coming soon, please visit

**millsandboon.co.uk/nextmonth**

MILLS & BOON

# MILLS & BOON®

## Coming next month

### THE NURSE'S ONE-NIGHT BABY
Tina Beckett

Serena waited for him to say something. To respond to what she'd just told him. None of this was happening the way she'd wanted it to.

But now that she'd said it, she couldn't take the words back.

He blinked as if not quite sure what to say. "Sorry?" He shifted her on his legs, easing out of her.

She hated the feeling but understood that he was probably in shock. Maybe she should backtrack and try this again.

"I...I..." She took a deep breath. "I haven't been feeling quite right for the last couple of weeks, and I couldn't figure out why."

"You didn't look like you felt at all well when we were running. And add that to what you said before we parted ways..."

Her teeth scraped against each other a couple of times as she tried to drum up the courage to say again what she needed to say. "I couldn't get up the nerve to tell you what was wrong that day."

"And now you want to."

He looked confused. Maybe Toby hadn't actually heard what she'd said a minute ago. She hadn't exactly shouted out the news. "Yes. As I said, I wasn't feeling well and realized my cycle was later than it had ever been. So... I decided to take a pregnancy test."

"I see."

He was calm. Too calm.

A sense of horror and foreboding rushed over her. "I'm pregnant."

"You're pregnant?"

*Continue reading*
**THE NURSE'S ONE-NIGHT BABY**
Tina Beckett

*Available next month*
www.millsandboon.co.uk

# LET'S TALK

## Romance

For exclusive extracts, competitions
and special offers, find us online:

**f** facebook.com/millsandboon

**𝕏** @MillsandBoon

**◎** @MillsandBoonUK

**♪** @MillsandBoonUK

Get in touch on 01413 063 232

For all the latest titles coming soon, visit
**millsandboon.co.uk/nextmonth**

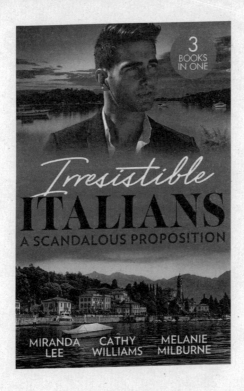

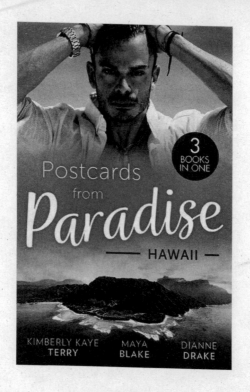

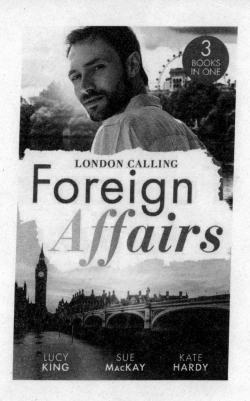

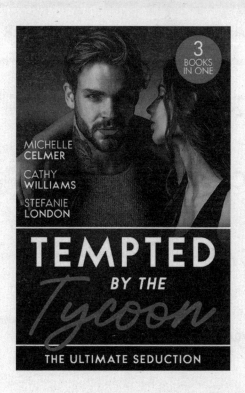

# MILLS & BOON

## THE HEART OF ROMANCE

## A ROMANCE FOR EVERY READER

**MODERN**
Prepare to be swept off your feet by sophisticated, sexy and seductive heroes, in some of the world's most glamourous and romantic locations, where power and passion collide.

**HISTORICAL**
Escape with historical heroes from time gone by. Whether your passion is for wicked Regency Rakes, muscled Vikings or rugged Highlanders, awaken the romance of the past.

**MEDICAL**
Set your pulse racing with dedicated, delectable doctors in the high-pressure world of medicine, where emotions run high and passion, comfort and love are the best medicine.

*True Love*
Celebrate true love with tender stories of heartfelt romance, from the rush of falling in love to the joy a new baby can bring, and a focus on the emotional heart of a relationship.

*Desire*
Indulge in secrets and scandal, intense drama and plenty of sizzling hot action with powerful and passionate heroes who have it all: wealth, status, good looks…everything but the right woman.

**HEROES**
Experience all the excitement of a gripping thriller, with an intense romance at its heart. Resourceful, true-to-life women and strong, fearless men face danger and desire - a killer combination!

To see which titles are coming soon, please visit

## millsandboon.co.uk/nextmonth